I0604510

BOOK OF YOU & I

bookofawriter.wixsite.com/severinopublishing

Published by Severino Publishing House, L.LC.
Book Cover and Illustrations by GSeverino
Editing by Jennia D'Lima
ISBN 978-1-0882-2645-2
Paperback. First edition: 2024

*This story explores life and love as well as loss and grief.
There are discussions of assault, includes minimal sexual/
mature content, and has depictions of alcohol and/or drug use
throughout the book. Please read with care!*

To myself, to my characters, to my stories—I wouldn't be here
without us.

I'm telling this story to heal, share with the world, and connect
with others who are going through the same pain.

To the boy who this story is about, the one I loved so deeply that
I forgot myself. The one who broke me, but taught me what it
was to feel and heal.

To you, the reader, for picking up this story and inviting it into
your life. I hope it helped you find the love within yourself,
helped you heal, helped you live again.

This is for you...

THIS IS A LONG STORY TO TELL, FULL OF MEMORIES AND LOVE—the story of how we began and how we ended.

Did we cheat destiny by meeting and falling in love? I don't know... I choose to believe in fate and the "meant to be;" that the stars aligned and conspired for us to find each other.

And yet, here I am, about to tell you our story as thoughts of him fill my head, replaying over and over: the first time we ever laid eyes on each other, our first touch, our first kiss, and getting swept off our feet—a love too strong to ignore.

To which I ask myself, ask him: How can we live on without knowing if we were destined to finish the *book of you and I?*

Chapter One

"The story of a lonely heart that only wanted to be loved."
~ Stage 1: Naivety, Alexandra Kessler.

OLIVIA – OCEAN CITY

THE WAVES WHISPER TALES OF MEMORIES AS I SNAP A PICTURE. I capture my sister, Ella, against the backdrop of the Ocean City shore, a moment forever frozen in the sands of time.

The day couldn't be more perfect for a photo shoot at the beach: clear skies with small clouds, crystal blue ocean, and white waves on the warm east coast water. A light wind blows Ella's short brown hair back, and the sun shines bright behind us, creating the ideal ambiance for these shots.

The best part? Few people are here today, only a few surfers and couples walking along the shore.

"Can you change poses? You've been in the same one for the last five shots," my best friend, Maia, suggests to my sister, losing her patience. The warm sun starting to tan our already golden skin.

The wind isn't being very kind to Maia, blowing her long, blue-dyed hair all over the place.

"Dude, *cállate*, I'm no experienced model. I've been doing this for one day, so chill." Ella raises her voice. "Can you hurry and finish taking the pictures already?" She turns to me, a playful look in her eyes. "I have places to be, friends to meet."

"You do understand we're doing this as a favor to you, right? The only reason you're not actually paying us is because you're my sister. But we won't rush, and we'll keep going until we're all satisfied, *¿entiendes?*" I say to her while snapping a couple more pictures. I love my sister to death, but I swear to God, sometimes she really gets on my nerves.

The best photos are taken when you least expect them—all-natural, candid. *Or to use as blackmail later.* Maia has her posing from different angles, positioning her hands on her hips and looking over her shoulder. I snap at least twenty more shots as she switches between them.

"Okay, now we're finished. It'll take us a few days to go through and edit all of them, but I'm confident they'll look great on your page. You'll definitely attract some clients," I say.

"Or maybe we could stay a little longer..." Ella says as she subtly glances behind us. "Don't look now, but it looks like a really handsome *papi* is coming this way."

Maia and I quickly turn our heads, the wind blowing my hair to the side in long, dark waves that obscure my vision. Ella's right—walking out from the water is a tall guy with slightly tanned skin carrying a surfboard. He pushes his dirty blond hair back, lifting his head and catching us gawking at him.

We try to play it cool and act nonchalant, each of us giving him a slight smile while quickly looking away and trying to act inconspicuously. Something about him feels familiar, but I can't quite put my finger on it: is it his short, dirty blond hair, his smile, or maybe his muscled physique? I don't know.

Stopping before us, he says, sounding out of breath, "Hey, you're Olivia and Maia, right? From Ocean City High? I'm Sam, Sam Walker." He looks between us, running his hand through his wet hair. "Can't believe it's been so long since we've last seen each other."

I look at Maia, my eyes wide open as I recall our old high school friend and our quick chats in those bright hallways. *He was definitely not this toned back then.*

"Oh my God, yes, how are you? It's been like, what, four years?" I smile at him, leaning my hip to the side.

"Yeah, I guess time flies. I didn't know you girls still lived here. I thought you would be long gone by now." His body seems to relax, muscles unclenching.

"I could say the same thing about you. I figured you were somewhere out there working for some big investment company or something." I nudge his shoulder, but he tenses up a little. *Touchy subject?*

He quickly relaxes and looks down toward our cameras. "And I see you stayed with the photography thing. Are you guys doing a photoshoot?"

"Her sister's starting her own clothing line, and we're helping her with the website's content," Maia says while pointing to Ella.

"Congrats, Ella! That sounds amazing," He smiles at her, and she nods as a thank you. "So, you work at a studio now? That's pretty cool." He turns to face Maia and me.

"Well, kind of. We started our own company a year ago. It's called Sunkissed Studio." I take a business card from my camera case and hand it to him.

"That's awesome!" He gives us a charming smile. "I have to go, but it was great seeing you again, girls. And Ollie, I'll try to stay in touch this time." He winks at me and chuckles. *Ollie…*

We say goodbye, leaving me smiling as he jogs away, and then Maia and Ella help me gather our equipment. As we start walking back to my car, I turn to Maia.

"Sam has changed a lot, hasn't he? I honestly didn't recognize him right away. Did you see his arms? Good thing he came up to us. And how did he recognize us that easily? You with your dyed hair and growth spurt. And me with…well, I guess I haven't changed much." I say with a chuckle.

"I'm pretty sure he had a crush on you in high school." She nudges my shoulder.

"No way. He would've confessed or something at some point, right?"

"Are you girls done *chismeando (gossiping)*? I have to go, and you're making me late," Ella says, then flips her hair.

"You're not famous yet, and you're already stuck up. You should be thanking us instead of whining," Maia says, narrowing her eyes at Ella. "Don't make us regret letting you live with us to finish high school. I bet your mom would take you back to Florida before we could even finish asking."

I carry a tray of what can only be called a laughable attempt at homemade cappuccinos, the foam definitely not having the correct consistency, and place it on our coffee table. We each sit on the sofas, spread out but facing each other. I pull one of our light brown blankets over my legs.

We're wearing matching pajamas on a Friday night, talking about our days, and making our plans for spring vacation. It might seem boring, but this is our sacred tradition—sitting together once a week and discussing everything happening in our lives.

"So, a new guy came to school this week," Ella blurts out. "His name is Noah Miller, and I think he transferred from New York. And he's so, so nice. We got paired up for a science lab three days ago and got along pretty well."

"Oh, really? Go on, *cuéntanos*." Maia rests her chin on her drawn-up knees.

"And he's really cute. Like, *Pinterest cute*. You know...tall, plays lacrosse, has dark curly hair, adorable dimples when he smiles," she says with a dreamy gaze.

Maia and I exchange knowing looks. *This girl has a crush*; I raise my eyebrows, and she mimics me.

"Also, next week is spring break for me, right? We're camping at the Huckleberry Hill Campground for our junior trip. And you'll never guess who's coming!" Ella exclaims.

Maia gasps. "*No me digas*, let me guess—Noah?!"

"Yes," Ella screams.

"Oh, wow, what a surprise. I was not expecting that at all." Maia's tone drips with mockery.

"Why do you have to be so sarcastic all the time? You could give it a break, you know. It won't kill you," Ella says, returning the attitude.

Maia opens her mouth to snap back, but my phone rings, interrupting her.

"Saved by the bell," she mutters, giving Ella the stink eye.

I answer the call. "Hello, this is Olivia."

"Hey, Ollie, it's Sam."

"Oh, hi. Wait, how did you get this number again?"

"I have your card, remember?"

"Oh, yes! I forgot! What's up?"

"Is Maia also with you?" He asks.

"Yeah, she's right here."

"Could you put me on speaker so I can speak to both of you?" His voice sounds serious.

"Sure, no problem, go ahead."

"Okay, some of my friends from college started a band called Reputation about a year ago. They're doing some gigs over spring break season and need photographers to cover the events. After going through your website, I thought you would be perfect for the job, and we'll pay you, of course. It's in the

Rockwood Music Hall in Manhattan. Are you free?"

Maia jumps up on the couch and looks at me. "Oh, my God, Rockwood Music Hall?! I've heard that's where all the best indie bands play!" Her brown eyes are wide and pleading for me to accept.

How could I say no to that face? "Count us in, Sam. When do we leave?" I ask.

Maia squeals, knocking our coffees onto the floor and splashing our ivory couches.

Damn it! Note to self: clean up our mess.

"We leave next Saturday. Does that work with your schedule?" he asks.

"That's perfect, Sam. Yes, we'll do it!"

"And don't worry about transportation and where to stay; you can ride with me, and we can find you a place to stay."

"Thank you so much, see you next week." I try to conceal my excitement before hanging up, then immediately turn to Maia, screaming and jumping with excitement.

"WE'RE GOING TO NEW YORK!" I knock my phone off the table as we hop on the table, and I hear the screen crack. *Damn it.*

Ella joins in as we hug and squeal, thrilled at the thought of finally traveling to our dream city to do our dream job.

Note to self: repair my phone before leaving for the trip.

The week passes by in a blur since we are extra busy tying up loose ends before the trip. Between Ella requesting some reshoots, our product shoots for our clients, and arranging our schedule for the upcoming week, it's been hectic, to say the least. So, as we sit around our living room waiting for our ride, our worries are nonexistent.

"Remind me again about your relationship with Sam? If it were any other situation, wouldn't we find his hospitality a bit creepy?" Ella asks as we sit around.

She does have a point... "We weren't close in high school, but you could say we were friends. Especially after one time after school when some stupid jocks were pushing him around, and Maia and I intervened," I say.

"Come on, you two against a group of buff jocks? Not believable enough," Ella snickers.

"Excuse you, but we were definitely forceful enough to scare them away," Maia scoffs defensively.

"All right, all right, you two, don't spoil a perfectly good morning before our trips," I hold back a laugh.

"Fine," Ella sighs dramatically. "Oh, I almost forgot to tell you guys. Noah is picking me up soon, too. He offered to drive me and my friends on the camping trip."

"Ooh, Noah," I mock her using a sing-songy voice.

"Ollie, *no*. It's not like that. Just go already and text me when you get there safe," she rolls her eyes, brushing me off as her annoying older sister.

"Okay, love you, have fun. Oh, and don't forget to use protection!" Maia teases.

"Maia!" Ella screams before we close the front door.

We push the down button for the elevator, and a couple of minutes later, it arrives at our floor.

"What do you think he drives?" I ask Maia, filling the silence.

"Hmm, I bet he owns a big car or maybe a Jeep. Don't surfers own those?"

The doors open on the ground floor, and we quickly reach the parking lot. Sam waits for us right outside the complex, leaning against what looks like a brand-new Jeep Wrangler.

"Figures. He is a surfer boy, isn't he?" Maia says, and I roll my eyes while I laugh. *I mean, what else did we expect?*

"Hey, girls, ready to go?" Sam asks, pushing himself off his car. "I can take your things. Go ahead and find a seat." *Who said chivalry is dead?*

We hand him our bags. We might've packed a little too much for this trip. But who knows what we might need?

"I call shotgun." I run to the front passenger seat.

"You do know you don't need to run if you already called it, right?" Maia raises an eyebrow.

"Oh, shut it. You're just jealous I'm in the front, and I'll have control of the music." I stick my tongue out while looking at her in the rearview mirror.

"Oh, sticking your tongue out? Real mature, Olivia," she says while fighting a laugh.

Before I can answer, Sam opens the driver's door and gets in. "Okay, we're all set. Let's hit the road!" He turns the key in the ignition and the engine purrs.

"Here's what I was thinking: we can put on Reputation's album, and that way, you can get in tune with their music," Sam suggests. "Is that okay?"

We agree, and he starts playing their music on his phone, turning up the volume before driving off. Music blasts through the speakers and the guitar riffs hit me like a storm—beautiful transitions between the chords accompanying the beats and the bass rhythm.

"Damn, Sam, how have I never heard of them before? They sound amazing, particularly the guitar." I turn to him in surprise. "Are you sure they're from here and are your friends?"

"Guitar?! Did you not hear those vocals? I would pay for him to teach me how to sing like that. And the bass? The song would be nothing without it," Maia says enthusiastically.

Sam laughs, tossing his head back. "I told you these guys are good! Wait until you hear them live; that's when I think they're at their best. And you may not have heard of them because they're new, only started playing professionally and publishing their music a couple of months ago."

We listen to the rest of their album on repeat for the next couple of hours, and I like what I hear. If the guitar sounds like that in a studio, I can't wait to hear it in person. I also can't help but wonder what he looks like. Or is it even a *him*—what if it's a *her*?

"We still have two more hours, but I need to stop for gas. I'm not sure if we'll have a chance to stop inside the city." Sam looks between us.

"Great, because I have to pee. Unless you're okay with something happening to your car..." Maia jokes. *Okay, ew?*

"I just want a snack. You don't have to worry about me ruining anything." I cringe at the thought.

Once we arrive at the gas station, Maia runs inside—I guess she really needs to go. I walk into the convenience store, head straight to our favorite snacks, and pull out my phone to text Sam.

Olivia:
hey, do you want anything

Sam:
i'm okay with water
but I would be down for some chips

Olivia:
got it, we'll be back in a few

I put the phone back in my pocket and take the chips and the drinks to the cashier. As I hand her the money, I suddenly get this weird feeling. Like a subtle shiver, an unspoken tingle with a mix of curiosity and awareness: a sensation that makes me question if it's just a trick of my mind or an instinctive acknowledgment of a lingering gaze.

I turn around and catch a guy looking right at me. He's tall with lightly tanned skin; maybe he goes to the beach a lot. I wish I could see the color of his eyes, but he looks away before I can, brushing his hand through his dark brown, wavy hair.

I quickly turn away, not wanting to seem creepy. *Oh, he's cute.* I look back at him and catch him staring again. I flash him a smile, and he gives me a shy grin while combing his hair. *That's twice in a row now.*

"Excuse me, miss, your change," the cashier calls to me.

I look at her, blinking a couple of times. "Right, sorry!"

"Don't worry about it."

I can feel my cheeks redden and heat up. I put the change away and grab my bags, intent on looking for him again. But when I turn around, I don't see him. *Did he leave?* I spin around, trying to catch his eye somewhere in the store.

I see him at the back, by one of the drink coolers. I gather the courage to walk up and introduce myself as I hear the jingle of the door opening.

But my vision's interrupted by Maia standing in front of me. "Ollie, what are you doing? I've been waiting outside for about five minutes. We're leaving." She takes my free hand and drags me to the car.

I glance back, hoping to see the mystery guy again, but I don't. I guess it wasn't meant to be. *But why am I left feeling that maybe he's more than just a cute face?*

∞

Two hours later, we're entering the tunnel into Manhattan.

"Well, it looks like this might take a while." Maia exhales.
"Sam, tell us about yourself. What have you been doing all these years?"

"Well, I met the guys during college and became pretty close. When they decided to start the band, it was a pretty easy decision to help them with all the managerial duties. Mostly because of my economics degree."

"And what about surfing?" I sit up, remembering Sam carrying a board everywhere.

He sighs, pausing for a moment. "I tried, I really did. But my parents didn't think of it as a viable life path. If I wanted to pursue it as a hobby or on my personal time, I'd have to agree to study what they wanted for me, or else they wouldn't cover my tuition," Sam answers with a slight look of disappointment.

"Yeah, I remember you being at the top of our class when I took AP math. The worst week of my life, I tell ya," Maia says in a relaxed tone. "I can't talk for Ollie, but it looks like I haven't aged much since high school, or else you wouldn't have recognized us back at the beach."

"Sure, there's that, and also, I had a bit of a crush on you, Ollie, back in school. I wouldn't miss your face in a crowd."

I let out a nervous laugh, not because it's funny but because I don't know what to say.

"Hey, you weren't supposed to laugh." He laughs, but I notice him slightly blushing as I turn to face him.

"No, I'm sorry, I didn't mean to." I fidget with my fingers. "But it's all in the past now anyway, right?"

"Umm, yeah. But then again, it's because of that silly crush that I recognized you at the beach, and we wouldn't be here if I hadn't. So, ha-ha, the joke's on you."

"Well, thank God for nerdy Sam." Maia chuckles.

"Yeah, I guess that's true. We should be thanking your old self then." I nudge his arm.

Sam lets out a breathy laugh but says nothing else; *maybe we should go back to the easier-going mood.*

"Anyway...how long until we arrive? I'm getting hungry. Maybe we could stop for hot dogs at one of those carts," I say.

"Yes, please, I'm dying to try one of those. I've never had one before." Maia places her feet on the armrest, and I push them back down. "This is our first time in New York, so we are for sure doing all the iconic stuff."

"What? Neither of you has ever been to the greatest city in the world?" Sam asks, looking at her in the rearview mirror. "It's good that we're staying for a week. We're going everywhere!"

I grin from ear to ear, seeing Maia do the same as I turn around in my seat, excited to walk around the city and visit the go-to spots together.

"I'm sure we'll find a couple of stands around Rockwood. We can park in the back and get something to eat while the band rehearses," Sam says while driving.

"Great, because now I'm hungry too," Maia says, smiling.

We arrive at Rockwood about an hour before the gig starts. From the outside, it seems like a regular, dull, red-brick building, just like any other in the city. We park in the back next to a van with a logo reading "Reputation." *I'm guessing that's how the band brought their instruments.*

"You can leave your equipment in the Jeep, and we'll take it in after we eat. Is that okay?" Sam asks us.

"Yeah, we're good. It looks safe enough." I shrug after quickly looking at our surroundings.

We walk around the corner, and just like he had said, we immediately find a hot dog cart. After we order, I pull out my wallet to pay when Sam sticks a hand out and shakes his head.

"No, don't worry about it." I don't have time to protest before he hands the cash over.

"Don't even think of whining, Ollie. Enjoy the free hot dogs." Maia nudges me.

"Fine, fine. Thanks, Sam." I smile at him before taking a bite of what I can only say is the best hot dog I've ever had.

The world is right—nothing compares to New York dogs. I cannot wait to try pizza next. It's not long before we're all done, and Sam and Maia order seconds.

"No more for me, thanks. I guess the snacks made me fuller than I thought. I'll see what we're working with," I say.

Sam hands me his keys after taking a bite. I take the cameras and a tripod from the Jeep and walk up to the security guard. I show him my ID and business card, letting him know I'm taking pictures for the band. He wraps a red-colored band around my wrist and lets me in through a staff-only door.

I'm immediately taken aback by the décor when I walk in. *I guess it's true—you can't judge a book by its cover.* The walls have a rustic feel, with the bricks exposed and painted dark brown. A small stage sits by the far corner with padded walls. High-top tables line the walls throughout the hall, leaving space right in the middle for the audience. A second-floor balcony sits across the stage, and a full bar with stools stands underneath it.

I turn around, not paying attention to where I'm going since the hall is nearly empty, and bump into someone, almost dropping my camera.

Damn it, this cannot be happening. An involuntary gasp leaves my lips as I look up, coming face-to-face with him.

"It cried itself at night, and it dreamed of you in sleep."
~ Stage 1: Naivety, Alexandra Kessler.

OLIVIA – NEW YORK

WHOA, CAREFUL THERE. You might hurt yourself if you don't watch where you're going." A pair of hands steadies me before I fall. "Are you okay?"

I cannot believe my eyes. In front of me stands a tall, dark-haired guy with a pink cap on his head, *the guy from the convenience store.*

"Well, fancy seeing you here," he jokes. "Brandon, pleasure to meet you properly."

"Hi, Olivia. I'd shake your hand, but, you know." I lift my arms, holding my cameras higher.

Dios, derríteme ahora (melt me now). He laughs and takes his cap off to fix his hair. *That's the third time he's done it, but who's keeping count?*

"I'm assuming you're here for the concert too. I heard the band is good, but I won't be sure until I see them play." I showcase a playful smile.

He gives me a slight smirk. "Yeah, you could say that... They're excellent; I'm sure you'll like them. But I'm friends with the band, so I'm a little biased."

He nods at my hands. "What's with the badge and the cameras? Don't tell me you're one of those obsessed paparazzi... should I get security?" He steps back, acting as if he's leaving to get them.

"Oh, definitely, but please don't blow my cover." I wink, making him laugh. "No, a friend of mine also knows the band. He got me and my partner a job to cover their gigs this week."

"*Sunkissed Studio*, nice name. Why did you pick that? Does it have to do with your style?" He reads it off the badge as I hold it up.

"We're from Ocean City, Maryland, so most clients want pictures by the beach. We like to play around with the sunlight so it looks like the sun is kissing the models or subjects. Guess you could say it's what we're known for back home."

"I would love to see your work sometime." He slips his hands into his pockets. "And you mentioned a partner?"

"Yes, I did. She and the friend who recommended us are outside. We just got here and hadn't eaten anything. I assume they're coming in soon."

And speaking of the devil and her minion, Maia and Sam walk up to us.

"Ollie, I need the car keys to get the equipment." I hand them to her, and she gives me a weird look. "Well, well, well, what do we have here?" she says in a singsong voice.

So subtle. "Brandon here more or less saved our jobs. I almost tripped and broke our cameras," I quickly say.

Interesting, Maia seems to say as she raises her eyebrows. I give her a look back that says, *Girl, shut up*.

Sam immediately goes in for one of those bro "handshake-pat-on-the-back" hugs. "Dude, what's up? I missed you."

Brandon laughs. "It's been a day; stop being such a baby. But I missed you too." He hugs him back.

They keep laughing and doing their thing while Maia and I just stand there staring at the whole interaction, confused and wondering how they seem to know each other. She coughs, calling their attention back to us.

"Right, sorry. This is Brandon. He's the guitar player for Reputation. Also known as my best friend and roommate since college. We're missing our other roommate, but I can't find him…" Sam looks around.

Of course, he's in the band. Why didn't I figure that out before? Brandon gives me a knowing look. *The day keeps getting better and better… Stop it, Olivia. You'll get in over your head.* I realize I've zoned out for too long when a group of people comes to stand in front of us.

"Great, now that you're all here, I can introduce everybody. This is Drew, the drummer." Sam points to a slender, messy-haired blond guy wearing a ripped jean jacket.

"What's up, ladies?" he says in a flirty tone and sly smile.

The girl next to him nudges him in the ribs. "Stop it, Drew. You'll scare them away," she says with a laugh. "Hey, nice to meet you. I'm Layla! I'm on the keyboards and the backup singer."

She's so cute with her long, light brown hair and petite figure. She reminds me of an adorable squirrel for some reason.

"And thank God you're here. I've been waiting for some female company. Too much testosterone up in here!" Layla says with what sounds like a sigh of relief.

Maia and I each let out an honest laugh. *I like her already.*

"And last but not least, this dumbass over here…I mean—" Sam points to a tall guy with curly black hair and tattoos on his arms.

"Hilarious, Sam… thanks for the intro, dude. I'm Scott. Lead singer, bass player, and a total badass," he says smugly.

"A self-proclaimed badass, how humble of you," Maia snickers, eyeing him up and down.

"I like her," Layla blurts out.

"And what kind of groupie are you?" Scott crosses his arms

and scoffs at us. *Umm, excuse you?*

Before Maia can give her trademark rude comeback, Sam jumps in. "Well, I can see everyone's getting along perfectly so far. And they're not groupies. They run Sunkissed Studio, the photographers I told you about."

I notice him containing his laughter, appearing amused by the whole interaction. *Let me save him some embarrassment.*

"I'm Olivia Woods, but you can call me Ollie," I wave.

"What if someone wants to call you by a different nickname?" Brandon asks, tilting his head like a curious puppy. *Focus, focus, focus.*

I look down, shifting my feet. "I just prefer Ollie."

Maia notices my reaction and jumps in. "And I'm Maia Brooks, but you can call me whatever you want. It's nice to meet you all."

"And the mouth has a name… who would've thought?" Scott snickers. *With these two going at it already, this will be a long trip…*

Sam covers Scott's mouth before he can say something else. "And Scott, here, is our other roommate," he says, pulling them into side hugs. "You'll get used to the effect his…peculiar… personality has over people."

One of the stage managers calls the band up for soundcheck and rehearsal. While they do that, Sam, Maia, and I sit on barstools by the back and set up our cameras.

A few minutes later, I notice Sam standing up from his seat with a suspicious look and walking back and forth while on a call. For over five minutes, he paces the floor and mutters on the phone.

"Sam, what's going on? You're acting weird, and it's freaking me out," I call out to him after he hangs up.

"Yeah, why do you look like you just killed someone? Did

you forget to hide the body, and now you're in trouble?" Maia eyes him up and down.

Sam's face is priceless, staring at her wide-eyed and with a panicky look in his eyes. "Umm, no, but we might have a problem." He taps his phone with his index finger.

"What do you mean *we*?" Maia squints.

With a guilty look on his face, he stares at his phone.

"Sam, come on. What is it?" I urge him.

"Do you remember when I told you not to worry about finding a place to stay? That I had it all covered?" He's still not looking at us. *How bad is it that he can't even do that?*

"Yeah…?"

"Well, as it turns out…I don't…but it's not my fault, kinda." Sam looks at us sheepishly.

"…what did you just say?" Maia quickly gets up.

"Sam… please tell us you're lying, that this is some sort of sick joke." I let out a dry laugh. "Just tell us what happened; it'll be fine."

Sam looks a bit more relaxed but still frightened. "Okay, the place I reserved for you, well, that's gone. Apparently, the owner mixed up our dates with someone else's and sent over the refund with the cancellation."

You have to be kidding me. I brush my hands through my hair, looking at him in disbelief. I let out a dry, sarcastic, and not-amused laugh. I shake my head, sitting back on the stool.

"Damn it, and what do you suggest we do now?" I say while looking at Maia, who's leaning on the bar. "It's not like we can just book a hotel room for a week; we just started the business."

"Yeah, not much savings right now," Maia sighs. "And not to pile on the stress, but we forgot to text Ella that we got here. Or our moms." *That's the least of our problems.*

I press my face against my hands, frustrated. The loud music from the band playing doesn't help either.

"I need to take a breath and see what I can come up with." I stand up to leave. "Can you text them and tell them we're fine?"

Sam steps forward, but Maia stops him. "Give her a moment. She'll come back when she's ready," I hear her whisper.

The security guard opens the back door, and I walk up to the Jeep and sit on the hood. I prop my elbows on my lap, then press my head into the palms of my hands, letting out a frustrated sigh. How can everything be fine one second and upside down the next? I did not sign up for this.

"Are you okay? You ran out of the club so fast and seemed very upset. I thought maybe I could see if you needed something," I hear someone say as they walk up to me.

Even though it sounds familiar, I can't quite recognize who the male voice belongs to.

"Yeah, I'm fine. Just a little stressed." I look up to find Brandon standing in front of me.

"Here, let me help." He leans in to take my forehead into his hands, and I move back.

"What are you doing?" I stare at him.

"It's a thing I do to relieve stress; is it okay?"

I stare at him for a few more seconds, questioning whether I should let him. *You know what? What do I have to lose? Maybe it will help.* I lean forward into his hands, silently giving him permission. He puts pressure on my temples with both hands and to my surprise, it helps calm me down a little.

"Where did you learn to do that?" I breathe in and let out a sigh of relief.

"My mom's a nurse. She taught me some things that could be useful in my everyday life."

I can't believe I'm letting some stranger touch my head. But something about him makes me trust him. And I guess I surprisingly do because we stay like this for a long while, losing track of time.

"Are you feeling any better? I can stay for as long as you need." Brandon softens the pressure.

"Yeah, I do. Thank you." I smile at him. "So why did you come out here?"

He stifles a laugh and brushes his hair back—*that's the fourth time.* "I heard you guys fighting from the stage. You looked upset, and I thought someone should check on you."

Damn, are you trying to make me fall for you this soon?

"Nothing you should fret about; it's silly." I fake a laugh. "We forgot to text our moms and my sister to let them know we got here alive. They worry a lot."

"Yeah, I get it. I would worry too." He nods and seems to believe me. "Do you want to go back inside or need more time?"

"No, it's fine. I don't want Maia and Sam to worry more than they already have." I get down from the hood. We walk back in comfortable silence.

Maia approaches me when we enter and Brandon returns to the stage. "Are you feeling any better?"

"I'm fine. Brandon came out and helped me relieve some of the stress."

She gives me a knowing look, raising her eyebrows and smirking. "Ooh, did he now?"

"Oh, stop that, it's not what you think, *no fue nada.* Don't we have other things to worry about?"

We walk up to Sam, the worried expression still plastered on his face.

"Dude, it's fine, chill. We have time to figure it out. Right now, we need to focus on the concert." Maia says. "And I'm pretty sure they're about to open the doors to the public." *No pressure, huh?*

I check the time on my phone: eight p.m. The concert's supposed to start in half an hour.

"We haven't even started setting up." I sigh; now we have to rush. "Which shots do you want to take?" I ask Maia.

"I can take up close, and you do the sides since you have a better eye for those angles."

"Then let's make sure we have the right settings for their light show; don't want to interfere with what they already have."

"*Sí*," she agrees.

Let the show begin...

"It wanted to be wanted, but no one else could see."
~ Stage 1: Naivety, Alexandra Kessler.

MAIA – NEW YORK

PEOPLE ARE POURING IN, filling up all the seats. *Damn, I guess the band's more popular than we thought. Or maybe people just like music...*

The stage is built on one of the far corners, raised with a platform, leaving more space for the audience. It's the perfect size for just the band, so people have space for dancing in front of it. The stage's lights perfectly match the ambiance: a mix of red, orange, and a little blue, setting the mood.

I'm taking a couple of shots by the stage before they start playing when Scott kneels toward me.

Too close, dude, way too close.

"Umm, hi?" I ask, adding an exasperated sigh for the drama.

"Are you prepared to see me in action? It's the best thing you'll ever see, darling," he says with a cocky look on his face.

This dude is as smug as they come. "Sure, honey, whatever you say." I give him my best fake smile. "You know what? Here." I hand him a stick of mint gum. "You need it more than I do."

He scoffs while taking it, and I nudge his face away from mine. He didn't have bad breath, but I had to bring his ego down a notch.

The lights over the audience dim just as he takes his place with the rest of the band, letting us know the concert is starting.

The announcer introduces the band, and they immediately begin with "Twisted;" I remember it from the drive over. What's different from how I remember it is that, while Scott's singing, the music hasn't started yet.

I turn to Ollie, confused about what's happening. *Maybe this is a special version for when they sing live?* Then, in a split second, everything comes to life, and the lights switch from a soft blue to a deep, all-encompassing navy. The guitar comes in along with the beat of the drums, and Layla beautifully harmonizes with Scott's voice.

I snap pictures of everything, from Drew flipping his drumsticks to Brandon on the guitar and throwing in some sick chords. I focus on Scott for a second, and as much as I hate to admit it, he's one talented asshole. And in that exact second, he looks into my camera and flips it off.

Not gonna lie...that's one cool-ass shot. *Damn, here I am, complimenting this jerk in my head.* If he could hear me now, I'm pretty sure I'd never hear the end of it.

I move over to Brandon and Layla's side and swear I can see sparkles in his eyes. Following his stare, I turn around and spot Ollie. And, of course, it wouldn't be me if I didn't try to annoy and embarrass her. I approach her as she takes faraway shots of the stage and audience.

"Hey, you know what angles would look great? The left side." I nod over to Brandon playing the guitar.

She gives me a questioning look, not buying my weak excuse. *Not like I was trying to be subtle.* "I'll go, but only because I like that spot," Ollie says.

"Are you sure? No other reason?" I nudge her arm.

She shoves me away and sticks out her tongue but goes to him anyway. And it would be a waste if I didn't take advantage of this situation. They're stealing glances at each other, with Ollie holding back smiles and blushes. I take the opportunity to snap a couple of pictures of them; they look so adorable.

It's only the first day, and she already has a love interest.

After a couple of songs we don't recognize, they play "Restless," the first one we heard in the car. Ollie looks at me, wide-eyed: *that's the one.* And I have to admit that they're pretty good, especially Scott.

I shake my head as soon as his name pops into my thoughts, not giving him the satisfaction of proving him right, even if it's just in my mind.

Okay, but he doesn't know what I'm thinking anyway.

I focus on taking pictures instead of on the song, acting as if I'm indifferent to Scott's, let's face it, undeniable talent. But in reality, I'm enjoying these vibes and the mood, letting my body sway to the rhythm.

A whole week of this? I am definitely not complaining.

∞

"Woo-hoo, let's go celebrate! We're in the city that never sleeps, my peeps." Drew slings an arm around Layla, drumsticks in hand.

"Yes, please, let's go out and do something fun," she agrees, clapping her hands.

Olivia walks up next to me. "Yeah, sure. But we need to leave our stuff somewhere first, no?"

"Of course, no problem. Where are you guys staying?" Brandon asks after placing his guitar back in the case.

"Yes, good question. Where *are* we staying, Sam?" I raise my eyebrows at him.

"Umm, about that. Do any of you have any spare rooms the girls can use?" he asks with a guilty look.

"Dude, did you seriously forget to find them a place to stay?" Brandon asks Sam, looking at him as if he lost his head.

"Oops?" Sam shrugs. "Technically, it's not my fault. It's just a misunderstanding with the owners."

"First time in New York, and the day keeps getting better by the second." I sigh.

"What?! It's your first time here?" Layla gapes at me.

Didn't I just say that? Whatever, it's too soon to burden her with my sarcastic remarks.

"Aha, the first time." I give her a tight smile.

"We would offer our place, but we're already cramped in Layla's sister's apartment. She also lives with a roommate. I mean, I'm not complaining, but we have no space left. Sorry, girls." Drew gives us an apologetic smile.

I turn to Ollie, frowning. *Are they a couple or something?*

Layla catches our stares. "Oh, no, no, we're cousins! And Drew's sleeping on the floor like the pig he is, just FYI."

"Ahhhh," we say and laugh at the same time.

"Okay, fine, listen. My parents are out of town vacationing at their lakehouse," Scott sighs reluctantly. "Brandon and Sam are already staying with me, so might as well lend the girls a room. But no funny business!" he says in a fake serious voice.

We both quickly look at Brandon and Ollie. *I guess I'm not the only one sensing their chemistry.*

Sam coughs, getting our attention. "Should we get going?"

"Okay, yeah… Let's do that, and you can settle in before we decide on a plan for tonight." Brandon claps his hands.

"Well, since we all came in my van, and we're not staying in the same places, Sam, can you take Scott and Brandon with you too?" Drew chimes in.

"Do you think they'll fit? I mean, you have all your bags with you," Layla asks with genuine concern.

"The bags are in the trunk, so space is not a problem." Sam shrugs. "It's a new Jeep, one of the latest models with extra space. Perfect for traveling, you know."

"Okay, GEICO, thanks for the ad," Scott mumbles, but we all hear him and laugh at his comment.

"Could we skip to the end when we finally get in the car?" I add to the joke, making us laugh harder.

As we leave through the back entrance and walk to the cars, I turn to Ollie. "Lakehouse?! This dude has to be rich-rich," I mutter under my breath.

"I know, right? Who even has that kind of money, anyway?" she whispers back.

"Remember how to get there?" I overhear Scott ask Sam.

"Umm, no, I don't even remember the last time I visited."

We pile into the car: Scott sits in the passenger seat, Brandon sits behind Sam, Ollie stays in the middle, and I get stuck behind Scott. *Lucky me.*

We leave the parking lot, and Scott plugs in his phone. "You guys don't mind, right? Pretty sure I have the best taste."

We scoff at his comment. *It will certainly be a long week.* "Why'd You Only Call Me When You're High?" by Arctic Monkeys starts playing. *Well, damn, he does have good taste.* He starts singing along, hand-drumming the beats on the dashboard. By the chorus, we all join in and hum along.

I rest my head against the window as the music keeps playing, and I feel like I'm in one of those cheesy movie scenes. It's too cliché for me. But I can't help it; New York is a beautiful city—The lights, the streets, everybody focusing on living life.

I can see how people would either love it or hate it here, though I'm pretty sure I'll love it. Then I realize I'll be spending a week here with my best friend, and I can't help but smile. I catch a glimpse of Ollie and Brandon talking and acting shyly toward each other. *I mean, that's fair; we all just met.*

A call comes in on Scott's phone, the loud ringtone making us jump. "Sorry guys, I'll turn it down," he says with a wince. "Hey, Layla, what's up? You're on speaker."

"Oh, okay. Hi, everyone!" Layla's chirpy voice echoes in the car. "My sister's roommate told me about a party at one of her friend's apartments. She lives in a super chill building, and they're always throwing the best rooftop parties. Wanna come?"

"That sounds great. Thank you!" Ollie answers for all of us after we nod in agreement. "Count us in."

"Cool, text us the address." Scott hangs up before Layla can say anything else. *What the hell, dude? Rude.*

Okay, but this seems like a fun idea. A free rock concert we'll get paid for attending and an after-party? It's the perfect first night in the city.

"Turn right here. It'll be the first one on the right."

Scott points out through the window as Sam drives down the street, the buildings getting taller and fancier, each with a concierge standing outside their doors.

Chapter Two

"I can fall for you in a minute. Thousand promises in that time limit."
~ Lovesick, Alexandra Kessler.

OLIVIA – NEW YORK

E PULL UP IN FRONT OF A TALL BUILDING, cream-colored with marble details on the door and a red marquee canopy with the building's name written in gold. *If this is how it looks from the outside, I can only imagine the inside.*

It's not what I pictured when Scott mentioned his parents' place. Is this what it means to "not judge a book by its cover?"

"You can use my dad's spot in the underground lot." Scott points to a gate. Sam pulls in, and we quickly leave the car after parking.

The guys offer to help with our bags, and Maia leans into me, whispering, "I knew they'd be rich-rich."

"I know, right?"

We enter the lobby, and I can't describe how beautiful it is. Maia and I must look ridiculous with our mouths hanging open, admiring the details surrounding us: white marble walls, crystal-clear windows, and white furniture with gold accents. I've never in my life seen a lobby so elegant.

I don't realize I'm zoning out until the elevator dings, and Brandon calls from where he's already waiting inside. "Are you guys coming or what?"

We don't even get a chance to answer before Scott says, "Come on, move it." He pushes the button for the 20th floor and inserts a key. I turn to Maia, both of us in shock.

Sam notices our reactions. "Yeah, they live in the penthouse. Just wait for it."

The doors open directly into the apartment. I cannot believe my eyes: white furniture, gold and marble decorative pieces, hardwood floors, a gorgeous spiral staircase, and a wall of windows overlooking the New York skyline. *This apartment is breathtaking.*

"Quick tour. That's the living room area, the kitchen is to the left, rooms upstairs, and outside to the far right, we have a small pool with a barbecue. And…that's it." Scott shrugs.

"That's it? I thought there would be more to it." Maia lifts her eyebrows while looking around the apartment, not trying to hide her sarcasm.

"Yes, there is; thank you for reminding me. We also have a hot tub next to the pool," Scott says with an unimpressed tone.

Oh my, anything else you want to add?

"Maia and Olivia, you can stay in the guest bedroom. It's the first one to the left. You two can use Dufus's room, and I'll stay in mine; I don't want to touch anything of my parents." Scott leads us upstairs and points to each room before going straight to his. *Well, this is a man on a mission.*

"Who's *Dufus*?" Maia asks.

"Oh, that's his little brother. He lives with us back in Ocean City," Sam answers as we enter their room.

As we all walk into ours, Brandon calls out, "Oh, Scott. We forgot to call N–"

We close the door before we hear him finish. *He wasn't talking to us anyway.*

Immediately after, we jump up and down. "Oh, my God, Maia, this is amazing! Can you believe we're staying here?!" I hug her as I scream out. "This will be the best week ever."

"What the hell? No way it's real! I'm about to pinch myself," Maia squeals. "Thank you, nerdy Sam!"

I try shushing her, but it's too late. Sam opens the door slowly as soon as the words leave her mouth.

"Umm, I just came to see if you need anything…" He trails off. *Well, this is awkward.*

We try to play it cool, as if we weren't jumping around like little girls just now.

"Nope. We're good, Sam, thanks for asking; just excited to be here." I stretch my arms in front of me.

Yeah, right. Real cool, Ollie.

"Great, then. Meet us downstairs in thirty?" He still looks confused, a frown on his forehead.

"Yep, no problem!"

He closes the door, and as soon as he leaves, we look at each other and burst out laughing.

∞

I'm finishing my makeup, standing in front of the bathroom mirror while Maia fixes her hair. I check the time and notice the 30 minutes are up, so we grab our purses and head downstairs.

As we reach the bottom of the stairs, Scott dramatically struts down, taking his sweet time right after us.

"Took you long enough. Were you getting ready for your beauty pageant, princess?" Sam fake-bows to Scott.

"You know I had to make an entrance." Scott shrugs and fixes his collar. "Y'all ready to go?"

We agree and pile into the elevator, standing silently as we descend to the parking lot. Once by the car, Brandon gets ahead of me and opens the door, smiling as he motions for me to slide in and then get in behind me. *Am I blushing?*

"Did Layla send you the address?" Sam asks Scott.

"Yeah, it's only half an hour away."

"So, we know Sam from high school, but how did you meet?"

"We're friends from college, but Scott and I met at a music camp the year before. We stayed in contact and studied music together," Brandon answers.

"And how did you two meet Sam?"

"Right, well, we met him at a frat party freshman year. He was living with his parents while Scott and I stayed in the dorms. Flash forward to sophomore year. Sam told us he was moving out, and we decided to get an apartment together. Scott's brother has also moved in to finish high school since we had a spare bedroom. What about you girls?"

"Come to think of it, you two were always very close in high school," Sam adds, looking in the mirror.

Maia and I look at each other. "Well, that's a funny story," she says as she smiles.

"We've known each other since birth, more or less. Our moms have been best friends for almost three decades, and they're practically joined at the hip. So, we grew up together." I smile back at her.

"We're like those cliché stories in romantic comedies." Maia's grin widens. "Minus the romance." The car fills with laughter, drowning out what I assume is a crude comment from Scott.

I rest my head on her shoulder as they turn on the music and enjoy the view out the car window. Bright lights, big and flashy signs, people-filled streets, and food carts on every corner— *everything that makes New York the best city on Earth.*

Twenty minutes later, we arrive at the party, and the music is so loud that we can hear it inside the car.

We're definitely not in Maryland anymore… The Wizard of Oz, *get it? No? Okay, moving on.*

"Hey, dude, we're here. Who's letting us in?" we hear Scott say on the phone. "Okay, cool. We'll wait." He hangs up. "That was Drew. Layla's coming to get us."

After a couple of minutes, she walks out to us. "Hi guys, I'm so glad you made it!" Layla pulls us into a hug.

A few long seconds later, she lets us go, and we enter the building, taking the elevator straight to the rooftop.

We haven't been to this kind of party in a long time. Maia and I go out sometimes, but not college-party style. *At least not for some time…*

The doors open, and it looks like your typical fraternity party: red cups everywhere, people dancing, beer pong, and more people scattered around talking.

"Hey, meet my sister Dani and her roommate, Ronnie," Layla says. "These are Ollie and Maia, our new photographers."

She and her sister look very alike, and I would've guessed they're related even if no one told me. Ronnie is a stark contrast to them with her curly hair and dark complexion.

"It's so nice to meet you. Layla hasn't stopped talking about you two." Ronnie offers us her hand.

"Aww, thanks! It was very nice of you to invite us tonight." I say, shaking her hand.

"Yes, it already looks like so much fun." Maia shakes it too.

"Well, the drinks are on the kitchen island, and you can use the chairs by the ledges if you'd like to chill." She smiles at us, and we smile back. "Great, so we'll see you around. Have fun!" Dani and Ronnie show us around before moving on to enjoy the party.

"Where's Drew?" Scott asks.

"He's playing beer pong. You should join him; he's missing

his lucky charm." Layla points him to the table.

"Lucky charm?" I ask Scott.

"Let's just say I've never lost a game before." He smiles smugly before walking over to Drew.

"Let's get some drinks! What do you girls want?" Sam looks between us.

"I could have a beer," I say, smiling at him.

He asks Maia, but she shakes her head. "No, thanks, I'm good. We do this thing where only one of us drinks in social settings, so at least one of us is like *the mom* for the night."

"Anyone else wants anything?" Sam asks.

"I'll take a beer too. Thanks, bro," Brandon answers.

"I'm good. I already have one." Layla lifts her cup.

As I follow her movement, I look behind her and realize someone's watching her. She stands by the drinks table and seems involved in deep conversation, beers in hand. Although, the way her eyes keep darting to and fro, focusing on Layla, tells another story.

Whoever this girl is or whatever she wants with Layla, I can certainly see the appeal: with long, raven black hair and ebony skin, she looks like a warrior princess.

"Hey, I don't want to freak you out or anything, but I'm pretty sure that girl has been staring at you since we got here," I lean closer to Layla.

She turns around, giving her a quick look before turning back to us. "Oh, that's just my ex."

"I don't think she wants to be your ex anymore," Maia smirks as she raises an eyebrow suggestively.

"I–It's a complicated relationship." Layla stumbles on her words as she tries to explain, but I can see she wants to leave from the way she shifts around to look back at her ex.

"You can go. Don't worry about us."

"Are you sure, Maia? Okay, thanks." She gives us another quick hug, not waiting for our confirmation. "Y'all are so cool. I owe you one!"

As she leaves, Sam comes back with our drinks, and we thank him.

"That's smart of you, what you said before. It's nice to see how you take care of each other," Brandon says as he nods to the one drink.

"Do you always do that?" Sam asks after taking a sip from his cup.

"Not always, but we don't usually drink together at places we haven't been before," I say.

"It also depends on our moods, and I don't feel like it tonight," Maia adds.

"Hey, you made it! How's it going?" Drew stumbles over to us. "Are you having fun?!"

"Hey, friend! Yes, we are." I match his excited tone. "Are you okay?"

He pulls Sam into a side hug. "Yeah, I'm good." He's almost falling over.

"Okay, buddy, let's get you some water." Sam chuckles as he excuses himself and leads him away.

"Wasn't he playing with Scott, though?" Brandon asks as we move to the beer pong table. "Dude, what did you do?"

"His weak ass couldn't handle the drinks. But he was already tipsy when we got here," Scott says, fighting back a laugh. "And now I don't have a partner, so who's playing with me?"

"I could do it, but I'm not drinking tonight so you'll have to do it for me." Maia looks at him as she answers.

"Sure, I can afford to lose once in a while," Scott says with a smirk.

"Ugh, shut up." She takes the ball out of his hand. "Who else is playing?" She gives Brandon and me a challenging look.

"We can go against you. Can you handle your drinks?" He looks at me with a pleading smile and a glimmer in his eyes.

"Well, I can handle my beer. What I can't handle is my aim, which is why I've never played beer pong." *I hope I don't embarrass myself too much.*

"Nah, she can't. But we're on vacation, so we'll let it pass." Maia winks at me, and I stick my tongue out.

Sam comes back with a more sober-looking Drew. "Damn, you left me out? Dude, you know I'm good at it." *Oops! Well, at least he looks alive.* "Which rules are you playing with?"

"What do you mean, *which rules*?" I ask, my hands getting slightly sweaty.

The guys glance at each other with mischievous looks.

"Oh, this will be fun." Scott smiles mischievously. "As a tradition, we always like to play with some 'house rules' like Death Cup and Behind Your Back," he continues. "We usually have a couple more, but we'll leave it at that because it's your first time."

"The 'what' cup?" I ask and look at Maia. What the heck did we get ourselves into?

"Don't worry about it. Just focus on getting the ball into the cup," Brandon tries to reassure me.

"Then I guess I'm getting more drinks." Sam gets up as if he's about to leave.

"Wait, I almost forgot! Get a bottle of vodka. We're also doing 'Russian Roulette,'" Scott hollers after him.

"Are you sure? You're the one drinking for your team..." Brandon asks, looking at him with a worried expression.

"I'm good, dude. It's just a couple of drinks." He brushes the comment off, seeming sure of himself.

Sam comes back with, "How many are you doing?"

"Two each, but switch them up so we can't know where they are. Everyone turn around." Scott gives his back to us.

The rest of us face the other way, and I angle my head toward Brandon. "Okay, so, what's going on?"

"We're adding some vodka shots to two cups, but we won't know which two. So, when the balls go in, it's like Russian roulette but with alcohol."

"You guys play by some weird rules, don't you?" I laugh, and we all turn around again when Sam finishes.

"So, who starts?" Maia asks.

"Rock-paper-scissors?" I ask.

"Two out of three."

Rock-paper-scissors shoot. I win. *Rock-paper-scissors shoot.* Maia wins. *Rock-paper-scissors shoot.* I win again.

"Great, we get to start." I confidently shoot first and miss by a long shot. Fuck, this shit's more challenging than I thought.

"You really haven't played before, huh? I can see why," Brandon says with a smirk as he effortlessly makes another shot.

This little bi– "Hey, give me a break. It's not my fault I have sucky aim."

Maia and Scott both make their shots, which means they can go again.

"Pure luck." Scott snickers.

"Sure, honey." Maia rolls her eyes.

Damn, how are they so good? Note to self: ask Maia when she's been practicing.

A quick movement calls my attention. I look to my side and

notice Brandon sniffing some cups; *that's weird*. I look back to the table and throw again, but the ball bounces off the table. Brandon lunges forward and grabs it.

"Look, this is where 'behind your back' comes from." He turns me around and bends my arm behind my back. "Now throw the ball and hope for the best."

Maia hides under the table. "I need to prepare myself." *Oh, come on, bitch. I'm not that bad.*

Surprisingly, I make the shot, and I scream out of excitement while hugging Brandon. Tiny shivers travel down my back as he hugs me, his hands on the small of my back.

"I need another drink." Sam gets up again, no longer sounding sober. *Should we start getting worried?*

"Yo, lovebirds! The game..." Maia teases. We pull away from each other and clear our throats.

"Right..." Brandon shoots but misses, and now it's Maia's turn.

She makes the shot, and Scott makes his with a simple flick of the wrist. *I swear, these two...* Brandon picks up the cups, discreetly sniffs them, and hands me one.

"Why are you doing that?" I whisper to him.

"Making sure you don't get one with vodka. We don't want you getting hammered, now do we?" He gives me a slight smirk as he whispers.

Splash. Another ball goes right into my cup.

"Did you just..." Scott stutters.

"Did she just..." Sam stands still as he returns with his drink.

"Yes, she did! And that, my friends, is the Death Cup," Maia says, bowing.

"Okay, okay, not bad. I might give it to you," Scott says in an impressed tone.

"That was the Death Cup?!" I say a little too loud and with

my eyes wide open.

"Damn right, it was! Now you have to drink everything on the table." Scott winks at us.

"ALL OF IT?" I exclaim.

"Sowwy, Ollie," Maia mocks me.

Damn, I'm getting the whole experience, and it's only my first time playing. How will I handle so many drinks?

"I can help out if you want." Sam walks up to us, his steps a little slow, but he still sounds clear-headed.

"Go for it. The more, the merrier." I hand him a few cups, and he curses under his breath.

"What?" Brandon eyes him.

"Bro, I've gotten both the vodka shots. I swear, my luck today..." He sighs.

"Can you guys get the rest of my cups? I think I'm getting tipsy." I involuntarily slur my words a little. Sam and Brandon share what's left of the drinks.

"Damn it." Sam gets the last one with vodka.

Poor boy, it really wasn't his day. And he doesn't look that great either. I guess I'm not the only one feeling loopy.

He pushes us onto the dance floor, jumping around and bobbing his head. *Is that his way of dancing while he's drunk?*

"Looks like they patched things up," Maia says with a smile. She points to a corner where Layla and her "ex" are full-on making out.

"Well, that's Layla for y'all." Drew throws all his weight on us, hanging off our shoulders.

I lose my balance and fall forward, but Brandon catches me. "So you can't hold your drinks or yourself, huh?" He laughs, and I start giggling.

"Hey, not my fault! I did not count on the extra body on me." I snort a laugh, and Drew nudges me.

"Let's play flip cup! Come on, guys." Drew pulls Sam and Scott with him. Sam looks like he's being forced along.

"I'll make sure they don't die." Maia winks at me. "Go and have your fun," she whispers in my ear, but I shake my head and brush her off.

"I should sit down for a moment." I squint, my head spinning.

Brandon nods toward the chairs and away from the crowd. Once we reach the chairs, he helps me sit down. I'm pretty sure I would've fallen otherwise.

"So," he starts.

"So," I mimic him.

"How do you like the trip so far?"

"Other than not having a place to stay…" I bump his shoulder. "I like it; I'm having fun. We came here without expectations, so what we've done has been great." I give him a thumbs up. "But how about you? Were you expecting anything?"

He purses his lips, apparently thinking. "From what Sam told us, you girls would be good photographers. But other than that, I'm just hoping for the best."

"Hey, not nice." I chuckle. "I still can't believe it's only our first night here, and we've done so much already."

"Now you can say you know how to play beer pong." He lifts his hand, signaling for a high-five.

I go for it, but because of my current state, I miss, and my body pulls me forward and into him.

Brandon laughs, steadying me. "You're only getting water from now on." He starts to get up, but I sloppily pull him back.

"Let's play a game," I suggest.

"I still think I should get you some water, but sure. Do you want to play twenty questions?"

"Yeah, I'm down. Let me think." *Hmm, what should I ask…? Got it!* "What's your dream place to live?"

"I've always wanted to live in Spain. You know, *sunny Barcelona*," he answers, using a higher-pitched voice for the last part. "You?"

"Well, that one has different answers." I chuckle as I think. "During high school, I would daydream about living in L.A. But for about a year now, I've considered moving to London in the not-so-far future."

"I've never been to England, but I've heard London is a great city for photographers."

"Yeah? Do you have friends who live there or something?"

"Oh yes, they're brilliant, and they know a little about everything," he says with a smile creeping onto his face.

"Hmm, what's his name then?"

"Google."

We can't contain our laughter as it echoes over the loud music. I try to stop laughing, but we glance at each other and start again. I nudge his shoulder in an attempt to get closer, the shadow of a glint dancing in his eyes as he looks at me.

"Umm, sorry to interrupt…" I hear Maia muttering.

I quickly look up, still feeling Brandon's lingering gaze on me, and see Sam and Drew slumped over Scott and Layla, the two of them almost falling from holding up their weight.

"Oh, no, poor Layla! You'll crush her," I blurt out, laughing once again.

"Shhh, no more talking." Brandon covers my mouth and nods to Maia. *Don't blush, don't blush, don't blush.*

"As I was saying. we need to get these *children* some food."

"Oh, yes. Food!" I exclaim after pushing Brandon's hand off my mouth.

"I want McDonald's!" Sam lifts his head. *Someone woke up.*

"Yeah, McDonald's is the best. Let's go!" Drew joins in, his head bobbing up and down like a child's.

Brandon looks at Drew with worry.

"He's fine. He just always gets like this, don't worry about it." Layla shrugs. "Also, my sister is our designated driver; she doesn't drink."

"But what about McDonald's?" Drew asks with puppy eyes.

"No, honey, we have to get home. It's already late and there's food there," she says in a sweet voice. "Well, bye, everyone! Thank you for coming; I had so much fun."

We wave goodbye as they carry Drew to the car and stay back as we decide where to go.

"Okay, here's my idea. We can go to a McDonald's drive-thru and Fort Tryon Park until sunrise. It's one of the best places to see the sunrise in the city," Scott suggests.

"Yay, I love sunrises," I squeal.

"But who's driving?" Brandon looks at each of us.

"OH, I will! I drove us here safely, didn't I?" Sam slurs his words, taking out the keys.

"Are you even sober enough?" Maia looks into his eyes, which are red and glossy, even though we all know he's not.

"I'll say that I am *moderately* functional." He hiccups.

"Yeah…that's a no. I'm driving. I know these roads better than anyone here, anyway." Scott takes the keys.

"Uhh, no, you're not. I will. Better safe than sorry since I'm the only one who didn't drink." Maia grabs them from his hands.

"It's her first time in New York, and we're letting her drive. I–great, just great." Scott slaps his hands on his legs.

"Ever heard of Google Maps and a license, genius?" She smiles triumphantly as we walk to the elevator.

Scott opens his mouth, but Brandon pushes him in before he

can reply. "Let it go, bro."

The rest of us get in the car. Sam, Brandon, and I stay in the backseats while Scott sits in the front.

Maia types in the address to the nearest McDonald's and starts driving. But Scott keeps giving her alternate routes.

"I'm from here, remember? I got it." He groans as he tries to make her pay attention to him instead of the map by talking over the GPS.

"Just shut up and let me drive!" Maia slaps his hand away from the screen.

"Fine, but I get the aux then." He plugs in his phone before waiting for an answer.

Sam leans on my shoulder, his breath reeking of alcohol. "Hey, you smell nice. Has anyone ever told you that?"

"Oh, well, thanks." I giggle. Maybe I'm a little drunk too.

"Whoa, dude, not weird at all..." Brandon looks uncomfortable, shifting in the seat. But Sam is so far gone that he doesn't even pay attention.

"Hey, Sam? Does your car have a sunroof?" Maia asks. *Oh, that's a great idea! Let's get some fresh air in here.*

"Yes, it does, Maia. My Jeep is freaking amazing." Sam reaches over, presses a button twice, and the roof folds back.

And as every drunk does, he stands up, raises his arms, and starts singing along to "Empire State of Mind" by Alicia Keys as it plays.

Or more like screaming. Scott turns the volume up, and we all start singing at the top of our lungs.

This will surely be a moment forever imprinted on my mind. *Small disclaimer: it may also be the alcohol making everything feel so magical. But I guess I'll never know.*

About ten minutes later, we reach the drive-thru, and it has a line stretching out to the street.

"Ugh, how is this drive-thru busy? It's almost three a.m.," Maia groans. "Should we wait or go somewhere else?"

"Hi, guys, we're getting bruggers!" Sam shouts.

"Did he say brugger? What the fuck is a brugger?" I burst out laughing.

Brandon reaches over to sit him down but pulls his pants instead. That's when everyone completely loses it.

Sam sits back down, his pants now back in place. "Did you enjoy the view, my friends?" he asks, slurring his words.

"We need to find another place to eat. The quicker, the better." Maia says to Scott.

He points to the right. "Turn here. You'll see a Wendy's at the end of the street." We drive by it, but it's also too busy.

Maia finally finds another McDonald's. They take our orders immediately, and everyone grabs their bags as Maia types in the directions to Fort Tryon Park.

We arrive at the park shortly after, and Scott directs her to the highland, where we'll have the perfect view of the sun rising over the park.

"See? We made it here alive, dumbass." Maia nudges Scott.

"Yeah, I guess," he mutters.

We leave the car and walk up to the wall that overlooks the park. I notice Maia getting too close to the edge while taking a picture. *That's weird; she's terrified of heights. But anything for the perfect shot, I guess...*

Scott stands behind her and fake pushes her while holding onto her shoulders, making her scream bloody murder. "Don't do that ever again." Maia goes all out on him, hitting him with everything she has.

"Hey, chill, *Rocky*, I was only joking around." Scott puts his hands up in defense.

"Wow, congrats, man. You have the whole crowd laughing.

How about a round of applause for you?" Maia fumes at him.

"Okay. How about we sit and eat while the food is still hot?" Brandon stands between them, sensing the storm brewing and placing himself in the line of fire.

"I met him in the park; I asked for a drag of his cigarette."
~ Cigarette, Alexandra Kessler.

OLIVIA – NEW YORK

BRANDON AND I SIT ON THE HOOD OF THE CAR while Sam, Scott, and Maia stay in the backseat with both doors open wide. Sam eats his whole burger in seconds, lies across the seats, and falls asleep while the rest of us take our time to eat our food.

"I think we lost one," Maia says as she munches slowly.

"Aww, poor Sam. He's had a rough day; he deserves a nap," I say.

"His luck just kept getting worse and worse today." Brandon chuckles and shakes his head.

"Maybe a nap will do him some good tonight, and he'll be good as new tomorrow," I sigh as I look back at Sam and Maia inside the car.

Once she's finished with her food, Maia gets out and takes the camera with her. *Once a photographer, always a photographer, right?* Scott gets out of the car too, following her, and starts walking on the ledge a few feet in front of the car, their voices low given the slight distance.

"I'd tell you to get off, but you won't listen to me anyway." She rolls her eyes.

"Wow, I didn't know you were that smart." Scott sports a smug look on his face. "And correction, I don't listen to *anyone.*"

Maia ignores him and continues taking more pictures as the sun rises, painting a beautiful streak of yellow, orange, and purple in its trail.

Scott starts posing in front of her. "Yo, take pictures of me! You can't deny it; those would be some cool-ass shots."

"Your ego can't take *not* being the center of attention, can it?" Maia sighs but still snaps the pictures.

"Only a day has passed, and you already know me so well, congrats!" He gives her a round of light claps.

"Hey." Brandon nudges my arm, drawing my gaze away from them. "We never finished our twenty questions."

"Right." I lean against the windshield and look up at the sky. "So, you don't care about validation, huh?"

He mirrors my actions. "No, not anymore. Once you realize people's opinions don't add value to your life, you learn to let that go. The only opinion that truly matters is your own."

"So, what, you only listen to yourself?" I ask, my tipsy ass forgetting about filters. *Come on, control yourself.*

"No, not only myself. I pay attention to the opinions of people who value and love me for who I am."

"That's one way to view it. But I don't believe that's the only way to see yourself. It's not that I care about validation, but at the end of the day, everyone has some kind of reputation to hold up."

"As long as you respect yourself and stay true to who you are, that's something I could get behind."

I stay silent, taking in the power behind his statement.

"Next question." I lay my head on my hands, my elbows propped up on my knees. "What inspired you to start the band? To start playing?"

"I see it as an escape from reality, from my mind. A better way to express my feelings and put them down in words."

"I wish I had that. It sounds like music is the most important thing in your life. I never learned how to play anything and always left it halfway. I love to sing, though. Sometimes it calms me down."

I turn to him, finding his gaze already on me, the intensity of it burning into me as we let the silence of the night surround us.

Eventually, I feel shy, my heart beating rapidly, and I look away. "Your turn to ask."

He clears his throat. "On a scale from one to ten, how did you like the band?"

"Can I use negative numbers?" I shift to my side, smiling.

"Ha-ha. Come on, seriously, what did you think?"

"Honestly, I'm surprised we haven't heard of you before—Maia and I listen to that type of music, and you're based in Maryland too. But yes, I think you sounded amazing," I stop. "The band, I mean, and your lyrics are nothing like I've heard before." I try to hide my blush by looking away.

"Not a number, but I'll take it. Thank you." He lies back down on the window. A small smile forms on his lips as he stares up at the brightening sky, the sun still not high enough to dull the vibrant colors of the sunrise. "Your turn."

Hmm, what should I ask? As if the universe gives me the answer I was looking for, I notice Brandon twirling his necklace.

"What's something you treasure the most? Like an item or something personal," I look at him as he smiles, gazing at the sky.

"My mom made me these two necklaces when I was a kid and having trouble believing in myself. And my best friend from home in Salisbury, Jordan, made me this wool bracelet before he moved to Texas."

"Oh, wow, that's a beautiful thing to keep close to your heart. How long have you had the bracelet?"

"About six years, give or take. I haven't seen him since." His smile is still very present as he turns toward me.

"Damn, that's a very long time. Do you still stay in contact?"

"Yeah, we talk."

"And how did you guys meet?"

"We used to skate together in a park near our houses." He looks back up at the sky. "We were around twelve years old. I was trying to learn a new trick where you skate down the railings, but I kept falling over."

"Oh, so he taught you how to do it?" I ask, looking at the stars too.

"Nope, he kept falling over too. It made me feel less stupid, though." He laughs, and I join in.

Our laughter dies down, and we quietly watch as the sun comes up and paints the sky a beautiful mix of orange and pink. I release a sigh of relief, witnessing everything change colors. Maybe it's the sun or having Brandon next to me, but warmth spreads through me, like a feeling of peace.

"Give me the keys," we hear Scott say to Maia. *That's one way to ruin a moment.*

"Huh?" Maia asks.

"The sun's coming up. I have to match the vibe," Scott says.

"HUH?" she asks again.

"Ugh, just give them to me!" Scott holds out his hand, staring her down before she hands them over, looking back as he walks away.

He gets in the driver's seat and turns the key without starting the car. He plugs in his phone and plays "Are You Bored Yet?" by Wallows and Clairo.

"Now we're talking!" he exclaims, running to sit on the edge.

We all watch the sunrise in a peaceful quiet, enjoying how it lights up the sky and the clouds, letting my feelings sink in.

It's been a long day, so we decide to go back to the penthouse. Brandon hops off the hood, and while I try to do the same, I lose my balance, *again...*

He grabs me around the waist, smirk at the ready. "I'm kinda getting used to catching you."

"I have to gather myself," I mumble, trying to hide my face as a blush creeps in.

"Or don't...I'm not complaining." He shrugs, his hands lingering at my waistline.

"Hey, let's go." Scott's voice breaks me out of my trance as Brandon and I pull away.

I see Scott jumping off the ledge and standing over Maia, who fell asleep on the bench.

"What do I do?" he asks us.

"Just bring her here or try to wake her up."

A look of sheer terror appears on Scott's face. "You realize you're telling me to wake up a tiger, right?"

He pokes her as if she's some sort of wild animal about to attack at any given moment. "Umm, she's not moving."

"Carry her, it's fine," I tell him.

"We also need to deal with Sam over here," Brandon whispers next to me.

"We?" *Hmm, that sounds like a you problem...*

Scott carries Maia bridal-style for precisely one second before she wakes up. "What are you doing?" She jumps down.

"You, sleep...and we're leaving...don't kill me?" he says, blocking her punches. "She told me to carry you."

I nod, and Maia stops hitting him. "Okay, fine. Give me the keys and let's go." She opens her hand, signaling for him to hand them over.

"No, I can drive. I'm good to go, and you're tired. So, better safe than sorry, am I right?" He mocks Maia with her comment from earlier.

She groans before going straight to the passenger seat. Brandon moves Sam's sleeping body so he's resting his head against the window. Scott starts driving, and Maia takes the aux, playing songs that match the new vibe.

"You two can't complain—the day has been one hell of a ride," Scott says.

"Not gonna lie, it has! We haven't had this much fun for a long time, so thank you," I say.

"No, don't thank them. You three are the ones who can't complain. You got to meet us amazing women," Maia gloats.

"Look who's smug now..." Scott says with a smirk, and I laugh a little.

"Okay, I'll admit it. You guys are pretty cool," Brandon says, his piercing hazel eyes connecting with mine, and I give him a shy smile.

After a while, I start falling asleep and end up leaning my head on Brandon's shoulder. He doesn't react or push me away, so I assume it doesn't bother him. When we arrive at the penthouse, we find ourselves with an issue: Sam is still out cold.

"Okay, who's carrying him?" Scott looks back.

Maia and I step out of the car right away. "Well, don't look at us," I say.

"Rock-paper-scissors?" Scott turns to Brandon, smiling cheekily at us.

"Two out of three?" he replies with a smirk. *Hey! Are they copying us? That's kind of funny.*

Brandon wins, so Scott's stuck helping Sam up. A few minutes in an elevator ride later, we walk into the penthouse. Maia and I go straight to our rooms, leaving them to help Sam.

"Night, guys!"

"Good night!" Their voices echo down the hallway.

We close the door and collapse on the bed. "This is...unreal. I am so exhausted," I say with a sigh.

"We haven't had a day with so much chaos in a while."

"Tell me about it... I kinda missed it, though."

Maia laughs, throwing a pillow at my face. "Come on, let's go to sleep."

We get ready for bed and close the blinds, blocking out the sunlight coming in through the massive windows. *Oh, New York, what a day. I can't wait to see what happens next...*

Chapter Three

"He said you shouldn't be sharing lips with someone you just met."
~ Cigarette, Alexandra Kessler.

OLIVIA – NEW YORK

OKAY, BUT WE'RE HIRED, RIGHT?" I hear Maia's voice as I start walking down the stairs. I don't hear or see anything else before going over the last steps. Maia then jumps out of her chair, doing her little celebratory dance.

"¿Qué pasa?" I ask, rubbing the sleep out of my eyes.

"Hi, *dormilona (sleepyhead)*, I got us a job as Reputation's social media managers!" She jumps up beside me.

"*Qué*, for real?!"

"Yeah, I know, I'm an angel."

"Or I'm just used to your demonic ways." I hug her tight.

"Tomayto, tomahto."

I drop my arms seconds later. "Wait, I'm tired. I need coffee."

"Coming right up," Sam says, his voice coming from somewhere in the kitchen.

"Me too, please," Brandon says in a raspy voice and then turns to me. "How did you sleep?" I guess *he also just woke up. Wait...where's his shirt...?*

"I slept fine." I stretch my arms above my head. "Has anyone checked on Drew?"

"Don't worry, Layla will call us when they're up and they can hang out. He always gets like that, anyway," Brandon says.

Sam comes back, bringing our coffees with him, and all of us are now at the table. "I'm hungry, guys. What are we eating?" he asks.

"I heard about a new diner that opened a few streets down. We can go check it out instead of staying in," Scott suggests, shrugging.

"Yeah, sounds good. Let's go!" Brandon claps his hands.

Sam throws the keys in Brandon's direction, but Maia jumps between them and catches them midair.

"Come on, I'll drive." She confidently walks to the front door.

Scott takes the keys back from her, but not without her holding them even tighter, fighting back.

"Nope, we're taking the subway. You need to get the full New York experience."

I don't bother arguing for her because I kind of want to try it out too. "Umm, guys..." I casually interrupt.

"You do realize we're all in our pajamas, right?" I catch them exchanging glances. "And half of you don't even have shirts on, just thought you should know."

I can't help but steal a glance at Brandon's shirtless, firmly toned body, tearing my eyes away before he catches me blushing. *If I wasn't already swooning...*

We all start to head to the stairs, but the doorbell rings, stopping us in our tracks. By our confused expressions, no one expects anyone, but I assume it's Layla and Drew. *I wonder if they'd actually come without calling first, or is that just me?* Scott goes to open the door, and I follow Maia to the kitchen as she jumps on the counter and grabs her computer.

"What are you doing here?" we hear Scott say.

"What? Isn't it a nice surprise?" a female voice with a British accent responds. *So, not Layla...*

A girl with red, shoulder-length hair and oversized, heart-shaped sunglasses enters the room, pushing past Scott. Maia and I face each other; *who the heck is she?*

"Hi, baabee!! Surprise," she sings with arms stretched out.

"Babe?" I whisper to Maia. My body stiffens, and my hands twitch, making me fold them into my arms across my chest.

"Anna, what are you doing here? And how did you even know where we were?" Brandon asks, appearing dumbfounded.

I look at Maia, and she slams her laptop shut. *The fuck?*

"What a warm welcome… Hi, love! I wanted to surprise you for your concerts. So, here I am. Surprise!" Anna pulls him into a hug. "And does it matter that I knew you were here?"

"No, I guess not." He hugs her back, the same dumbfounded look still on his face. *What is going on?*

"Surprise, indeed," Scott mutters while leaning on the kitchen island beside us.

"Hey, who is she?" Maia whispers to him.

"*Apparently*, Brandon's girlfriend," he answers.

"Apparently?" I ask, confused, but he ignores my tone.

She pecks him on the lips before turning to us. "Oh, hi! And who might you be?"

"Umm, we are—" Maia starts, but Sam interrupts her.

"Olivia Woods and Maia Brooks. The photographers we hired for the band."

"Hey," we say and awkwardly wave.

Anna looks at us like she's confused. "And they're staying here too?" *What does she mean by "too"?*

Sam nods. "Yes, there was a mix-up with the place they were staying at, so Scott offered up a room for them."

She gives us a fake smile. "Oh, I see. Well, it's nice to meet you girls. I'm Annabelle, but my friends call me Anna." She hugs Brandon again. "I'm Brandon's girlfriend from London."

Asshole…didn't he say he didn't know anyone in the UK?

I can feel his intense gaze on me, but I refuse to meet it, fully aware that he must know what I'm thinking.

"Nice to meet you too," Maia and I say simultaneously.

"Hey, can I talk to you for a minute?" Brandon asks Annabelle, grabbing her hands.

"Of course, babe," she answers. They go outside to the balcony and close the door behind them.

"Hey, rockstar." Maia crosses her arms and hollers at Scott as he is about to walk up the stairs. "Elaborate."

"Anna is Brandon's long-distance girlfriend of over a year. They've been on and off for some time, and he's told us that the relationship is toxic. I thought they were in the *off stage* right now."

"It sure doesn't look like it," Maia mumbles.

"And I think she's staying over." Sam nods to her luggage.

Maia notices my silence and that I'm starting to feel uncomfortable. "Well, we're going to get ready now. I'm getting kinda hungry, so we'll meet you back in fifteen."

She hastily grabs her laptop and pushes me up the stairs and into our room.

I can't take it anymore, the words bursting out of me as soon as we walk in. "What the fuck?!"

"¡LO SÉ (I KNOW)!" she exclaims. She runs her fingers through her hair.

"Okay, I don't want to seem like I'm overreacting. But Brandon *was* flirting with me, *sí?* Like, hardcore." I pace back and forth across the room.

"Totally," Maia says while opening her laptop.

The first thing I see is a picture of Brandon and me at the concert; *and it is a cute one, damn it!*

"But he's in a relationship." I fall forward onto the bed.

"Dude, why are *boys* so disappointing?" Maia groans.

"Ugh." I bury my face in a pillow, my skin feeling like it's boiling with anger.

"Listen, it doesn't matter. We just met them, so we shouldn't get in over our heads."

"It is what it is, right?" I mutter against the pillow.

"Yeah. *Lo siento*, Ollie," she says. "But we do have to get ready now, or I'll die of starvation."

Ugh, fucking stupid. Why did I wish to know what would happen next?

"We're ready," I announce while we walk downstairs.

"Ready for what?" Anna asks.

"Right, you weren't here... Well, we're going to a diner for breakfast-slash-lunch. We haven't eaten anything today," Scott explains in a bored toned.

Anna looks at Brandon. "It's like two in the afternoon. Why have you not eaten yet?"

"Umm, we didn't get back to the apartment until about seven in the morning after the concert and the party." Scott scratches the back of his head. "...and the sunrise thing."

"Party? Sunrise thing?" Anna looks at Brandon with a questioning look, and he gives her an innocent smile.

"Bro, you have a big mouth, don't you?" Sam slaps Scott's back. "And when did we watch the sunrise?"

I pat his head. "Aww, poor thing."

"No, I'm not," he says, grinning like a fool.

And now my hand can't reach his head anymore. "You are freakishly tall, man." I didn't realize how much taller than me he is.

"Ollie, you're five feet tall. Everyone is freakishly tall to you," Maia says.

"Hey, that's bullying, you know that?" I give her a slight push.

"It's not like you can talk." Scott comes over and rests his arm on Maia's head.

She's of average height, but he still towers over her. And come to think of it, everybody here is very tall except for Brandon. But I'm still way shorter than him.

Maia pushes Scott's arm away. "Can we just go, please?"

"Anna, Brandon, are you guys coming? Or should we leave you behind for the welcome gift exchange?" Sam jokes with a teasing look on his face.

Thanks for that image, Sam. To even think about it makes my stomach turn.

"We could stay, hun." Anna hugs Brandon, a sultry smile on her face.

"Honestly, I'm pretty hungry too. Let's just go?" He takes her hand, not returning the smile, quickly glancing at me and I look away. *You don't get to do that now.*

"Oh, yes, of course." She sounds disappointed.

We all walk to the nearest subway station and get our metro cards.

"Oh, we're using the tube? Brilliant!" Anna's smile gets brighter, and she holds Brandon's hand even tighter.

Tube? Maia and I look at each other.

"Right, you're Americans. That's what we call it in London."

"Ahh, that's cool!"

We walk in, and almost all the seats are taken. Scott, Sam, Ollie, and I have to stand.

Ollie and I stand in the middle while they grab onto the handles, looking at us like they're confused.

"What?" I shrug.

"Hold on," Scott whispers from behind me.

"But I'm fine." I stare at him, not understanding.

Ollie listens to him and grabs onto the handles. *What a baby!* The train starts abruptly, causing me to lose my balance and crash into Scott's chest. *Ew, why?*

"You were saying..." He gives me his trademark smug look.

Okay, I guess my pride got the best of me. Everyone starts giggling as I put my arm up and hold onto the handle next to Scott's hand.

I struggle to hold on and stay in place, and I feel his hand getting closer to mine, keeping it from letting go.

Who would've thought? He's capable of being considerate, and I'm capable of accepting it.

∞

After a silence-filled ride, in which, thankfully, we all found seats, we arrive at our stop. We all follow Scott since he's the only one who knows where the diner is. No more than five minutes later, we're walking through its doors, the smell of freshly made burgers and fries wafting around us.

The place is charming and homey, with enough room to create personal spaces for each party sitting on the red-colored, leathered booths lining the windows. Few people are inside, and the atmosphere is calm and quiet, just the sounds of the kitchen staff echoing through the white walls.

We take our seats in the booth, and everything is a little more awkward since Brandon is facing me. I immediately take a menu, using it to block his intense stare and try to figure out what to get. Maia does the same, sliding closer to me.

"What are you getting?" she whispers.

"I'm thinking of a cheeseburger with fries, and we can share a milkshake—"

"And dip the fries in it," we say simultaneously.

"Can we be more cliché?" Maia laughs.

"No, you really can't," Scott mumbles, and we roll our eyes.

"Hi, everyone. My name is Heather, and I'll be your server today. Do you know what you're having?" A brunette with a ponytail stands at the edge of our table, notepad and pencil in hand.

"We're good to go. And we would like to split the bill." Maia says, smiling.

"Sure, no problem. What would you like to order?"

"We're both having a cheeseburger and fries. What are your best milkshakes?" I ask.

"Our clients' favorites are salted caramel and s'mores."

"We'll share the salted caramel shake."

"Sure, and what about the rest of you?"

"Yes, thanks, love. What would you like, B?" Anna looks at Brandon with a smile.

Could she be more cringy? No, stop it, brain! She hasn't done anything wrong—*yet*.

"I'll have a BLT, and she'll have a grilled chicken wrap," he answers stiffly while closing the menu.

"Babe, you remembered my order." She rests her head on his shoulder, her lips slightly pouty as she bats her eyelashes.

Just like us last night in the car. He glances at me, and I look away but still feel his piercing gaze.

She writes everyone's orders before we hand her the menus and walks back to the kitchen.

"So, Anna. How long have you known the boys?" Maia asks, leaning back on the leather booth.

"Oh, dear, we go way back, don't we?" She sighs as if

reminiscing. "We met at a music camp years ago—"

"Oh, the one where Brandon and Scott met?" I interrupt her. *Okay, maybe that was a little rude.*

"Yes, the same one," she continues in a bitter tone. *Damn, it seems like we're all on edge today.*

"It's an annual thing. We met Anna and her band the last year we went." Scott shrugs, seemingly acting indifferent. "That's also when we met Drew and Layla."

"We're called Starlights; it's a pop girl group," she continues in a chipper voice.

"Cool." I smile. *Dios, ¿a quién le importa (who cares)?*

"I like the name," Maia tells her. *Yeah, right.*

"Thanks, loves! But anyway, after that, we stayed in contact. And a year ago, I came to the US for a month to visit a few friends in Maryland and reunited with B." She hugs his arm. "We've had some proper chemistry ever since we saw each other. That whole month was magical, wasn't it, love?"

"Yeah, wonderful." He seems to be forcing a smile as he hugs her back.

"I even stayed a month longer so we could spend more time together," Anna continues.

"Wow," I mumble.

"We became an official couple right then, and here we are!" She rests her head on his shoulder again. *I should stop paying attention to them.*

"Here they are," Scott says in a girlish tone, making the rest of us hold back chuckles.

I feel someone kick me under the table. "Ouch, what the heck, dude?" I exclaim.

"Shit, sorry, Ollie. I didn't mean to hit you. I was trying to get this dumbass." Brandon reaches for my hand, but I jerk it away before he can touch me.

"Hey, it's my bad. I kicked Scott first and he thought it was Brandon, so he kicked back the wrong person. I didn't mean for you to get kicked." Sam gives me a side hug.

"It's okay." I hug him back, releasing a sigh.

"If you were trying to play footsies with me, you could've just said so." Scott winks at him.

"Here you go, guys." *Saved by the bell.* Heather returns with everyone's food and places Maia's and my plates down first.

"Gosh, good thing we're walking," Anna mutters while nodding to our plates.

"Did she just..." Maia whispers to me. I glance at her, giving her a *do not get me started* look.

"So, what did Drew and Layla say?" Scott asks Sam.

"Oh, right, I forgot to tell you. They're meeting us later tonight at the penthouse instead."

"Okay, cool."

"Oh, I have an idea! You should throw me a welcome party!" Anna squeals. *What?*

"Umm, sure. We can make it a pool thing and buy some snacks and drinks," Scott says.

"We could also have a barbecue. I'll tell Drew to bring some things." Sam takes out his phone, presumably to text him.

"Isn't it a bit too cold for the pool?" *I'm not getting frostbite.*

"Fine, the hot tub, then," Scott smirks.

"To be rich..." Maia mutters in a dreamy voice, and Scott scoffs at her comment but doesn't lose the smirk.

"So, lads, you need to catch me up. How's Noah?" Anna asks, taking a sip of her Coke.

"He's doing fine, living with us now. He's on a road trip with his friends for spring break." Scott gives her a tight smile.

Ooh, looks like someone else isn't a big fan either.

"Oh, that's lovely! We should do that." She claps her hands, sporting a wide smile.

"How long are you staying for?" Sam asks.

"Only for the week. I guess we won't have any time for a road trip...bullocks." She sighs.

Yeah, how very sad...

We finish eating, pay our bills, and decide to take a walk around the neighborhood, enjoying the city during the day as the sun shines brightly above.

Gotta love a cloudless sky and a cool spring breeze.

"I have to say, I'm loving New York," Maia says, taking my arm in hers.

"And I love being here with you." I pull her closer as we walk down the sidewalk.

We must look like full-on tourists, gazing at the tall buildings, the beautiful parks surrounding us, and the bustling locals.

"I am so knackered! Do you mind if we cut it short?" Anna asks, looking at Brandon.

"I want to walk around for a bit more," Maia protests, gazing at everything around us, avoiding looking at Anna.

"We also have to buy a few things for tonight." Sam nods.

"But you guys can go, and we can meet up later at the house." Scott throws the apartment keys to Brandon.

"Sure, see ya, guys." He gives us one last sad and longing look before pulling his girlfriend along.

"Thanks, loves, you're the best!" Anna blows us a kiss.

"Text us if you need anything," Sam says as they head toward the subway station.

"So, what are we buying for tonight?" I ask.

"I think the apartment has a full pantry. But we should buy more snacks, just in case." Sam throws his arm around my shoulders. And I let him, needing the comfort.

"There's a store around the corner; they should have all we need." Scott starts walking, and we take it as a sign to follow.

"But in a moment, a thrill. It's all finished."
~ Lovesick, Alexandra Kessler.

OLIVIA – NEW YORK

OH, LOOK, A DISPOSABLE CAMERA! I've wanted to get one for so long." Maia dashes toward the display, a grin on her face.

"You're a professional photographer, and you want to buy a disposable?" Scott leans closer, reading over the packaging.

"It's the aesthetic, okay? I need it to document our trip," she says as if it is the most obvious answer. And it is…at least to us.

"Damn, now I kinda want to buy one," he says as he picks one up from the shelves.

"Copycat." Maia gives him the side eye.

"Hey, guys? Is it just me, or does Brandon seem off today? I mean, what do I know? I know we just met, but he's acting weird," I say while pretending to browse through the cameras.

"No, you're right. Annabelle came as a surprise to us, so I guess he could be in shock." Scott shrugs it off. *I wonder why he called her by her full name.*

"I don't know, man, he might just be tired. We did just pull an all-nighter." Sam turns away as he tries on some sunglasses.

We brush it off as him staying up all night and move along with our shopping. Still, something feels off to me.

We get everything we came for, check out, and leave the store. Sam gets a call, and we stand to the side to wait for him, not wanting to block other people's paths.

"Okay, great, thanks. See you soon!" He hangs up and walks back to us. "So, Reputation has two more concerts for the week."

"Dude, that's great!" Scott high-fives him.

"That's so cool," I say in a chipper voice.

"When, where?" *Trust Maia to ask the important questions.*

"Wednesday in Central Park for a mid-spring break season festival. Then we're back to Rockwood on Friday to end the vacation week." He checks his notes on his phone. "So that means we go back home on Saturday." He looks at.

"Okay, sounds good to me," I say for the both of us.

"We should start promoting the band, then. Starting with this week's concerts and fixing up your socials. No offense." Maia gives them a serious look before smiling.

"Guess we'll see if you girls are as good as you say." Scott places sunglasses over his eyes as he turns to Maia and me.

"We are," Maia answers for both of us.

"I trust them." Sam raises his hand. *Don't know why he's raising his hand, and I don't know why I find it cute.*

"Of course you do." Scott punches his shoulder.

"Come on, let's go." I start walking without waiting.

"Wrong way," Sam hollers at me, and Maia pulls me back by the arm. *Of course, it is...*

We sit in the living room while the boys leave the snacks in the kitchen, propping our feet on the table. I'm so exhausted.

I nudge Maia. "We should call Ella. We haven't talked to her since we got here."

We excuse ourselves and head up to our room, closing the door behind us. I take out my phone and immediately video-call her.

"Ugh, finally! Where the heck have you been? What's up? How's it going?"

"Oh, it's going."

"What do you mean?"

"We'll tell you the ugly details later. Tell us what's up with you first," Maia says.

"Fine, I guess your lame thing can wait. Our trip is going perfectly! The lake view is amazing, and I love my friends," she says in a chipper tone.

"Ella, blink twice if you're okay. You're using the word love and seem oddly happy…" Maia says with wide eyes.

"Oh, Maia, *tú y tu sarcasmo (you and your sarcasm)*."

Maia and I look at each other. "And where's Noah?" We raise our eyebrows at her.

"Shh, *no*, it's not like that." She blushes.

"Yeah, right. I can see it on your face, stupid."

"Yo, what's that background? It looks like you're using a green screen," Ella asks, ignoring my comment.

"Right, we forgot to tell you," Maia answers. "We had a problem with the place Sam had booked for us, so we're staying at Scott's penthouse; he's one of the band members."

Ella looks at us with wide eyes. "A pent–what?! Damn, you guys are lucky as heck! Give me a tour right now. Go, before my internet connection stops working."

We show her the room we're staying in, and her jaw drops.

"I mean, we can't blame her. We did the same thing, didn't we?" I say as we laugh at her reaction.

We head downstairs to finish the tour of the house.

"Dude, that place is freaking huge!" Ella exclaims.

Scott hears her from the living room, and we see him look down at his pants. "I know, right?"

"Ew, you are disgusting." Maia looks at him with a nauseated look, taking the phone from me.

"Damn, dude, a little too far." Sam shakes his head.

"Who's that?" Ella asks.

"Hi!" He walks up to stand next to us and waves.

"Hey...Sam?" she says like it's a question.

"Yeah, that was him," Maia mumbles as he walks away.

"And I don't get a proper introduction? How mean!" Scott scoffs as if offended, coming up to us. "You girls have no respect for my flair for the dramatics."

"After that comment, you don't deserve one." She pushes him.

He pries the phone from her hands and runs to the kitchen, and Maia follows. "Hi, Ella, I'm Scott."

Brandon takes the phone from him. "A cocky stupid-ass. And I'm Brandon. It's nice to meet you," he smiles, "here you go," and hands me back my phone, our fingers touching it. *Calm down, Ollie. The phone's not that big; your fingers are bound to brush.*

"Okay, so you're telling me you're staying with three hot guys in a luxury penthouse...in New York...for a week?" Ella asks.

"Sounds about right," I answer without even thinking.

"Oh, and Anna's also here," Maia adds with a tight smile.

"Who?" Ella gives us a confused face.

"Oh, hi, love! I'm Anna, Brandon's girlfriend," she says from the couch, waving at my phone.

Ella must notice my smile switch to a frown. "What's with the face, Ollie?"

"We'll leave that for next time; that will take a while."

The doorbell rings, cutting into our conversation. *It must be Layla and Drew unless they have another surprise visitor... Scott* opens the door, and, indeed, they walk in.

"OMG, hi, girls! I feel like I haven't seen you in so long." She pulls us into a tight hug.

"Oh, jeez. Who sounds so happy?" Ella mumbles.

"Layla, meet my sister, Ella. She's on a school trip with some friends and classmates."

"That's so cool! And it's so nice to meet you. I hope you're having the best time," she says excitedly.

"Thank you! Are you in the band too?" Ella asks her with a genuine smile.

"Yes! I'm on keyboards and sing backup for the boys. And this is Drew, my cousin. He's the drummer." She points to him.

"Hi, nice meeting you, Ella. Maybe next time you can come too." He smiles at the camera and winks.

"For sure!" She smiles back.

"Hey, Ella, we're leaving." Someone calls out to her.

"Oh, is that—" Maia starts, but Ella interrupts her.

"Shh, yeah, yeah! I'll talk to you guys later when we get back from the lake."

"Hey, no fair, you met everyone here! You should let us meet *your* new friends," I say.

"Bye." Ella hangs up.

"Ugh, this girl." Maia rolls her eyes.

"Hold up, is that Anna?!" Layla shrieks, making us jump.

"Layla, love, I've missed you! Come hug me." She matches her excitement.

"What are you doing here?" Layla asks while almost squeezing her.

"I'm visiting for the week. I needed to see my B. Right, babe?" She turns to Brandon.

"Yes, and I missed you too," he replies with a smile, but it doesn't seem sincere to me. *Not that I know him all too well ...*

"Okay, can I have everyone on the couches?" Sam says, and we all sit down. "Great, so you guys have two more concerts this week. I got a call on our way back earlier: Wednesday at Central Park and Friday at Rockwood."

Drew joins in, high-fiving Brandon and Scott.

"Also, meet your new social media managers, on a trial basis, but still. Glad to have you girls onboard," Sam continues.

"OMG, guys, for real? That's so exciting!" Layla jumps from her seat and hugs us.

Drew sits between us after Layla goes back to her spot and throws his arms around us. "Alright, now we're having some serious fun!"

"Oh, so it's a new thing?" Anna asks, looking between Brandon and us. *Qué te importa (why do you care)*.

His eyes connect with mine in an apologetic and pleading way before reluctantly returning his gaze to Anna.

"Yeah, as of this morning," Sam answers, and she nods, not saying anything else.

"Before I forget. Here's the barbecue stuff you asked for." Drew hands him a couple of grocery bags. "I don't know how to cook, though. So, who's going to get greasy?"

"I can do it!" I say.

"You can cook?" Brandon asks with a glint in his eyes. *Stop that, please.*

"Oh, definitely, but she can only cook meat. For some reason, it's the only thing she learned how to do. You do not want her doing anything else, or she'll burn the kitchen down." Maia snorts a laugh and I punch her shoulder.

"Awesome, I'll put these in the fridge so they don't go bad, and we'll start cooking later. We still have food babies from lunch. Or at least I do." Sam takes the bags into the kitchen.

"Lovely! Well, if you guys don't mind, I should catch up

with Layla." Anna takes her hand and pulls her upstairs.

"Come on, Maia, I have some cool picture ideas." I take our disposables, and we walk out to the balcony. *There's no way I'm letting this impressive view of the skyline go to waste.*

Chapter Four

"Should I let you know the truth, the way I really feel about you?"
~ Should I, Alexandra Kessler.

OLIVIA – NEW YORK

I STAND IN FRONT OF THE GRILL, staring at it like nothing about it makes any sense. *What's with all the buttons? How do I even turn on this shit? I'm used to charcoal.*

"Ollie, it's a modern grill. It ain't that hard."

"What's your point?"

"That you only need to do this." Scott turns it on just like you'd do a stove.

Damn, it was that easy? Or am I just dumb?

"Let's call you an assistant, but not because I doubt you or anything." Maia looks between me and Scott.

"On it. Yo, Sam!" he hollers without missing a beat. "He usually works this grill."

"What's up? Do you need any help?" Sam walks out, hands in his pockets, immediately looking at me. Maybe it's because I clearly look lost and out of my game.

"Yes, please," I say in a baby voice.

"Sure." He chuckles.

"Okay, I'll be back in the kitchen making a salad. I leave you in good hands, I hope." Maia clasps her hands together like she's praying, and Sam assures her on my behalf.

"Okay, so, we're missing the seasoning." I look at him.

"I'll get them. Try not to burn yourself in the meantime."

"Yeah, yeah, go be useful."

He goes back into the house, and I just stand still, mesmerized by the fantastic view. We truly are lucky to be here right now; this is beautiful.

The sun sets in the background; its rays stream through the clouds, and the sky changes into a beautiful pink and purple.

"Hey!" A deep, masculine voice pulls me back from admiring the scenery.

"Huh?" I turn around to find a confused-looking Brandon.

"I've been calling you for a while." He rubs the back of his head, appearing uncomfortable.

I guess I was a little too lost inside my head. I blink a couple of times before answering. "Sorry, my bad. Did you need anything or...?"

"Umm...do you want some help with this?" His guilty eyes say that it's not the real reason.

"Hmm, no, not really. Sam's already doing it, but thanks, anyway!" *There's no way I can be alone with him. Especially now that I know he has a girlfriend...who's here.*

As I say his name, Sam comes out with his hands full of condiments. "Don't worry, dude, I got it."

"Yeah, it's fine. You can go. And it seems like Anna wants to spend time with you." I nod behind him to her running up to us, trying not to look upset.

She jumps on his back when she reaches him. "Babe, let's go to the hot tub!" He sighs and reluctantly accepts.

∞

"Okay, great, now put the steaks on, and I'll get some drinks. Do you want a beer?" he asks.

"Sure, thanks." I open the grill, and all the smoke comes straight to my face.

I jump back to avoid burning myself, crashing into Sam. *What's up with me today?*

"Shit, are you okay?" He steadies me, holding my waist.

"Oh, yeah, I'm super. I did that on purpose, you know."

"Right, I guess you wanted a charcoal facial." I laugh.

"Okay, okay, go get the drinks."

"Try not to die while I'm gone, okay?" *Ha-ha.*

I quickly finish placing the steaks inside and close the grill. A few minutes later, I startle when he tickles me from behind.

"Do you *want* me to burn myself?" I joke as he passes me a can. "So, Sam..."

"So, Olivia..."

"How is it we didn't hang out in high school?" I ask, and he looks at me like I've grown two heads. "What?"

"Ollie, I was a huge nerd. And, let's be honest, as cliché as it sounds, we weren't in the same social circles. Not that I had much of a circle anyway..." He sighs. "Don't get me wrong, being alone for most of my high school years wasn't that bad."

"You had a hard time then? I remember people messing with you for no reason, and I've always thought that was very fucked up. But I didn't know how bad it was for you."

"Yeah, it was. But I guess that made me the man I am now. If I didn't struggle and go through the things I went through, I wouldn't be here and have this life now. I'm in a good place because of that," he says with a proud look.

"I get that, but it doesn't excuse what people did to you."

"True, but that's in the past now." He clicks his can with mine.

"True too." I nod. "Maia and I wouldn't be here if it weren't for your high school self."

"Nerdy Sam. Who would've thought?" He nudges my arm, and I nudge him back.

"Can I ask you something? But promise me it won't be awkward or weird."

"Should I get another beer first?" He gestures to the kitchen, and I smirk. "Okay, no, I'm kidding. Pinky-promise!" He holds up his finger and links it with mine.

"Why did you have a crush on me back then? Like, we didn't hate each other or anything. But we weren't that close either, so was it a superficial thing or..."

"I *do* need to get another beer then." He laughs, but it sounds forced.

"Hey, come on." I push his shoulder.

He puts his hands up. "Kidding! But yeah, sure, it was a superficial thing. I thought you were hot; you know, I was a teenager. Boy stuff."

"Oh." I furrow my eyebrows and look away. *Why does it hurt?*

"Disappointed, huh?" He lets out a dry laugh, apparently noticing my change of mood. "I'm sorry, it wasn't like that at all. It started around junior year..."

"So, what...you liked me because I inspired you to start your surfing career?" I smile at him as he finished the story.

"Hey, don't get ahead of yourself. I was going to do it eventually. Let's just say you pushed me at the right time."

"Sure. So, you liked me because I was nice and helped you stand up against your bullies?"

"Something like that," he says with a shy smile.

"Aw, you're blushing," I say in a sing-songy voice. "You're such a cutie."

"No, I'm not," he immediately protests with a serious look.

"Yes, you are. Look at you." I pinch his cheeks.

"We're grilling steak. It's hot!"

"Umm, sure."

"Shut up." He pushes me with his left hip.

It's been a while since I've laughed this much, and I genuinely enjoyed it. Oh, how I needed that today...

"I've been down these roads so many times, falling in love to a stranger's touch." ~ Him – Not Again, Alexandra Kessler.

BRANDON – NEW YORK

SCOTT TURNS THE MUSIC UP and touches a button that changes the pool's colors. I'm too focused on Sam and Ollie's hardcore flirting to get excited about it.

"Babe, hello?!" Anna waves a hand in front of my face.

"Sorry, what?" I brush my hand through my hair. *I swear, someday, my hair will start to fall out.*

"What's going on with you, love?"

"What do you mean? I'm fine." I hug her, trying to comfort her in an attempt to appear like everything's normal.

"You've been awfully quiet today."

"I'm fine, I'm just tired." I give her a peck on the cheek. *Honestly, I don't know what's going on with me. Do I even love her anymore, want to be with her?*

"Hey, dinner's ready!" Ollie yells from the grill area, Sam helping her carry the food inside. *Could he be more transparent with his flirting?*

She lets out a giggle as he whispers something in her ear.

"Let's go, hun." Anna nudges me.

I get out of the hot tub and take her hand, helping her out of habit. *How will I get through this week when I didn't even know she was coming?*

∞

"Okay, okay, even if you almost burned it, I have to give it to you guys; it was pretty good," Maia says as Sam hugs Ollie. *Why do they have to hug so much?*

"Yeah, it was so good!" Layla relaxes on the couch along with everyone else.

"Yo, I have an idea! This is starting to get boring, so what about a game of truth or dare?" Drew sits up as he announces his new "brilliant" idea. Everybody agrees in a rush of excitement.

"Cool," I reply without any emotion.

Anna holds my arm tighter. "Okay, but nothing risky, please." That's not the Anna I remember. What's changed?

"But first"—Layla stands up—"everybody put on their swimsuits, now!" *How can that much energy fit in that tiny body? And why do we just always agree with her ideas?*

Scott, Sam, Anna, and I sit close to the hot tub's edge, waiting for the girls. Layla and Drew are already in the water.

Scott's eyes drift to the glass door. "Oh, fuck me..." he says under his breath.

I look back to see Maia and Ollie coming to the balcony with their bikinis on, and I have to stop my jaw from dropping. Goddamn, is Ollie gorgeous...

Brandon, shut up! You have your girlfriend sitting right next to you demanding your attention.

"Dude, where did you find these girls?" Drew says in an amused tone.

"Yo, shut up!" Sam splashes water on his face.

"Yessss, work it, beauties!" Layla shouts at them. They laugh and walk toward us. *Is it the tub, or why is it so hot in here now?*

"I have that same bikini in pink," Anna mumbles next to me.

"Shit, it's fucking cold," Maia says while wrapping her arms around herself.

"Yeah, we should get our hoodies," Ollie suggests. They turn around to go inside and retrieve them, but Sam stops them.

"Here, take it." He gives his to her. "Scott, take yours off."

"Huh?" he says, coming back to reality.

"Your hoodie," Sam repeats in a sterner tone.

"Seriously?" Scott groans, throwing his head back for dramatic effect.

"Never mind, I'll just get mine." Maia starts to go back inside.

"No, wait, it's fine. But only because I want to start the game." He hands it to Maia, sitting down next to me afterward.

"Be careful, or you might start drooling," I tease him quietly. *Shit, I should take my own advice, or I might start drooling.*

"Shut the fuck up." He pushes my shoulder.

"Okay, now that we're all here. Who starts?" Layla looks around at everyone.

"NOSE GOES," Drew yells, and everyone but me touches their nose.

"Wait, no! I wasn't paying attention!" I groan.

"Too bad, bro. Truth or dare?" Drew leans back.

"Dare," I say with a sigh.

"A brave soul." Drew nods. "Do four cartwheels in a row."

"Come on, dude, that's easy." I get up and stand where I'll have more space. On the fourth one, I get dizzy and stumble. *Damn it!*

"Come on. That's easy, dude!" Drew mocks me.

"The floor was wet," I groan as I sit back down.

"Sure, sure," he taunts. "Anna, truth or dare?"

"Truth," she says confidently. *Now that's the girl I knew and fell for, so sure of herself.*

"Have you ever thought about cheating?"

"Damn, Drew's coming in hot," Scott hollers.

"Always, sweet pea." He bows his head.

"What kind of question is that? Are you mental? Of course, I haven't!" Anna exclaims in a defensive tone, hanging harder onto my arm. *Someone's a little dramatic today.*

"Not even with a hot celebrity?" Drew looks at her, waggling his eyebrows.

The girls start naming different male celebrities.

"Nope." Anna shakes her head furiously.

"Dude, she's loyal. Congrats!" Sam high-fives me, but I frown at him. *Why is everyone acting so weird about her answer?*

"Drew, truth or dare?" I ask.

"Dare."

"Yell the first word that comes to your mind right now."

"Shrink?" he blurts out.

"Yeah, you sure need one." Maia snorts from next to him.

"Yeah? Are you interested?" he says in a flirty tone.

"Okay, next one, please," Ollie mumbles, breaking the awkwardness.

"Layla—" Drew starts to ask.

"Dare, I choose dare!" Layla bobs up and down.

"Too much energy for me," Ollie mutters under her breath. I quickly stop myself from laughing as I notice Anna glaring at me from the corner of my eye.

"Attempt to do a magic trick," Drew says.

"OMG, yes! I have the perfect one; give me one second."

Layla gets out of the water and runs back into the apartment.

She soon comes back with a deck of cards in her hands. *Nothing she did would surprise me at this point.*

"Do you carry that in your purse?" Maia asks, appearing completely baffled.

"Yes! You never know when an opportunity might arise. Like right now," she answers.

She attempts to guess Maia's and Ollie's cards but fails and makes us all die of laughter.

"Sam, your turn." Layla turns to him, acting like her "magic act" did not just flop.

"Truth."

"Damn it, I got nothing." Layla sighs after looking around.

"I have a question!" Drew raises his hand. "Among all the people here, which guy or girl would you like to date?" *Now, this just got interesting...*

"I'm getting another drink." He ignores him and stands up, walking to the door.

"Oh, come on, man, answer the question!" Everyone stares at me. *Did I say that out loud?*

"Ollie," Sam mumbles and then abruptly closes the door.

"Coward much," I say under my breath.

"Okay, Ollie, I guess it's your turn now." Layla smiles wickedly.

"Truth."

"Why do you hate it when people don't call you Ollie?" I ask, raising my eyebrows.

"Dare," she says with a cold stare.

"Really?" I internally sigh. *What are you hiding, and why do I feel like learning all your secrets?*

"Kiss the person to your right," Anna challenges her.

"He's not even here," I mutter, annoyed at this stupid game.

As if on cue, Sam enters with a Coke can in hand, and Ollie goes up to him and pecks him on the lips. "Done," she says while looking at Anna. "You're welcome, *love*." She winks at her.

Sam tries to act nonchalant about it, but he's blushing. *Why am I even mad?* My back stiffens as I shift uncomfortably.

"I like your blush, Sam. What shade is that, cherry tomato?" Scott mocks him in a childish voice.

"Okay, my turn! I choose dare," Maia cuts him off.

"Umm, okay. Sell a piece of trash to someone in the group. Try to be the best saleswoman you can." Drew says.

Maia looks around and then grins at Scott and stands up. "Okay, guys, I have this brand-new statement piece right here." She grabs his shoulders.

"To be honest, it doesn't have much value. I mean, if you consider trash talk valuable, then this is the item for you! We found it brand new from the garbage, so get it while you still can," she says with a smile.

"Damn, dude just got burnt," Drew mocks him as we all laugh.

"Sure," Scott scoffs, a sour look on his face. "I choose dare, by the way."

"I dare you to jump in the pool for the rest of your turn...on this cold New York night...on a balcony," Sam dares him, and he stands up confidently.

Maia lets out a slight laugh. "My pleasure." He picks her up.

"Fuckkk, no, no, no. Don't you dare; put me down!" Maia lets out a scream as he jumps into the pool with her.

"Wait, I want to do it too!" Drew yells, jumping in with Layla following right behind.

"They're risking it all, huh?" Ollie says in an amused tone.

Sam takes his shirt off and turns to her. "Life is short,

right?" He picks her up and then jumps into the pool too as she squeals into his shoulder.

Come on, man. I roll my eyes and mutter under my breath.

"Do we really have to?" I look at Anna. *Fucking damn it.*

"We kind of do, love."

"Alright!" I pick her up, and we jump in with everyone else.

We stay in the water for a while, swimming around and splashing each other. But it gets too cold as the night passes, so we all get out and grab some towels from the pool rack to dry ourselves.

"Oh Lord, I'm freezing!" Layla says, her voice trembling and her body shaking.

"Me too," Maia and Ollie reply at the same time. *That's kind of cute.*

"I'm going to take a bath before I die from hypothermia," Anna says before walking upstairs.

"Hey, it's getting pretty late. Shouldn't you guys stay over?" I ask Layla and Drew.

"Can we? Neither of us feels like driving that far this late." Layla turns to Scott, who is still shivering.

"If you don't mind sleeping on the couches." Scott dries off.

"Dude, they're like beds. Wait, that one's bigger than my actual bed." Drew snorts a laugh.

"You can stay with us, Layla. It's a king-sized bed, after all." Ollie shrugs, the towel slipping with the movement.

"Thanks, girls! But that's calling my name." She points to another enormous couch.

"I don't blame you; it looks comfy as hell." Maia nods.

"Achoo! Ah, great, I better shower too; I don't want to get a cold." She runs up the stairs.

"You could use ours too and go after Maia. I'm not that cold," Ollie tells Layla.

"Awesome, you're so cool! I'll wait upstairs if you don't mind." Layla runs up without waiting for confirmation.

"I'll go ahead too." Sam walks to his room, and Drew leaves for the one downstairs.

"Well, then, I'll leave you two alone," Scott walks up the stairs. *How subtle of you, dude.*

I let out an exhaustive sigh, as if finally being alone with Ollie releases a tension in my shoulders that I didn't know I was carrying since Anna's arrival. But this is the first time we've been alone, and I'm desperate to know where her head is at, even if the idea of hurting her crushes me.

Why do I even care so much? We've only just met. And why does it feel like I'm living only for her attention? This doesn't make any sense. It was never like this with Anna.

"So, Anna is...nice," Ollie says while shifting on her feet.

"Yeah, but I wasn't expecting her to show up."

"I noticed," she says while tidying up the kitchen.

I decide to help her, don't want her thinking I have no manners. *Not that it should matter to me...but why does it?*

"Doesn't seem like communication comes easy. Must be hard to maintain a long-distance relationship," she asks, not looking at me.

"What can I say? It's not easy if both parties aren't fully committed. to the relationship"

"You make it sound like it's a business deal," she jokes in a dry tone.

"No, I mean, it's not like that. It's just been a long time since I've seen her, and I guess time changes people. So, I'm getting used to this changed version of her."

"She hasn't always been this way?" she asks, picking up more trash, still not looking at me.

"No, not at all. When we first started dating, she was looser, free-spirited, and didn't care for others' opinions. She was independent. I don't know what happened. Where did all that go?" *When did everything change? Anna's almost unrecognizable to me, like she's weighed down by something, but she won't tell me about it. But I'm acting strange too, so maybe it's me. I'm the one who's changed.*

"I mean, she did just arrive today. She might just feel exhausted," she says without emotion.

She feels off; this is not the same person I've been talking to for the past two days. But I get it, yesterday I overstepped boundaries that a person in a relationship shouldn't have crossed. Should I even bring it up with her? She keeps cleaning and hasn't looked at me since we started talking.

"Ollie, can you look at me?"

"What?" She lifts her head, her gaze a combination of frustration and hurt.

"Umm, about last night—"

"It's fine," she interrupts me.

"No, it's not. And I'm sorry if I did anything that made you uncomfortable." I occupy my hands with picking up trash as they ache to reach for her, but I know I shouldn't.

"Let's leave it in the past. And we don't have to bring it up ever again." She sighs, her shoulders sinking and drops the bags on the floor. "Let's just ease this weird tension between us and start over."

"One hundred percent! You could've cut it with a knife."

"Yeah, no, Brandon. Jokes aren't your thing." She shakes her head and laughs under her breath, making me smile.

"Noted." At least we're getting somewhere.

Maia comes downstairs. *Are you kidding me? She had to come right now?*

"Hey, guys! I'm making hot cocoa. Does anyone want

some?” Her eyes shift between us. “You know what? Never mind.”

She starts to go back up, but I stop her. “It’s fine. I should go shower anyway,” I say.

I jog upstairs, and Maia walks into the kitchen with Ollie. I know it’s wrong, but my curiosity wins. So, I stay on the stairs where they can’t see me but where I can still hear them.

“What’s up with that?” Maia asks, and I hear her moving some things. I’m assuming she needs to find cocoa ingredients.

“We had a conversation, or at least I think it was supposed to be a conversation.”

“What do you mean? How did it go?”

“Shit, it went like shit,” Ollie answers in a bitter tone. *That bad, huh?*

“Really?” Maia asks, sounding surprised.

“Yeah, but don’t worry, it’s all flushed down the toilet.” Ollie snorts a laugh.

“Look at her, she has a sense of humor.” Maia laughs.

“Everything’s fine. I’m pretty sure he noticed how tense I was since this dude was flirting with me. While in a relationship! And here I thought he was genuine,” she says, sounding even more annoyed.

I was acting genuine, but I guess I wasn’t entirely truthful from the start either.

“Anyway, he sort of apologized.” *She sounds relieved.*

“At least he’s self-aware,” Maia says.

“It’s fine, I guess. We only met yesterday, and it’s not like we hooked up or he cheated with me, so...” *Damn, it was just yesterday? I feel like I’ve known her for months.*

“It’s been two days, and it feels like a week. But thank God everything’s fine now; remember that we’re also working with these guys for a while,” Maia reminds her.

"Yep." Ollie sighs. *How am I so disappointing?*

"Dude, what are you doing?!" Scott startles me as he approaches from behind. "Are you eavesdropping?"

"No, maybe, possibly…yes." *I'm disappointed in myself.*

"Dude, go and shower. Preferably with Anna, your *girlfriend* of a year. The one who came to surprise you and is staying with you." Scott emphasizes almost every word while keeping his voice down.

What am I even doing? I don't even know who I am anymore.

I go back into our room with my head hanging from embarrassment, lying on the bed and sighing. It's been such a long day; I need it to end.

Chapter Five

"I'm planting a rose to remind me of my worth, on how things take time to grow." ~ Stage 4: Acceptance - Planting a Rose, Alexandra Kessler.

MAIA – NEW YORK

DAMN, SOMETHING SMELLS GOOD," Sam says as he strolls downstairs. "What's happening? Ollie's not cooking, right? No offense."

"Ha ha, no. Maia's making breakfast." She laughs as he tries to hug her.

"Morning, thanks for feeding us," he walks up to me in the kitchen. "Want any help?"

Olivia's phone rings before I get to answer. "It's Ella," she says before answering the call. "Hey, what's up?"

"Good morning! Nothing much here; going on a hike in a bit. What about you?" Ella's voice echoes through the phone.

"Oh, that's cool. We're making breakfast for everyone."

"WE?" Ella and I say in an accusatory tone.

"Okay, okay, *Maia* is cooking for everyone," Ollie says, rolling her eyes.

"Thank God… no offense." Ella snorts a laugh.

"Hey, no fair! Why is everybody coming after my cooking skills? Damn," she cries out with a groan.

"What skills?" Ella says, and I start laughing. Even Sam does a little, earning a glare from Ollie. "Kidding, kidding, you know we love you."

"I used to, but now I'm not so sure." She sticks her tongue

out at us.

"Ella, you ready?" A male voice comes through the phone, making me run up to it to see who it is.

"Oh, is that—" Ollie asks in a sing-song voice.

"Hi," he replies, and I run to Ollie's phone.

"Well, hello! Nice to finally match a face to your name," Olivia says in a sad attempt at a joke. I nudge her, making her look at me as I frown as if saying, *what was that?*

A boy with wavy brown hair fills the screen. Why does he look so familiar?

"I'm Noah, Ella's friend," he says with a smile.

"We know, I mean—" I start saying.

"It's nice to meet you too," Ollie says, swooping in.

"Are you trying to burn the house down?" Scott walks down the stairs, dramatically waving his hand in front of his face like there's smoke. *And there's not...*

"Good morning to you, too." I look at him before turning my attention back to the phone.

Wait, oh my God, the food. I turn around to go to the stove but Sam's already there.

"Wait, who was that?" Noah squints at the screen.

"Hello...?" Scott stops dead in his tracks, a confused look on his face. "Hold up, Noah?!" He comes closer to the phone.

"Scott?!" Noah screams.

"What the fuck? Why are you video-calling?" Scott yells as he jerks the phone away.

Ollie, Ella, and I look at each other, not understanding what's happening.

"Can someone explain what's happening?" Ollie asks for the three of us.

At that moment, I remember Scott talking about his brother and Anna mentioning his name at dinner.

"Wait, is Noah—" I start asking.

"My little brother," Scott finishes for me.

"Dufus?!" Ollie and I ask at the same time.

"Wow, Scott, really? How nice of you," Noah groans. "Why are you still calling me that?"

Sam walks by after checking the food and glances at the screen. "Yo, what's up, Noah!" He takes a double look. "What?"

Scott still appears confused, mouth agape. "Stole the words right out of my mouth."

"Noah and Ella, my sister, are in the same class. They went on their junior camping trip together." Ollie blinks a few times as she wraps her head around it. "Don't worry, we're as lost as you."

"Oh…" Sam and Scott mumble, finally getting it.

"And what's happening there, *dufus*?" Scott asks with raised eyebrows and a smirk.

Noah and Ella's cheeks turn bright pink, avoiding each other's gazes, and Noah quickly answers. "Nothing! We're just friends, don't be weird."

"Sure, Elmo, whatever you say," Scott mocks him—only making Noah blush harder if that's even possible.

Ella interrupts him. "Anyway, this was fun, but we really need to go now. Bye, guys!"

We say goodbye right before they hang up.

"They are so cute!" Ollie squeals. *Okay, calm down now.*

"Dude, it *is* a small-ass world." I sigh while laughing and going back to cooking.

"Tell me about it," Scott mumbles and brushes his hair back in what I assume is disbelief.

I finish cooking, and Drew and Layla wake up. "Geez, this smells great. Thanks, Maia!" she says while jumping off the couch.

Now they wake up?! Not from all the noise we made?

"How are you so chirpy this early?" I ask while handing her a full plate.

Layla giggles as she stretches her arms up. "Am I?" *Should we even answer that?*

As we sit down, the two *lovebirds* walk downstairs to join the rest of us at the table.

"Wow, you went all out, huh…" Anna mutters with an unimpressed look on her face.

Does she ever have any other face?

"I guess," I reply, noticing Brandon looking over at Ollie, who's still avoiding him. *This guy, the CEO of giving mixed signals.*

"I didn't know the deal came with a personal cook, but I ain't mad about it," Scott smirks at me as he waits for his food.

"I do like cooking, but don't get used to it." I wink while handing him his plate.

"So, what's the plan for today?" Drew asks with a mouthful. *Boys will be boys, I guess.*

"We could go to Times Square. I love that place!" Anna squeals before taking a bite.

"We can't, we need to work today. But you guys can go have fun," Ollie answers for both of us.

"That's so good of you girls! Working hard, I see," Anna says in a tone that annoys me.

Can she just shut up? I look at Ollie to see if she thinks the same, and I try to keep a straight face.

"Are you sure? It's not going to be as fun." Layla pouts.

"Aww, but don't pressure them, love," Anna talks over her.

"It's fine, she wasn't." I look at her, frowning, feeling annoyed.

"Why don't we go at night? Maybe you'll be finished by then." Sam turns to us with a smile.

"Sure, sounds good." I smile back, and Ollie does the same.

After we finish breakfast, Sam stands up and starts cleaning up. "Oh, thanks! You didn't have to do that," I say to him.

"Of course I did." He grabs the boys' dishes. "But we're all going to clean up while the girls work. Right, guys?"

Layla and Anna agree. "Oh, yes, that's a great idea!"

"Kiss-ass," Brandon mutters while rolling his eyes at Sam. *Well, someone's bitter.*

"Huh? Dude, it's my house," Scott groans and throws his head back.

"Exactly, and you treat your guests with kindness." Sam stands his ground, enunciating each word. *Yeah, you go.*

"That's not a word in his vocabulary." Brandon snorts, and Scott playfully punches him.

"Well, I'm a guest here too. You guys go ahead and I'll supervise." Drew leans back on his arms. But Sam pulls him up and makes him clean. *Oh, I'm here for this bromance.*

We take our computers and sit in the living room with Layla and Anna. I open up my laptop for everyone to see. *Fuck, I completely forgot about the picture of Ollie and Brandon.* I quickly take it off the screen before anyone notices. *Fingers crossed, at least Anna didn't.*

"I hope Sam likes your work because I really want you to stay with us," Layla says with a hopeful tone.

"Oh, I'm positive they will. You know, since Sam has a crush on Olivia." Anna turns to look at her.

"What?! No, he doesn't." She looks at Anna as if she has lost her mind.

"Oh, come on, it's pretty noticeable." Anna winks at her like this is a game. "Don't fight it, love; you guys would look so cute together!" She stands up. "Well, I'm going to shower and change. I also might take a little nap. Last night was exhausting if you know what I mean."

Oh, we know, but we didn't need to hear that.

"Okay..." Ollie mumbles and gives me a *look*.

"I'm sorry for her, girls. I don't know why she's acting so strange," Layla pleads with us after Anna walks upstairs.

After they're done with the dishes, which weren't many, the guys throw themselves on the couch as if they came back from war or something.

"Wow, guys, five minutes. That's a new record." Ollie pretends to check the time on her wrist.

"Yeah, that's impressive. Four men putting plates in a dishwasher... Damn, that must've been hard," I say sarcastically.

Scott lays his head on my lap and looks up at me. "That's not very grateful of you now, is it?"

"Stop it." I push him off. *Umm, personal space?*

"What, are my looks distracting you?" He raises an eyebrow and starts to smirk.

"You wish," I roll my eyes.

"Ouch," he says while placing a hand on his chest. *Like I could even dent that ego of his.*

"Well, if you guys don't mind, we have to work. So, could we have the living room, please?" Ollie asks.

"But it's my house." Scott groans, reluctantly doing what he was told.

"It's alright, sweetie. We have to go back to the apartment anyway." Layla hugs us.

"Yeah, text us what time we're meeting and where." Drew man-hugs the boys.

"Sure, we'll see you there!" Brandon pats his back.

We yell our goodbyes from the couch, and Sam walks them

to the door. The boys leave us to do our own thing, and we start working on the photos and their upcoming posts announcing their gigs, letting time fly by. It's not until they place some pizza for us on the table that we notice the time. *Is it already three in the afternoon? Damn, we're in the zone.*

"Ollie, room, now!" I exclaim as a memory pops into my head and I shut the computer.

"What?"

"Come on." I pull her by the hand and skip upstairs. We walk into the room and close the door behind us.

"What's going on?" she asks.

"Do you remember what we agreed on early this year?"

She looks up, trying to remember what I'm saying. *I love my best friend, but she's the most forgetful person I know.* She looks at me wide-eyed as she realizes what I'm talking about.

"Oh no…"

"Oh, yeah!" I nod enthusiastically.

"The *no more bullshit* thing," she sighs.

When we started the year, we had a whole tipsy rant about how we would embrace our true selves this time. Do the things we've always wanted to do; no more bullshit.

"Why now?"

"Why *not* now? I mean, we're on vacation! It's the perfect time to start, so let's go." I grab my bag and put on my shoes.

"Go where?" she asks with a questioning look.

I stop and look her dead in the eye. "To get my blue hair dye, of course."

"Of course," she mimics me but follows me anyway. *Not like she could say no, we did make a promise.*

∞

We arrive back at the apartment and run to the room, ignoring the weird glances from the guys and Anna. *Who even cares that she's staring?*

"Try not to make a mess, okay?" I pretend to be bossy.

"I'm not you, Maia." She squints her eyes at me.

"Funny." I give her an unamused look. The joke fires back on my face as Ollie lathers up the hair dye on my head without any drops on the floor.

"Okay, put on a thirty-minute timer?" I ask her and take this time as an opportunity to ask some critical questions. "So, what's up? We're going with Sam now, huh? Hoe."

"Shut up, Maia." She shoves my arm playfully, even though I know she's annoyed.

"I'm kidding!"

"It's just weird!" She groans. "Brandon seems so off since yesterday, you know? It's like he's completely turned off or something, and Anna is all over the place, all over him. And it also bothers me that they keep making all these comments about Sam and me!" She lies back on the bed.

Ugh! Oh no, I poked the stress beast.

"For example, during the game last night. Anna dared me to kiss Sam, and Brandon pressured him to answer Drew's question. What the fuck is up with that?" She lets out an exasperated sigh.

"But Brandon keeps sending these mixed signals, and it's messing with my head. I know I can't let it get to me, but it does. And we also had that moment at the park, which I can't stop thinking about." She groans, covering her face with a cushion.

"I know! Everything's so crazy right now. Like, dude, what about the Noah and Ella coincidence? And don't you think it's insane that he decided to move out at seventeen…with his brother and roommates? Also, it's the second semester; that seems off to me." I laugh. "Though Ella's been living with us, we shouldn't find that *too* weird."

"Yes, it does. Maybe you should ask Scott," she suggests with a sly smile. "You two seemed…cozy…this morning."

"Ask the embodiment of arrogance? No, thanks, I'm good." *Not that he would tell me anyway.* "And, no, we were not getting *cozy* or whatever. He just has a problem with respecting personal space."

"Hmm," she hums, obviously not agreeing with me.

I pick up my phone and notice the number of notifications from the Reputation account. "Look, the posts are getting so many likes already!"

"The power of social media," Ollie says with a smile.

"And two badasses who know what they're doing!" I high-five her.

"We should show the boys once your hair's ready."

"Yeah, about that…has it been thirty minutes yet? The smell is starting to bother me."

She checks her phone. "No, you still have ten more minutes to go."

I pause for a second and look around. "Are we not going to mention that this looks like a freaking hotel room?"

She looks around too and laughs. "Look." She points to the bathroom.

I follow her finger and notice a blow dryer and curling iron. "Dude, what?"

"I'm going all hairdresser on you now." She stands to set it all up on the counter.

"Sure, be my guest!"

"Let me be your favorite song, play me all day long."
~ Symphonic Orchestra, Alexandra Kessler.

OLIVIA – NEW YORK

I OPEN MY EYES, yawning and stretching my arms, and instinctively check my phone: Wednesday, 10:30 a.m.

Finally, the day of the festival. The last few days have been pretty uneventful with the guys rehearsing and us working. *Well, if you don't count Anna getting more annoying by the second.*

I get up from bed, trying not to wake Maia. I walk straight into the kitchen and start the coffee maker; the smell of coffee fills the air in a matter of seconds. *If this doesn't wake people up, I don't know what will.* I close my eyes, taking a deep breath to savor it.

"Is it safe for you to handle that, or should I call the fire department?" I hear Brandon ask.

I open my eyes, finding him leaning against the counter, and I take a subtle step back. "Oh, come on, give me some credit! I'm not that useless."

"Emphasis on *that*," he jokes and moves back to avoid my incoming smack.

"You think you're so funny, don't you?" I prop my elbows on the counter, lean my head on my hands, and give him an accusatory look.

"At least people laugh at my jokes," he answers with a smug smile. I open my mouth but can't think of any comebacks. "I guess that means I won," he says.

"Don't get used to it, mister. I rarely ever lose."

We give each other challenging looks but then start laughing. We keep looking at each other for longer than we should, the intensity behind his eyes making me slightly shiver. I break eye contact when I turn around to get some mugs.

"Are you the only one up?" I ask with my back still to him.

"Yeah, I think so. Do you need help with anything?" I can hear him walk closer to me.

"Nope, I'm good. Thanks." I start pouring our coffee, and he passes me the sugar.

I thank him while turning around and looking up at his face. *Why is he standing so close to me? And was his hair messy all this time? How did I not notice it before?* Something about the just-woke-up-look on a guy hits differently.

He stretches his arms, and his tank top rises, showing his lower abs, and I let my gaze drop for a second. I quickly look back up; he's staring right back at me, raising his eyebrows. I turn away, embarrassed. *Could I be more awkward?* I add two scoops of sugar to my coffee and then pass the jar to him.

"I like it, by the way." He nods to my oversized shirt.

Shit, I completely forgot this is all I'm wearing...in a house full of boys. Wait, did he steal a glance at me too? Stop it, Ollie; his gaze is on your legs, not you, his non-girlfriend.

"Thanks, it's from the Star Wars prequels."

"I didn't think you'd be a fan." He sips his coffee.

"And why not?" I ask, drinking mine.

"You don't seem like the geeky type to me." He shrugs and leans on the counter again.

This dumb ass guy takes one step forward and two steps back. "Oh, and what type do I seem like, exactly?" I ask.

"Rom-coms?"

"You do know a girl can have more than one interest, right?" I answer, trying not to get annoyed at the comment.

Before he can say anything else, Sam and Maia walk downstairs. *Saved by the smell of fresh coffee.*

"The best way to wake up, hands down," Sam sighs with a delighted smile.

"Tell me Brandon made the coffee, or I might walk back upstairs." Maia stops on the last steps.

"Don't be ridiculous and come get your coffee." I laugh.

"But what's the fun in that?" She smiles, walking up to me.

"Slight change in topic, but how are we doing with our social media? Any changes yet?" Sam asks as he sips his coffee.

"I don't want to brag… But ever since we took over, your engagement has been through the roof. "The best post so far is the one about the festival."

"Then we made the right choice. Thank you, girls!" Sam pulls us into side hugs.

"No problem," I say with a small smile.

We hear footsteps coming downstairs. "Dude, I want to skate so badly, I even dreamt about it. Good morning, by the way," Scott says as he reaches the last steps and stands behind Maia.

"Morning to you too. Honestly, same. We should go today." Brandon says.

"Umm, today's the concert, guys," I say matter-of-factly.

"Yeah, but isn't it in Central Park? We could leave early, spend the day riding for a bit, and still have plenty of time before we play." Brandon says.

"Morning, everyone! What are we talking about?" Anna walks into the kitchen. *I knew this calm morning was too good to be true.*

"Nothing much; we're going skating before the concert." Scott sips his coffee.

Anna rests her head against Brandon's shoulder. "Babe, we

can have a picnic date," she says while batting her eyelashes.

"You do know we're also here, right?" Maia frowns.

"Of course, hun, I meant for all of us," Anna says, raising her voice. *Sure, you did.*

"Okay, here's my idea. Scott, do you have any baskets?" I ask, ignoring Anna.

"My mom has some, yeah."

"Great! Let's take some food and have a little brunch at the park. Who's in?" I clap my hands together and get a round of *yes, sure,* and *let's do it.*

We get right to it: packing some sandwiches, juices, bottled water, and extra snacks for later in the day.

Is this even going to go well or be fun? Everyone's been so tense and on edge since Anna's arrival. I just hope this helps us— or, well, me—relax before the big concert.

The last thing I need today is to be stressed the whole time and take bad pictures.

We walk around once we get there, taking in the beautiful scenery of tall trees, winding hills, and vast green grass as we search for the perfect spot to set up our picnic. We decide on a small hill overlooking a lake near some old-looking buildings towering over the trees. *I could stay here forever with just my best friend and some food.*

We start to unpack everything, and a few minutes later, we see Layla and Drew walking toward us.

"Hi, guys! Oh, this is just the perfect time for a picnic. Whose idea was it?" she asks with her usual chipper tone.

"It was Ollie's. She sort of set everything into motion today," Sam explains while throwing an arm around my shoulder.

I smile at him while tucking my hair behind my ear. "I wouldn't say that, but thanks."

"We didn't bring anything. Sam told us you brought enough?" Drew says while sitting on one of the blankets.

"Don't worry about it. I always pack extra anyway," I answer. "But I didn't bring a lot of beer since you guys are playing, and we're taking pictures later. You know, being professional and all." I say as we sit down.

As birds chirp around us, we eat slowly and chit-chat about what we've done over the past few days—working on the band's pictures and social media.

We finish eating and cleaning up, sipping our drinks, and enjoying the quiet breeze that blows through the park; it all combines to give the moment a serene feeling.

"Maia, OMG, your hair, I just noticed it! You look like a skater girl now; I love it so much." Layla opens her eyes wide and smiles as if mesmerized by her.

"Thanks, Ollie actually dyed it last night before going out," Maia says.

"Oh, that reminds me! I brought my sister's penny board in case any of you wanted to skate." Layla pulls it from Drew's backpack. "And it's purple!"

"No way!" Anna shakes her head.

"Yeah, no. I'm out too," I say. *The first time I agree with her.*

"I want to!" Maia takes it.

"I thought you would say that. You've done it before, right?" Layla asks cautiously.

"Nope, not once."

"Really? I thought you did, you know, from your vibes and all." Layla frowns, shock and confusion written on her face.

"Don't judge a book by its cover, I guess." Maia winks at her.

"Are you girls going to keep talking or skate?" Scott gets up, clearly eager to start skating.

"Are you going to take that stick out of your ass?" Maia smiles at him. *Oh, if looks could kill…*

"Cute," Scott smirks.

"Come on, I'll teach you!" Layla stands up, and they walk to the concrete pathway.

Brandon scoots closer to me as the others leave. *Why couldn't he leave the space between us? Why does it feel like we're pulled toward one another? We can't be.* "So, why don't you like skateboarding?"

"I'm not a sporty or active person, have no interest in it."

He looks at me like I've grown a second head or something. "What? But it's so fun, so freeing."

I shrug. "Hmm, I don't know. I honestly don't think I'd like it."

"Come on, what's that saying, you don't know until you try it?" He nudges my shoulder. *Did he forget his girlfriend is here? What is this?*

I groan, throwing my head back and laughing. "Sure, let's say I do try it. Are you volunteering to teach me? A skateboarding rockstar?"

"Layla would do it. She's teaching Maia, isn't she?" Anna gets up from her spot and sits on Brandon's lap. "Right, babe? She could even do it right now. Olivia can use your board while we stay here."

Well, someone wants me out of the way.

"Don't force her, Anna. She doesn't have to if she doesn't want to. It was just a suggestion." Brandon looks at her with a confused look.

Weren't you doing the same thing right now? Make up your damn mind.

Sam must pick up on me feeling uncomfortable because he comes up and sits on my lap. *Is this dude crazy? He'll crush me.* I shake my head and laugh at his absurdity, making him do the same, shifting his weight on me.

"No, yeah, you're right." Anna nods. "Layla?" she calls out.

"What?" Layla responds, apparently forgetting about Maia, making her roll down the hill.

Scott stops her with his foot and grabs Maia by the waist. She holds onto his shoulder and immediately gets off the board. She pushes him away while muttering *thank you* and walks up to us. Scott picks the board up and follows her.

"So, I think I'm done skating for now. Thank you, Layla, for the traumatizing experience. I'll be scarred for life," Maia jokes as she sits beside me.

"I'm so sorry, Maia! Anna called me, and I spaced out for a moment," Layla says in an apologetic tone.

"It's fine. I'm just messing with you," Maia says with a smile.

"Now that Layla's free, she can teach Olivia, no?" Anna hugs Brandon, pulling him tight against her, and stares me down with a pointed look.

"No, thanks. With my luck, I'll fall on my face." I shake my head, and I think I hear Anna scoff. *What the heck is her problem?*

"And there goes your aspiring modeling career," Maia sighs dramatically. "How sad."

"Hey, no fair! You know that's my life-long dream." I fake gasp. My legs start to stiffen. "Sam, no offense, but you're not as light as a feather." I try to push him off.

"Oops." He laughs while getting up and sits next to Drew.

"Ugh, finally, I can feel my legs," I groan while stretching.

"That's what she said," Drew yells, and we all laugh.

Maia gets up once the laughter stops and grabs the board again. "I'll make sure she doesn't die," Scott mutters and follows her.

She practices her balance by standing on the board, and Scott puts a foot between her feet. Not sure if that's helping, but she hasn't fallen yet. I'd take that as a win.

"Hey." A guy with long hair and a baseball cap approaches her out of the blue. *Is it me, or do his eyes look a little bloodshot?*

"Umm, hi," Maia says, almost like it's a question.

"I've been watching you for a while." He shoves one of his hands into his pockets. *Wow, not creepy at all, dude.* I watch cautiously. "I dig your moves." He gets closer, stepping into her personal space and taking off the cap.

"Oh, thanks! Cool design, grungy." She points to his skateboard while taking one step back. Maybe she feels the weird vibes too.

"Yeah, so, I was wondering—" he starts saying while getting even closer to her, leaving Maia with barely any space, and she leans closer to Scott.

Suddenly, Scott discreetly kicks Maia's board in the opposite direction, sending her barreling toward the grass. I hope she figures out how to stop, or it won't end pretty.

"Sorry, buddy, I guess she wasn't interested." Scott shrugs.

"You think?!" The guy leaves, a shaky hand running through his greasy hair while his friends laugh a few steps behind him.

Umm, okay, no need to yell, dude. All she said was hi. Why is he getting mad?

"Dude, what was that?" Maia gives up on skating, storming

back and confronting Scott.

"That's the thanks you give me?"

"What?" She frowns while regaining her breath.

"It seemed you wanted to get out of that conversation, so... you're welcome," he says as if stating the obvious, and even shrugs in an exaggerated manner.

"And the only way you thought of helping was by pushing me down a hill? I didn't need your help!" Maia's fuming.

"I guess you kinda did need the push. You learned how to skate, girl." Drew lies on the grass, arms crossed under his head. "It was pretty hot, though, not gonna lie."

Layla punches his shoulder. "Shut up."

Maia pushes past Scott and sits beside me, leaving him standing and confused. "Hey, come on, he did what we were all thinking. That dude creeped me out too," I whisper to her.

"Yes, he was giving me the creeps, and *maybe* I was trying to get closer to Scott. But still, he's an asshole for doing that. And I could've defended myself without his help, you know."

"Oh, trust me, I know; it wouldn't be the first time either." I lean my head on her shoulder as I whisper that last part.

I hope we can just enjoy the rest of the day without killing each other. Or at least trying to...

"I no longer depend on your reign, nor your watering, nor your pain."
~ Stage 4: Acceptance - Planting a Rose, Alexandra Kessler.

OLIVIA – NEW YORK

TEN MINUTES BEFORE THE SHOW STARTS, Maia and I walk to the front of the stage, standing in front of the first row.

The band that was playing finishes their set, thanks the crowd, and goes backstage. I turn around to snap some pictures and cannot believe how many people are here at the festival. The people in the park fill up the hills and the picnic tables surrounding the area.

How on earth will we walk through that later?

The lights dim while the presenters introduce Reputation, and I turn back around to face the stage. A spotlight turns on Brandon as he starts the song with a guitar riff, and part of the crowd goes wild.

Then, another spotlight hits as Drew joins in with the drums. At last, Scott starts with the bass, and Layla starts singing. That's when the crowd loses it, screaming, cheering, and clapping as they play.

I snap pictures of each of them as the spotlight first hits them, the lights turning red, purple, and a hint of orange. They go through a couple of their songs, highlighting their talents.

At one point, Brandon and Scott get close to one microphone, harmonizing over the song's bridge. *Damn, and he can sing too? No wonder Anna's obsessed with him...or am I thinking of myself too?* As if the crowd can hear my thoughts, they whistle and clap until the song ends. I take advantage of this moment and snap the perfect picture. *They look adorable sharing that microphone.*

"Hi, everyone; thank you for welcoming us tonight and for being such an amazing crowd! And for that, we have a gift for you. We'll be playing a brand-new song that's coming out next week," Scott says into the microphone.

That's so cool! I mouth to Maia.

"It's called 'Elixir.' We hope you enjoy it." Brandon glances at me, and my heart skips a beat.

"This guy never stops, huh?" Maia whispers to me. *Tell me about it.*

I switch to recording mode to create a promo video for the song and a recap of their gig. The music starts with a bass riff from Scott and, surprisingly, Brandon's singing as the lead.

> I wake up, and you're on my mind,
> I wonder if I am on yours,
> I've been feeling lost and confused.

He looks at me, staring into my soul. I try to focus on the video and the camera, making sure my trembling isn't noticeable on the feed. The crowd is quiet this time, feeling the lyrics just as we are. I can still sense his stare as he goes into the chorus with Scott and Layla.

> I'm in a daze, and you're my elixir,
> I am crumbling down,
> But you pick up my pieces.

"Damn, who hurt them?" Maia whispers while leaning into me.

I shake my head. "I don't know. But Brandon has to stop staring at me..." *What about your girlfriend, dude? Where the hell is she and is she noticing this?*

I sigh while looking through my lens after switching back to picture mode to take more shots of the band. Scott sticks his tongue out at us, and Maia snaps one of him. He'll love it.

They reach the chorus again and play it more up-tempo as they do a medley with another song. Scott and Brandon start dancing around to the rhythm. Then, a drum solo starts, and Drew's going all out with it. Screams fill the air, earning some smiles from the others and a wink from Drew.

Suddenly, cannons go off from all sides of the stage, filling the sky with red and white confetti. Smoke starts to come out from behind Drew, and with the lights, it looks like the band members are walking out from inside the clouds.

I capture the moment Drew throws his sticks in the air, and the lights go through the smoke. I then turn around to take some shots of the crowd with the confetti falling on them. They're going wild: cheering, dancing, and some even try to catch the confetti.

"Thank you, New York; you've been amazing. We're Reputation. Have a great night!" they yell into the microphones, waving goodbye and blowing kisses to the crowd.

A concert to remember...for more than one reason.

"So, what now?" Drew asks, leaning against the car and wiping his sweaty forehead with a towel.

"The artist lineup looks pretty cool. Maybe we should stay and watch some of it." Brandon looks at us over his shoulder as he helps pack up the instruments.

We decide to eat something first, so we walk down to the food area, after making sure everything's in the van and the trunk of Sam's Jeep.

"Maia, so, the *no-bullshit* thing," I whisper as we sit at one of the tables.

"What about it?"

"What if we both drink today? We both let go for a while." I shrug, liking the idea of drinking wiht my best friend.

"Who are you, and what have you done to my best friend?" She squints at me.

"What?" I ask, acting fake-surprised and smiling wickedly.

"Nothing. You know what? Sure, let's do it! But someone has to watch out for us."

"We're getting some drinks, girls. Do you want anything?" Sam turns to us as he stands up from the far end of the table. We turn to him with sneaky smiles. "Why are you staring at me like that?"

We tell him our plan for the night, and he agrees. And, with that, we walk up to one of the beer stands. We then make our way into the crowd, jumping and vibing with the music and other people. And since it's getting darker, the hanging lights between the trees shine even brighter above us.

"Hey!" Maia shouts over the loud music. "I'm getting another drink. Do you want anything?"

"Sure, surprise me!" I see her go to one of the drink stands close by; *good thing we're not very far into the crowd.*

I keep dancing under the strobing lights, feeling the beat of the music. I glance beside me and see Brandon vibing along to the song too. We look at each other for a moment, and my breathing gets heavier from the intensity in his eyes. But in a split second, Anna walks up to him, coming from the drink cart, and starts grinding against him.

Why do I keep getting my hopes up, only for her to shut them down? It's not like I can blame her; she is his girlfriend, after all.

I look away to the stage, watching the band playing. I turn to where I last spotted Maia, but she's talking to the creepy guy from earlier. Again, he leans too close to her, backing her up against the cart and giving her no choice but to finish the conversation. I squint in an attempt to see them better, noticing his hand is dangerously close to her drink.

"Umm, what was that?" I ask as she approaches me.

"Nothing, he was asking me about what happened at the park. I told him that Scott kicked my board. Did you notice his eyes were kind of red before? Well, now they're fully bloodshot and weirdly wide. He might be *on* something."

"Not at all." I shake my head. "I think you missed it while you were skating back, but he got pissed, even yelled."

"Well, here's to avoiding him while we're here." She takes a sip of her drink and hands me a beer.

"It's adorable!" I look the can over; it's so colorful.

"I knew you'd like it." She winks and smiles.

Well, it's better than whatever she's drinking. It has so many colors that it looks like a potion or something.

"Hey, don't look at it like that. Why don't you try it?" she offers as she catches me eyeing it.

"No, thanks, I'm good; that shit looks weird as fuck." *Like the greasy guy from before.*

We keep on dancing, and the rest of the group joins us. I close my eyes, taking in this moment with my best friend and this new group of people. We just met, but I feel these friendships will last a lifetime.

The band on stage says they're playing one of their first songs, and the crowd goes wild. Everyone's singing at the top of their lungs, jumping and hugging each other.

"Are you okay?" Sam approaches me, rubbing my arm,

taking that take-care-of-me thing too seriously.

I'm tipsy, but I'm fine. He keeps staring at me, and I realize that I might've only answered him in my head. "Sam, I'm fine." I giggle. "Don't worry."

"Maia seems to be doing okay too." He nods over to her. *Wait, when did she even leave my side?*

I look to where he's pointing and see her dancing with the greasy dude and his creepy friends further into the crowd.

Huh, that's weird... She told me that guy felt off to her. I guess the no BS list included ignoring the warning signs...

"Are you fucking kidding me? I thought we all agreed that guy was sketchy," Scott shouts over the music and chugs down his drink.

"Guess she likes creepy." Drew shrugs as if trying to make a a funny comment.

"And where's Layla?" I ask, looking around; I can't see her anywhere. My pulse quickens at the thought of losing her in the crowd too.

"Over there." Sam points behind him.

I see her climb up a treehouse between some trees, built just for the festival, dancing with other girls. "That girl truly is the life of the party," I say in an amused tone.

After a while of dancing alone, I can't shake the bad feelings in my gut, the feeling that something's wrong. *Maia...why hasn't she come up to me, asking if I'm okay, checking in, or even telling me she was going to dance with him?*

I turn to where she was just now to make sure she's okay. But when I look over, I don't see her anywhere. Spinning around, I enter full panic mode as I approach the guys.

"Hey, have you seen Maia? I can't find her!" I ask, my voice shaking and my hands trembling. *Am I too drunk or just dizzy with panic?*

"What?!" Scott yells.

I look behind him and finally see her leaving with that creepy guy and his friends. "What the fuck?"

"What happened?" Brandon asks in a worried tone.

"She's probably having fun, sweetheart. Let her be free," Anna says like it's not a big deal while leaning on Brandon.

God, just shut up already! Why are you even here?

"If it were anyone else, I'd believe you. But this is my best friend we're talking about here; she never does these things! Excuse me," I bump her shoulder as I tread in Maia's direction with the guys following behind.

When we're near them, my heart drops. I can see that Maia's not well: she's not just drunk, she looks completely gone.

"What do you think you're doing?" Sam confronts them, Scott trailing right behind him, both fuming.

"Nothing, dude. She wanted to leave with us," the creepy guy answers, a mischievous look on his face. She doesn't even object; she just stands there.

"Maia," I call out, and she looks at me with a blank stare.

"Wait, did you guys fucking drug her?!" Scott yells, moving closer to them.

One of the guy's friends runs away. Scott throws his beer can on the ground and jumps the creepy guy in a split second, beating the crap out of him. But he doesn't give up without landing some punches too. Even if I wanted to get in on it, I wouldn't be of any real help. It doesn't take long until the creepy guy's other friends follow in the first runaway's footsteps.

Sam takes Maia's hand, and she willingly follows him, but it's clear she doesn't know what she's doing. A security guard comes up to us after the others have run away. Scott tells him about the guy, and the guard chases after him, calling backup.

"We're going home to take care of her. Make sure Layla is

okay too, and let us know when you're home," Sam tells Drew, and we leave for the car as he goes after his cousin.

Maia passes out beside me on the seat, and I can't help but feel like the shittiest friend ever. "Guys, I think we should go to the hospital." I almost sob as I try to contain my tremors.

"Turn right here. There's an ER on that street," Scott instructs Sam, his leg bouncing up and down like mine.

We arrive at the emergency room, Scott carrying Maia in and calling over to the nurses. Sam holds me as a group of nurses and doctors bring in a gurney, laying Maia down on it. I drown out the noise and voices as Scott explains what we witnessed, even though he's unsure what happened. I shake in Sam's arms, tears streaming down my face at the thought of losing my best friend, of what could've happened if we were even just a second later.

They wheel her away and into an examination room. Scott's voice sounds distorted as he says something about tests being done. We sit in the waiting room, all of us on edge and shaking with the dread of bad news. I'm not sure how much time passes until we all stand as a doctor approaches.

"From the looks of it and the test results, we determined that she had a small dosage of Rohypnol, commonly known as the date-rape drug." My breath hitches as he starts explaining. "Mixed with whatever she was drinking, it was enough to make her amenable, susceptible to suggestion, but not enough to knock her out completely.

"Take her home, monitor her recovery closely, and let her rest. Make sure she eats and drinks lots of fluids. And if she's not fine by tomorrow afternoon, bring her back and ask for me. My information will be on the discharge papers."

"Thank you," I say, taking it with a shaky hand.

"You, young man, should let us bandage you up." He looks

at Scott and signals over a nurse.

"No, I'm good," he barks out before grabbing Maia by the hand, who follows his lead silently. He doesn't wait long before walking off toward the car, us trailing behind them.

Once we're back at the house, we wake her and make her drink water. She does everything we're telling her to do, which infuriates me more. *There are some sick people in this world.* Maia passes out on the couch again, and Scott's cuts keep bleeding, but he refuses anyone's help.

"Fuck, why the hell would someone do that? No wonder people say men ain't shit," Scott groans, breathing heavily.

"Thank God you saw it at the right time, Ollie," Brandon says to comfort me while Anna quietly holds onto him. *Thank God she stayed quiet at the hospital, or I would've lost it.*

"No, it took me too long; who knows what could've happened?" I say, on the verge of tears.

Scott gets up and punches the kitchen counter, releasing a scream and startling everyone.

"Hey, dude, calm down! You're not helping her by hurting yourself," Sam says to him.

I doubt anything will have a calming effect right now.

Scott looks back at Maia, chest rising with each huffing breath, guilt washing over his face, and then storms upstairs.

"We should all get some rest," Sam mutters while helping me carry Maia upstairs.

Tonight will be a long and sleepless night, at least for me.

Chapter Six

"And I was gasping for air. I tried to scream, and nothing came out." ~ Scary Nights, Alexandra Kessler.

OLIVIA – NEW YORK

EVERYONE WAKES UP EARLY, waiting for Maia to come downstairs. I'm pretty sure none of us slept at all last night; I can tell from the tired looks on everyone's faces.

After a while, Sam starts to get restless, so he decides to make the biggest cappuccino in hopes of helping her feel better when she comes downstairs. Even Anna seems to be on edge about the situation, maybe she regrets some of her comments. And then there's Scott, all bruised up but seemingly unfazed by it.

Maia walks down the stairs. "What the hell happened last night? My head's throbbing." She stops at the last step and stares at us, wide-eyed. "Why do you all look like you're going to hold an intervention?"

"Maybe you should sit down." Sam gives her a tight smile. She sits beside me, he hands her the coffee, and she puts her legs up on the couch.

"Okay, what is all this?" she asks, clearly confused. She turns to Scott. "And what happened to you? Are you okay?"

"It's not me you should worry about." He gives her a concerned look.

"Guys, just tell me what happened. And can someone give me something for my head?"

"Umm, last night...someone...they..." Sam stutters.

"Sam, get to the point, please," Maia says in an exasperated tone.

"I don't know how else to say it, but you were roofied last night." He looks like he's fighting back some tears. "It was that creepy guy from when you were skating. He was dancing with you, and then he and his friends tried to take you away from the park. We stopped him before anything else happened, and we believe the police caught up to them."

After a while, Maia answers, "Oh. So that's why that asshole was distracting me when I was getting the drinks."

"What? That's all you have to say? You're not scared?" Scott almost yells, a pained look on his face. Maia sighs heavily and then takes a painkiller that Anna hands her with the coffee.

"Here's the thing. I experienced this a few years ago. An old friend of ours did it—if you can even call that a friend." She pauses, looking at me. "And once at a party in high school. This world is very fucked up. And for some reason, I've grown sort of numb to it," she says with a cold stare.

I know how bad this hurts her deep inside, and I hate to think she had to go through it again. She might be acting like it's nothing, but I know it's killing her inside, just like it is me.

"Fuck, man, I'm sorry." Sam sighs, rubbing her arms in a comforting way.

"But I am very grateful that you guys were able to help." She weakly smiles at each of us.

"Of course, Maia, always." I sniffle while hugging her.

"So, what happened to you?" She looks at Scott again once we let go.

"Oh, me? You should see the other guy." He says, shrugging and acting nonchalantly.

"He beat the shit out of that asshole," Brandon says.

Scott shrugs like it was nothing, but we can see that he's still pissed. The room settles in profound silence, and no one seems to know what to say.

"So, I have the biggest hangover. Can we order Chinese?" Maia asks, as if trying to show everyone she's fine and breaking the silence.

I laugh in an attempt to make her—or me—feel more comfortable. "On it!"

∞

We all eat in silence, walking on eggshells around Maia. But I get it. It's not every day that something like this happens, especially to someone close to you. Maia and I have been through this before, but last night was different.

I can't believe I left her alone with that guy—if I had been paying more attention; if only I was there with her...

"Hey, *no es tu culpa (it's not your fault)*, okay? And stop looking at me like that. I know what's going through your head," Maia says, grabbing my hands and snapping me back.

"I can't help it; I should've been more careful. It's not the first time, and I should've seen the signs," I cry out. *I'm the worst friend ever.*

"Okay, listen, let's do this: we'll put on our swimsuits, get in the hot tub, and have the day to ourselves. Talk, rest, and get it out of our systems." She caresses my hands.

I agree, and with that, we walk upstairs to change. When we walk back down, Maia goes straight outside while I go to the kitchen for drinks. I find a bottle of white wine and put it in the freezer.

"Umm, Scott, do you have one of those ice buckets?" I ask.

"I don't think so, but we have a small cooler you could fill with ice. I'm assuming it's for the wine you just took?" He leans against the counter.

I give him a sheepish look. "Yeah...you don't mind, right?"

"Not at all, go nuts. Join Maia, and I'll bring it to you in a while." He says with a light laugh. *Go nuts? Who says that?*

"Are you sure?"

"Go, it's fine. I got it."

I nod, walking out to the balcony. "Scott's bringing out the wine later. We're going to need our liquid courage," I try to joke.

"You don't have to act so strong with me; I can see through your walls." She forces a small smile.

I get in next to her, resting my head on her shoulder. "*Lo siento tanto*, Maia. I'm sorry that this keeps happening and I'm never there to stop it before it does." I wipe away some tears. "It's not fair. So, why is it happening? Why won't it stop?" Now I'm full-on sobbing, and Maia pulls me into a hug.

"Hey, relax. *Respira*." She rubs my arms. "It sucks, you know? Those people exist to harm someone only for their own benefit." She pauses. "I mean, everything happens for a reason, right? It made me stronger, in a way."

"No one deserves this pain."

"No, no decent human being deserves it when real shitty things happen to them. But that's life, I guess," she says.

I groan, throwing my head back in frustration. "What were we doing back then? How could we associate with people like that?" *I just wish we could erase that part of our lives.*

After pouring our souls out, we let it all out: crying, holding, and comforting each other. I don't even know how much time passes. All that matters is that she's here, she's safe, and we'll do all we can to prevent it from happening again.

I don't know what I would do if I lost her. Last night was a close call, and I can't let us go through that again. We both can't drink in public anymore; there are too many things we cannot control.

"Umm, am I interrupting?" A very confused-looking Scott walks out with a cooler in his injured hands.

He's so bruised, and all because of that douchebag. Scott went all out for Maia.

"No, *no*, you're good. Thank you, Scott," I answer while getting out of the tub to take the cooler from him.

"The glasses are inside." He turns around to walk back in.

"Wait, can I talk to you?" Maia stops him.

He sighs, his back still to us, and then turns around.

"Sure, but make it quick." He casually slides his hands into his pockets, as if acting relaxed.

"This sounds serious... I'll come back," I mutter while getting out, not giving them a chance to protest. *Though it's not like she won't tell me about it later...*

I walk back into the apartment, drying my lower half, and bump into Brandon walking into the kitchen.

"Oh, sorry, didn't know anyone else was in here," I say, backing away and heading for the stairs.

"Wait," he calls out. "You don't have to go."

The sweetness in his voice stops me, making me turn around and face him. A hint of worry, care, and tenderness dances in his eyes; *but for who? Is it wrong if I hope he has a little concern for me?*

"How's Maia? Is there anything I—we—can do?" *Right, I'm not the focus of today.*

"Better, we talked and comforted each other. Though I'm not sure just talking will help calm down the thoughts of what could've happened," I say, still standing in the same place.

Brandon takes a step closer, my heart skipping as he does. "And what would help *you*?"

I blink the tears away. "I—" my voice cracks. "I don't

know." *Do not break down in front of him again.*

He takes two steps closer, taking my stillness as a sign that it's okay. "I know it was scary for you too, the possibility of something happ—"

"Please don't finish that sentence." My voice cracks again.

"Okay, okay, I'm sorry." He puts his hands up, halting mid-step. "What I'm trying, and clearly failing to say, is that I'm here for you. If you want it." His arms come down a little, opened, offering a hug without having to say it.

And, God, do I want that hug. My hands shake as I feel myself, my walls, breaking; needing comfort more than anything. His hands start to descend more as if giving up on me taking him up on his offer.

Before I can process what I'm doing, I feel myself taking three wide steps toward him, my arms reaching up to his neck. I hold onto him, my face snuggling in his chest, and his strong arms wrap around my waist, pulling me closer. I feel like I can finally exhale, and all of the concern, anger, and guilt are finally lifting from my shoulders. Brandon leans into me like he needs our embrace as much as I do.

"It's okay," he whispers, his head resting on mine. "You're okay. She's okay."

My body slowly stops shaking, his hand rubbing up and down on my back, the falling tears coming to a stop.

He lifts his head, pulling away and creating a few inches of space between us. "Maybe all you needed was some comfort." He wipes away the tears sitting on my cheeks with his thumb.

"Thank you, Brandon." My voice sounds small, the softness of his soothing me.

I look up at him, the tenderness in his eyes knocking the breath out of me, my heart skipping another beat. *How does he have this effect on me?*

"Anytime, Ollie," he whispers, his minty breath fanning my face, making me inhale deeply. *I don't think I've ever felt more at peace than in this moment, even though it should feel wrong.*

"I—" Words fail me as his eyes flick down to my lips and then back up to my eyes, an unmistakable shine dancing in them.

A clear, loud bang of a door closing upstairs brings us back to earth. I step back and pull away first, the warmth of his body quickly disappearing, leaving me feeling cold.

He clears his throat. "I think that's Anna. We were going to take a walk." His eyes lose the glimmer from when he held me. *Why is he still holding back? Why do they lie to themselves?*

"Yeah, right." My voice still sounds small, barely above a whisper. "I should go back out anyway."

I don't wait for a response before turning around and heading toward the balcony door. I see his reflection on the glass, halted mid-step again, a longing look in his eyes, and then he steps back into place just as his girlfriend takes her last steps toward him.

"Talk later, yeah?" I overhear Scott as I slide the door open.

"Yeah, thanks, Scott," I hear Maia. "But please, don't hurt yourself for me anymore. It makes you look desperate." I can sense the playfulness in her voice. *Hmm, what is that about?*

"Noted." Scott chuckles as he walks toward me, and I can't unsee the smirk on his face as he reaches me. "She's all yours."

"Thanks, and thanks for talking to her." We nod to each other as we pass.

"What?" Maia asks, brows furrowed, as I walk up to her.

"Oh, nothing. Just wondering why you were nice to Scott..."
I waggle my eyebrows.

"Nothing happened, Ollie. The dude beat the shit out of an asshole for me. The least I could do is be a tiny bit nice in return, right?" She shrugs.

I shrug; *just asking.*

"I'm worried he's not getting his cuts checked. What if they get infected, or he fractured something important? It's not safe." She sighs, looking down at her hands resting on her thighs.

"Ooh, someone cares..." I sing-song. "And it seems like he does too. You didn't see him last night, but he was so freaking mad. He scared every single one of us. Did he tell you he punched the counter?"

"He did." She scoffs a laugh. "It's so weird. He acts so tough, smug, and sarcastic. But then he goes and punches some asshole for trying something with me. Why did he do that?"

"I don't know, Maia. You'd have to ask him. But I'm pretty sure he won't give you a straight answer."

"He won't; even I can see the big-ass wall he puts up. And I'm not even close enough to try and break it anyway, so..."

"Let's just stay here for the rest of the day and relax. Because we fucking deserve it." She leans closer to me. "And why haven't you poured the wine?"

I throw my head back, laughing. "And she's back." I hand her a glass. "But what about the pictures and videos?"

"Let's worry about that later. We have plenty of time before the concert at Rockwood tomorrow tonight. Today is just for us to relax. You, me, this wine, the hot tub, and the wonderful view of the city. No better way to make me forget..."

"¡Salud y amén!"

"All I am is music, and you're my favorite fan. But all you are is stupid, for loving me so bad." ~ Symphonic Orchestra, Alexandra Kessler.

OLIVIA – NEW YORK

BRANDON STORMS INTO THE APARTMENT after dropping his girlfriend off at the airport, a fuming look on his face. Sam and Scott exchange weird glances and take off after him as he stomps up the stairs.

What the fuck was that? Maia and I stay still, looking at each other as we finish cleaning up after breakfast.

"Do you think they're just going to blow over whatever shit this is?" she asks, but it sounds more like a statement.

"I'd be more surprised if we ever find out." I sigh, still stunned.

Shortly after, Sam walks down to help us with the clean-up. He's quiet, adding to the awkwardness.

"Hey, Sam?" I call out to him. "Is he okay?"

"Yeah, it's nothing important. Just some stuff about the band for when we get back." He rubs the back of his head.

Damn it, Sam, I want to know.

"Okay."

Scott and Brandon come back, bags in hand. We all head down and put everything in the trunk. Then we settle in.

"Let's go home," Sam says with a sigh.

"We're not buying that, right?" Maia whispers to me as we drive off.

I shake my head. "Nah, they wouldn't have looked worried if it were about the band. I'm not sure what it is, but something's off," I whisper.

I take out my phone to tell Ella we're on our way back, and she tells me they're leaving soon.

"Do you think we'll meet Noah?" Maia asks teasingly.

"This whole Noah thing is so funny. Like, what are the odds that he's Scott's brother?" I say a little too loud.

"What's that about my brother?" Scott turns to us. *Ooh, someone's protective.*

"It's nothing, just laughing about the whole thing with him and my sister." I shrug.

"I guess that is a pretty big coincidence. He lives with us too. He kind of got as sick of our parents as I did."

"Don't know if that's a good thing or a bad thing..." I trail off. He shrugs and turns back around to give Sam directions.

I notice Brandon's been quiet for a while, so I nudge his arm to get his attention.

"Hey, are you okay? You haven't said a word since you got back from the airport." I lean closer to him and whisper.

"Nothing you need to worry about. It's just band stuff," he whispers back.

I sigh, not believing his answer. *This has nothing to do with you; let it go.* I give him a slight smile. *But what if it is...?*

"Did you and Maia at least have fun on the trip?" he asks.

"Oh yeah, we loved it. I don't think we'll ever get tired of New York; we took so many pictures that we could fill the walls of our studio. It was about time we got new material for our portfolio," I smile as I answer, and Brandon chuckles.

"What?" I can feel my cheeks getting red.

"No, no, it's nothing. Just that you got so excited about the pictures," he quickly replies. "I think it's kinda cute." He smiles, and we look at each other a little longer than we should, *again*.

"Anyway, we need to get most of them developed. Hope we didn't have our fingers on the lenses," I joke, but he barely lets out a puff of air—*lousy comment, dumbass*.

"Well, let me know if at least one of them comes out decent," he tries to joke back, and I can't help but chuckle at how stupid we sound.

"Are you going to make those terrible jokes the whole drive home? If so, I'll turn up the music," Scott complains.

"Ugh, thank you! One more, and I was going to jump out of the car," Maia groans, throwing her head back on the seat.

I lean back too, closing my eyes and enjoying the drive home as the music echoes in the background.

OCEAN CITY

"Hey, we're almost there." I hear someone say while slightly shaking me.

I open my eyes, stretch my arms, and yawn. The sunset's by the bay as we cross the bridge into Ocean City. I'll never get tired of this view. The sky is beautifully colored with blue, red, and orange tones, reflecting over the water.

"Home, sweet home," Sam says with a hint of a smile.

I take in the views through the window as we drive by, completely zoning out. Every time we cross this bridge, I'm reminded of why I love living here and how peaceful this marvelous oceanic scenery is.

"Ollie, do you need me to drop you off right away, or can we take a detour?" Sam asks, pulling me back from the trance.

"No, there's no rush to get home. Ella's class took off around the same time as us, but they're still on the road. Why? What do you have in mind?"

"Thought we could show you where we live?" He looks back at me through the mirror, waiting for an answer, and I nod.

Now that he mentions that, I notice he was already driving right toward the marina, where we live. Maia and I look at each other. There aren't many buildings around that area. Meaning: they could be our neighbors, and we didn't even know.

"Hold up. You live by the marina too?" Maia asks.

"What do you mean, *too*? You guys live there?" Scott turns around in his seat.

"Yeah, in the White Marlins."

"And we're in Emerson Towers..." Scott trails off as he slowly turns to look at Sam.

"Sam! How could you not tell us that you're practically our neighbors? You even picked us up," I exclaim, baffled by this brand-new information.

"Umm, I guess I was so overwhelmed with everything else and getting ready for our trip that I forgot," he says with a guilty expression. *Boy, how can you forget where you live?*

We all burst out laughing. As the laughter dies down, Sam pulls up in front of their building; right across the dock from us.

It has beautiful blueish-gray tiles, white frames, and cozy balconies overlooking the docks. The building's also surrounded by little gardens and bushes, giving it a homey feeling. Their view of the sunrises and sunsets must be amazing.

"And this is us. How do you like it?" Brandon asks, leaning closer to me.

"Looks nice! We can see it from our apartment." I laugh.

"So, where are you guys?"

"Look to your right. Do you see that white and brown building across the dock? That's it!" I point through the window.

"Oh, yeah! We considered that one, but these apartments

had more rooms. And you know…we're four guys." Brandon shrugs. "We need the space."

"That's understandable. We got lucky to score one with three rooms. You guys would've been very cramped."

Ping. My phone's notifications interrupt our conversation. "It's Ella. They're crossing the bridge, and Noah's driving her home," I read out loud. Sam heads back to our building.

"Aww, look, even your little bro is more of a gentleman than you… What went wrong there?" Maia teases Scott.

"Well, he has a reason to: he wants to impress Ollie's sister. Meanwhile, I don't have to impress anyone here," he says without looking back at her. *Ouch.*

"Oh, so you're only nice when you want something? What a gem of a human being," she replies sarcastically.

"Okay, we're here! Scott, help me with their bags. Thanks," Sam cuts them off and gives Scott a *shut-up* look. He turns off the car, and we get out.

I breathe in, looking up at our building and already feeling calmer now that I'm back home. I must've zoned out again because I didn't notice Brandon standing before me.

"Huh, sorry, were you saying something?" I blink.

"Just how weird it is that we've never met yet live so close." He pushes his hair back. *I've lost count of how many times he's done that at this point. I've lost count of how many times it's made me blush.*

"We would've met eventually, crossed paths or something." I shrug, kicking up some dust with my shoes. "Who knows? Maybe we weren't meant to meet until now."

"Hmm," he hums. "Do you believe in destiny, then?" He tilts his head, a dreamy smile on his face, sporting a confidence he wasn't showing off before. *Where was this until now?*

I open my mouth to answer, but Maia interrupts before I can

say anything. "Here comes the lovebirds," she says in a sing-song voice.

We turn around to see Noah pull up in his car, parking a little further from the door. They get out, he takes Ella's bags out of his trunk, and they walk toward us. Very close to each other, might I add...

I look at Maia: *So, he is cute.* She looks back: *I know, right?*

He looks like a mini version of Scott but with less curly hair. His expression looks bright, like he has no worries in the world. They're laughing, probably at us, and how creepy we all must look while staring at them.

I assume she rolls her eyes at Maia and me for giving her suggestive looks. *We need to have our weekly girls' night, like right now.*

"What's up, guys? So nice to finally meet you." She smiles. "And—"

"So, this is Noah, the new student?" Maia cuts her off. "I bet he taught you a lot about camping..."

"Of course he did. I'm sure my little bro did everything I taught him!" Scott throws an arm across Noah's shoulder. "You work fast, little man. You just came here and already have a girlfriend. I'm impressed." He ruffles his hair a bit, clearly annoying him, doing his job as older sibling.

"Shut up, dumbass." Noah pushes him off, but he keeps roughing him up.

"Come on, let's go home." Scott starts walking backward to the car. "Nice meeting you, Ella. We'll probably see a lot more of each other." He throws her a wink before turning around.

"For sure. See you around, guys! And guess I'll see you Monday?" Ella laughs it off before looking at Noah.

Noah hugs her goodbye. "Of course!"

"Hey, listen! Thank you so much for helping us out this

week. You'll receive your payment by tomorrow," Sam says as he hugs us goodbye. "Also, we have our weekly meetings every Monday in the recording studio at four. Does that work for you?"

"Yeah, that works!" I smile. "Text us the address."

"Sure thing," Sam replies as he gets in his car.

"See ya Monday." Brandon smiles as he opens the passenger door. "Don't forget you owe me an answer," he hollers at me from the car. I shake my head as we watch them drive.

"What was that about?" Ella asks with a confused look as we walk into the building and toward the elevator.

"Something stupid he asked me right before you walked up to us, and I didn't get to answer," I say, brushing it off. "And don't think you can distract us with questions; you're telling us everything that happened on your trip, okay?"

"But not before you tell me what went on during yours! I saw a lot of tension going around today. We all need to spill the tea."

"Okay, hold up! Let me see if I got this right…" Ella blinks a couple of times. "So, Brandon is the same guy you chickened out on in the gas station and who you bumped into at his concert. And you had all these moments, flirting, touching, and even almost kissing?!"

"*Sí*," I nod.

"But then his 'girlfriend' from London came back to surprise him and acted all weird? And he pretended like nothing happened between you two? This shit's a lot to process, dude." She lies back in the chair. *Ugh, you're telling me!*

"*Sí*, it's all a big mess. But he did apologize for the confusion and acting weird." I take a sip of my wine.

"Yeah, because that makes everything better," Ella scoffs.

"What was the question? The one you owe him an answer to," Maia asks.

"We were talking about how weird it is that we've never met, even though we're neighbors. I said maybe we weren't meant to meet yet, and he asked if I believed in destiny."

"But why would he ask that if he's supposed to be dating this Hannah girl?" Ella exclaims.

"Anna," Maia and I correct her at the same time.

"*Lo mismo (Same thing).*" Ella waves her hand around.

"He might not have meant it romantically, you know? Sometimes you feel that way when you form friendships spontaneously. But he was acting pretty sketchy this whole day," Maia shrugs.

"Right? He came back from the airport looking like someone died but didn't say anything about it to us."

"Yeah, the guys just told us it was just band stuff, but we're not stupid. Something happened, and they won't say what it is," Maia snickers.

"What about Sam? He was being kinda flirty that day on the beach, no?" Ella waggles her eyebrows.

"Funny story, he told us he had a crush on Ollie all through junior and senior year. And I'm pretty sure he's still crushing on her," Maia teases me, and Ella immediately agrees.

"No, come on! I'm pretty sure he got over his silly high school crush; it's been years. Also, he was just being nice to me. He was *so* not flirting," I protest. *But was he?*

"Hmm," they both say with pursed lips, and I roll my eyes.

"I just need to figure out this Brandon shit. He's been confusing me since day one." I sigh and lean back.

"I mean, you do seem pretty interested in him," Maia teases.

"Shhh, I'm done! Your turn now. How was your camping trip?" I ask Ella. *I need this conversation about my lack of a love life to be over already.*

"Well, you better pour yourselves some more wine…"

Ella smiles at Maia and me as we stare back, mouths wide open. "And that's what happens when you're not too scared to make a move."

"*Ayy, cállate.* You did nothing. It was all Noah." I cross my arms over my chest.

"At least I got kissed and had cute little moments at the lake and campfire. You got played, and Maia just got insulted by a rock star."

"Do not drag me into this! I am not the one with boy problems; that's on you guys. My love life is simply nonexistent," Maia protests, and Ella shrugs.

"I still can't believe all that happened… We kissed again before he dropped me off, but I can't process that yet."

Maia and I look at each other as if saying, *aww.*

"Nah, I can't get mad. That's the cutest story anyone has ever told me. I will admit it makes me just slightly jealous, but you will not see the light of day if you tell anyone outside this room," Maia laughs. "Cheers to at least one of us having a love life!"

"Cheers to that!" Ella almost squeals. *Oh, how I missed my girls' night this past week.*

Chapter Seven

"I've never been in love, never even tried. Not because I don't want to, but because I don't know how to act." ~ Lovesick, Alexandra Kessler.

OLIVIA – OCEAN CITY

MAIA LOOKS AT MY OUTFIT AS WE GET IN THE ELEVATOR. "Huh."

"*¿Qué?*" I give her a side-eye.

"Are you dressing to impress, honey? I know the first meeting got canceled, and we haven't seen the boys in a week, but this is another level."

"I have no idea what you're talking about. Who would I even want to impress, anyway?"

"I was just teasing! Yes, we dress for ourselves, but I wasn't expecting you to get all shy and shit."

"Let's just go."

We settle into my car and set the GPS, realizing the studio is just a few blocks away. *We could have walked. But we're too lazy today.* During the entire drive, I could sense Maia's accusatory gaze, but I was still hung up on my outfit choice.

"Maia, this is ridiculous. All I did was put on a simple dress and a jacket. Is it really that different from my usual?"

"Girl, yes. We wear jeans, T-shirts, and sneakers to our office."

"Can't I dress nice?"

"Yes, you can! But don't lie to my face and say that you *don't* have any ulterior motives." She narrows her eyes at me.

"I am not." I avoid all eye contact as we're stuck at a red stoplight; *just my luck*.

"You are so gone." She laughs, knowing me better than I know myself.

I don't answer as the light changes to green, and we make one last turn before pulling up to the studio.

"Oops, we're here, too bad we can't finish the conversation."

"Sure, you keep telling yourself that if it lets you sleep at night." She winks at me as we walk out.

Sam greets us at the door. "Hey girls, how are you? Come in."

"We're doing fine, thanks. What about you?" I answer as we hug him.

We walk into the studio, a big open-spaced warehouse with lots of windows that bring in some natural light. The instruments and recording equipment are in the far back corner, acting as a performance space with a living room set facing them.

"What's up, groupies?" Scott nudges Maia.

"Don't start." She points a finger at him as a warning.

As I look around, I get the feeling that someone's missing. *Brandon. Where is he? Wasn't he supposed to be here already? And what about Drew and Layla?*

"Okay, girls, let's sit and start with the official business." Scott sits on a chair and props his feet on a desk. Sam stands beside a rolling whiteboard.

"So professional, huh." I point to the board, a slight smile on my face. "And shouldn't we wait until everyone's here?"

"Yeah, it was our best purchase! It's how we write songs and propose ideas. Even though some of us like to write random notes all over the place..." I hear Brandon say in an accusatory tone to Scott. He comes in carrying coffees and hands one to each of us.

"Thanks, and hi," I say, and he smiles. *That smile*. "That reminds me of Maia in high school. I could never understand her notes. It was like her brain exploded."

"Hey! I understood them, and that was all that mattered," she protests.

"Yeah, yeah." I brush her off with a *pfft* sound. "Can I ask how you guys got the money for this place?"

"It wasn't that much. It just seems like it would be because it's so big. And to be honest, we found a very cool deal." Brandon shrugs as he takes a seat close to me.

Is it just me or did it get hotter in here?

"One of my surfing friends used this to teach the basics at the school since it's right by the beach, but he left for Hawaii and got married. So, he gave it to us practically for free." Sam smiles, appearing very proud of this deal.

"And with my lovely parents' don't-die money, we turned it into a recording studio!" Scott continues, a tight grin on his face. *Touchy subject, I see.*

"Damn, you guys really are investing!" I exclaim with a whistle.

"Yeah, I guess." Scott shrugs, propping his feet up on the coffee table.

We all startle when the door bursts open and turn around to see Layla and Drew rush through.

"Hi, guys," Layla says while panting. "I am so, so, so sorry we're late!"

"It's okay; we also just got here, but why are you out of breath?" I ask.

"Because airhead over here decided we needed to walk—or run—instead of driving over..." Drew says, out of breath.

"Anyway...let's get started," Sam interrupts them.

We go over our monthly social media plan, explaining how this will boost their numbers along with engaging with their audience and alternating the types of content that will build up their image. Sam explains their writing and production process and how we fit their style perfectly.

"Okay, guys, I have news!" I clap my hands together once Sam is done. "So, a record label from New York called New Sound Records contacted us through your social media last week. They want to hear a sample of your EP and set up a meeting with you. And if all goes well, they would like to sign you. It's not set in stone, but they seem very eager and interested in the band."

"Dude, no way! We've tried to get signed for so long," Drew exclaims as he sits up.

"That is awesome! Send me the contact, and I'll schedule a meeting for this week." Sam nods to me with a huge, bright smile.

"Perfect, will do!" I salute him, saying *aye, aye, captain*.

"We also have a new song we've been working on. We'll play it for you, and you can tell us what you think," Scott says as they pick up their instruments. "It's called 'Nosedive'."

They start playing an upbeat rhythm, with Drew going at it on the drums and Layla on the keyboards. Then Brandon comes in with the guitar as Scott begins to sing and play the bass. I like how they blend their sounds and that you can still hear how they play on their own. They finish with a drum and a keyboard solo and stare at us with expectant looks.

"I really liked it! I think it could totally be in the EP for the record label." I smile as we clap.

"Thank you. I'm glad you liked it." Brandon only looks at me when he says it, making the butterflies in my stomach go crazy. *He can't keep looking at me like that.*

"Guys! Okay, so, going off-topic," Layla starts but then stops, waiting for confirmation to continue.

"Yes?" Maia asks.

"One of my friends told me about this new club opening on Friday, and we should totally go! She's even friends with the owner and can get us some bar discounts."

"That sounds cool!" I say. *Drinks for less? Let's go!*

"Yeah, I'm in!" Scott agrees.

"Wait, do they have live music?" Maia gasps.

Layla seems to think it over before answering. "Umm, yes. I think so."

"Could you talk to your friend and see if Reputation can get a gig?"

"Oh, that's so smart," she squeals, and we stare at her. "Oh, yeah, yeah, now!" She walks outside to make the call. After a long while, she comes back into the room and sits down next to us but starts humming instead of talking.

"So..."

"Oh, yeah! Oh, wait, they're dating now. I mean, I thought they were since she promoted that club so much like she was personally proud of it. That's so cute, right? Like–"

"Layla!" we all yell in unison.

"What?" she gasps.

"The gig..."

"Yeah, we got it! It opens at 10, and the gig is at 10:30. We'll only sing three songs, though, since they also hired a DJ."

"Perfect, thanks, Layla!" Everyone high-fives or hugs her.

"Well, see you Friday! We have some errands to run," Maia says as we pick up our stuff.

A round of *bye, girls* calls after us as we leave the studio. After the short drive home, Maia and I get in our elevator, and I give her a knowing look.

"*Now* we will dress to impress." She winks.

"You got that right!" I high-five her.

Now, what should I wear that will knock them dead?

Maia runs from her room to the living room and then back. "Dude, where did I leave my high-heeled boots?"

"In here!" I shout back as I put on my heels.

She runs into my room. "Oh, thanks! Wait, why were they here?" She asks.

"I don't know…" I try to lie.

She glares at me intensely, knowing very well that I wore them without telling her. Then she looks me up and down. "Damn, girl, you look hot!"

"You too! Look at yourself, Maia." I whistle at her.

We stand in front of the mirror and look over our outfits. I'm wearing a mesh top, a black bralette underneath, and a black skirt paired with my black platforms. Maia has a body-con dress and high-heeled boots topped with a leather jacket. I just know she'll regret the jacket later because of all the sweating while dancing.

Ella enters the room and crashes on the bed with a dramatic sigh. "What now?" I ask.

"You guys look great, by the way. But you're going to a club while I stay here, alone! That's not fair," she whines like a five-year-old.

"Girl, you just came from hanging out with your friends!"

"Plus, you have the house all to yourself, and Noah's probably free." Maia waggles her eyebrows.

"Oh, God!" Ella presses a pillow to her face.

"You know what? Maybe you should hang out in his

apartment instead. That way, we don't have to clean up your mess." Maia feigns disgust and gags.

"Maia!" Ella and I exclaim at the same time.

"What? You're the ones taking it the wrong way." She puts her hands up. "Shit, we're going to be late! Let's go; the guys are waiting downstairs."

We say goodbye to Ella and take the elevator down. We walk outside, and like the gentleman he is, Sam gets out of his car. He opens the door for us, and I feel his gaze linger on my outfit; *or is it on me?*

"You girls look great," he says to us.

"Thanks! Sam, how are you so nice and have such rude friends?" Maia fake sighs, and he laughs.

"Oh, he is not that nice! Just get in, or we'll be late," Scott urges us from inside the car. *Ugh, rude.*

We get in, and I sit between Brandon and Maia. *What a surprise...*

"You look nice, Ollie." He smiles at me, and I try not to blush as the intensity behind his eyes makes me tremble. I barely mumble a *thank you* in return, his gaze still burning into me, like he's struggling to look away. And if I'm honest, I don't really want him to.

When we get to the club, the line's longer than expected. That can only mean that Reputation will get more recognition— and that's great!

I gaze at the people in line and do a double take; *what the hell?* I reach for Maia. "Is that—"

"Hey, over here!" Layla calls out to us from the backstage door and distracts my gaze.

It doesn't matter. I'm pretty sure I was mistaken.

Layla comes up to us and ushers us through a side door. We walk into the backstage area, where we can see the whole club.

The stage is not as big as the one in Rockwood, but it leaves more space for the dance floor and VIP sections. They set up the bar in the far back with a few bartenders, taking up the whole wall.

"Damn, girls, you look smokin'." Drew winks and whistles as his eyes trail up and down our bodies.

"Yeah, I might have to agree. We kinda look like your groupies this time," Scott says, coming up behind Maia.

"Yeah, I got that because you haven't stopped drooling since we stepped out of the car..." Maia smiles sarcastically.

"You wish," he says closer to her ear, but even I can hear what he says.

"Aha, right," she pushes him away.

"Okay, everyone, get in place. It's almost time," one of the staff members coming up to us says.

∞

The band starts with "Nosedive," the new one they played for us on Monday. They also play "Fallen Obsession," one of their first songs. Maia and I take pictures with one of our smaller cameras that fit in our purses while they're playing.

"For our last song, we're playing a new one called 'Façade.' Hope you like it," Brandon says in a very low voice.

The song starts with Brandon singing and playing the guitar while the rest of the band claps to the rhythm. Then Drew comes in with the drums, and Layla plays a soft tune on the keyboard. The song is slower than usual but still has a slightly upbeat rhythm.

Listening to the lyrics, I realize it has a deeper meaning. You can feel the raw emotions in Brandon's voice as he sings the chorus, and his eyes bore into mine.

> *I was blinded by the you in my mind,*
> *You were faking it because of our past,*
> *I guess this was our expiration date.*
>
> *I will miss you but not my emptiness,*
> *It took a day to realize we lost it all,*
> *A day I will never get out of my head.*

Confusion fills my mind as the song ends. Isn't he in a relationship with Anna? What's going on? Is this why he's been acting flirty and touchy these past two weeks? Or maybe it's about another ex?

I swear, this guy is going to be the death of me. It feels like two steps forward, two steps back—going nowhere. The intensity behind his eyes makes me shiver, driving me mad as I try to figure out who he's singing to.

We go to the bar for drinks, and as soon as they finish playing, Scott almost sprints toward us. "Calm down, the drinks won't run away," Maia says when he reaches us.

"Ha-ha," he laughs sarcastically.

"Here, miss," the bartender calls me, and I thank him while taking my drink.

"Hey, quick, pretend to be my date," I hear Maia say as she gets closer to Scott. *Huh?*

"What?" Scott asks, dumbfounded, as the bartender hands him his beer.

"Just do it," she says in an anxious-sounding tone. *What the heck is happening?*

"I knew you liked me, but I didn't think you were that desperate," Scott pretends to flirt. *I swear, the chemistry between these two...and the denial.*

"Ugh, fine, forget it!" As she turns to leave, he grabs her hand and embraces her. *Can they be any cuter?*

"Don't get too excited there, buddy." She glares at him.

"Okay, but what's going on?" I ask Maia, matching her tone.

She nods for me to look behind me. I turn around and see him, immediately feeling my face pale.

Tell me, please, that this is not true. This shit is not happening. Please, not tonight...

> *"Can't close my eyes, a scary night. The pressure is eating me alive."*
> *~ Scary Nights, Alexandra Kessler.*

OLIVIA – FLASHBACK, TWO YEARS BEFORE

I SEE MAIA RUNNING FROM CONNOR'S FRIEND, Jacob. He's been obsessing over getting with her ever since we met about a year ago. I swear this one's a step away from getting a restraining order for harassment.

"Are you even listening to me?" Connor shouts in my face.

"What more do you want me to say?" I answer calmly. "You cheated on me and broke me into pieces. I have nothing else to say."

"You think this is easy? Do you think you're the only one hurting? Has it ever occurred to you that I'm breaking too? You've barely talked to me the past few weeks, doing whatever the fuck you do. You don't even have the decency of telling me what you're up to."

"Well, now you can tell them that we have. Sorry to be such a burden to you." I start to walk away.

"Hey, hey, stop! Don't go." He grabs my arm so tight I can see the skin whitening around his grasp.

"Let go, Connor. You're hurting me." I stare him down, breathing heavily, and he reluctantly releases me, closing the sliding door behind him.

"I'm sorry, I fucked up, I know. But I don't want to lose you, Livy, please." He almost kneels in front of me as he begs.

"I'm sorry, it's too late. You already did." I walk away from

Connor, and I never look back.

PRESENT TIME

"Brooks, Livy. Long time no see," Jacob says in a coy tone, walking up to Maia. "And you changed your hair? I have to say, blue suits you."

I notice Connor from the corner of my eye, appearing embarrassed by his friend's approach. But *he's still an asshole...*

"So, what's up? What are you guys doing here?" Jacob asks while poking Maia on the arm. She tenses up, and Scott hugs her from behind, moving her further away.

Connor walks up too close for my liking and asks me how I'm doing. I don't want to deal with him right now, so I look around. I see Sam standing not too far away from the stage. He gives me a knowing nod and starts to walk toward us.

Hands hugging me around the waist pull me away from this awkward situation. I turn around to meet Brandon's eyes, immediately melting into his embrace. *Where did he even come from?* I can see a flicker of anger mixed with care as he stares down at Connor, the protectiveness behind them making me feel safe. I turn my head back to where I saw Sam, but he's gone. *Maybe I should talk to him later.*

"Hey, what's going on, boys? I'm Brandon, and this is Scott." He pats Scott on the back.

Scott's still holding Maia like she's a fragile flower. *Something I would never use to describe her...*

"We're some old friends of the girls. We go way back, don't we?" Jacob smirks, keeping his distance.

"Yeah, you could say we have history. Right, Livy?" Connor's grin starts to creep me out, and I feel Brandon tense up as he calls me *Livy*. Instead of showing our panic, Maia and I refrain from responding and lean further into the embraces.

"Well, if you don't mind, we'd like to dance with our girls. Excuse us." Scott and Brandon pull us away from that nightmare without waiting for a response.

On the dance floor, Maia and I thank the guys, though we can still sense Connor and Jacob staring and seething at us.

"Hey, don't worry about it. Those guys give me a bad vibe." Scott sounds almost pissed.

"More than that, they *are* bad vibes." Maia scowls.

"Well, bad vibes are looking at us right now. Let's dance and distract them a bit?" Brandon suggests and moves us further into the crowd.

The DJ puts on a slower song, changing the club's mood. Some people around us pair up to slow dance, and others leave to get more drinks.

Brandon puts his hands around my waist while I put mine around his neck to pull him closer, his scent washing over me and calming my nerves.

"So, *Livy*, huh? I guess that's why you don't want people calling you that. There *is* a story behind it, after all," he whispers into my ear as we sway to the rhythm, his hands sending chills down my spine.

He hasn't let me go since the moment he came to my rescue, as if the moment we break contact, the spell will be broken, that he's not even capable of doing so.

"Well, that, and it sounds like *willy*," I sigh. "Can we not talk about it? I'm not in the mood."

"*Willy*," he says in a mocking voice. "Sorry, sorry, what do you want to talk about while we keep the *facade* going then?"

"Oh, exactly that, your song. What's it about, if you don't mind me asking?"

"Well, you remember Anna, right?" he whispers, and I nod.

"We had a very long-distance relationship going for a while. At first, it was fine. We thought we could make it work despite it being hard. But, spoiler alert, we weren't fine," he says in a bitter tone.

"I realized I started falling in love with the idea of her rather than her, and I'm pretty sure she did the same thing with me. So, when we reunited, it was all a *facade* because we weren't feeling it anymore."

He stops to breathe before speaking again. "We broke up after the trip, the day she went back home."

"Oh, I am so sorry, Brandon."

"For what? You didn't do anything." He takes a dramatic pause. "Well, actually..."

"What did I do now?" I pull away.

"No, no, please don't take it the wrong way. You just made me realize I didn't want to be in a relationship with her anymore." He grabs my waist and pulls me back again. *Don't stop doing that.*

"You made me feel the urge of wanting to be with someone for who they are. To know what they're doing, you know? That infatuation. Something I lost with her; I didn't feel the sparks anymore and I just couldn't stay together."

"All that because of me?" I take a deep breath. *Calm down, tiger. That doesn't mean he wants that with you.*

"No, not because of you, necessarily. Those feelings weren't there a long time ago. I just needed to accept it, and let's say you helped me achieve that."

"You're welcome, I guess." I shrug. *Try not to sound so happy, will you? Stop, he didn't even say it was because of me.*

"Hold on, there's more," he adds, and I raise my eyebrows.

"She also confessed she was seeing this other guy in England.

That's why she was so clingy and jealous during the trip. Guilty people tend to blame others for the same things they do."

"Jinx to that, friend," I reply in a bitter tone.

"Huh?"

"Connor there." I nod back at him. "You know, *bad vibes*? He's my ex; we were together for a year. He cheated and used me for longer than I was aware of. But I guess you have to go through a few bad relationships to find a good one."

"You didn't deserve to be cheated on, Ollie." He brushes some hair from my face, and I slightly shiver under his touch.

"Neither did you, Brandon." We move to the rhythm of the slow music.

"Agreed, and as terrible as it ended for both of us...we should always—"

"Find the good things they left behind?" I finish for him. His hands move to my hips, and he looks at me like he'll never let me go.

"It's like you read my mind," he whispers breathlessly.

His eyes flicker to my lips, lingering for what feels like ages. He pulls me in, closer than we've been so far, and starts to lean down. *Is this really about to happen? Are we going to kiss?* My breath hitches in the back of my throat as I lean in too, his hand pulling even me closer.

A drunken Layla stumbles into us, breaking us apart. "Hey, guys! Are you having fun?" The DJ changes the song to something more up-tempo, and Layla gasps.

"Oh, my God, this is my favorite song. Come on, guys, let's dance!" She starts to dance, and I stumble back a little as I carry her weight. "Whoops, careful. Maybe you've had a lot to drink, Owie."

"I think that's you, honey." I hug her. "We should sit you down in one of the booths. Don't think your friend would mind?"

"Aww, come on, don't be such a downer. I want to keep dancing." She grabs my hand and starts dancing with me.

I look for Maia and see her dancing with Scott. She sees my pleading eyes and instantly knows to come over.

"What's up?"

"Maia, hi! Oh, my God, why aren't you dancing, girl? Come on, don't be lame. Scott, you too, stop it with the stuck-up face all the time," Layla says with a slur and stumbles around.

"I do not!" Scott protests.

"No, she's kinda right," Maia joins in.

"Yeah, so. As you can see, Layla is a little...you know." I give her a knowing look.

"Yeah," Maia nods.

While we try to figure out what to do with her, Sam comes to us. *Shit, I forgot he was here. I even signaled him over before. What a lousy friend I'm being.*

"Hey, are you guys alright?" he asks in a tone I've never heard him use before, as if he's annoyed.

"Yeah, yeah, we're fine. Thanks for the late arrival." I nudge his shoulder.

"It doesn't matter anymore, does it? It seems like you had everything under control." His voice cracks in what seems like anger or frustration.

What's the matter with him?

"Anyway...I think Layla here needs help." I do my best not to drop her.

"I can help her. That's what I'm here for anyway, right?" he almost barks at us.

"Could you guys please take care of her? Ollie and I need to take some quick time outside, if you don't mind," Maia asks the guys.

"Please." I give them puppy-dog eyes.

"Yeah, of course." Brandon nods and rubs my arms.

"Come on, I saw a little terrace not that far back." Maia grabs my hand, pulling me behind her.

She leads the way as we try to move through the maze of people; the red, blue, and purple lights make it harder to see where we're going. We're weaving between sweaty bodies, trying not to bump into people grinding and dancing. We walk across the dance floor until we reach a door by the bar. I take a big gasp of air as we walk outside, finally able to fully breathe without all those people around me.

The first thing we notice is that it's nearly empty. Some people smoke on the far right, and others sit on the chairs scattered around the middle. But the left side is empty, so we walk up to the railing and lean on it, sighing deeply.

"Of all the people in the world we could've run into, it had to be those two assholes?" I let out an exasperated sigh.

"I mean, they still live here, and so do we. It was stupid of us to think we would never see them again," Maia says.

"It's good to dream, though."

"Damn right." She laughs sarcastically.

"Honestly, Brandon and Scott pulled through for us."

"Yeah, but it's not like Brandon wouldn't do anything in his power to get a dance with you..." She smirks.

"Oh, stop." I feel my cheeks heating up, and I try to hide it.

"You know I'm right!" She gives me her trademark *I-told-you-so* look.

I resist her for as long as I can, but I cave. "I wish you were."

"I know." She smiles, and I roll my eyes at her.

"Was it me, or did Sam seem different to you? Like, weird?"

"Yeah, he was kinda moody. So unlike him."

"Right?"

"So, we were right; you girls were bluffing." I recognize the bone-chilling voice.

Fucking Connor. We turn around.

"Great, so it's you assholes again." Maia glares at them, clearly over it.

"Oh, she's got a sassy mouth since the last time we saw her." Jacob grabs her chin.

Maia jerks away. "It's not like I could talk, could I?!"

"What about you, Livy? Why did you have to go through all that trouble to get away from me? Are you afraid your feelings for me might resurface?" Connor inches closer to me, and I narrow my eyes.

"You two need a reality check. Or a permanent stay in a ward," Maia barks back, balling her hands into fists.

"What the actual fuck, Connor! Did you forget why we broke up? You're delusional if you think I could have any feelings for you again."

"Livy, never say never." He gets even closer.

How can someone be so out of their mind? They both inch closer and closer to us, and I feel something in my hand. I look over, and it's Maia handing me the pepper spray she bought after the New York incident.

As I take the mace, everything that happens next feels like it's in slow motion. I bust the cap open and spray it right into his eyes. Finally having this much power and control over him gives me such an adrenaline rush. To my surprise, I feel somewhat confident. My hand's not trembling, and I can feel my blood pulsing through my veins.

From the corner of my eye, I see Maia kicking Jacob in the groin. He crouches down in pain, screaming like the little bitch he is. We leave them in their excruciating agony and run back inside, crashing right into a furious Brandon and Scott.

"You bitches, you'll pay for this!" They scream after us, crying and groaning on the floor.

"What the fuck? I'm going to fucking kill those guys." Scott tries to push through, and Maia stops him.

Brandon tries to go in their direction. I place my hand on his chest, making him look at me, the outrage vibrating through his body.

"No, please don't. They're not worth it," I plead. He breathes in and gives me a slight nod, but I can still see the anger floating in his eyes.

"Come on, man. I think they got it covered," he sighs, nudging Scott.

"No, I know they deserve worse." Scott keeps pushing back. "Maia, get off!"

"No. You need to calm the fuck down." She pushes his chest. "I understand you're worried, but it was our fight, not yours. And we just kicked their asses, so please, let's go. And fast, before we get kicked out."

After some reluctance from Scott, we round up our group, thanking Layla's friend for having us, and walk back to our cars. We say goodbye to Layla and Drew, and they take off. The rest of us pile back into Sam's car, sighing as we sit down and finally relax after that whole mess.

"Are you girls okay?" Sam asks, acting like his usual self.

"Yes, we're fine. It was intense. But we're okay." I give him a comforting smile.

While looking ahead, I notice it's barely past two a.m. *Damn, this night ended early. I'm not even tired yet.*

"Here's an idea! We could chill in our apartment for a while." I look around the car. "Also, my sister's in yours with Noah."

"Oh, is she? More reason to leave them alone then," Scott says in a sing-song voice and leans forward to avoid me slapping his arm.

∞

"Home sweet home," I sigh as we enter the apartment.

"Finally," Maia exhales as she drops her purse on the table.

"You guys can"—Scott crashes on the couch, propping his feet up—"get comfortable."

"We're going to change; give us a second," I tell them as I push them off my table.

"Okay." Brandon nods as he and Sam just stand around, unsure of what to do.

After slipping into more comfortable clothes, we go back out to the balcony where the boys were already waiting.

"Thank you so much for helping us out tonight. Again." I brush my hair behind my ear.

"Not that you needed it." Brandon laughs and gives me a little push on the shoulder.

"If you don't mind me asking, what's the story between you and them?" Sam asks, scratching the back of his head. *He sure does that a lot, huh?*

Maia and I look at each other, knowing what we're about to say might piss them off even more.

"Okay, the one with brown hair and blue eyes," I start, a heavy feeling in my chest.

"Yeah?" Sam whispers while the other two listen intently.

"He's my ex. We dated for a whole year, and he was what you would call a master manipulator. By the end of the relationship, I found out he was cheating on me, using me. I only knew about one girl, but who knows how many more times there were? And to top it all off, he blamed it all on me."

"He did what??" Brandon stares at me again, his eyes looking darker.

"Yeah, don't be surprised; common sense is something he clearly lacks."

"And the other guy?" Scott asks, gripping the railing.

"That's Jacob," Maia answers. "His best friend and an even dumber version of Connor. I'm pretty sure he only wanted to be with me just because I didn't have feelings for him. Whenever we hung out, the guy never respected personal space or women."

"Fucking asshole." Scott's knuckles start turning whiter.

"Yeah, and it gets worse." Maia sighs.

"How?" the guys ask at the same time.

"Well, after I broke it off, we went to a mutual friend's party about a week later. I got a bit drunk and felt nostalgic for our time together. Of course, he manipulated me into believing that what we had was true love. So... we kissed again." I sigh and let my head hang, ashamed.

"Ollie—" Brandon starts.

"But I came back to my senses right away and went looking for Maia, finding her all loopy in one of the rooms. Jacob wasn't there with her, but it's probably because he was in the bathroom or something."

"Jacob spiked my drink, and Ollie found me just in time. We went home, but what we found out later was a mess." Maia pauses to take a breath.

"Jacob and Connor decided that Jacob had to roofie me. He did it to manipulate Ollie into getting back together with Connor. You know, get her drunk and have me out of the way. Who knows what else he could've done..."

Maia looks at me. "Thankfully, Ollie got her head back in the game fast."

"So, this is what you meant when you said it's happened before?" Scott looks genuinely concerned.

"Yep," she says, pulling her legs onto the chair.

"We thought we wouldn't see them again. This was over two years ago, and so far, we were safe—or so we thought." I say with a sigh.

"Fuck, man. This world's twisted." Brandon brushes his fingers through his hair. *I lost count of how many times he's done that...*

I stare into the sky, flashbacks of those nights flooding my head. The feeling of a hand on my shoulder startles me and brings me back to the present.

"I hope you know nothing that happened is your fault. His mind seems disturbed in ways we can't understand. They were the ones that did this to both of you, so please don't torture yourself over it," Brandon whispers to me.

Instead of answering, I let him pull me into a hug. His hands caress my back, and I breathe in as his touch soothes me. And suddenly, I wish we were doing this with the salty waves of the ocean surrounding us. *What if...*

I pull away, his hand still on my lower back. "What if we have a beach day on Sunday? I feel like I need it, like we all need a break."

"Yeah, sounds good! I could even bring out a couple of surfboards. It might be fun watching you girls learn." Sam smiles brightly now, appearing happy to move on to another topic.

We all laugh at the thought of trying to surf but agree to the plan anyway. The sound of the front door opening startles us. We all relax once we see Ella and Noah. But since we're on the balcony, they can't easily see us.

"Thanks for walking me home," she says to him sweetly.

"No problem." He grabs her by the waist and kisses her. We

all burst out laughing, and they pull away.

"That's my baby brother." Scott walks up to them and pats him back.

"Shit, guess we forgot to tell you we were going back home," Ella says with a groan.

"Well, finally! Now they can stop acting like we don't know shit." Maia claps her hands together like she's praying.

"Well, we're taking off. See you, girls." Sam and Scott hug us.

"Bye, see you Sunday. Again, thanks for everything. Oh, by the way, you guys did great on the opening!" I smile at them.

"Thanks." Brandon walks up to me and gives me a peck on the cheek. "See ya soon."

They all leave, and I stand there with my breath caught in my throat, holding my cheek, trying to keep his touch there as long as possible. I'm pretty sure I'm going to dream about this tonight.

Chapter Eight

"Change the pitch to all your dreams, and make them about me."
~ Symphonic Orchestra, Alexandra Kessler.

OLIVIA – OCEAN CITY

*P*ING. I GET A NOTIFICATION and pick up my phone after packing snacks and drinks for the day.

Hey, it's Brandon! Are you girls ready?

Wait, did Sam give him my number…or did I? It doesn't matter; he's texting me!

Ollie:
hey back, almost!

Brandon:
cool, come down when you're ready
we parked by the door

Ollie:
give us like five more minutes
what time did Sam set for us?

Brandon:
the whole afternoon starting at 2:30
we still have a little time :)

I check the time, my phone reading 2:20 p.m. I quickly grab my bags, and Maia picks up hers, opening the door for us.

"Ella, let's go! The guys are waiting downstairs," I yell from the door. "Come on, what's taking you so long?"

She walks out of the hallway wearing her classic beach

outfit. *No wonder she took so long.* Maia and I roll our eyes at her; we're always waiting for her.

"What? I couldn't go wearing just anything…" She waves her hand over her outfit: a white bikini, a white skirt cover-up, a brown beach hat, brown sandals, and oversized, round sunglasses.

"We're going surfing, Ella," Maia reminds her.

"I can still look fabulous." She walks past us and calls the elevator. Once inside, we take mirror selfies. "You guys look fire."

While posing, I look over Maia's and my outfits. I'm wearing a black one-piece with a slit stopping right above my belly button. I pair it with a beach hat, cream sandals, black sunglasses, and my long, white, open kimono wrapped around my waist.

Maia's wearing her brown suede bikini, a cream dress shirt, and white shorts. The shirt is open down to her belly button and tied in a knot. She completes the look with brown sandals and bold, cream-colored sunglasses.

"Need some help with that?" Brandon walks up to us as we near the car, taking the baskets before I can refuse.

"Not like I had a chance, right," I joke; *dude, shut up.* "Hi, by the way."

"Oh, yeah, hi, sorry!" He stumbles and pecks me on the cheek again. *Damn it, Brandon, you have to stop doing that.*

"O—okay, umm, let's get in. Ella and Noah can sit in the back this time." *Stop acting like an idiot, Ollie.*

The drive to Sam's surf school is no more than five minutes. Funny, we've lived here for so long, and I don't think we've ever seen it.

He set us up with some umbrellas to put down our towels and everything we brought. We sit farther away from others doing the same but still close to the water.

"We should take some pictures before going in." Ella looks at Mia and me.

We find a cute spot further down the beach: a couple of small palm trees and rocks, a little secluded as if it's meant for photoshoots. We each take turns posing on the rocks, against the trees, and lying on the sand with leaves reflecting on our backs. After a while, we call Noah to take some of us.

"Damn, Noah, maybe we should hire you as an intern!" We whistle as we check the pictures he took of us.

"Oh, yeah, for sure! Next time you have a photoshoot, I'll be your lighting guy," he joins in with the joke.

By the time we walk back, Sam already has surfboards and wetsuits lined up on the sand.

"Okay, before I let you in the water, you need to learn the basics while we're still on the sand. So, put down your stuff and come up to the board." He claps his hands.

We all do as he says, each standing next to one another and putting on the wetsuits.

"Y'all set?" he asks, and we all nod.

"Perfect, let's begin! Before doing anything, make sure your strap is tight on your dominant leg. After that, we move to step one: mastering the prone position. Lie down on your belly like you're paddling and get comfortable. Lie on your surfboard, balanced and centered. Feel the surfboard, move around, and try to master it before you go into the water."

We all follow Sam's instructions, and some of us giggle because of how silly we must look paddling on the sand. After a few minutes of practicing, feeling the board, and finding our balance, we move on to step two.

"You're doing great, everyone! But that's the easy part... the prop-up is the tough one. It should be swift and seamless, jumping from the prone position. Think of it as a push-up, then jumping to your feet and landing in a squat position. When you land, keep your feet apart, centered, and balanced. Trust me, you don't want to fall out there."

"I have to be honest—you'll fall a lot at first. But it's important you bend your knees and not your back. And don't put your weight too far forward on the board, or you'll nosedive," he says as he walks around and helps us practice our prop-ups. "Another tip is always staying perpendicular to the water, so you break it with the board and your body when a wave hits.

"Also important: keep your distance from one another. We won't want any accidents with the boards hitting your face when you fall. Make sure you fall sideways, too, so your board doesn't hit you. And please always double-check that your strap is on!"

After going over all the steps, we all feel confident enough to go in. Sam walks around, having one-on-ones with each of us as he wants us to be safe in the water. We review all the steps one last time and clap when we finish.

"Awesome, y'all are ready to go in the water!" We all cheer, picking up our boards, but he stops us. "But you're still missing the most important step of all…"

We all glance at each other, confused by what he means. "Come on, guys, it's obvious," he says, but we stare blankly. "Have fun!!"

We all laugh at his lame-ass joke, and Scott play-punches him. We pick up our boards, run toward the water, and spread out as Sam instructed.

Right before getting in, Ella stops dead in her tracks with Noah next to her. "You know what? Maybe I should sit this one out, you all have fun."

"Oh, come on, you'll be surfing; there's no way you'll touch any fish. Also, how are you *just* realizing this?"

"Well…I was focusing on the lessons, so I did not have time to think about *the fish*." She whispers the last part.

"I'll be right next to you the whole time; I promise no fish will go near you." Noah holds her hands and looks into her eyes. After giving her pleading looks, she agrees, and he kisses her. *Aren't they so adorable?!*

We follow Sam's instructions as we get in the water, lying on the board and paddling out to a clearing in the sea. As the waves grow, the salty water splashes my face—a refreshing contrast to the heat on my back.

"Before we ride the waves, let's all sit on our boards. And with our backs to the ocean, let's take a moment to relax. Feel the water as you shuffle your feet, the sun on your face, and the salty air as you breathe. Take a moment to connect with your body and listen to it. Let it guide you every step from riding the wave to the shore." Sam's soothing voice reaches out to us as we stop.

A few minutes pass, and the water is calm and cold. I close my eyes, breathing in and out, moving my feet—connecting to the board, to the soothing feelings that come with it—*preparing myself for falling on my face more times than staying on.*

Sam interrupts my train of thought as he yells. "Here comes an easy one! Lie on your bellies and paddle, then pop up when you feel the wave getting closer."

I quickly swim forward, waiting for the wave to hit. After a few seconds, I push myself up the board and try to jump onto my feet. The wave hits harder than I expected, throwing me off balance. The next thing I know, I'm flailing underwater while the wave passes over me.

I come up for air to find most of the others also fell over. Sam, of course, is already swimming back to the clearing, and

Scott trails behind him. I scan the water for Ella, making sure she's okay. I find her next to Noah, the two of them splashing water on each other and helping each other back on their boards, paddling away.

I flip mine to try and hop back on, failing miserably. *Being short sucks.* Two hands snaking around my waist hoist me up onto the board. I turn and meet a pair of brown eyes staring back at me. *Brandon, of course, it's Brandon.*

"Thanks." I give him a small smile.

"No problem, Ollie." He brushes some hair out of my face. "Next time, try popping up faster. Unless you want to fall on your face again…" I stick my tongue out at him and swim away instead of answering.

For what feels like over half an hour, we spend our time falling off the boards over and over again. Attempt after attempt, I fall forward, backward, and every other way imaginable. Water and sand are sticking to every part of my body. By now, there's more saltwater in my lungs than air.

I hop on my board again, lying down and resting from falling so many times. If I can just get it right one time, I'll call that a success. I look over at Maia, determination written all over her face. We're so close that I could reach out and hold her hand. We look back as a wave starts to build up, not big, but not small either.

Everything moves and feels like it's happening in slow motion: paddling forward, closing my eyes, and feeling the water. We look at each other, nodding as the wave gets closer. We push ourselves up, lifting our bodies in a swift, clean motion. I hop on and look at Maia next to me, and a look of surprise sits on her face as we find our balance. We hit a minor wave, stumble a little, and instinctively reach over to each other.

"Oh, my God, we're doing it! Maia, we're doing it!" I

scream, my fists punching the air.

"Whoohooo," Maia yells as we ride out the wave, reaching over the space between the boards to hold each other. The wind blows in our faces, salt in our hair, and water on our skin, her blue hair glistening under the sun.

It's not long until we reach the end of our short-lived celebration, with me falling and knocking Maia down. I gasp for air as soon as we break the surface. I look at Maia, curling over in laughter as I see her hair everywhere.

"Why are you laughing? Yours isn't that different from mine," she says while laughing at me.

I lift my hands to feel my hair, and indeed, it's a knotty mess. We splash each other, laughing.

But our laughter's interrupted by Ella yelling over to us. "Watch out!"

We swiftly turn around, coming face to face with her falling off her board and onto us.

"Shittt," we all yell out before going underwater.

The three of us flail around while trying not to drown, which is kind of hard to do when the boards' straps pull us around. We take off the straps and get out of the water—gasps of air and coughing up water are the only sounds we hear. *Well, at least our hair looks good.* Now, we can't contain our laughter.

"Y'all okay?" The boys walk up to us with worried looks on their faces.

"Yeah, yeah, we're good. Don't worry about it," I answer. Brandon offers me his hand to help me up, and this time, I take it. "Thanks...again."

"I got you." He gives me one of those loopy smiles, making me forget we're not alone *and that I'm still holding his hand.*

"Umm...I should take my board back. I think I'm done for now." I drop his hand and turn around. "What about you?"

"No, you go ahead. We're staying." Maia and Ella give me a weird look. "Right, guys?" they ask the other boys.

Scott and Noah agree on cue while Sam takes a little longer but agrees too. Brandon takes our boards, putting them back on the rack. Meanwhile, I take off the suit and dry myself with a towel.

From my peripheral vision, I notice Brandon doing the same thing next to me. "Hey, want to take a walk with me?"

"Uhh, yeah, sure," I answer as I put on my kimono, leaving it open. We grab a couple of water bottles and start walking on the shore away from everyone.

For the first few minutes, we walk in silence, dragging our feet in the sand and appreciating the feeling of it—the cold water splashes against our feet and legs.

"So," he mumbles.

"So." *And we're doing this again.*

"Did you like it? Surfing, I mean." He looks at me.

"It was fun. But spending most of the time flailing underwater is not my thing..." I laugh while looking down.

"Oh, come on, it wasn't that bad. You stayed on a couple of times. And that thing you did with Maia, holding hands, that was pretty cool."

"Sure, sure, until I fell on her, and then Ella almost killed us," I huff as I hold in a laugh.

"If that's not a success, then I don't know what is." He shrugs.

"Well, you didn't do so bad either." I nudge him while walking, almost tripping over my own feet.

"Oh, yeah, I did pretty well. Had some practice too. Sam has taken us surfing before." He gives me a smirk—*that damn, charming smile.*

"You think you're so smug, don't you?" I look at him, and

the wind blows my hair in my face.

"Maybe." He stops us, brushing my hair behind my ears.

The feeling of his fingers against my cheeks sends shivers down my spine, and I draw in a shaky breath as he stares deep into my eyes. *Come on, say something, don't be embarrassing.* His touch makes me so nervous that I'll become a stuttering mess if I try to say anything.

"I—" cough. "We should go back; we don't want the others worrying about us too much."

"Sure." A hint of disappointment fills his eyes.

As we walk back, his hand grazes mine, sending a jolt through my body. *Boy, what are you doing to me?*

Note to self: I need to talk to Maia and Ella ASAP.

MAIA – OCEAN CITY

I START TO TAKE MY SUIT OFF OUT ON THE SAND as Sam and Scott come out of the water, doing the same as me, our boards on the ground.

"Sam, honestly, you are such a great teacher. Thank you for the lesson!" I say as I struggle with my arms. "I think it's safe to say I wanna try this again."

"No problem! You girls are fast learners, too. I'm actually impressed." He bumps my hip, a smile on his face.

Scott stands next to me and, without warning, shakes his wet hair onto me.

"Hey, come on!" I try to push him away, clearly not as strong as he is.

"What? Am I bothering you?" He pokes my stomach.

"When are you not?" I playfully push him away, successfully this time. "I think we need to have a talk about personal space."

"You mean getting rid of it? I never would've guessed you wanted less of it with me," he smirks as he finishes shimmying out of his suit.

What is he even trying to prove with his little quirky dance? I look to my left, trying to ignore his usual antics, and notice Ollie and Brandon walking toward us, still out of earshot.

I know Olivia likes him, but I don't want her to get her hopes up without knowing what he feels. Should I ask? No, but—

"Hey, guys?"

"Yeah?" Sam lifts his head after dropping his suit, and Scott does the same.

"What do you think of them?" I signal over to the lovebirds by the shore.

"What about them?" Sam glances at them and then quickly looks away. *Hmm...*

"Well, do you think Brandon likes Olivia?" I finish drying off, and I can see Scott's eyes wander down my body.

"Hey, up here, rockstar!" I snap my fingers by his face and he bats it away. "If you're so interested in my bikini, I could tell you where I bought it. I think it would look so much better on you anyway."

"Yeah, Scott. You'd look so pretty," Sam sings mockingly.

"Actually, you know what? Yeah, I would totally rock it!" Scott laughs it off and poses, modeling. "Send me the link; I'll get it right now. Do they have it in blue?"

I laugh and roll my eyes, swatting his arm playfully. *Okay, enough niceness already, back to normal now.* "Yeah, yeah, back to my question, thanks. Does he or does he not?!"

"Fine, fine, I think so, yeah. But Brandon was never one to

go all the way for girls, at least back in college. The only person that got him like that was Anna when they first met, but we know how that ended up going." His eyes quickly glance at Sam as if he said something wrong. *What's that about?* "So, yeah," Scott answers in a confident tone.

"Maybe he's just being nice? Ollie is a wonderful person. Who wouldn't treat her like the best all the time?" Sam shrugs as he rambles.

"Well, between you and us. In Brandon's song, 'Façade,' if you listen closely, he talks about something that made him feel what he had lost." Scott whispers, leaning closer.

"That's about Ollie?" I whisper back, eyes slightly wider. *Well, she definitely did not tell me that. Does she even know this?*

"Yep," Scott answers as he nods. "I mean, maybe." He looks at Sam with a questioning look.

"Yeah, it's about her," he says in a disgruntled tone as he looks back at the shore. "I'll put the boards and the suits back. See you guys back at the car." He quickly grabs them all.

"No, let us help." I attempt to take one from him.

"No, don't worry about it. It's technically my job anyway," he says, running off with everything before we can reply. *What happened to his excitement just two minutes ago?*

I share a questioning look with Scott. "No idea, man," he shrugs as he says to me.

We hush and try to act normal as we see Olivia and Brandon walk up to us after their stroll with a sheepish look on their faces.

"Hey, guys." Olivia can't seem to look Brandon in the eyes as their hands brush past one another. *Well, well, well, would you look at that… I guess we're having a talk later.*

"Hey," we answer together, *because that's not suspicious*

behavior at all.

"Umm, okay... Where are Ella and Noah?" Ollie asks, looking around, her hand brushing Brandon's from the movement. *Okay, I see what you're doing.*

"They wanted to walk home, so they left," I shrug, trying to hide my knowing look.

"Those two can't get enough of each other, can they?" She laughs and shakes her head, now avoiding *my* gaze.

I do have to admit, to myself, that Ella and Noah are the most adorable couple. Though I would never tell her that, or she would never let me hear the end of it.

We're back home resting in the living room, exhausted from the day and hydrating ourselves when Olivia sighs audibly.

"Yes? What's wrong now?" I sigh back in an attempt to mock her.

"I like him, Maia." She grabs a cushion and groans into it. "I like Brandon," she mumbles.

"Finally!!" Ella and I exclaim exasperatedly, throwing our heads back on the couch.

"Shut up, they're going to hear," she whispers, lifting her head. *What?!*

"Bitch, they live in a whole other building!" I whisper back, looking at her like she's finally lost her mind and making her groan into the pillow again.

"So, what are you going to do about it?" Ella asks, leaning her head on her hands and smiling wickedly.

"I don't know." She drawls out the last word. "All I know is that I have all these feelings. And that I'm fucked because I don't know what he feels."

"I don't know, Ollie. He might surprise you." I shrug. *Well, I know*. I *could* tell her, but watching this unfold is more fun.

Instead of answering, she throws the pillow at my face and storms off to her room. *Very mature, Ollie, very mature.*

"Can we stop the hands of time? Can I be yours 'till the day I die?" ~ My Confession, Alexandra Kessler.

OLIVIA – OCEAN CITY

"HEY, GUYS. WHERE'S SAM?" I ask as Brandon sits next to me and hands me a coffee. "Thanks," I whisper.

"Saw him taking a call outside," he answers. "And you're welcome," he whispers to me.

"Is everything okay with him?"

"Yeah, yeah, all good." He nods. "How was your night?"

"Had some strange dreams, but other than that, all good."

"What was it about?" *Not the kind of dream you want me to share in front of everyone.*

I open my mouth, but Sam comes rushing into the studio before I can say anything, his breath shaky and eyes wide.

"Whoa, what's going on?" I sit up, my heart still racing from thinking about Brandon's question.

"New Sound Records called!" He pauses to slow down and breathe properly. "They recorded the audition from last week and showed it to the executives." He looks around with wide eyes. "Guys, they loved it!"

"Hold up, what does that mean?" Brandon asks, leaning over on the couch.

"We're in. They're signing the Reputation!" he cries out.

"What?! Oh, my God!" we all scream out and jump with with thrill and excitement.

"They want us to come in this Saturday to sign all the papers. They're having a signing party for us too. Shit, it's happening!!" Sam jumps up and down like a kid.

We're cheering, screaming, hugging—celebrating this huge milestone we achieved together. I feel someone spinning me around and wrapping their arms around my waist. I breathe in Brandon's cologne as he pulls me into a hug.

I even recognize his scent now. I hold on to his neck as he lifts me off the ground. The feeling of being so close sends shivers through my entire body, like sparks of electricity flowing in my veins.

He puts me back down, hands still at my waist, and stares into my eyes with a glimmer shining in his. His look is so intense that he could pierce into my soul, knocking my breath out.

"Congratulations, you guys deserve it!" I whisper, staring back at him with the same intensity.

"Couldn't have done it without you," he whispers back, giving me a slight smile. Maia coughs and brings us back down to reality. "Without both of you, of course," he says, slowly letting me go.

I look at Maia, and she gives me a knowing look. *Stop it.* I roll my eyes at her.

I can't take all this confusion; I need to talk to Brandon. I have to tell him how I feel, even if he doesn't feel the same. *And maybe, just maybe, this trip is exactly what we need to forget about Connor and Jacob and the bullshit they pulled before.*

NEW YORK

"Damn, I know you showed me the apartment, but that video call did not do it justice. This place is fancy as hell," Ella

whispers as we enter the penthouse.

"We told you, his family is rich-rich!" I whisper back. "Where are your parents, by the way?" I turn to Scott.

"I have no idea, dealing with business somewhere..." he answers with a hint of a bitter tone as we walk up the stairs. *Touchy subject, I see.* "Anyway, Noah and I are taking their room. The rest of you can take the same ones you had last time."

"Will the three of us fit in one bed?" Ella asks us. Instead of answering, we smirk and open the bedroom door.

"Holy shit, it's like a hotel suite!" Ella walks around, starstruck, as she stares out the big window. I still can't believe how amazing it is myself.

"We told you." Maia shrugs as we sit on the bed.

"We still have a couple of hours before we need to start getting ready. Want to see—" Before I finish the question, Ella's already dragging us out the door.

We show her the whole place: The huge kitchen, the beautiful living room with the window wall, and the terrace with a barbecue area, pool, and hot tub. All that time, Ella's mouth is agape, and she fawns over everything. We move to the wall overlooking the New York skyline, enjoying the feeling of the wind on our faces, blowing through our hair.

"Do you realize tonight we'll be at a party with a freaking record label?" I let out a breath of disbelief. "The press will be there. They're taking pictures of not only the band but of us too. Like, what the heck?!"

"Holy—" Maia lets out a dry laugh. "Oh, shit!"

I pull them into a hug, hollering with excitement.

"I'm going to be famous now!" Ella squeals.

Only she would have that on her mind. And it's not even about her tonight.

"Come on, let's start getting ready. There's only one

bathroom, and there are three of us."

"Ollie, can you pass me the red lipstick?" Ella asks as I apply the finishing touches to my makeup. I smack my lips together after handing it over to her.

I walk over to the full-body mirror, brushing my hands through my straightened hair. Taking my time to appreciate my outfit, I glance over my reflection: a white romper with wavy frills and a surplice neckline, gold heels, and gold accessories.

I look at Ella as she curls the tips of her hair and flips it back, the waves falling onto her black dress with long lace sleeves and a heart-shaped front. She pairs it with platinum heels and accessories, and a black pearl purse.

"How do I look?" Maia stands in front of us.

She signals over her outfit: a tight black two-piece set, a black leather blazer on top, and black heels. It looks so good on her that she doesn't need to accessorize.

"Like you're the one getting signed." I wink at her.

Ella whistles as we stare at ourselves in the mirror. The sound of knocking on the door startles us. We turn around as I say, "Come in," and meet Brandon's gaze.

"Hey, sorry, girls. Are you ready?" His eyes find mine after looking around the room.

His mouth slightly opens, his eyes drifting over me. He meets mine again with a look that I can't quite distinguish—so intense, so much emotion dancing in his eyes. I feel my face burning, and a shiver runs down my back.

"Yes, we're good to go." Maia's voice pulls me back down.

Brandon moves aside, clearing his throat as we walk through the door. I take a moment to look him over and discreetly suck in a breath. *Something about guys in suits just makes me lose it.* His black pants and dress shirt make the white blazer pop. If he looked good before, now he's blowing up the standards.

"Damn, guys, we look so hot!" Layla squeals and fake fans herself with her hand as we walk down the stairs. And indeed she does too with her long, white two-piece set: flared pants and a crop top with a short slit on the front.

"I'm so glad we met you." I give her a side hug.

"Ugh, of course, they get the grand entrance... I've been overlooked," Scott says dramatically, earning a snort from Drew.

I look over the guys, all dressed in suits. An array of colors varies between them: Scott's in full black and Noah's in a gray suit with a white shirt. Drew goes classic with a white shirt, black dress pants, and a black blazer.

My eyes stop at Sam, standing out between them. His pants are a simple black, but he wears a navy blue shirt that matches his blazer's blue accents. I don't know why, but the way it fits and looks on him makes my eyes linger. But why is it making my breath hitch?

"Guys, the executives sent us a limo," Sam says as he reads a text from his phone.

"No way, dude! This sounds too good to be true." Drew gives him a wide smile.

"Not really, you guys are very talented! You're finally getting the recognition you deserve." I say with a smile.

"Thanks, Ollie; we appreciate the work you girls do!" Drew smiles and winks at me, earning a slight glare from both Brandon and Sam. *Weird, but okay.*

"Okay, let's stop talking and go to the limo!" Layla pipes in with a shrill voice. She even does little jumps.

"How does she have so much energy all the time?" Ella whispers to Maia and me.

"I ask myself that every day," I mumble as I shake my head. *And yet, we love her as she is.*

Pop. The champagne's cork flies across the rooftop as one of the executives opens it. We all cheer, beaming after they sign the contracts and pose for promo pictures. They pour us a glass each, except for Ella and Noah since they're seventeen.

"Here's to a great partnership and an even more amazing future ahead of you," the executive hollers, and we click our glasses together. And with a unanimous "cheers," we take a sip.

"I still can't believe this is happening," Brandon mumbles, an incredulous look on his face.

"Why not? This is what you've been working for. Own it!" I place my hand on his upper arm, giving him a reassuring smile.

He opens his mouth to say something but closes it as one of the junior executives walks up to us.

"Hello, guys! My name's Oscar; it's nice to meet you all. How are you all enjoying the party?" He shakes our hands and lingers on mine, giving it a light squeeze.

"I'm Olivia." I give him a slight smile, and Brandon stiffens beside me. *Let's see how far I can push him for a reaction.* "How long have you worked here?"

"A couple of years. I've seen a lot of artists come through here and take off in their careers. I have a feeling you guys will blow up pretty quick." He looks at Brandon this time.

He mumbles a low "thanks" before downing his champagne.

"And what do you do?" he asks me with a curious look.

"My friend Maia and I own a photography studio, and we also work on the band's social media presence."

"Interesting! Glad you worked your magic on them; that—

and their talent—is what brought you here." He winks at me.

I'm about to say something else when Brandon interrupts the conversation. "I'm sorry; I would love to continue this *wonderful* chat. But isn't this your favorite song, Ollie?"

"Oh, my God, yes!" I gasp. "Sorry, Oscar. It was nice meeting you too." I smile at him, and Brandon moves us to the dance floor setup.

I smirk and let out a dry laugh while Brandon glares at Oscar.

"What?" he mumbles, looking back at me.

"Nothing, just testing something out." I slightly shake my head.

"Hmm. Can I know what it is?"

I shake my head, to which he glares more. "What, you don't trust me?" I bat my eyes at him.

He purses his lips, taking a moment to think. "Not right now, no," he says in a high-pitched tone.

I fake gasp as if shocked and insulted by his answer, batting his arm away from mine. He laughs and snakes his arms around my waist, pulling me in. We slow dance as the songs play, not caring if it's not the right rhythm. We spend what feels like hours dancing, talking, and laughing at whatever lame jokes he tells. And whenever I throw my head back, his hands pull me closer.

At one point, he has me pressed up against him, and I can hear his heartbeat. And I'm sure he can hear mine, beating so fast it could break free from my body. His hands caressing my back and brushing the hair out of my face are not making this any easier either.

His face is so close I could confuse his heavy breathing with mine. He keeps flickering between my eyes and my lips with such intensity that I could kiss him right here without hesitation.

Scared and going against my instincts, I lay my head on his

shoulder. He sighs, but his arms hug me around my waist, and he moves us to the beat of a slow song. *Well, about damn time they played one. We must've looked stupid all this time, slow dancing to the wrong rhythm.*

"Ollie," he whispers in my ear.

"Yeah?"

"Can we sit for a moment?" He pulls back a little to look me in the eyes.

I nod, and he grabs my hand. *Shit, shit, shit.* The feeling of his hand on mine makes my head spin and my heart flutter.

Once we reach a more secluded area, we sit down, and he lets go of my hand. *No, grab it again!* I want to beg and shout at him.

"What's up?"

He takes a deep breath. "Ollie," he whispers, grabbing my hand. I breathe in as his deep voice pronounces my name.

"Brandon," I whisper. His thumb is now caressing the back of my hand, drawing small circles.

"I don't know where to start, honestly. But you make me very nervous when I'm near you. You make me want to be next to you all the time." He takes a shaky breath. "And you look so beautiful tonight. The way we danced together, how it felt to hold you close. I could dance with you all night if you let me."

The way he looks at me while caressing my hands melts me, as if all he wants to do is to kiss me. My breathing, my heartbeat, my mind: everything's going all over the place right now. I focus on how he looks at me, smiling, and his gaze flickering down to my lips. The way his hands spark a fire in me whenever he touches me and how it lingers after it's gone.

My breath hitches, my heart feels like it's about to explode, and my mind goes a mile a minute. The only thing keeping me from bursting is his hand on mine.

"I—umm." A stutter breaks out of me.

And now that look is back, like he's about to kiss me. *Why can't he just do it? Why does he torture me by prolonging this moment?* I've been waiting for it ever since we met. Every time he smiles at me; when he brushes his hand against mine; when his hands hold my hips; I want him to kiss me like the world's about to end, and we won't ever get a chance again.

I press my hand against his cheek, brushing my thumb back and forth. Biting the inside of my bottom lip, not knowing how to go into it, I lean in. Taking a deep breath, I see him do the same. His nose brushes against mine, and his lips are so close that I can almost taste them.

"Shit, sorry! So sorry, I didn't see you there until now," Oscar pipes in. He bends down next to the chairs, grabbing something from behind them. He's too quick for me to see what it is.

"The big guys needed this..." he says awkwardly and then walks away.

I suck in a shaky breath, pissed off at this dumbass. *Could you not see we were in the middle of something? What a way to ruin the mood, dude.*

I pull away from Brandon, laying my hands on my knees, and he doesn't resist. I knew this was too good to be true. I turn away from him, feeling cold from his absence.

"Fuck it," I hear Brandon mumble.

Without processing what's going on, he turns me toward him. And before I can say anything, his lips are on mine— expertly moving against them, partly opening them and matching my pace.

One of his hands glides to the back of my head, tangling in my hair, earning a hum from me. I move my hands to his neck, pulling him in a little more and turning my head to the side, deepening the kiss—a kiss so intense it ignites my body on fire.

My skin burns wherever he places his hands. Every emotion, our burning passion, everything we couldn't convey with words, is felt in this searing kiss.

We stop to take a breath, his gaze burning into mine, and it's not long until he pulls me in again. Weeks of anticipation, missed opportunities, and pent-up feelings—all fueled by this kiss. A kiss with so much intensity I didn't know could spark so many emotions.

"I'm not here; I'm not here. Continue, pretend I'm a ghost. Don't stop on my account!" Oscar walks by again.

I don't even want to see what he's here for this time! The sound of our lips disconnecting resonates in my head as we pull apart.

"I'm going to kill that little shit," Brandon mutters. His heavy breath fans on my face as he rests his forehead on mine. I let out a dry laugh, still coming down from the high of the kiss. "He won't stop interrupting, won't he?" He lets out a sarcastic huff.

"The universe has proven that so far, yeah..."

"I would not stop kissing you if it was up to me," he whispers, caressing my face. I close my eyes, enjoying the feeling of being near him. "Come on, let's join the rest of the party!" He gives me a not-so-short kiss on the lips.

"Tell me that you guys finally kissed..." Maia sighs as we reach them. Brandon and I look sheepishly at each other.

"Yes, we did. We almost killed someone to make it happen, but, yes, we did..." He hugs me by the waist.

"Umm, what?"

"Nothing. Just life playing one of its tricks." He snickers, and I muffle a laugh. Everyone gives us weird looks, staring like we lost our heads.

"Come on, I haven't seen you since we got here. Let's go dance!" I pull Maia and Ella to the floor.

Hours go by with us jumping and dancing like nothing else matters as we sing along with the songs. This party tops every milestone we've ever gone through: the feeling of accomplishment, of making it with your best friend for life. Nothing can take this spark of joy away, a perfect moment that will forever remain in our memories.

"Guys, I need a break." I stop dancing, taking a breath to calm my beating heart. *Is it the dancing and jumping or the kiss? Or the excitement of tonight? All of the above.*

"Are you okay?" Brandon stops too, standing in front of me and caressing my arms. *He's adorable, melt me now.*

"Yeah, yeah." I quickly peck his lips. *Can I do this a million more times?* "I just need a quick trip to the bathroom."

"Want me to walk you over?" he whispers, kissing me. *Please, do that again.*

"No, no, it's okay. I'll find my way." Looking behind him, I signal Maia that I'm going to the bathroom. She gives me a thumbs-up and goes back to dancing.

Giving him another quick peck, I walk inside to find the bathroom. Looking up, I see a sign pointing to the far left and follow it.

Once inside, I do my business in one of the stalls and step out in front of the mirror. I take my time: washing my hands, wiping a paper towel on my skin to refresh myself, and then fixing my makeup.

A rattle on the door makes me jump in place, leaving me startled and my heart beating erratically. "Sorry, it's busy! I'll be right out." I yell out to them.

But they don't seem to hear me, the rattling continuing with a hard push to the door. "Hey, hey, alright. Hold on, I'm out!" I run to the door, open it, and I stop breathing, my palms getting sweaty.

"What are you doing here?" Mustering all the bravery I have in me, I look straight into his eyes with my best poker face. Disdain drips out of my mouth with every word.

Without saying a word, he bursts in, grabbing my throat and pushing me back against the wall behind us. I gather all my strength, trying to pry his hands off. He tightens them, making my throat close, and it gets harder to breathe.

"No, stop. Please," I barely get out, my voice raspy. My vision blurs, and my head gets heavier. I drop my purse and try to lift my hands in an attempt to push him away.

I don't get too far before he catches it and holds it above my head. His voice whispering *shut up* is the last thing I hear before everything fades.

"I'm sorry I can't fix you. There's nothing I could do for you."
~ Drown, Alexandra Kessler.

BRANDON – NEW YORK

*H*OW LONG HAS SHE BEEN IN THE BATHROOM?

"Hey." I nudge Maia's shoulder. "Is she still not back?"

"No, why?" She stops dancing and frowns at me.

"I don't know. I just think it's been a little too long."

She takes out her phone, her hands shaking slightly after seeing the time. "Wait, how has it been an hour? Where is she?!"

"Shit, okay." I put the drinks down on a table and rub my face. "I'll go check on her. I'm sure it's fine."

I waste no time, almost running toward the bathrooms. I reach the ladies' door and lift my hand to knock. Without using much force, it squeaks open. *What the hell?* Why isn't this closed? Did something happen?

I walk in, close the door behind me, and look around inside the not-so-small space: a cracked sink, shards of glass on the floors, broken mirrors with a smear of blood, and running water spilling onto the floor.

"Ollie, where are you?" Silence. "Shit, Olivia, come on, answer me. Please, tell me you're okay!" I walk around the lobby space, glass crunching under my shoes. *What the fuck happened here? Is she hurt? Why isn't she answering?*

"Olivia, please!" I run to the back and check the open stalls. *Come on, come on.*

I rush through, pushing each door until I reach the last one. My breath leaves my body as I find her lying on the floor, unmoving. Kneeling next to her, I quickly check for a pulse. *Thank the Lord!*

"Shit, Ollie, what happened to you?" I brush the hair off her face, revealing the bruising around her eye. There are also some minor scratches on her cheeks and arms, maybe from the broken mirrors.

"Please, please, wake up. I just had you, Ollie, don't leave me!" I try shaking her awake to no avail.

"I'm so, so sorry, Ollie, I should've just walked with you. If I did, then you wouldn't have gotten hurt." I cradle her body against mine, hugging her and caressing her hair.

"Come back to me, Ollie, come back," I whisper as I kiss her forehead, tears dripping on her.

Wait, what am I still doing here? I need to get her out of here—take her to the hospital. Ollie's not waking up; she needs a hospital!

I should call 911…but what if they take too long? I could drive her myself. Shit, we didn't drive here. The limo!

The line keeps ringing and ringing. *Come on! Pick up the damn phone, man, we need you here.* The call goes straight to voicemail, and I hang up to call Sam again.

After two rings, he answers. "Brandon?"

"Sam, something's wrong with Ollie. She went to the bathroom alone, but she was taking too long. I—I'm not sure if she's breathing well." I ramble on and on, trying to explain as much as possible. "I didn't know who else to call, Sam. I need you. Ollie needs you. Can you please come quick?"

"Whoa, whoa, slow down, man. What the fuck happened?" I hear some rustling as he pushes through people.

"Please, just get here. I'll tell you what I know then. How

fast can you get the limo to drive us to the hospital?"

"Hospital?!" he yells. "I'm on my way. I'll ask the driver to meet us downstairs!"

"I can't lose her, man, I can't. I just got with her." My voice breaks, and a sob escapes me.

"You won't. Don't go there, okay? You won't," he says in a stern voice, but I notice his shaky breathing. "Just hang on, man, I'm almost there."

I cradle Ollie in my arms, shaking as I cry and hold her to my chest. I hear footsteps rushing through the door after it bursts wide open.

"Where are you?!" Sam's voice echoes through the halls.

"In the last stall!" I cry out.

"Shit, Brandon, what happened?" His voice trembles as he looks at her.

"I don't know, man. We were dancing, and she took a bathroom break. She was supposed to only take five minutes, but an hour went by, and she still wasn't back. I came here to look for her and found the door open. The bathroom was a mess, with glass everywhere. Someone hurt her." My voice breaks again. "I'm so sorry!"

"She's going to be okay. We'll take her to the hospital; she'll be fine. And I promise you, we'll find the bastard who did this."

"Help! Anybody, I need some help over here," I cry out as we burst through the emergency room's doors. A group of doctors takes Ollie from my arms, placing her on a gurney.

"Sir, I need you to calm down so I can ask you a few questions. Can you do that for me?" A kind nurse stands in front of us with a clipboard. I breathe in and out, calming my nerves and nodding.

"Can you tell us what happened?"

"I'm not sure. I left her alone in the bathroom at a party. She was only supposed to be there for a couple of minutes, but an hour went by, and we got worried. When I went to look for her, the bathroom was a mess, and I found her on the floor like this."

"And did you find any more wounds or some bruising around the stomach?"

"Shit." I close my eyes, exhaling out of frustration. "No, I did not." I shake my head. Something flips in my brain, making me stare at the nurse. "Is that a bad thing? Do you think she might be bleeding internally?"

She shakes her head, a calm look on her face. "There's nothing to worry about right now. These are just some procedural questions. I will tell her doctors when they check her into one of our examination rooms."

With a serene voice, she urges us toward the waiting room. "Please, take a seat. One of the receptionists will give you some forms to fill out, and I'll update you as soon as I can."

We thank her and sit in the far back since it's empty. I can't deal with strangers right now. I lean over, pressing my face into my hands. Sam rubs my back as my body begins to shake from my sobbing. People must be giving us those awkward, sympathetic looks right now. But I couldn't care less; all I want is for Ollie to be okay.

"Excuse me," someone says in a low voice, barely above a whisper, and places something next to me. I lift my head to ask what it is, but she's already gone.

"Probably some forms... Fuck," I mutter under my breath, realizing that we forgot a lot of things.

"What?" Sam asks, lifting his head.

I sit straight, leaning my head on the wall. "We didn't bring her things; her ID, health insurance card, and I don't know her Social Security number. Maybe Ella…" I trail off.

"Brandon, we forgot her sister and Maia. You sounded so scared that I just took off without telling anyone." Sam leans over too, sighing.

"I am so *fucking* selfish. How could I forget about her sister and best friend? They need to be here, not me. You know what? I should just go. I'll take a cab and tell them everything so they can come here with her things," I begin to stand, but he sits me back down.

"You are not selfish. You found her in a very delicate and time-sensitive situation. You acted quickly and brought her in, which was the most important thing," he says. "I'll go pick them up in the limo. You stay here in case they have any updates."

Overwhelmed with all that's happening, I nod and breathe, closing my eyes. *In and out. In and out. Everything will be fine. Ollie's going to be okay.*

I yawn, and I start to feel droopy. Unable to open my eyes, I leave them closed and rest for a minute. But only for a minute; I need to stay awake for her. *My Ollie…*

∞

"Hey!" I jolt awake after someone yells in my face and slams their hands on the chair.

I sit up straight and face a red-faced Maia and Ella. "Ollie is in the ER right now, and you dare to fall asleep?!" Ella yells.

"Sam and I brought her here; I have the right to rest my eyes. And I only closed them for a second; not my fault they stayed that way," I whisper-yell at them. *I am so dead!*

My stare drops to her hands, and I notice they brought Ollie's purse. "Here, I'll fill these out. Just hand me her ID," I say.

"How could you leave her alone like that?" Ella roughly passes me the documents.

"How did—"

"Sam filled us all in with the details."

"And why would I ever think that letting her go alone to a bathroom would lead to her getting hurt?" I fight back while scribbling everything down.

"How the hell would I know?!" Maia attracts pointed glances from strangers as she yells. "Sorry." She shrugs at them.

"Listen, take a seat. I'm already done with the forms; I'll hand them in and wait for updates. I know we're all worried, but there's nothing else we can do." A nurse at the desk takes the clipboard before I retake my seat.

"Brandon?" Ella calls me with urgency in her voice. I turn to her, letting her know I'm listening. "Is she going to be okay?" Her eyes well up.

Taking a deep breath, I take her hand in mine to comfort her. "Everything will be fine. I promise."

"Come here." Maia taps the seat on her right while Scott sits on her left. Ella moves over, and they hug with Noah on her other side. Drew and Layla do the same next to them while Sam stays with me.

How long has it been? How long did I sleep? And why the fuck is no one coming to tell us good news?

I tap my feet incessantly, bouncing my knee up and down. I check my phone for the time: it's been over an hour. *Ugh.* I throw my head back on the wall. *I can't handle it anymore. I need answers, good news.*

Walking up to the desk, I get the nurse's attention behind it. "Is there any news on Olivia Woods?"

"What is your relation to the patient?" she asks with a

serious face.

"Her boyfriend, but I'm the one who brought her in," I say.

"I wish I could help you, but we can only release information to the immediate family. Is there anyone in your group who's a family member?" She has her folder in hand.

Ella. "Yes, yes!" I say excitedly. "Her sister, she's right here." I turn around and wave for her to come.

"What's going on?" She shifts between us, a scared look in her eyes.

"They can only release patient information to the immediate family, and that's you."

Her eyes open wide. "Is she okay? Did something else happen?"

"Your sister's okay now. After running some tests, the doctors determined she has a concussion and mild internal bleeding. She's now resting in the examination room as the doctors are monitoring her symptoms. We will let you know when you can go in to see her."

Oh, my God, we breathe out as some tension leaves our bodies. We thank the nurse and go back to our seats with calmer minds. I let Ella fill the others in as my eyes feel droopy, and my head gets heavy.

"Hey." Someone shakes me awake. "Get up. We can see her now." I rub my eyes, coming face-to-face with Ella. "Come on."

I groggily follow her into the hallway, past other examination rooms, nurses' stations, and quiet patient rooms. We finally reach hers, pushing open the door and finding everyone else already inside. Sam's moping in a chair, Maia's holding her hand, Scott's in a corner with Noah, and Drew holds

Layla in the opposite corner.

My heart breaks as I see her on the bed: IV in one hand, a breathing tube in her nose, bandages on her arms, and stitches over her eyebrow.

"Oh, Ollie." My voice falters as I reach her, taking her free hand in mine. "I don't know if you can hear me, but if you can, I'm so sorry. I'm sorry I didn't think to walk with you. It was so stupid and so not the gentleman's way of doing things. If I had known that you—that someone hurt—if I would've known."

A sob wracks my body, making me shake all over and forcing me down on my knees next to her bed.

"It's my fault, Ollie, all my fault. And I promise I won't let anything like this happen again. We'll find the bastard who did this to you and make them pay."

I wipe my tears with my other hand. "And I won't leave your side until you wake up. Day and night, 24/7, I'll be right here. And I'll stay because I care about you, okay? So, so much." I hear sniffles around the room.

"I wish you could hear me right now," I mutter against her forehead. And I don't know if it is God, pure luck, or the universe, but her hand clasps tighter around mine.

"You can hear me? She can hear me!" I turn around and look at everyone, then back to her. "We're here. We're all here for you. You'll be fine, just fine."

Chapter Nine

"My eyesight is full of broken glass." ~ Scary Nights,
Alexandra Kessler.

OLIVIA – NEW YORK

ER VITALS ARE STABLE FOR NOW. Her wounds are healing nicely, and she'll wake up any time soon. We also notified the police ..."

A voice I don't recognize drifts off, sounding far away. I try to listen, but the pounding in my head overpowers my strength to do so. It smells funny too, clean and with a hint of bleach. *Maybe too clean...¿dónde estoy (where am I)?*

"She should be heading home within a week, given how well she's responding to treatment." The voice keeps talking, fading in and out inside my head. *What does that mean? Am I not at home? Where am I?*

Shit. I hiss as I try to open my eyes and close them again after getting hit with blinding, white, fluorescent lights. Muffled voices come from all around, and my head spins as I try to understand what they're saying.

"And what if she doesn't heal that fast?" A distorted voice in a higher pitch interrupts the other one.

"How long until the authorities respond?" A deeper voice starts talking now.

My mouth feels dry; why does it feel dry? *I need water.* And these sheets feel weird, rough against my hands. *This is not my house. Where am I?* I try lifting my arm and feel a pinch on my wrist. *I'm in the hospital... Why am I in a hospital? And how long have I been here?*

"This is all I can tell you at the moment. I wish I had more information. Meanwhile, you could all help out by…"

I need to get up and get out. *I want to go home.* A wave of nausea hits as I lift my head, forcing me back down.

My body feels heavy and tired. My vision's blurry, and my mind's fuzzy. *Am I even awake? Why can't I move? Quiero a mi mami (I want my mommy)…* I suddenly need to cry, but my body's not cooperating. So I lie there as tears run down my cheeks, trickling down my neck.

Why can't I remember what happened? How did I get here? My head is throbbing, and my mouth is dry. I can't open my eyes…I want my mom. *Why isn't she here?*

"Oh, no, Ollie, please don't cry! We're here for you, right here," a soft voice I recognize as Ella whispers to my right side.

"Yes, yes, everyone is. We're all here for you." Maia sounds cheery but worried, as if she couldn't believe that I was awake— *barely awake.*

The sound of a door shutting and rushed footsteps pulls me away from the conversation.

"Is she okay? Is she waking up?" A husky voice resonates from my left side. *Sam?*

"W–" I start to breathe out. "Where's"—I continue with bated breath, my chest feeling heavy—"Mom?"

A minute of silence engulfs the room, and then the door opens again. A voice echoes, but it starts to fade as it comes closer. I try my best to hold on, to stay awake.

"Is she up?" The voice sounds distorted as my body starts to give out. I can barely make out the deep tones of a male voice. *It might be him.*

"Are you okay, Ollie?" He takes my hand in his—*Brandon.* "Squeeze my hand if you can hear me." I try my hardest to do so, but all I can manage is a weak movement with my fingers.

"Rest, Ollie. Just rest." His voice fades until it's nothing more than a dream. *Or a nightmare...*

"Let go of my arms." I try to push him off. "You're hurting me."

"But aren't you this strong and independent woman now? Come on, push me away." His alcohol-filled breath hits my neck. I squirm under his hold, trying to get out but failing miserably.

"This is not funny, okay? Let me go now!" I do my best to sound powerful and confident.

"I'll never let you go. You'll always be mine." He brushes my cheek with this thumb, holding my hands above my head.

"I am not yours anymore. I haven't been for a long time. Now, let me go." I lift myself from the wall but get knocked back again by his weight.

"I said." He squeezes my face, forcing me to look at him. "You're mine." He presses his lips hard on mine.

"Stop," I mumble. "Let me go." My voice starts to break. "Please stop," I cry out.

"Mine, all mine." He holds my head in place as his lips leave sloppy kisses on my neck.

"Let me go." I struggle against his grip. His hands travel down from my torso to my pants. "No." I thrash around, trying to shake him off.

"No!" I jolt awake, sitting up straight and opening my eyes. I'm in the hospital now with shaking limbs and sweaty palms.

"Hey, hey, it's okay, Ollie. You're safe." I stare frantically at a blurry silhouette of a male, backing away from him.

"What's wrong?" His voice sounds softer now, and his face is no longer blurry, resembling the one who captured my heart.

"Brandon?" I whisper in a shaky voice, my eyes welling up.

"Ollie." He slips into the bed, snuggling me into his side. "You're okay. It was just a nightmare." He rubs my arms.

[Hands sliding, groping, touching.]

I can't stop shaking, my breath is erratic, and my eyes are wide open. Anything I try to say comes out incoherent.

[Stop, let me go...you're hurting me.]

"You don't have to say anything, okay? Breathe in, breathe out." He mimics the motions. "Come on, let's do it together. In, out."

[Mine, only mine.]

I follow his instructions, regulating my breathing with his. After several times, I can feel myself relaxing and controlling my frantic behavior.

[You are not leaving me.]

"Yes, like that, keep going." He does a couple more with me. "You're doing great."

After a while, I calm down enough to hug him back. "Thank you," I whisper.

"You don't have to thank me for anything." He kisses the top of my head. "I'm just relieved that you're okay."

"I want to go home," I mumble, on the verge of bursting into tears again.

[Glass crunches under my back, making me hiss as it pierces me through my skin.]

"We will, soon." He shushes me, combing his fingers

through my hair.

I stay quiet, listening to the sound of his heart. His breathing technique calmed me down, but there's still something nagging me in the back of my head.

[*If I can't have you, no one will.*]

"Hey, Brandon," I whisper.

"Yeah?"

"What happened to me?" I tilt my head to look at him. "Why am I here? And where are we?"

He looks at me, confusion written all over his face. He stares back. "Ollie," he says in a quiet voice. "You don't know?" I shake my head no.

"Shit," he hisses. "What can you remember?"

I blink quickly as a memory or a dream flashes in my mind. My head starts to hurt again from trying to recall everything; memories get blurred. I'm not sure what's real and what's a dream or just my imagination.

[*Get off me;* I feel my body squirming.]

If I can't have you, no one can; the feeling of clammy hands sliding over my legs burns my skin.

"Us dancing, and then me going to the bathroom. Everything that happened after feels distorted; it doesn't make sense." I take a shaky breath. "What happened to me?"

[*Glass flies across the bathroom lobby and shards scratch my skin. The sink cracks, making me flinch.*]

He closes his eyes, taking a moment to compose himself. "When I went looking for you in the bathroom at the signing party, it was a mess, completely trashed. Broken glass everywhere, blood smeared on the mirrors, cracked sinks. I couldn't find you, and I got so, so scared." He releases a shaky breath, trying not to cry.

[My ears begin to ring, a shrill scream echoing in my head, as if my body is crying out, but my mouth stays closed.]

"And when I finally found you in one of the stalls, lying on a shard-covered floor..." His voice breaks. "I don't know what happened to you or who did it, but they hurt you badly, Ollie."

"Oh," I say in a low voice. "Wait, are we still in New York?"

"Yeah, we are." He breathes in and out slowly. "We rushed you to the nearest hospital we could find."

We? I look around, realizing it's only him with me. Noticing this, he says, "Everyone went back home, mostly to keep the band's momentum going. Ella and Noah had school and practice, Maia didn't want to leave Ella by herself and said something about a client. And, well, you know Sam, he had to see them back safely."

"And you stayed?" My voice sounds small and my heart swells at the thought.

"Of course I did. I couldn't leave you behind like this, especially since it's all my fault..."

"What?! No, it's not. Brandon, you did nothing wrong."

He shakes his head, fighting back the unshed tears in his eyes. "I left you all alone; if only I had walked you over and waited for you, this would not have happened."

"Please, don't think like that." I slowly try to raise my hand to touch his face, but the pain makes me drop it.

He grabs it, holding it to his heart. "I just hate to see you like this. I'm so sorry, Ollie." He kisses my hand tenderly.

The feeling of his lips on my skin makes me shiver, but not in a good way. And then something awful lights up in my head.

But who would do that? I recall the dream I just had, and a horrendous thought pops into my head.

"Brandon, was I…you know?" My voice comes out strangled. *No, ni pienses así (don't even think like that).*

He closes his eyes, taking in a sharp breath. "I'm sure you were not…let's hope not." He hugs me tighter, brushing my hair.

"Could you ask the nurse to find out for sure?" I mumble against his chest.

"Sure, Ollie, anything you need." He continues to rub my arm, taking his time. "Hey," he calls me, and I look up.

"Yeah?"

He moves one of his hands to my face, caressing my cheek. "I want you to know how happy and relieved I am that you're awake and safe. Because I like you, and I care about you, so much." Looking deep into my eyes, he mutters the words I didn't know I wanted to hear: *"Te quiero (I like you)."*

I suck in a breath, not expecting him to say it after all those missed moments, the push and pull. To think that a few weeks ago, we couldn't even look into each other's eyes for long. And look at us now, holding each other so tight that we could become one.

"Wait, when did you learn to say it in Spanish?"

The idea of him learning it for me melts my heart, the emotions behind the words meaning more than the fact that he really likes me. It's as if his whole world is in his arms, the woman he's falling in love with.

A hint of blush appears on his cheeks. "Maia and Ella. I asked them before they left."

With my gaze shifting between his eyes, I look for a hint of mockery or fake sentiment but find none. He holds my gaze, looking at me with such tenderness that it could make me melt.

And I can't stop myself from saying, *"Te quiero."*

"Became a slave of my own damn thoughts. Couldn't seem to escape, couldn't work it out." ~ Alone, Alexandra Kessler.

OLIVIA – NEW YORK

"CAN YOU STAND?" Brandon asks as he holds my arms. My legs tremble as I try to stand up.

Using Brandon's arms for support, I manage to stand up. "I got it." He lets me go but stays close by.

As I take a few steps forward, it isn't long before my body can't take it anymore, and my knees start to buckle. As I search for something to grab, shapes distort and blend. In my attempt to steady myself, I reach out but can't get a hold of anything. Another second and—

Brandon catches me in his arms before I hit the ground. "I'm sorry, I—"

His hands slip under my legs as he picks me up. "It's okay, Ollie, I got you."

He settles me down on the bed, covers me with the sheets, puffs up my pillows, and sits down.

"You don't have to do all this," I whisper, shying away.

"And you don't have to do this alone," he says, placing his finger under my chin. "We all need a little help sometimes."

"Well, I don't," I whisper in a mocking tone. "Unless it's from you, then I'd think about it."

"Oh, you think you're funny now, do you?" he says to me as he props himself up on his elbows.

"Are you now realizing this? Come on, you can't be that

slow..." I stare back with fake disbelief.

"Well, it did take me weeks to realize that I like you. So, I'd think that's a pretty good guess."

I let out a fake gasp and try to push him off. "You are such an asshole, Brandon!"

He holds his position, not budging even a little from my attempt at getting him off me. I need to exercise. This is embarrassing even for me. *Or maybe it's the fact that I'm in the middle of recovering.*

"I'm kidding, I'm kidding," he says as he kisses my forehead and looks into my eyes.

He looks at me with such intensity, holding my gaze for what feels like an eternity. The trace of his fingertips on my face, brushing the hair from my face, sends shivers down my spine.

"How can I not like you? How could I have been so unaware not to see how much you mean to me?" He exhales, rubbing his nose against mine. "*Te quiero*, Olivia."

I suck in a breath, still not used to the sound of it and how my body reacts to his words. My whole body tingles, butterflies flutter in my stomach, and my heart races. This remarkable man in front of me genuinely adores me. All my flaws, the way I think, everything that makes me who I am. He likes me and cares about me.

Grabbing his face, I pull him toward me and kiss him. Somehow, I can best describe how he's making me feel with a soft and tender kiss. It doesn't take him long to kiss me back, laying me back on the pillow.

"*Te quiero, te quiero*," I mumble between kisses.

His hand cradles my right cheek, deepening the kiss. He covers my body with his arms as he purrs through his bated breath, saying, "Not more than me."

We move in sync, touching and caressing each other.

Although I'm still healing, he is mindful of my wounds.

His hand slides up my sides, stopping at my hips. Then, I remember what I'm wearing: a flimsy, uncomfortable hospital gown. I tug it down as it starts to ride up my legs, suddenly feeling self-conscious in front of Brandon.

A weird feeling settles on my stomach, making me uncomfortable, and my skin itch. It feels like something's crawling over me. *What is this?*

The sound of our lips disconnecting echoes in this empty, white-walled, bleach-smelling room.

"Maybe it's better if we don't do this here. Nurses or doctors could walk in at any given moment." I bite my lip while looking down.

"Is something wrong?" He lowers his head, trying to catch my eyes. "You can talk to me, Ollie, whatever it is." He holds my cheek again, stroking it with his thumb.

"I don't know." My voice falters. "I can't remember anything about that night, and it's scaring me to the point that I can't sleep. I close my eyes, and these images run through my mind, but I can't distinguish anything, like it's not even happening to me. But I can feel everything as if I'm reliving it."

"Ollie." He hugs me tight in his arms.

"Why can't I remember anything? Why can't I figure out what happened that night?" I cry out, not able to hold in the sobs and tears any longer.

He shushes me and hugs me tighter. "It's okay. Everything's going to be okay. You don't have to remember anything right now; it's not your fault."

I nod against his chest, breathing in and out to calm myself down. "I'm sorry," I whisper.

"Hey." He lifts my face, staring straight into my eyes. "You have nothing to apologize for. You went through something very traumatic. Time to heal is the only thing you need right now, and I'm not leaving."

"You promise?" I say in a low voice and with shaky breath.

He smiles in a gentle, comforting way. "I promise." He places a tender kiss on my head, cuddling me into his side.

"Can you sing for me?" I ask, looking up at him.

He nods, holding the back of my head and bringing me to his chest, over his heart. Its beating calms me down, reminding me of how I used to fall asleep on my dad's chest as a kid.

He starts singing, his sweet but raspy voice lulling me to sleep. I recognize the song, "Elixir," from the festival. It reminds me of how it all started, how we stole glances at each other and blushed when we noticed. How my heart would beat so fast every time we bumped in the kitchen. *And look at us now.*

He sings in my ear as I drift into a peaceful sleep. Safe to say, this is the first time in days that I've slept, cuddled in the arms of the man I'm falling for as he whispers sweet nothings.

OCEAN CITY

"Here." He places his hand on top of mine as I struggle to enter the key and open the door to my apartment. "Why don't you let me do it?"

I breathe out and nod, giving up after only a few tries. *So weak...*

I stumble back and blink as an unrecognizable voice whispers in a low tone. I look around but find no one else, only Brandon and me. *It sounds familiar.* I should know who that voice belongs to.

"Hey, are you feeling alright? You're looking a little pale." Brandon's voice pulls me out of my thoughts.

He comes closer, placing a hand on my forehead. "Should I take you back?"

"I'm fine," I grab his hand, taking it off my face. "Just tripped on my own feet; it's nothing."

He stares deeply into my eyes, like he's trying to figure out if I'm telling the truth. Finally, he brings my hand to his mouth and kisses it.

"Come on, people are dying to see you." He nods toward my apartment.

"Brandon..." I trail off. "What did you do?"

He shrugs, and a mischievous smile appears on his face. "Go in, and you'll see..."

I walk inside, leaving him behind to handle the bags. What I see when walking in is far better than I could have imagined.

The living room and kitchen have beautiful decorations. My eyes well up as I look at everyone that's here, standing under a handwritten sign.

"Welcome home, Ollie! *Te extrañamos (we've missed you)*," Maia cries with open arms, inviting me into them. I don't waste a single second before running to her.

She cuddles me tightly into her, both of us forgetting my body's still a little sore. I let out a sob as everyone joins in on the hug and traps us in their embrace. Ella squeezes in, pulling me to her chest as we all cry it out. The boys even sniffle.

"Oh, sweetie, I'm so glad you're finally home! Leaving you in New York felt like torture." Layla wipes her tears away as we part from the hug. "Have they found the bastard who did it?"

I hang my head as I sigh. "Not yet, no. I can't seem to remember anything, and I'm their only lead."

"It's all going to be okay. I promise." Brandon throws an arm around my shoulder. "Stop putting so much pressure on yourself. You'll remember once you're ready, and whenever that happens, we'll be here to support you."

I feel more than safe as he hugs me closer and places a kiss on my head, his way of assuring me of his promise.

"Alright." Drew claps and startles me with how close he is. "How about we end this pity party and start properly celebrating? Let's get some drinks!"

A round of *yes, let's do it*, and some hollers echo in the room as the group disperses.

"I'm not drinking; I don't think it's safe for my healing." I relax in Brandon's embrace. "But I'll take a Coke, please." I give him my best, innocent, convincing smile.

"Coming right up, milady." Drew bows his head.

As everyone starts doing their own thing, I take my time to look around my apartment. Flower petals decorate the tables, shelves, and kitchen counter. The coffee table has an assortment of sweet and salty snacks, from chips to mini cheesecakes, fruits, and crackers with cheese.

I can also see from here that the balcony has fairy lights hanging from the sliding door like a curtain. Plush bean bags and blankets replace the usual wooden chairs and table set.

"You guys did all this"—I turn to the group, my eyes glistening—"for me?"

"Of course we did."

"Why wouldn't we?"

"You deserve nothing less."

"You're my sister," Ella and Maia answer in unison.

People might not believe it, but Maia is more than my best friend. She's like a sister to us, our third musketeer since we can remember. And I wouldn't want it any other way.

"Oh, but you didn't have to." My voice comes out in a tender tone.

"You'd kill us if we didn't. Don't deny it." Maia gives me a fake accusatory look.

I take my time, pretending to think about my answer. "Fine, you're right, I would've." I let out a laugh. "But I am thankful; this is beautiful."

They bow down as if they were at the end of a show, continuing the playful mood.

"Hey, Ollie?" Sam whispers as he walks up to my side. "Can you come with me outside for a talk?"

I look at Brandon, who's still hugging me, letting him know he has to release me so I can move. He lets me go, and I turn to Sam.

Let's go; I nod to the balcony. The lock clicks as we close the sliding door behind us, and we sit on the bean bags, letting them swallow us.

"So."

"So." He avoids my eyes, staring at his hands.

"Sam." I place mine on top of his. "Everything okay?"

He breathes out. "The night Brandon found you was my life's scariest night. The thought of losing you overcame every sense in my body. I didn't think; I just reacted. Nothing else mattered but getting you to safety when I got his call."

He's the one who arranged the limo rides? My breathing becomes frantic as I listen to him. Finding out they put aside their responsibilities for me, for my safety, is a lot after being in the hospital.

"I even forgot Ella and Maia and everyone else. Brandon left your purse." He lets out a nervous, dry laugh.

"But none of that was important to us because you were safe. You were away from—" He stops himself from what I assume is profanity.

I squeeze his hand, letting him know it's okay, and he continues. "We thought we'd lost you, Ollie. When I saw you limp in his arms, my heart broke into a million pieces." His voice trembles and his hands shake.

"And to think I haven't..." he whispers.

"Haven't what, Sam?"

"I haven't told you how much your friendship means to me." He turns to me now, looking into my eyes.

I can tell his answer's genuine, but it feels like he's hiding something else. There's more he wants to say to me. I know it, but he doesn't do it. And he doesn't need to; I can see it in his eyes. I lean forward, placing my head on his shoulder, and he puts his on top of mine.

"You mean the world to me, Sam. You truly do, and I could never thank you enough for what you did for me." I lift my head to look at him. "You've saved my life now too. And for what it's worth," I whisper. "You could never lose me, and I could never lose you. You'll always be my *nerdy* Sam."

He laughs, as in, a loud-as-an-alarm laugh, throwing his head back on the window.

"I hate that nickname. Not from you, though. You don't say it with hate."

"I could never." I also lean back on the window, staring out into the night sky.

"Beautiful, isn't it?" He pauses. "There's an infinite number of stars, yet you can see them all shine as bright as the others."

"Shine bright like a diamond," I sing out. *I love that song.*

"Ooh, the girl has some vocals." He sits up and looks at me.

I shrug, acting nonchalant. "I try."

We look at each other, staring for a couple of seconds until we burst out laughing. I'm sure the people in my neighboring building can hear us, but I don't care. We're having fun, even after these traumatic few weeks, and I'll cherish this moment forever.

A knock on the glass makes us jump. The door opens, and Brandon pops his head out.

"Sorry to interrupt the fun, but I'm supposed to tell you they need you inside…" He points his thumb in that direction.

"Right, we're having a party." I look between the two boys in my life.

"And it's not a party without the guest of honor." Brandon extends his hand to me.

I look at Sam before taking it. "Are you going to be okay?"

He blinks a couple of times. "Oh, yeah, I'll be fine."

I stand up with Brandon's help, but Sam stays put. "Go, go, don't worry about me. It'll just be a minute."

With a weird feeling in my gut, I give him one last look before walking inside.

"Aye, I was looking for you!" Drew shouts as soon as we close the door. "Do you still want your Coke?"

"Yes, thank you! I forgot about that," I say as I reach him in the kitchen. "But I'm already here, so I can serve it myself."

"No, I'll do it. I offered." He takes a glass from the cupboard.

"Drew, it's fine." I grab it from his hands.

"Ollie…I'm a gentleman. And that's what we do: serve the ladies drinks." He takes it back.

"I can do it myself. I'm not in the hospital anymore." I fake laugh and grab the cup again.

"But I want to do it."

"But you don't have to, Drew."

"Could you please stop being so stubborn? It's just a drink."

"I told you, it's fine!"

The next thing I know, the cup flies out of our hands and onto the ground. I stumble back from the force of this stupid back and forth and knock myself into the kitchen wall. A flash of light and images hits me like a freight train, playing in my mind like a movie trailer.

A rattle on the door makes me jump in place, leaving me startled and my heart beating erratically.

"Sorry, it's busy! I'll be right out." I yell out to them.

But they don't seem to hear me, the rattling still going on along with a hard push to the door.

"Hey, hey, alright. Hold on, I'm out!" I run to the door and open it, and I stop breathing, my palms sweaty.

"What are you doing here?" Mustering all the bravery I have in me, I look straight into his eyes with my best poker face. Disdain drips out of my mouth with every word.

Without saying a word, he bursts in, grabbing my throat and pushing me back onto the wall behind us. I gather all my strength, using my hands to try and pry his hands off. He tightens them, making my throat close, and it gets harder to breathe.

"No, stop. Please." I barely get those few words out, my voice raspy. My vision gets blurry, and my head gets heavier. My hand drops my purse, and I lift it in an attempt to make some noise and see if I catch anyone's attention as to what's happening.

I don't get too far before he catches it and holds it above my head, his voice whispering, "Shut up," the last thing I remember before everything fades.

"Connor...why?"

"Damn it, Ollie, are you okay? I'm so sorry." Drew's face comes into my line of vision. "I should've let you pour your drink. I—" He stops babbling.

"Hey, are you okay? You're starting to look pasty. Brandon, doesn't she look pale to you?"

"Baby, what's wrong?" Brandon's soothing voice and presence wake my body up.

With shaky breathing, I mutter the words I've been yearning to say. Except now, it's not what I feel anymore.

"It's Connor. I remember." A single tear escapes my eyes. "H–he's the one the authorities are looking for." I look around the dead silent room. "He's my assailant."

"How is it that the ones who always give are the ones
who suffer the most?" ~ Alone, Alexandra Kessler.

OLIVIA – OCEAN CITY

THE WORDS THAT COME OUT FEEL FOREIGN TO ME, and I can't comprehend these newfound memories. I haven't moved from my spot against the wall, too shocked to muster up the courage. If they're talking, I can't hear any of it. The ringing in my ears blocks every sound.

The pounding in my head, in my chest, makes it hard for me to breathe. It knocks out the air from my lungs, making me dizzy.

Will I ever rid my life of this man? What kind of fucking sick game is he playing with me? Assaulting me in some twisted version of marking his territory? Right now, red is all I see, and fumes are coming out of my ears.

I see faces moving in and out of my line of vision, and yet I can't distinguish who's who. I'm sure their intentions are pure, mumbling words like *sick bastard, make him pay,* and *break his face.* The ringing starts dying down, and my hearing comes back to me.

"Ollie." Brandon grabs my hand, squeezing it in his. "What do you want to do?"

"Yes, whatever you want to do, we're here." Sam comes into my line of vision.

I shake my head; I don't know. I need more time. Brandon lifts my head, holding onto my chin like he always does.

"Do you want us to go over to his house? Because we can, but only if you approve." He holds my gaze.

I know Brandon; behind that calm persona is a sea of rage waiting to create a tsunami. But his comment does make me laugh. He knows my answer will be *no*, but he still goes ahead and asks things like this. I shake my head as an answer. No words are strong enough to represent what's going through my head. *Not even I know.*

"I have a bat in the van. We can get it right now," Drew suggests, and I think Layla smacks him in the head.

"Please, no violence, okay? That's what got me in this mess in the first place," I mumble, wiping away some tears.

"Come here." Brandon pulls me into his chest, moving me from my stuck position on the wall. It wouldn't surprise me if I left an imprint from how long I stood there.

"Everything will be fine. It'll be okay soon." Brandon leaves a kiss on the top of my head. The type of kiss that makes me feel wanted and cherished.

"I'm scared," I mumble against his chest. "Why can't I get rid of him?" My voice breaks.

"You will." He rubs my back in a comforting way. "But I promise you, we will do everything in our power to make sure he can't get near you ever again."

"You promise?"

He cradles my head to look into my eyes. "I promise."

My breath hitches from the sheer intensity of his gaze. Never have I ever felt this cherished and cared for, this protected. The fights, the disagreements, nothing else matters right now. At this moment, all I want is to be in his arms, away from danger.

"Can everyone go home? I need time to think, process this, and decide in the morning." I cuddle back into his embrace.

"Of course, whatever you need," he whispers in my ear and

rubs my arms. "How about this? Take a bath, get ready for bed, and I can make sure everyone leaves. I'll put away your stuff from the hospital before I leave."

"You're not staying?" I mumble while taking a step back to look at him.

"Oh no, Ollie, of course, I'll stay. I'm sorry, I will." He nods frantically. "Go, I'll be right there."

"Okay, thank you." I stand on my toes, reaching up to kiss him. "*Te quiero*."

Te quiero, he mouths back to me before letting me go.

"His name is Connor Owens." I breathe heavily, my hand shaking as Brandon holds it on his legs. "We dated for a year about two years ago. I ended the relationship after finding out he was unfaithful to me multiple times."

"And was that the last time you saw each other?" the detective, whose name I think is Danielle Rogers, asks me as she takes notes.

"No, before the assault, we ran into him and his friend, Jacob Lawrence, who we filed a restraining order against for stalking my best friend, Maia Brooks Garcia. It was the last Friday of April; we were at a club opening, and the band was playing. Nothing happened then, but we maced them once they stood too close to us. We didn't want to risk it."

I gather the same bravery I demonstrated that night as I tell the stories. It feels easier with Brandon by my side.

Detective Rogers looks up from her notes. "And after that night, did he try to contact you again? Did you see any signs of him before the night of the attack?"

"No." I shake my head slowly. "No word or sight of him

until the night he…" I take a shaky breath.

"Take your time." She smiles apologetically at me.

Breathe in, breathe out. One, two, three. "It was the first Saturday of May. We were at a signing party with New Sound Records. I don't know how he found us or managed to slip into the building, but he did. I remember now how his breath reeked of alcohol; he was clearly inebriated past his limits."

I quickly wipe away a tear that slips from my eyes before continuing with my report. "The memories of what he did are still fuzzy. I don't remember exactly how he hurt me, but the nurses said no signs of sexual assault were present, only physical. I just know he went straight for my throat when I opened the bathroom door."

"What else can you remember? Any detail you can remember counts."

"I remember him smashing my head on the bathroom mirror and one of the sinks cracking. Don't recall how it cracked, but it did." My voice breaks as I tell the story. "And at some point, he dragged me to the stalls after I attempted to escape."

Detective Rogers jots down every word, nodding to let us know she's listening intently.

"Any idea of where he could've run off to, where he escaped to?"

I contain my sobs as I shake my head. "No idea. I'm sorry."

"There's no need to be. None of this is your fault; what you told us helps greatly." She smiles at me, offering me a tissue. "I believe we have everything we need to proceed with the investigation. We will keep you updated through the process and need you to stay in the country or at least be reachable. Can you do that?"

"Yes, detective, we can," Brandon answers, holding my hand.

"We will also place a very tight restraining order against him for you and your family. We'll also extend Mr. Lawrence's restraining order to you in case they're in some sort of contact."

"Thank you very much for your help, Detective."

We stand up, shake her hand, and take our leave toward the car. Once inside, I can't hold it in anymore, and I sob uncontrollably. Brandon doesn't waste a second, holding me tight to his chest as he comforts me.

"Shh, it's okay. It'll be okay." He rubs his warm hands on my arms. "It's done, it's over now. Justice will do its job, and he'll be out of your life forever."

It's okay, it's okay. I'll be okay. It's over...finally over.

Chapter Ten

"Chant my name, and I'll scream my mind to you. Dance to the rhythm of my heart." ~ Symphonic Orchestra, Alexandra Kessler.

OLIVIA – OCEAN CITY

THE SOUND OF BIRDS CHIRPING OUTSIDE WAKES ME.

The bright blue sky is clear through my window, the shining sun peeping in.

My see-through curtains allow its rays to reflect on my face. It usually bothers me, but this morning, it's different—today— feels different, like I'm finally back home. Not even the looming thought that Connor is still somewhere out there, running from the law, can hinder this newfound feeling.

Maybe it's because you'll see Brandon again today. Even though he's been by my side these past weeks… No, I don't think so. *Then why did you blush when I said his name?* Great, now I'm talking to myself.

Note to self: stop having conversations in my head.

Pushing the covers off, I walk up to my window and open the curtains, closing my eyes and breathing in fresh air that smells like sea and salt. The sun shines on my face, making me feel revived with light and energy—the day's bright and beautiful, and it's meant to be enjoyed. *I should walk today.*

The smell of waffles fills my nostrils as it reaches my room. It's not long before I leave my room and into the kitchen, following the deliciously-smelling trail.

"Good morning," I say in a chirpy voice, serving myself a

cup of coffee and sitting at the table to eat what Maia made. *She's getting good at making these homemade waffles.*

Ella and Maia give each other weird looks, as if I were a stranger in their home. "What?" I answer with a mouthful.

"Why are you so chirpy?" Maia eyes me up and down.

"Yeah, it's *Monday*!" Ella says with a hint of disgust.

"So?" I take a sip of my coffee and shrug. "It's a beautiful day today. We should take advantage of it."

"Is this because you're going to see Brandon again?" Ella asks with a smirk.

"I–I don't know what you're talking about..." I look down, biting the inside of my cheeks.

"Girl, we saw how he acted around you and cared for you during your recovery. You can stop hiding your blushes." Maia throws a blueberry at my face. "Are you sure you're not just avoiding having to talk or think about Connor? Three weeks is not that long to move on."

"Oh, stop it! I'm not hiding anything; it *is* a beautiful day. Can't I just be happy that everything's back to normal?" I push my chair back as I swallow the last bite. "In fact, I'll walk to the recording studio today."

"Just because?" Maia asks with amusement on her face.

"Just because!" I state and start to walk away. I slam the door before they can even think of a better comeback.

Good one, Ollie. Thank you, voice in my head, who's me...

The walking distance from our apartment to the recording studio is relatively short, even more so if I take shortcuts. But I want to enjoy this day with the wind brushing against my skin and the sun shining brightly on my face. So I take the longer route:

the sidewalk right in front of the boardwalk—buildings, houses, trees, and bushes line the path.

I take my time looking around, noticing how flowers decorate almost every tree or bush. How many birds fly around, building their nests, and chirping as they do. *How have I been so unaware of all this beauty? Have I been so deep into work and in my head not to notice them?*

People say that liking or developing feelings toward someone opens your eyes to this world's natural beauty. I always brushed them off, saying how ridiculous that sounds.

"How can I not notice nature? It's all around us. It would be stupid of me not to see it; of course, I see it," I used to say. But I didn't. I've been ignoring it, taking it for granted, and focusing on work and myself within my little bubble with Ella and Maia.

They've always been my world, so why would I leave that to notice anything outside of it? It's not like I didn't see colors or enjoy living on the beach. I adore sunsets and sunrises; my phone's full of those pictures. But was that all I saw? The sky? Now, I'm like all those people: chirpy, appreciating nature more, and noticing those little things God created.

If they could see me now, almost skipping as I smell the flowers along the way. I don't know if they would laugh or welcome me into "the club."

"If I had a flower for every time I thought of you since that kiss, I would be as full as that bush!" Brandon's presence overpowers my senses as he comes up from behind me. Plucking a flower, he brushes my hair back and startles me.

"Aye, warn a girl before scaring the crap out of her!" I swat his arm away, then look at his hand. "But I will have the flower because it's gorgeous." I give him a sheepish look as he places it on my ear.

"Not more than you." He wraps his arm around my waist,

turning me around and pulling me in.

"Is that the best you have?"

"I'm just starting." He leans down.

"But what if I stop you?" I whisper, dropping my gaze to his lips and looking back into his eyes.

"Trust me, you could never stop them from coming." And his mouth is on mine.

His soft lips move against mine, building the fire that ignites us. He deepens the kiss a little more, not caring that we're on the street and that other people might see us. *It's like he can't get enough, like he can't control his lips.*

After a few minutes, we pull away, and he presses his forehead against mine. His breath brushes my face, and I giggle as it tickles me.

"How did you know I was here?" My breath is shaky.

"I didn't. I just decided to walk today. I don't know why, but the day called for it. I woke up wanting to enjoy the scenic routes more often. You were in my way, I guess." He tries to act nonchalant.

I shake my head in response, laughing internally at life's humor. *Nice one, world, very nice move!*

"Let's go, or else we'll be late." I leave his embrace and start to walk away. "Are you coming?" I look over my shoulder to where he's still standing. He zones back into reality, doing a little run to catch up to me, grabbing my hand.

"What's up, guys? What did we miss?" Brandon hollers as we walk in, using a deeper voice.

I hit his arm, embarrassed for being late and his entrance.

"Dear Lord," I whisper to him, but he laughs it off.

He props himself on a couch, brings me down with him, and sets me on his legs. I look at Maia and feel her stare. *Well, that was fast,* she says with her eyes. I give her a blank stare.

"Nothing important, we were just talking over our coffees. Here are yours, by the way." Sam nods to the table in front of us.

"Thanks," we answer, taking the cups in our hands.

"I was talking with the executives at the party, going over everything, what would change because of your deal. First, we don't have to be in the city all the time, just two weekends a month to record. Second, once the EP is developed, we might have more movement—interviews, press releases, and, fingers-crossed, collaborations. In which case, we might have to move there for a couple of months," Sam explains as he gets into it.

We might have to move for a few months—the last sentence resonates nonstop in my head.

We just got together, and he might not even be here soon. Okay, no, stop it, Ollie! Don't go to that dark space; you do not need that yet. *Yet…*

"That's amazing, man! It's way more than I ever expected," Drew bursts out.

"Yeah! And we can all crash in my parents' apartment whenever necessary. They're doing some consultancy tours throughout the country. So, they're not using it." Scott shrugs, trying to hide his excitement. Though we all know he's in it for the long run.

Isn't it weird how they're never present? I know it's prying, but it makes me curious about his story.

"Our dreams are becoming a reality, boys. And it's all because of you two!" I jump a little as Brandon's hug startles me and brings me out of the trance. "Are you okay, Ollie?" he asks as he tries to read my face.

I shake my head. "Yeah, yeah, I'm good. I'm just so happy for you!" I hug him back, my face turning away from him. I'm glad he can't see my face because my expression contradicts what I blurt out.

I'm still very happy for him, for them, for us. But I can't control the lousy feeling building and rising in the pit of my stomach. I don't know what any of this means yet, how far we'll take it.

Though I do know my feelings for him, maybe I don't know how *he* feels about *me*. But whatever happens, we'll work through this. So, I push out any uncertainties and focus on this win. Reputation signed in New York, and they'll go big!

"Want to go for a walk with me?" Brandon whispers from behind as I pack the last of my things into my bag. His actions force me to stop as he hugs me, his arms pulling me into his chest. I rest my head back, enjoying the feeling of being in his embrace.

"Does it include food?" I ask with a mocking tone.

"For you? Anything." He kisses the top of my head.

"Oh, anything?" I raise my eyebrows. "How about ice cream?"

"Deal!" He spins me around, landing a kiss on my lips. "Let's go." He takes my bag and grabs my hand.

Again, we decide to walk. We can't seem to stop enjoying this beautiful day for some strange reason. And we have no desire to waste it by getting in a car when we can walk everywhere and savor these moments.

The walk is a little longer than five minutes, crossing several streets and sidewalks. And all this time, we never let go of each other's hand, as if the moment we stop, they'll disappear. I don't understand this feeling of not wanting to let go—the feeling of being safe in each other, in our embrace. But I don't need to understand it to know that it's real, that it's happening.

Once we reach the beach, we take our shoes off and walk along the shore, letting our feet soak in the salty seawater and dipping them into the sand. Brandon's hand brushes against mine, and I grab it, letting it engulf mine. They fit perfectly, meant to be together.

"Random thought," he says, barely above a whisper. "We never finished the twenty questions."

After giving it some deep thought, I recall our first night in New York. "Oh, my God, you're right. And again...we got interrupted." I let out a dry laugh.

"It seems to be our theme, doesn't it?" His comment makes me give a genuine laugh.

"Okay, so, you go first. What do you want to know?" I turn my head to look at him; he appears to be deep in thought.

"Umm, I already know some of your tastes from the Star Wars shirt. But what else do you like?"

"My likes are very diverse, or at least I'd like to think they are. My favorites are Star Wars—that you already know—and everything Marvel and Harry Potter. You could say it's my geeky side." I shrug as I smile.

"I love The Godfather trilogy, anything by Martin Scorsese or Quentin Tarantino. I *hate* scary/horror movies, but give me anything psychological, and I'll probably predict the ending."

I pause to breathe. "But...my guilty pleasures are chick flicks, comedies, and romance. Just cheesy romantic comedies."

His mouth opens to say something, but I interrupt him. "Oh, and I live for musicals!"

"I knew it." He throws his head back with a short laugh. "I

mean, you're not that unpredictable, but it's a good mix."

"You could say that's a 'gift' from my dad. He raised me to appreciate the classics and what you would call 'oldies.' In music too, like Queen or the Beatles."

"Good job, *dad*," he mocks, making me laugh.

"But don't tell him; it's kinda my thing to not give him credit."

He shakes his head in fake disbelief, pretends to zip his mouth, then throws the fake key away. "Okay, your turn now, ask me anything you want!"

It doesn't take me long to figure out my first question. "When did you learn to sing and play the guitar? And why?"

"My whole family plays something or sings. So, they started to teach me everything when I was five."

"Everything? Does that mean you play more than guitar?"

He scratches the back of his head with his free hand. "Umm, yeah…about six or seven instruments."

"What?!" I stop dead in my tracks. "Which ones?"

"Guitar, all kinds. Piano, drums, ukulele, the flute, and bass. I also dabble in violin and the triangle."

I can't help but laugh at the thought of this grown-ass man standing in a corner, waiting for his moment to shine by hitting a triangle. But I hide the laughter from him; *maybe I'll save the mockery for later on.*

"So you could have a one-person band? Damn," I laugh.

He throws his head back. "You could say that. But it would be too much work; I'd be exhausted."

"Is that why you have the guys?"

"Oh, yeah, for sure! I couldn't keep a crowd on my own, so I thought it would be better as a band."

"You are impossible." I shake my head as he pulls me in.

"But you still like mc…"

"Umm, no…who said such a thing?" I give him my best attempt at an innocent look.

"You did, at the signing party. And then you kissed me! Just stating the facts here, honey." He shrugs and smirks.

"Umm, no, no. You kissed me after that guy—"

"Okay, okay, I remember now."

I laugh at his reaction, throwing my head back as his hands support me. "We're going to be telling that story for the rest of our lives, aren't we?"

"For as long as you let me." He caresses my cheek, looking deep into my eyes.

His gaze flickers to my lips, and he takes a slow breath. My eyes wander down to his, letting him know what I feel. He leans in, understanding the sign, and captures my mouth in his.

Seconds, minutes, or maybe even hours go by, our lips fighting for dominance. It's not long until his tongue brushes against my lips, asking for permission. The kiss gets more intense, with us exploring each other's mouths.

I keep waiting for someone else to interrupt, to break us apart. But no one comes; it's just him and me. Heat spreads through my body as his hands trace over it, leaving a trail of chills behind. From my hair to my neck, arms, and back, and then he stops on my hips. He presses a little harder, pulling me in closer if that's even possible at this point.

I don't remember stopping for air, completely consumed by each other's desire. Our breathing gets heavier and shorter by the second, hearing each other's heartbeats loud and clear. But all that matters right now is this perfect moment.

He grabs me by the waist, pulling me into a hug and lifting me off the ground. I laugh against his mouth, holding his face.

Pulling away, I look him in the eyes. "Did I not tell you I hate it when people carry me?"

"I don't care," he says while giving me quick pecks between words, making me giggle.

"Can we go eat now?" I whine in an attempt for him to put me down.

"Sure! But I got another idea…" He trails off with a sly smile. Before I can register what's happening, he swings me to the side and cradles me bridal style.

"Brandon, please never do that again! What if I fell?" I try to act threatening, but my breathy laughs give me away.

"You were not going to fall; I know what I'm doing!" He laughs. "You're safe with me, Ollie. I won't let anything happen to you. I can promise you that." He stops to look me in the eyes, getting serious now.

"Don't make promises you can't keep, okay?" I say in a shy voice and give him a sad smile.

Without missing a beat, he whispers, "I promise."

Who would've thought that this fleeting moment on the beach—a playful interaction between two people who like each other—would be the start of an endless exchange of promises? And yet, only time will tell whether these promises will come to pass or last forever.

*"I feel like I am good enough. Because I have you,
and that's good enough." ~ Mirror, Alexandra Kessler.*

OLIVIA – OCEAN CITY

*I*T'S BARELY BEEN A MONTH SINCE WE STARTED… whatever this is. But I can't stop smiling and gushing over every little thing before leaving my bed. Like, this morning, I daydreamed for so long that I was almost late for the shoot!"

I vent, each of us downing glasses of wine during our traditional Friday girls' night.

"You're really into him, aren't you?" Maia asks as she takes a handful of popcorn.

"It's just—" I breathe out. "I'm just constantly on cloud nine now that we're…well, whatever we are. It's as if every moment we spend together, time stops for us. And he's been so freaking sweet, leaving me these cute texts throughout the day. Picking me up from the office for coffee dates." I lie back on the couch with a sigh, leaving my glass on the table.

"Oh, that's so adorable!" Ella squeals as she also eats popcorn and drinks her soda.

"I know, right?!" A smile creeps up on my face. "I don't think I've ever felt like this before. Like it was meant to be all along, you know? I mean, that whole mess with Anna Band all the freaking mixed signals. But I don't know; it always felt like something was pulling us toward each other."

"Ollie, aren't you going a little too fast?" Maia asks as she eyes me up and down. "Also, are you forgetting the whole

Connor thing? You can't just ignore your trauma."

"What do you mean?" I sit up straight. "*No estoy 'ignorando el trauma' (I'm not 'ignoring the trauma')*. I'm trying to move on and leave it to Lady Justice, Maia."

She looks at me with a poker face, deciding whether she should believe me.

"It's only been a month now, right?" She pauses to wait for my confirmation. I nod, and she continues. "Look, don't get me wrong, I'm very happy for you and how he makes you feel. But I don't want you to forget that Connor also started like this. And that life is not always a fairy tale, you know?"

"It's not at all like that. I understand what you mean and why you're saying it. But with Brandon, it's different. There's no weird vibe or feeling when I'm with him. He cares about my feelings, what I think, what I want," I interrupt her.

"I know, I know. But we just don't want to see you getting hurt again, Ollie," she pleads with a reassuring smile.

"We've seen you get hurt and helped you get through breakups so many times before. We'd hate to see you get hurt again by falling too fast." Ella's mouth drops into a sad smile.

"Aww, you guys! That's so sweet." I cross over the table to hug them. The alcohol in my system seems to have taken effect already, and I knock over my glass on our tablecloth. "Shit. Oh, my God!"

We freeze, eyes wide, while staring at the mess: me on the table and wine all over.

"Well, that will leave a stain," I say while holding in a laugh.

We exchange looks, our tipsiness settling in, and we burst out laughing. I lose my balance again after tripping on air and fall on the girls' laps. *Jesus, Ollie, you want to knock over their glasses too?*

After what feels like an eternity of laughing, we manage to

make an even bigger mess by knocking down one of the bowls of popcorn. We are one hot mess. Shit, if the boys saw us now, I'm not sure if they'd talk to us again.

"Come on, let's clean this up and wash the cloth. Otherwise, it will stain." I get up from the couch.

Still laughing about who knows what at this point, I remember something. "Oh, oh! And I bought stuff to make cookies, too. You can get started on that."

"Chocolate chips?" Ella spins her head toward me, resembling a meerkat.

"Well, duh!"

Ella and Maia move to the kitchen, getting started on the cookie batter. I stay behind, cleaning up the popcorn mess on the floor and taking the tablecloth to soak it in stain remover.

When I cross the kitchen, I see another mess brewing—nothing major yet, just the flour flying everywhere. *Oh, my Lord, they'll be the death of me. I'm not cleaning that up.*

They must sense my stare because they turn around, flour on their faces. "Don't worry, we'll clean it!"

"Damn, these cookies are good! How many chocolate chips did you use?" I mumble and groan with a mouthful.

"Like, half the bag, maybe more." Maia shrugs after swallowing hers.

"Well, whatever, it's still good! How are you and Noah, by the way?" I ask Ella.

"Oh, we're doing so well! We walk together every day to and from school. And I know it's not on the way, but we stop for coffee every morning. Don't know where he gets the money to pay, but he does..." she babbles on and on after swallowing.

"Isn't that adorable?" *And there goes Maia with her sarcastic remarks.*

Ella is about to answer in her regular chipper tone when she notices me containing my laughter. Realizing she's mocking her, she rolls her eyes at Maia.

"I'm kidding, girl! It really is cute, though," she mumbles after nudging Ella's arm.

"Thank you! I'm very happy with him...he makes me happy." Ella sighs with a bright smile on her face.

"We can see that! You even wake up early now. I consider that a win!"

Getting distracted by my phone vibrating on my lap, I tune out their voices. A smile starts on my face as his name flashes on the screen.

Brandon:
how's the girls' night?

Ollie:
wine and popcorn spilled
all over the living room
flour ended up on the ceiling

I'm assuming he's taking his time to analyze what's going on as he takes a couple of minutes to reply.

Brandon:
are all your girls' nights this chaotic?

Ollie:
if they include wine yes

Brandon:
so all of them

I silence my laughs as I read his text, probably getting weird looks from Ella and Maia.

Ollie:

pretty much :)

Brandon:
what are you doing tomorrow?

Ollie:

finishing some things for work
but I'll be done by 2, why?

Brandon:
can I pick you up around 5 then?

Ollie:

tell me where we're be going?

Brandon:
nope, it's a surprise

Ollie:

can you at least give me a clue?
i can't wear the wrong clothes Brandon...

Brandon:
hmm don't wear heels?
come on it'll be fun, let me take you out!

Ollie:

okay fine tomorrow at 5

Brandon:
yes!! trust me you won't regret it Ollie

He's so sweet, how can I not fall for him?

Ollie:

then you better pray that I don't

Brandon:
see you tomorrow Ollie
and please don't spill more stuff
you'll ruin your apartment

Locking my phone, I hold it against my chest as if by doing so I can feel Brandon's embrace. I must look like a fool right now, all giddy and excited.

"What are you smiling at?" Maia throws popcorn at me, hitting me in the face.

"Hey!" I throw it back, missing her entirely. "Well, I have a date tomorrow," I reply in a sing-song voice.

"Ooh," they sing at the same time.

"Where is he taking you?" Ella asks with a smile and a glint in her eyes.

"I have no idea. All he says is not to wear heels?" I shrug.

"Oh, wow, super-specific..."

"Oh, yeah, for sure, he ruined the surprise by telling me that little detail. But it's not like he told me to wear a swimsuit. That would've been too much information." I serve myself another glass of the newly opened wine.

"Well, we can rule out anywhere fancy," Maia points out while grabbing more popcorn.

"That's true." I nod, giving it some thought. "But we can figure out my outfit tomorrow; we have time. Right now, I just want to be here in the moment with you guys!"

"Didn't know that included your phone..." Maia mutters and gives me the stink eye. "Kidding, I'm kidding," she says as she sees my unimpressed face.

"But you did miss a lot of my story..." Ella mumbles while munching on some popcorn kernels.

"Okay, okay, I'm all ears now. Tell me everything!"

Chapter Eleven

"Smiling at me, you pull me closer. Hand on your heart, head on your shoulder." ~ My Confession, Alexandra Kessler.

BRANDON – OCEAN CITY

ARE YOU SURE YOU DON'T WANT MORE NAPKINS?"

I extend my hand to Ollie as the ice cream melts and drips down the cone.

"No, no, I'm good. See?" she mumbles incoherently as she tries to catch every drip. Laughter erupts from her as she continues to fail—a laugh so contagious that I can't help but join in.

How can someone be so adorable? Some may see this mess as ridiculous or childish, but to me, it's the cutest thing. How she squints when she smiles or laughs, or how she doesn't care if anyone watches, even if we're in public.

Finally, getting rid of the mess, she notices me staring.

"What?" She blushes very subtly. "Do I still have ice cream on my face?"

"No, just admiring your clumsiness."

She narrows her eyes at me. "I am not clumsy! The ice cream just had an idea of its own..." Her face contorts in confusion.

"You're adorable." I smile at her.

"Thank you." She returns the smile.

"Come here." I pull her into my lap, hugging around her waist. I lean in, pressing my forehead to hers. "I am so glad we

met, Ollie. You ignite something in me that I didn't even know was missing."

"Then I'm glad you almost broke the cameras." She brushes her nose against mine.

"Umm, no. That's not how I remember it happening…"

"Well, they almost broke when I bumped into you. So, it would've been your fault if they did. No argument here." She wears her usual smug smile.

"You never stop, do you?" She shakes her head.

I bring my hand up to her face, caressing her cheek with my thumb. Then I lower my hand and hold a finger under her chin. I capture her lips with mine, savoring every second of our mouths moving in sync.

"Yooo, are you even alive? It's like eleven thirty, your breakfast's cold, man!" Scott bangs on my door and wakes me from what I think is a dream. *Or was it a daydream? That memory from three days ago felt very real.*

Wait…did he say eleven thirty? But the clock read nine when I checked it just now… How long was I daydreaming?

"I'm coming, I'm coming, damn! Please don't break down my door!" I throw on my T-shirt from yesterday, which was lying on my guitar.

Wait, that's weird. Wasn't I playing five minutes ago? The balls of paper surrounding it prove I was trying to write earlier.

I enter the kitchen, putting my breakfast in the microwave. Because who doesn't like reheated, soggy pancakes?

"Morning, princess. Did your royal highness have a good sleep?" Scott leans over the counter.

"Shut up, dude, I wasn't sleeping. I was…thinking."

"Let me guess…about Ollie? Were you daydreaming?"

"I was writing some new songs." I nod toward my bedroom. Turning around, I look at the guys. "Then I started daydreaming."

"Aww, who knew you were such a sweetheart?" Noah mocks me and then fake gags.

"I didn't either. It's different with Ollie." A small smile escapes my lips. "She brings that out of me, can't help it."

"But you're not that far from me, Noah. You're like the perfect boyfriend with Ella." Scott points to him while throwing him a napkin.

"Yeah, yeah, I'm a total goner for her. No shame in that, bro!" He throws it back, hitting Scott on the forehead.

"Hey, Sam? Can I ask for your advice on something?" I turn to him as I wait for my pancakes.

"Yeah, sure! What's up?" He follows me as I nod to the living room, where we will have some privacy.

Scott and Noah can still hear us. Still, the small space does its job.

"So, you've known Ollie for a long time, right?" Sam mutters a *yes*, and I continue.

"It's barely been a month, and I'm learning all these little things about Ollie. But there are some moments when she goes quiet when we talk about deeper stuff. Besides the Connor-Jacob situation, did something else happen to her? You know, that I should know about."

"Listen, man. I'm happy she's with you, and I know you'll treat her like she deserves. But it's not my place to talk about her past. Also, it's been a long time since we last saw each other, and we're just now reconnecting. Trust me, she'll tell you about it when she's ready." He gives me an apologetic smile.

"No, of course, I just thought that since you've known her longer, maybe it could help. And since I'm closer to you than to Ella or Maia, maybe you could give me some pointers?"

"Oh, well, yeah, I can do that," he answers in a lighter tone.

"First, she sometimes needs extra affirmations. I know she's been with some terrible guys, and it's hard for her to trust again. Well, that you do know. But that did not come from me!" He gives me an accusatory look. I raise my hands in surrender.

"Just be honest, man. Don't give her any reasons to doubt you, your feelings, or your intentions. Don't shower her with gifts or material things: that's not what she wants. Instead, just show up and give her those little details that tell her you care."

He pats my knee, letting me know that's all he has to say. And that, in a way, he too has my back.

"If you're finished with your girl talk, I have some news," Scott hollers at us. We give each other a *"What's that about?"* look and walk back to the dining room.

"Okay, so next weekend will be the last one before we go to New York. It's only twice a month for now, but I thought this could be the perfect 'farewell' weekend. The lake house in Steamboat Springs will be empty, and I asked my parents if we could use it. What do you think?"

"I'm taking Ollie out tonight; I can tell her then. I'm sure the girls will say yes. Maybe I should text her and see how her day is going." I take out my phone to text her.

Brandon:
how's your day going

Ollie:
hey, sweetie, pretty good so far
about to make lunch, what about you

Sweetie? Are we doing nicknames now? Should I use one?

Brandon:
*i tried to write a couple of
songs but nothing came out
oh and i'm sweetie now?*

Ollie:
*i don't know, it just sort of came out
does it bother you?*

Damn, you're already blowing it?

Brandon:
*no no it's okay!
i like it, don't worry about it*

Ollie:
*okay good
still on for today right?*

Brandon:
yeah I'll pick you up at 5

Ollie:
*perfect
see you later sweetie*

Sweetie... The word resonates in my head throughout what's left of the day, leaving me confused about how to feel about it right up to our date. Maybe I should workshop nicknames until I see Ollie...

∞

Parking outside her building, I text Ollie to let her know I'm here. What she doesn't know is that I'm driving my motorcycle... and I'm not sure if it's okay for her. Anticipation and nervousness

249

run through my body as I wait for her, helmet in hand. I don't know if it's because I'm excited to see her, but it feels like I've been waiting for ages.

Ollie walks out the door, and my breath hitches. She's wearing a white ruffled shirt and light blue shorts—so simple, yet so breathtaking. How can someone be so beautiful? So incredibly adorable with her bright smile, looking at me. Just me.

She frowns as soon as her eyes land on my bike. "Since when do you have that?"

"College. I haven't used it in a long time, and I thought tonight might be a good time. What do you think?"

"It's cool; I just don't really like motorcycles." She moves closer to me, squinting.

"Do you trust me?" I grab her hands.

"*Sí*, I do." She gives me one of her sweet smiles.

I put the second helmet on her head and kiss her lips. "Then hop on, baby!"

Calling her baby seems to calm her nerves about riding a motorcycle, and she carefully hops on behind me. The warm feeling of her arms circling my waist reaches my skin, even through my clothes. Her body trembles as I turn the ignition and the bike revs.

"I won't go too fast, okay?" I shout over the motor.

"You promise?" she pleads in a very soft voice.

"Yes, Ollie, I promise!" I smile at her through the round rearview mirror.

I lift the lever with my feet, balancing the bike before driving away. Ollie's arms tighten around me as we take off down the avenue. The pressure of her embrace is a little uncomfortable, but I don't have the heart to tell her.

I see the wind blowing on her hair in the mirror, making it dance in the air like it has a life of its own. Driving down the streets, I can feel her grip loosening. She rests her head on my back, her breathing slow and steady.

"Okay, this is pretty nice," Ollie mumbles against my back.

"So, you like it?"

"Maybe..."

"I'll take that as a yes then!"

"Whatever works for you, sweetie," she mocks me as we brake at a stoplight.

She lifts herself off my back, shifting around on the seat. *Why is she moving so much?* I can see her shaking her head and laughing to herself in the mirror.

"What's going on over there?"

"Got a text from Maia. It's so stupid," she says with a smile. "Look." She brings the phone up to my face.

Maia:
how's the date going
don't forget to use protection...

"Oh, damn it. I forgot to buy them, sorry, baby. Maybe next time?" I give her a fake hurt look.

"Okay, okay, I'll make sure to give her a heads-up."

"Looking forward to it." I wink at her as she puts her phone away. "Hold on again."

Before the light changes, her hands are already tight around me. I can't contain my laughter as I drive, and she holds on even tighter.

I think she notices me circling the avenue as we reach the boardwalk's parking lot. I smirk in celebration of my distraction working as planned.

"You think you're so slick, don't you?" She gives me a look of disbelief as she puts away her helmet.

"It did work, though." I lay against the bike, arms reaching to her.

Breaking through her facade, she smiles at me as I pull her closer. Her hand's on my chest, and her head rests on my shoulder.

"Yes, it did." She holds back a smile. "Now, will you tell me where we're going?" She lifts her head.

"Come on, I'll show you." I grab her hand, pulling her closer.

We leave the parking lot and step into the middle of the boardwalk, the welcome sign behind us. Her bright smile lets me know I brought her to the right place.

"Brandon, I—" she mutters. "Thank you. I haven't been here in so long!" She hugs me around the neck, standing on her toes.

"Let's go!" She plants a quick kiss on my lips. And just as quickly, she grabs my hand again and drags me toward her favorite place.

I didn't know it until now, but something told me this was where I had to bring her. The bright lights coming from the rides shine on her face, accentuating her smile and the sparkle in her beautiful eyes.

"Ollie, slow down. The park's not going anywhere." I laugh as I barely keep up with her. She's moving so fast that my hand's on the verge of slipping from hers.

"I know, I know. But I just can't wait to go on all the rides!" Her voice reaches an octave that I never thought possible.

We reach the entrance, and I pay for the tickets before she can pull out her wallet. She tries to protest, but I give her a smug look and grab her by the waist.

She wraps her hands around my neck, looking at me with such intensity that it sends shivers throughout my body. The very last second of the sun descending reflects on her piercing green eyes—every emotion dances around in them, expressing what she can't say with words.

"Have I told you how beautiful your eyes are?" I whisper, and her face lights up. "I could get lost in them for hours, just trying to make sense of the colors swirling in them."

"Well, thank you. You're welcome to do that anytime." She stands on her tiptoes and pecks me on the lips. "Come on, I want to do the roller coasters first!"

She drags me behind her and pulls me toward the looping roller coaster. I can already feel myself dying inside, and we're not even riding them yet. The ups and downs don't look that terrifying… until you reach the big loop that stops when you're upside down.

I fake excitement as they lock the levers. Not doing a good job at hiding my fear, Ollie notices and grabs my hand.

"I'm here, sweetie, and I promise I won't let go of your hand."

"Promise?" I plead. She nods and kisses my hand, then places it on her lap.

My body jolts as the ride starts without a heads-up. I throw Ollie a dirty look as she chuckles at my reaction. I don't know what's worse: the loop, the drop, or how long it's taking.

My eyes are so tightly shut, unaware of how close to the edge we are. And as if life's playing a sick game with me, right when I open my eyes, I see my feet dangling. That's when I know I'm dead, that it's too late.

A shrill, terrified scream leaves my mouth as we drop: twists, turns, and tilting sideways. My grip on Ollie's hand tightens with every move we make. Hopefully, I won't break it.

"Oh my God, oh my God, oh my God," I plead with my eyes closed in hopes of this ending soon.

After what feels like an eternity of rattling, we come to

a halt. Hoping it's over, I open my eyes. The realization that another drop is coming hits me right in the face. But that's not the worst part…we dangle off the edge, and the big loop is staring back at us. *Fuck, fuck, fuck.*

I close my eyes again, bracing myself. One more inch and the cart is moving faster than before. I can't even scream anymore. I now notice Ollie's been screaming too, but from excitement—enjoying every second of this ride. Laughter escapes her lips as our bodies rattle from side to side.

My head sticks to the headboard as we reach the loop and start to rise. As we stop right in the middle, our heads hang, and I can feel Ollie looking at me.

"It's okay, baby, it's okay. We're almost done," she encourages me as I squeeze her hand tighter.

After a few seconds—but if you were in my head, you would've thought it was hours—we drop again.

I'm going to die…Ollie's going to die…we're both going to die… It's now or never; I need to tell her how I feel before we splat onto the ground.

"Shit, shit, shit," I scream, my lungs starting to burn after doing so much of it. "I'm falling for you, Ollie. I think I'm falling in love with you!"

"What?!" She squeezes my hand as we go through another small loop. *Damn it, she didn't hear me.*

My body relaxes, letting out deep breaths as we finally reach the end. The moment the levers unlock, I pull Ollie out with me. There's no way I'm staying in that hell trap one more second.

I realize I might've said that out loud as Ollie muffles a laugh beside me. "I'm sorry, I'm sorry, but your reactions were so funny! You really hate roller coasters, don't you?" *Maybe she didn't hear me.*

"They are a death trap…" I whisper.

"You know it can't hurt you or hear you, right?" She laughs.

"How about we skip the other one and go to the bumper cars? And I swear you'll like the Hurricane; it's super fun!" Who can say no to the most adorable pleading eyes?

"Fine!" I slowly breathe in and out. "But I'm not doing the Slingshot! I know you've been thinking about it since we walked in."

"Okay, okay," she breathes out.

We wait in line to get in the bumper cars, and this time, Ollie notices my excitement as I bounce up and down. "You are such a kid! Of course, you'd like this one."

"Hey, it's fun!" I raise my hands in protest. "I bet you I'll win." I raise my eyebrows at her.

"Hmm, how about we make it interesting?" She gives me a devilish grin. "Winner chooses the ride after the Hurricane."

"Deal!" We shake hands to seal it.

"Whistle my laughs and drum to my heartbeat. I'll flow in your veins right through your heart, where you'll guard me."
~ *Symphonic Orchestra, Alexandra Kessler.*

BRANDON – OCEAN CITY

"COME ON, WE CAN DO IT. Let's blow up these freaking balloons!" Ollie's competitiveness starts to come out during one of the games.

And in her defense, it's the third cart we've tried, yet we haven't won anything. It seems that hand-eye coordination is not our forte.

"Game on!"

We put everything into it: shooting as much water as possible into the tiny hole. The time trickles down, working against us. The balloons are very slowly filling up, but our hopes of them popping are not.

With only fifteen seconds left, I press down tighter on the button. The water's precision seems to work better: my balloon grows bigger by the second. I don't know how Ollie's doing; only focusing on popping mine in these last five seconds. Water splashes on both of us as our balloons burst a nanosecond before the buzzer goes off.

"Yes, yes, yes! Oh, my God, we got it!" She jumps up and down. She reaches her hand to mine, giving me a very hard high five. *She really is competitive...*

We exchange the two small stuffed animals for one big one. I let Ollie pick, and she chooses a big, gray plush elephant. We hug it to get a feel of its texture, which is very soft, like a pillow. It's big enough to embrace comfortably but not so big that she can't carry it.

"Thank you so much." She gives me the sweetest kiss. The plush toy hangs from her hands. "I'll keep this forever, right beside me on the bed."

"You're sleeping with it?"

"Umm, it's *him*, not *it*. And he has a name…" she drawls out. Her smile twitches for a second. "How about Oscar?"

I close my eyes, the realization of the joke hitting me. "Ollie, I will kill you. Please do not mention him again. He-Who-Must-Not-Be-Named!"

She throws her head back, bursting into a deep laugh. *Good one, B, hitting her right on her geekiness.*

"You are insufferable." She shakes her head. "Alright, fine. What do you want me to call him?"

I give it a little thought and come up with the perfect name for the cutest stuffed animal. "Ellie."

Her face lights up as soon as she hears it. "I love it! Our cute little Ellie the Elephant."

"The cutest." I hold the side of her face, staring right into her shining eyes.

She reaches up to me, brushing her nose with mine. I lean down and steal a kiss from her lips. I don't know why, but every time I kiss her, it's like the world stops, and it's just us.

I can't get enough of stealing these perfect moments and having her in my arms.

She pulls away, leaving my lips feeling lonely. I pout, sort of begging for another one. She pouts back, copying me.

"Come on, let's get some cotton candy and take a walk."

Hand in hand, we walk down the beach. Ellie hangs onto Ollie's neck like a cape while we eat our cotton candy with our free hands. The moonlight reflects over the ocean, and the sand crunches under our feet. Nothing can be more perfect than this moment.

"So."

"So."

"I couldn't wait to have this nice, silent moment with you today. Don't get me wrong, this date was fun and a little scary. But I loved it," I smile at her.

"I loved it too. Thanks for the amazing night." She rests her head on my arm.

"Actually, can we sit down? I want to tell you something." I pull her with me, worry dancing in her eyes.

Taking a deep breath, I prepare myself, and her, for my confession. "Ever since that day I bumped into you at the concert, I couldn't stop thinking about you. I know, I know, I was with Anna. But it got complicated, and for me, it was already over with her. I was just waiting for something to wake me up and push me to break it off. That was you, Ollie."

Our breaths hitch, my heart feels like it's about to explode, and my mind goes a mile a minute. The only thing keeping me from bursting is her hand on mine.

"I—umm—"

"I understand if you don't feel the same. I'm okay with just letting you know my feelings for you. How I can't help but smile when you laugh, even if it's the lamest joke I've ever heard. How you get so focused when you're at work, but then you're so distracted when we're hanging out. The way you squint every time you smile... such a beautiful smile," I caress her cheek.

The way she looks at me while I pour my heart out, it's as if all she wants to do is to kiss me. My breathing, my heartbeat, my mind: everything's going all over the place right now. I focus on the way she looks at me, smiling at every sentence. The way her hands spark a fire in me whenever I touch her and how it lingers.

"Ollie...all I want is to know what you feel. Whatever's going on in your head. I want—I need to know." I try to give her a comforting smile. "Doesn't matter what it is, I can take it."

Taking a deep breath, I calm myself down as she speaks. "Brandon, I—" *inhale, exhale.*

"I have to admit that when I saw Anna walk into the apartment, calling you babe, it hurt. I wasn't expecting that after spending those days together and at the concert. ...And then after Connor. But I couldn't stop thinking about you either since I saw you at that gas station. And then, at the music hall, I felt that it was kind of like a sign. But I'm not entirely sure what I feel..." She places her hands on mine over her knees.

"All I know is that you haven't left my thoughts for one second. I can't explain why. And I've lost count of how many times you've brushed your hand through your hair." She lets out a dry laugh as I start doing it again, and I consciously stop.

Wait, she's counting how often I do it? Since when?!

"And when we were dancing in New York...the way you pulled me close to you. All I wanted to do was to stay like that forever, so close we could hear each other's heartbeats. Feeling safe in your arms." She caresses my hand. "I don't know what this is yet, what's happening, or what's going to happen. But what I do know is I'm glad we met. That I can feel like this after such a long time is something that also makes me glad."

I breathe out and close my eyes, enjoying the feeling of talking it all out—the feeling of having her so close and holding my hand.

"So, you do feel the same?"

"Brandon, of course, I do!" She keeps holding my hand. "And don't think I didn't hear you on the roller coaster. You were so adorable!"

"You did, didn't you?" I fake being offended. "And here I

thought I made a fool of myself."

My smile reaches my ears as I see and hear her laughing, her smile a mirror of mine. *She's beautiful when she laughs.*

I pull her closer to me and lay a kiss on her head. "Umm, listen, I have a proposition for you."

"Oh, that soon? I mean, I wasn't expecting it until at least a year. But hold on, let me clean my hand in the water."

After a small moment of laughter, I grab her attention again. "Come on, I'm serious." She nods for me to go on. "Scott's family lake house in Colorado will be empty next weekend, and he said we could use it. What do you think?"

"I love that idea! We definitely could use the break; it would be perfect. I'll talk it out with them, but I'm pretty sure we're on the same page." She stops herself from her never-ending rambling. "You know what? Just tell Scott that we're good to go."

Now it's my turn to hang my head back in laughter at that whirlwind of an answer. "Fine, fine, I'll tell him. But don't bail on me, okay? I'm counting on you!"

"You got it, sweetie, don't worry!" She raises our hands and kisses mine. "That's the last weekend before you start recording, right?" She smiles, but her eyes can't hide her sadness.

"Hey, what's wrong?"

"I know we haven't been together long, but our feelings for each other are strong. I mean, we just confessed them on a roller coaster." She sighs.

"I don't care if I only get to see you two weekends a month and sometimes during the week. All I want is to be with you whatever chance we get. I like you, Ollie; I'm falling for you. And there's nothing to worry about, I promise!" I kiss her cheek.

Around halfway through my speech, she lays her head on my shoulder while embracing Ellie.

"Thank you." She lifts her head to look at me, the moonlight reflecting on her eyes, making them look gloomy. "I trust you, Brandon. We'll be okay."

"Yes, we will," I mumble against the top of her head before slightly pulling away.

I caress her cheek with my thumb, leaning down and giving her the deepest kiss I've given her so far, fueling it with every emotion we're experiencing. I've lost count of how many times I've kissed her today. I get lost in this kiss, in her embrace, in her scent. Everything she is pulls me in deeper, with no slowing down in sight.

This moment, this night, this kiss feels like a promise—of holding each other tighter when things get tough and not letting go when one of us needs the other.

You may not hear my thoughts, Ollie, but I promise I won't make a promise I can't keep.

Chapter Twelve

"I want to feel the rush, the thrill. 'Cause I'm lovesick, and it kills me." ~ Lovesick, Alexandra Kessler.

OLIVIA – STEAMBOAT SPRINGS

WHOA, SCOTT, THIS IS BEAUTIFUL!" I say as the car stops in front of the lake house.

"Yeah, this house is beautiful. But can we talk about the fact that we just flew over in a freaking private jet?!" Ella squeals. "I have a rich boyfriend! A-private-jet-and-mansion-rich boyfriend."

Maia and I roll our eyes at Ella's vain rambles. But the girl's right—this is a whole other level of rich.

"Damn, maybe you should've dated Scott! He's got a plane," I whisper to Maia. "I mean…he's available, you know? You still have time." I give her a smirk.

"Wow, Ollie, who knew you had jokes? If we can even call them that."

Deciding not to push it further, I take a better look at this almost-mansion.

The house is made of painted wood and bricks. The ceiling is black, making the brown walls and details pop out. The columns are a beautiful mix of beige and light brown bricks. A vast lawn paves the way to the house with a soft and beautiful green color. Small flower gardens and potted plants line the brick columns and steps.

A balcony, or more like a terrace, overlooks the front and side of the house. And from down here, we can even see a small chimney. The morning views must be mesmerizing, with the forest and the mountains right in front.

"Wait until you see the back," Scott replies with a sly smile.

We step into the house, and the wind gets knocked out of me. If the New York apartment was impressive, then this broke all expectations. Like the outside, the brick columns are a blend of beige and light brown, and the walls are black and mahogany brown. The furniture is heavenly: an array of whites, grays, and browns that match the walls.

We leave the bags by the spiral staircase leading to the rooms and walk to the back of the house. Just like inside, the backyard has two levels. Below, it has a beautiful grass area with a bonfire and garden furniture. There are lounge chairs, another bonfire area, and a covered dining set with a bar on the upper level.

We follow a gravel path that leads to an astonishing view and what seems like the house's selling point. At the end of the trail sits a dock above the most beautiful lake I've ever seen. The sun even reflects over the water and gives it a heavenly look. Following our gaze to the end of the lake, we reach the view of the mountains. The sunset illuminates the sky and dreamy clouds with pink, purple, orange, and a fading blue.

"This is," I sigh, closing my eyes and slightly shaking my head, "breathtaking..."

Getting so lost in its beauty and my thoughts, I jump when Brandon's hands surround my waist. Instinctively, I lean back and settle in his embrace, resting my head on his chest.

"Now, this is a view I can get used to seeing. Waking up and having coffee right here on this dock," he sighs, his chin on my head.

I tilt my head, trying to look at him. "Me too. I don't think I can ever leave the beach, but I could for this."

"Let's do it then!"

I turn around with my eyebrows furrowed. "Yeah, because Scott's parents would just give us the house." I stifle a laugh.

"No, baby, not here. I meant that, I don't know, maybe one day we can have something like this."

The sunset shines on his eyes, making the feelings dancing in them more noticeable. He's looking at me like the world revolves around this moment, as if our friends are not right next to us. The sane part of my brain yells at me to ignore the feelings bubbling up. It's too fast to talk about growing old together, but my heart can't help encouraging it.

"Maybe," is the only thing I manage to whisper.

He leans down, but in a plan to tease him, I look away, his kiss landing with a muffled laugh against my cheek. "I hate it when you do that."

"I know; that's why I do it," I whisper with a laugh. "Also, there are people around, sweetie. I don't want to make anyone uncomfortable."

"Baby...Ella and Noah are down by the docks having their moment too. And no one seems bothered by their kissing."

I turn around, and indeed, she's having a make-out session with her boyfriend. Just what any sister wants to see... But at least they're good together.

"No, I know, but—" I stop myself as my gaze lands on Sam up in the higher part of the backyard. He seems to sense my staring and looks back at me, mustering a sad smile.

"But what?" he whispers, confusion dripping from every word. I look back at him, still feeling Sam's intensity.

"Nothing, never mind."

He cradles my face, making me feel protected, and engulfs my lips in his, tilting my head back. We forget about the world around us—time stops, and it's just us in this blissful moment. My whole body trembles as our mouths fight for dominance over the other. One of his hands trails down my back, stopping at my waist, and he pulls me in closer than we've ever been. Our bodies meld together, becoming one.

I let him guide me as he walks me back, taking careful steps on the rocky ground without disconnecting from each other. The feeling of wood on my back lets me know we've reached a tree. The kiss intensifies as his hand tilts my head to the side. His tongue skims over my lower lip, asking for permission.

I follow his lead, letting him take control of where this is going. My hand trails to the back of his neck, and I play with his hair. This encourages him more, his hand moving lower and stopping right before my bottom.

The sound of branches breaking makes us separate from each other. We turn our heads, our eyes landing on the faces of two very embarrassed teens. Ella and Noah give us the most sincere, apologetic looks and leave as quickly as they ruin our moment. Leave it to Ella to do her sisterly duties.

"We're always getting interrupted, aren't we?" Brandon breathes out against my neck.

I press my face into my hands, releasing a laugh. He pulls me into a hug, resting his head on mine, and joins in with me. He sways us side to side in our embrace.

He plants kisses on my head and forehead. "I mean...we're alone now." His voice trails off suggestively.

I look around and confirm that, indeed, it's only the two of us. "And what did you have in mind?"

Instead of answering, he kisses me with such passion that anyone would think it's our last day together, and he wants to be able to remember my taste once I'm gone.

∞

"Oh, look who's finally back! We thought you got lost in the woods or something," Maia mocks us as we enter the living room.

"We lost track of time." I avoid her gaze.

"Lost track of time… Girl, it's dark out now. What were you even doing?"

"Exploring," Brandon gives them a cheeky smile. Looking around at everyone, they're giving us annoyed, knowing looks.

Trying to get out of the spotlight, I change the topic. "So, what's for dinner?"

"Already thought of that. We're having a barbecue again. Sam already started on the grill," Scott quickly answers.

He positively looks like he owns the place, his feet propped on the table and his arms by his head. *I mean…he actually does.*

"Okay, cool. I can go help." I give Brandon a quick kiss and walk out to the terrace.

As expected, I spot Sam right in front of the grill, already halfway through cooking the burgers and sausages.

"Hey, what's up?"

"Hey. Heard you were exploring," he sputters in a weird tone.

"Umm, yeah, something like that…"

He doesn't laugh or even react to my comment, leaving us in uncomfortable and awkward silence.

"Hey, listen, is everything okay with you?"

He turns to look at me. "Yeah. It's all good. Why do you ask?" *Sure, very convincing.*

"I don't know. You've been acting weird since that night at the club. I didn't think much of it then, but now it's starting to worry me."

He stays quiet for a while, not looking at me anymore. His indifference toward me now fills my head with guilty thoughts.

"Shit, is it something I said? Or did?"

He whips around to face me as soon as I ask the question. "God, Ollie, no. Not at all; it has nothing to do with you. It's just…" He scratches the back of his head. "It's this complicated thing with my parents, and I don't want to burden anyone."

For some reason, his answer gives me a bad feeling. I don't believe his words. But I don't want to push it further than I already have. So, I nod and give him an apologetic smile.

We stay there in silence, cooking the burgers and preparing the plates for everyone. When we bump elbows, we don't look at each other; not even a glance.

A strong breeze brushes through, and not even being by the fire stops the cold from hitting me as I hiss. The shivers run up and down my body, making the spatula shake in my hand. After what feels like hours spent in a silent void, Sam looks at me. He disappears behind me, but only for a few seconds. The feeling of warmth spreads through me as he wraps a very fluffy blanket around my shoulders.

"Here," he whispers, careful not to startle me. "Don't want you getting a cold now, do we?" He lets out a short, dry laugh.

"Thanks." I glance back, expecting to find him a few steps behind me. But I suck in a breath of shock as I meet his face a couple of millimeters away from mine.

"No problem." His minty breath hits me.

I give him a small smile, waiting for him to return it. Another sad smile shows on his face before moving away from me, and now he's back to working the grill. I open my mouth only to close it again, having no words that can express anything but worry or pity.

A frown shows on his forehead as he breathes in and out slowly. "Ollie, listen, this might be the wrong time, but—"

"Hmm, baby, this smells amazing! Are they ready yet? We're

dying to try these burgers." Brandon's voice resonates as he comes out to us, and Sam quickly backs away, like he was never there.

"And I'm sure they taste even better than they smell." He kisses my cheek before embracing me from behind. *Talk about bad timing.*

"Almost done, man, like five more minutes," Sam adds without looking at Brandon or me.

"Do you mind if I steal my girl for a while?"

"Nope, she's all yours," he mumbles. Brandon and I give him a weird look, but we let it slide like we've been doing for the past week.

He takes my hand and walks me up to the balcony. A gasp escapes my lips as I take in the view: the moon and stars cast a magical light over the mountains and the trees in the forest. The sky is free of clouds, with the stars and constellations portraying a celestial picture.

"It's amazing how you can get the most beautiful and clearest of skies by just leaving the city." I lean my head back on his chest. "Beautiful," I breathe out.

I notice Brandon's hands shiver on top of mine, so I turn around and drape the blanket over us. His eyes catch mine with a stare so strong and deep I'm pretty sure we can glimpse each other's souls.

I brush off some hair that falls over his forehead, and he sucks in a breath. Every time I touch him, there's something about his eyes; how they seem to glimmer, like he's overwhelmed with his feelings for me.

And without any warning, his lips capture mine. I don't know if it's the blanket or the feeling of our hands all over each other, but my skin is burning with a fire so intense I might as well be right next to the sun.

Our hands and our mouths seem to have minds of their own as we roam them over each other. Our hands caress every detail and crevice of our bodies. Our mouths only disconnect to trail over our necks, cheeks, jaws.

We can't get enough of each other. As if the moment we stop kissing, we'll burn up and disappear. Deep down, we both know this won't happen. *But what if it does?* What if our feelings for each other burn so hot that they burn us out instead?

What is wrong with you, Olivia? Don't let your dark thoughts about your past dictate your present and future. Enjoy and cherish these moments with Brandon. He's good to you. He's kept his promises so far. Give him a real chance.

I listen to the voice in my head, pushing out the negative thoughts that consume my mind—only focusing on this beautiful, magical, and passionate moment.

"I wonder if sometimes, you talk about me with your friends."
~ Cigarette, Alexandra Kessler.

OLIVIA – STEAMBOAT SPRINGS

AND HE'S ALWAYS SO SWEET, SHOWING UP WITH COFFEE at the office or picking me up with a flower in his hand. He's even trying to teach me how to ride his motorclycle," Ella and Maia burst out laughing as the words leave my mouth.

"What?" I look at them, the hot tub bubbling even more from their movement. "What did I say?"

"You—" Maia tries to catch her breath in between laughs.

"You said motorclycle." Ella laughs again. "Instead of motorcycle!"

I open my eyes wide, embarrassed. Neither of us can contain ourselves now, the alcohol taking effect in our system. *Well, duh, we're like three bottles of wine down.*

"Oh, my God. Maybe we should stop drinking?" We all become silent, thinking. Seconds later, we're back to laughing.

"Anyway…" I say as I pour another glass for each of us. *There almost goes the third bottle. The guys might have to carry us up by the end of the night.*

"Don't you sometimes feel that things are going too perfect?" I ask, still coming down from laughing. "Like, in movies or a TV show, where everything is going so well and so beautifully. But it's too perfect, and you sit there waiting for the next bad thing."

"But what makes you think that something bad's going to happen?" Maia asks, brushing her blue-streaked hair over her shoulder and onto her back.

"Just a feeling. Thoughts that pop into my mind sometimes. Do you not feel that?" I shrug.

"Not really." Ella sighs as she leans back. "I prefer enjoying those moments instead of worrying about them ending."

"Yeah, maybe I should do that more often. It's probably just me worried about Brandon going to New York so often after this weekend."

"Hey, it'll be fine." Maia leans closer. "You two like and care for each other very much. Anyone would kill to have a guy look at them like he looks at you. You're going to be fine."

I return the smile and mumble a *thank you* before drinking almost everything in my glass. Then I remember what we were supposed to be doing...

"Oh, my God, the dares!" My shrill, excited voice makes Ella and Maia drop splashes of their wine in the water. "Oops." I shrug and smile widely at them. "Okay, I'll start! Ella, take an embarrassing selfie and use it as your profile picture."

"Dude, seriously? Couldn't think of something more creative?" She huffs.

"Well, if you decide to forfeit the dare, Maia and I would be more than happy to use some of the pictures we took during your photoshoot and post them online. Trust me, they are not flattering." I smirk, recalling the memory of our day on the beach and how awful those blackmail pictures look.

She groans dramatically before taking the selfie. "Okay, done." She sets the phone down by her towel. "Now, Ollie. Go into the living room and ask Brandon for his hoodie. Tell him it's freezing outside, and you're cold."

"¿Estás loca (are you crazy)? I'm not doing that!" I slur my words as I think of how stupid that is.

"It's the dare," Ella replies, and Maia shrugs as I look at her.

"Stupid," I mutter as I get out of the tub. Ella and Maia get out too and hide behind the wall behind me.

"Ollie? What's going on? Where's your towel? You're getting the floors wet," Brandon says, sitting up as I approach him.

"I came to ask you for your hoodie." I try my best to hold in my laughter.

"What?" Brandon asks, sounding confused.

"It's freezing outside, and I'm super cold. Could I please have your hoodie to keep me warm?"

"I, umm—" he stumbles, blinking rapidly. "Sure...here, take it."

I can feel Ella and Maia peeking their heads into the living room... I pull the hoodie over my head, kissing Brandon before walking back.

"Holy shit." I'm dying of laughter as we get back into the tub. The bottom half of the hoodie gets completely wet.

"Can't believe you actually did that." Maia breathes out as we laugh. "What are we, ten?"

"How can something so stupid be so funny?" I try to catch my breath.

"Maybe because we're drunk," Ella suggests, *and yet we keep on drinking*.

"Now it's Maia's turn," I smirk at her and sip my wine.

"Why me? You have nothing you can embarrass me with." She returns the smug look.

"What? Don't you think we've noticed you and Scott flirting all weekend? Scratch that. Since we met."

"No, I haven't! That's just him being arrogant and me talking back," Maia rolls her eyes

"He held your hand on the plane," Ella says with a wink.

"That"—she swallows—"was nothing. He was nice to me because I'm afraid of heights."

"Yeah, right. Come on, Maia, admit it. You like each other. Or at least *you* like *him*." Her stone-hard face stares back at me.

"Maybe I do, maybe I don't. So, was that my dare, me admitting my *feelings*?"

"Not exactly..." The mischievous smile is back. "The dare is to text that to Scott, to take the first step between you two."

She opens her eyes so wide they might pop out of her head. Her mouth drops open and closed as she fails to come up with anything to say.

"Hey, that's not a fair dare. It's not at all on the same level as the ones I gave you. And what if he doesn't feel the same? I'll look stupid."

"Then you can move on and go back to insulting his ass. And who said anything about dares being fair?" I move my glass to the middle, a smirk still on my face. I signal for us to click our glasses together and chug the wine.

"Fuck it."

Ella and I clap as she turns around and grabs her phone. She slowly unlocks it, bringing it closer to us, and pulls up his contact: Douchebag. *Would you look at that? She doesn't even admit it's a tell-tale sign of her crush.* Her fingers glide across the screen while she types as fast as possible.

"Yes, yes, that's perfect, keep going!" We encourage her as we read what she writes. Everything is in one whole paragraph.

"I'm going!" She reads over it one last time. "Okay, done." Her finger hovers over the send button.

"Come on, just do it. It'll be fine." I tap her shoulders.

Taking a deep breath, she closes her eyes and hits send.

Ella and I squeal, bringing her into a hug. As we pull her in, we startle her, and she jumps up.

"Shit, my phone!" she screams as we watch it disappear into the bubble-filled water. "Yo, help me find it," she pleads as we just stare in disbelief.

A few minutes go by, the three of us frantically moving around in the tub, trying to find it. I stand up after what feels like the most dreadful and painfully slow amount of time.

"I found it!" I say breathlessly

She takes it from my hands, trying to shake and suck the water out. The screen was already cracked, so the water went in from everywhere. Once it stops flowing out, she dries it with a towel and tries turning it on.

"Oh, my God, Maia, I'm so sorry!" I apologize over and over. "I didn't—we didn't—mean for that to happen!"

"It's okay, I know." Maia sighs. *Shit, fuck, I messed up.*

"One question, though," Ella interrupts us, and we turn to look at her. "Did he actually receive the message?"

We all stay silent for a second, staring at each other.

"I think so…" Maia trails off, seemingly trying her hardest to remember. "Maybe, maybe not. I'm not sure."

"Oh, I know! We should check his phone," I say, perking up.

"Oh, great idea, *Einstein.* Because Scott will lend it to me without a fight."

"No, listen to me; I thought of a plan. You distract him by talking or doing whatever while we try to unlock his phone," I whisper, getting very close to them.

"And how will you do that, *genius*?"

"Noah can help!" Ella claps her hands, then gives us an apologetic look for the loudness. "He might know his password, or his face could unlock it? They are brothers, after all."

Shit, that's even more genius! Or maybe that's just the bottles of alcohol talking…

"Fine, let's do it," Maia sighs. "But if this all goes to shit, I will blame it on both of you and haunt you in your sleep!"

We don't even acknowledge her threat as we squeal and cheer. If they don't get suspicious over all this noise, they're even more aloof than we thought.

We get out of the tub and dry ourselves before we go into the living room.

"So, I thought that for the EP, we can do some unplugged versions. And maybe—" Brandon stops talking as he looks over at me. I almost forgot I was wearing his hoodie, completely soaked in water.

"Baby, what the fuck did you do?" He tries to act mad but can't contain his laughter.

"What?" I look down at myself. "The water was cold." I don't see anything wrong with my logic.

"Come here." He rolls his eyes as we laugh. I sit on his lap and pepper him with kisses. Ella does the same with Noah.

Maia walks up to Scott, who is conveniently in the kitchen, while we do our part of the plan.

"Um, okay, here's the thing. We need your help. We dared her to do something super stupid, which fucked up her phone, and now we have to fix it," Ella says, looks sheepishly at Noah.

"We need one of you to unlock Scott's phone. Where is it?" I look over the coffee table, trying to figure out which one is his.

"This one, I think Noah knows his password. They have the same one." Sam leans over the coffee table from the couch across from us, handing over the device.

"Oh, my God, thank you, guys. You're the best! Please don't tell." Ella pouts as her boyfriend does his magic.

Ella and I open his messages and see Maia's, still unopened. *Yes, it worked!* We get in and delete only the latest one, so it looks like he never got it and won't get suspicious.

We silently celebrate as Maia walks back. "Got it, *vámonos*." She raises a six-pack of beer and nods to the terrace.

"Did it work? Did you see the text?" she asks as we get back into the tub.

"Yes, Noah got us in, and we deleted it." Ella makes a *phew* sound. "But we're not sure if he read it or not. He could've seen it from his notifications before going to the kitchen."

"Well, let's pray and hope that he didn't." She sighs. "It was a stupid-ass dare anyway." Ella and I give each other a look before turning back to her.

"What?" she asks in an annoyed tone.

"Maia, just admit that you like him," I say.

"I did. To you and him."

"No, you didn't. You said: *maybe I do, maybe I don't.* That's not admitting anything." *Why am I getting so frustrated over this? It's not like it's my relationship.*

She groans, throwing her head back. "Fine," she sighs, not looking at us. "I might, maybe, kinda, possibly…have feelings for his arrogant ass." She covers her face with her arm.

She doesn't even have to look up to know our faces light up with excitement as we smile and squeal. "I didn't say what kind of feelings. For all you know, I could have a strong feeling of wanting to attempt murder."

"Ugh, Maia, shut up." I nudge her shoulder.

"You know what? There's a fine line between love and hate." Ella points her beer at her as we keep giggling.

"Stop doing that, it's annoying!" She finally looks back at us. "This doesn't mean I want a relationship or that he even wants the same thing."

"Whatever, dude, you *like him*," I sing out to her, spinning like a ballerina. *Or more like a little kid…but that's what love feels like sometimes.*

Chapter Thirteen

"I see you staring at the mirror. What do you see?
Is it someone you love?" ~ *Mirror, Alexandra Kessler.*

OLIVIA – OCEAN CITY

DO YOU *HAVE* TO GO?" I pout as I lift my head from Brandon's chest, looking into his eyes.

"I'm sorry, baby, but you know I do." He kisses my forehead, returning the pout.

"But a whole week? It was only supposed to be two weekends a month."

"Well, it'll take longer than that. They have us recording all day and set up press releases. But this is a good thing." He caresses my cheek with his free hand.

"Yeah, I know, I know." I let out a breath. "I'm just going to miss you so much." My head falls on his chest again.

"I'm not leaving forever, Ollie. We'll be back on Saturday."

"Still, it's not fair that we just got here from the trip, and you're already leaving tomorrow."

"Baby, look at me," he whispers, and I slightly raise my head.

"You already knew this. We talked about it." He lets out a breathy laugh. "It's just one week."

"But—" He kisses me. "I—" He kisses me again. "You're not stopping, are you?" I mumble against his lips.

"Nope." His mouth is on mine again.

The kiss is not playful anymore; it's deep and gentle, letting out his emotions. It's his way of letting me know it will be okay, that we'll be okay. Seconds, minutes, hours—who knows how long we will go on like this? Time disappears as we melt into my recently made bed. *Well, not anymore.*

We part to catch our breath, our foreheads pressed together, and heavy breathing fans our faces. We cling to each other, not wanting this moment to end, and wishing for time to freeze at this exact point, lasting for eternity.

"*Quédate (stay),*" I whisper.

"What?" He frowns; *he probably didn't understand me.*

"Stay over, don't go tonight."

"I have to pack." He laughs, and I give him a funny look. "What?" he mimics me.

"Come on, you can do that in about five to ten minutes tops. Also, you're leaving at noon," I point out, and he gives me an acknowledging look. "We'll wake up early and have breakfast somewhere so we don't waste time cooking."

"God, you're so sexy when you're smart."

"I know." I give him a smirk.

"Come here." He sits up straight, pulling me with him.

He holds my face in his hands. His look is so fervent, like he can't believe this is happening. That we're sitting here, holding and admiring each other.

"Have I ever told you how beautiful you are?"

"A couple of times, yes." I give him a sheepish smile. "But don't you get tired of saying it?"

"I will never"—he brushes some hair out of my face—"get tired of telling you these things. One, because they're true. And two, I can't keep my feelings to myself, or I'll burst."

His stare is so intense, like a fire burning and consuming everything in its way. My head can't comprehend what's happening. I can't assimilate that this is real, that someone can feel like this about me. Have I been hurt so bad that I need these constant reassurances?

"And I will spend all day telling you this if I have to." He kisses my nose, and I scrunch up my face.

"Your stubble tickles." I giggle and try to back away.

"Oh, yeah?" He starts giving me quick pecks all around my face, making me laugh.

"Stooooop! I'm very ticklish." I try to pull away, but his hands on my waist stop me.

"Kinda the point, my love." His breath hits my neck, and mine gets stuck in my throat.

He stops his attack as he realizes what he's said. His nose brushes my cheek on his way to mine. One of his hands travels to my face while the other stays on my hip.

"So that you know"—his breathing gets heavy—"I'll miss you too." He tilts my head back, capturing my lips in his. "So, so, much," he whispers in between kisses.

His hand snakes to the back of my head, and I tilt it sideways, giving him more access. We move slowly and gently, cherishing each second. Chills run throughout my body as his hand moves under my shirt, his thumb making circles on my hip. His other hand leaves my face, joining the other at the base of my back, pulling me closer. His tongue grazes my bottom lip, asking for permission.

I trace one hand from his chest to the back of his neck, tangling it in his hair. I make my way under his shirt with the other, over his stomach and chest. He releases a shaky breath and kisses me deeper while my hand caresses his back. We embrace each other, clinging together as if at any given moment, we'll disappear.

His kisses grow hungry as his hands move over every part of my body, memorizing every curve and crevice. Our hands are under our shirts as though the layers itch, and they're an obstacle standing in the way.

"Wait, wait," I breathe out as his lips trace down my neck. But he doesn't stop. Instead, he continues over my hot skin.

"Brandon." I force him to look at me by holding his face up.

"Is something wrong? Did I hurt you?" He looks at me with panic in his eyes.

"No, baby, I'm good. Nothing's wrong." I smile at him. "It's just that," I breathe out, "Maia and Ella are in the rooms next to mine. Maybe we shouldn't do anything tonight."

"You're so adorable." He kisses my nose. "What if we're quiet? We can even put on some music." He waggles his eyebrows, making me throw my head back while laughing.

I bite my bottom lip as my laughter dies down. Looking deep into his eyes, I find nothing but affection and adoration swimming in them, making my decision easier.

"Lock the door."

I throw my keys on the coffee table by the door, feeling empty after my last breakfast with Brandon. God, I sound as if I'll never see him again.

"How'd it go?" Maia asks as I slump next to her.

"It'll be a very long week. I miss him already." I sigh. *I feel so stupid, childish.*

"Girl, he just left. What are you talking about?"

Damn, I sound ridiculous. I don't even look at her, realizing what I'm saying.

"You'll be fine; maybe this week apart will help you grow stronger." She taps my arm. "Don't stress so much about it. You won't have much time to do that anyway…" She trails off like she's about to reveal a mystery.

"Maia…what did you do?" I sit up straight.

"I got us a new client for the studio."

My jaw drops as she tells me the news.

"This new brand is launching its website in two weeks, and they want us to be their permanent photographers for their clothing line."

"This is so exciting. We can even get Ella to be one of their models and promote her too!"

"One step ahead of you. I told her the news while you were out, and she's already practicing her makeup." Maia smiles.

"And when do we start?"

"Tomorrow's the first photo shoot. We're doing dresses, rompers, jumpsuits, and two-piece sets. And then shirts, skirts, pants, and shorts on Wednesday and Thursday. We'll also fit the shoes in since they're wearing them anyway. Friday will be for purses and accessories; we won't need a lot of models."

"I love it, this is incredible. How did you even get this done?"

"They followed Ella on her brand's account and saw the pictures we took. Someone contacted her about it, and the rest is history." She shrugs as if she can't believe it either.

"Oh, wow…our work did pay off." I let out a chuckle. "How's Ella doing, by the way? She and I haven't talked about anything lately. I feel like a terrible sister."

"Well, you spend all your time with Brandon now, so it's understandable. But, yeah, she's doing good! Whenever she makes new pieces, she comes into the studio. We do the whole process of taking and editing pictures. Also, how do you think she's been paying for her stuff lately? From her sales!"

"Well, yeah, that makes sense." I scratch the back of my neck. "I've been a terrible sister, haven't I?"

"Yeah, kinda." She laughs as my jaw drops, and I push her arm. "Aye, you're the one who said it. I'm just agreeing with you."

"I should apologize, right?" I don't even wait for Maia's answer before walking to Ella's room.

Knock, knock. "How are you doing over here?" I don't wait for an answer before walking inside.

"You don't have to make the whole awkward, filler conversation. You guys talk loud. I heard everything from here," she says without looking at me.

"I'm still sorry." I shuffle closer to her. "I should've been paying more attention to you and how your brand is doing. I promise it won't happen again."

She turns to look at me with a tight smile. "Thank you. You'll do it again, but it's fine."

"Come on, no, I won't!"

"It's fine, *estás enamorada (you're in love)*, it happens." She shrugs. "I know what it's like; I'm in love too. It's not like I was sharing much with you either. It's okay."

"In love? I'm not in love. We've only been together for a few months, it can't happen that fast."

"Love is love, man. You can't help how you feel." She leaves me a confused mess as she goes back to doing her makeup. I'm guessing it's for a date... *Wow, I suck.*

"I'm not in love with Brandon..." *Or am I...?*

Yes, I have strong feelings for him, care about him a lot, and love spending time with him. But I'm not *in love* with him. *No, no, it's too soon.* It's just my mind playing games with me. These are ordinary feelings, not love.

I don't realize I am walking aimlessly until my knees bump into the front of my bed. Falling forward, I grab my pillows and cuddle them under my body, letting my thoughts run wild. *Come on, let's think this through rationally. What even is love?*

Feeling tingles every time we touch, the rush running

through my body when we kiss. The world stops when we're together, as if it's just the two of us—seeing the smile on his face when we see each other after a long day.

When he rubs his hand on my back and my legs or holds my hand... Any moment with him is magical and pure and free. I can be myself without feeling embarrassed.

And this is the moment when it clicks. What Ella and Maia have known all along: I'm falling in love with Brandon. *Shit.*

∞

"Morning, everyone," I say, walking into the kitchen, feeling like complete crap.

"Hey girl, want some coffee–" Maia stops in her tracks. "Olivia, what's wrong with you? Are you okay?"

"Huh?" I reply, and she points to a mirror.

When I see my reflection, I barely recognize myself. *This is a mess; I'm a mess.*

"I'm fine." My shoulders drop. "I just miss Brandon."

"Nah, no way, this is where you lose me! Olivia Woods, you cannot crumble because of a man, of all things. Are you kidding me? It's only been one week!" Maia gives me my coffee.

"First, he comes home tonight. Second, you talk every day, and third, you're an independent woman! So, take a shower and get changed. Breakfast will be ready by the time you're finished."

"Maia, I have not crumbled!" *Well, have I seen yourself? I certainly look the part. What's gotten into me?* I straighten my back. "You're right, I am all that!"

"Also, the new client's pictures are good to go; all there's left to do now is send and upload them to the page." I smile.

"Does that mean we're free for the day?"

"Yes, we can finally run our delayed errands!" I sigh in

relief.

"Okay, I'll send in the work while you get ready."

Walking into our favorite coffee place, we sit at our go-to table to the right of the entrance, right by the window with a view of the ocean.

"Who would've thought, huh? That we'd be doing all this." I exhale with a smile. "I can't wait for the page's official release!"

"Yes, this is an incredible opportunity! And I'm so glad we're doing this together." Maia smiles sweetly at me. "And are you feeling any better?"

"Yeah, of course; I don't know what's gotten into me these past few days."

"Well...I have an idea ..." She leans back in her seat, and I give her a questioning look. "You're in love, whether you want to admit it or not; you are."

"I guess so." There's no use denying it anymore.

"Gosh, finally!" She exhales, and we start laughing.

After we calm our breathing down, Maia straightens up. "So, I was talking to Scott—"

"Oh, so you're talking to him now?" I smirk at her and waggle my eyebrows.

"Oh, shut up, it's nothing," she brushes me off. "He said they'll arrive around eight tonight. And I thought we could surprise them with a little welcome party: some beer, wine, and snacks."

"That's a great idea! But I'm going to say I did it."

She laughs it off and shrugs. "I don't mind."

"Listen, I was thinking...if all goes well, we can save up and go on a trip to Paris, Rome, Milan, Madrid, London."

"Here she goes…" Maia mumbles. "But yes, I would love that. We definitely should!"

"And I can already picture us waking up to posters of the band: on our walls, buildings, sides of buses."

"Yeah…but let's not get carried away. Let's start with just planning the party."

"What do you think they're doing right now?"

"I don't know, probably hooking up with some groupies." She shrugs like it means nothing.

"Maia, come on, I don't need the stress." I give her a disapproving look.

She puts her hands up as her way of apologizing and mouthing "sorry."

"A chai latte for you." The waitress places a cup in front of Maia. "And a caramel macchiato for you." She sets the second drink in front of me.

Maia thanks her for both of us since my full attention is on the coffee. "If you keep looking at it like that, you might as well make out with it," she jokes.

Eyeing the cup as if it were my prey and I was a lioness, I start fake kissing it. *Am I really this lame? Oh, well!*

"And who do you call when the pain is too much?"
~ Poisoned Heart, Alexandra Kessler.

OLIVIA – OCEAN CITY

DON'T YOU THINK BALLOONS ARE A BIT MUCH?"
Ella asks as she picks up a bowl of chips.

"Yeah, I kinda agree; it looks like we're throwing a baby shower." Maia looks around at the decorations.

"What?" I shrug. "No, no, it's perfect! Besides, I like decorating and wasting time."

Before Ella or Maia can answer, we hear the sound of people bickering outside.

"I said, I can do it!" My Brandon's voice echoes into the apartment, sounding upset.

"Here, just take it, and open it yourself since you want to do it so fucking badly," someone yells back.

Weird, it sounds like Sam. I don't think we've ever heard him scream like that. We all look at each other, confusion plastered on our faces.

"Should we open the door?" I ask very slowly as I frown.

"Nah, I want to see what happens next," Ella mumbles while munching on the snacks. Noah nods, sticking to her like glue.

"Oh, shut the fuck up, both of you," we hear Scott snap while opening the door abruptly.

"¡Sorpresa!" We all shout, sounding more like a question.

The boys look more shocked than ever, so I guess we nailed it with the surprise. Sam's face falls; he looks tired and overwhelmed. Brandon's giving him side glances, and Scott seems over it while Layla and Drew try to ease the situation. *What the hell is going on?*

"What?! Oh, my God, this is so cool!" Layla fake-squeals while trying to lighten the mood.

"Yeah! We wanted you to have a little welcome party so you don't forget how fun we are..." I try to sport a wide smile to alleviate the tension.

"Thank you, this is amazing! Truly." Layla comes in and hugs all of us.

"Okay, okay, my turn." Brandon pushes past everyone, pulling me in and kissing me.

"Welcome back, baby," I whisper against his lips. "I missed you, so much."

He groans into the kiss, pulling me closer. "Not more than I did, baby."

Ugh, why did I think a surprise party would be a good idea? I want him all to myself now.

"Hey, let's play a game!" Layla screams, startling everyone and interrupting our moment.

"At least she's here to save the day." Maia lets out a dry laugh as she walks past us.

"Barely," Scott whispers as we sit in the living room.

As we take our places, I can't help but cling to Brandon's arm, wanting to be as close as possible after our time apart.

"Okay, I have a fun game we can play." Layla smiles, seeming overly excited.

"Here comes Layla and her amazing ideas," Drew mumbles against his drink.

"You know it, okay? It's called *deep or drink*, very self-explanatory." She takes a little box full of strips with what I assume are questions. "So, I read the paper, and if you don't want to answer or do what it says, you drink. And it's the same question for everyone."

Where the heck did she even get that from? She never ceases to surprise me.

"Yay, this is going to be a fun night!" Layla cheers as no one objects and pulls out a paper. "Okay, so, first question: What has been your longest relationship, and why did you break up?"

"For me, it would be Anna. We fell out of love, and she cheated on me," Brandon speaks first, and I tense up from hearing her name.

The room falls quiet as we all look at Maia, who's next in the circle.

"Oh, right." She clears her throat. "Umm, it only lasted a few months, and it was back in high school. His name's Jake, he was my first boyfriend. I found out he only dated me because of a dare to see how far I'd let him go, and I ended it before it went anywhere serious."

"Damn, Maia," Scott sputters, trying not to choke on his beer.

"What? It's a hell of a fun story to tell now." Maia laughs it out. "It hurt at the moment, but I don't think it lasted more than a few months."

"Well, he was a total jerk." Layla points to her with the paper in hand. *Trust me, his car paid the price with my keys.*

The room gets quiet again, and I take that as a sign to tell my story. "Connor. He cheated on me, and we all know he is a grade-A ass. Let's hope the justice system does its job."

"More than that," Brandon scoffs and pulls me closer.

We all look at Scott as I ask, "Who's next," but he stays quiet.

"Hello?" I gesture to him.

"Nah, I can't answer because I haven't been in a long relationship." He grabs the wine bottle after emptying his beer and drinking it straight out.

Wow, very classy. We all exchange a few questioning glances, but we ignore it.

"Okay, my turn." Drew sits straighter. "For me, it was Madeline. Or was it Kate? No, no, umm, I think it might've been Nicole. Or was it Cole?"

"Wait, what?" We all look at him with wide eyes.

"I'll get back to you on that." He winks at us, and we laugh.

"Her name is Sarah. She's a girl I met surfing while on vacation in Australia, but it ended as soon as I left." Sam speaks up right after, as if he needs to get it out now, a sad look on his face.

"Wow, very movie-like, points for having a main character vibe, Sam." I try to cheer him up. But it's a failed attempt to get rid of his bad mood.

"Yeah, but I don't get the girl by the end of it." He ignores my glance as he says it.

The rest of the game passes pretty quickly. Most of us don't answer the questions, so we get pretty drunk, laughing at everything and anything. Noah and Ella even leave for a midnight stroll to get ice cream. I don't know why because it's cold out, but whatever.

We forget the game's actual rules, so we just do it about random crap, more of a dare than a *deep or drink*.

"Next dare, everyone here must flash to the entire room," Layla reads out another paper. "Uff, so risqué!"

Everyone starts drinking, but Maia stands up. "So, apparently, all you rock stars are pussies," she states confidently. *You go, girl.* As she's about to pull up her shirt, Scott grabs her and throws her over his shoulder.

"Yeah, we didn't want to see that anyway," he mocks her and chuckles.

"Sure, right, you can put me down now." Her shirt starts to ride up a little, and we all laugh at them. "Scott, put me down."

"Chill, tigress," he says as he sets her on the kitchen counter. "That's enough alcohol for you, don't you think?"

"Says the guy with the whole wine bottle in his hand. I'm not a lightweight. I was just having a little fun."

"Sure you were."

"Yes, I was. You should try it sometime," she says with her usual sarcasm, jumping off. "Practice what you preach, superstar."

"Hey, the game?" Layla calls them over. "Next question." She opens the paper. "Ooh, this one's spicy. How many times have you said *I love you* and truly meant it to a romantic partner?"

And everyone stays quiet.

"Well, I said it once in a relationship and meant it. But you already know how it ended," I speak up first.

"I never did," Brandon says next. "And don't expect me to say it anytime soon, by the way." He turns to me, no hint of a joke in his voice.

"Excuse me?" I hiss at him.

"Yeah, it's kinda hard for me. Saying it, I mean." He shrugs like it isn't a big deal to him.

"What?" *Is Brandon trying to dig his own grave?*

"Dude, it might be different this time. Olivia's not Anna," Scott tries to reason with him.

"It all looks like true love to me," Layla shouts and laughs awkwardly.

"Bro, this sounds like you're playing her. I thought you were joking when you said that at the after-party," Drew blurts out and immediately covers his mouth.

Huh? I look at Maia.

"Come on, I'm not, and she knows that. I just mean that it's hard for me to say it if I don't feel it for sure," Brandon says.

I turn sideways, staring at him with a very prominent frown, but he straight up ignores it.

"Okay, next!" Layla shouts again, like she's trying to cool everyone down by interrupting him.

"Wait, what? What after-party?" I ask, but no one answers.

"Scott, your turn!" Layla yells.

"Huh?" Scott raises his head as if he is lost in thought.

"What the hell is going on?" I ask Brandon directly, but he ignores me and sips his beer.

"So, Scott. Have you ever said I love you and meant it?" Layla interrupts again.

"Stop avoiding my question, Brandon, and fucking look at me," I whisper-yell at him.

"It's nothing, okay? Just drop it," he whispers back but still won't look at me.

"*No,* I will not just 'drop it.' Why can't you tell me what's going on? What's Drew talking about?"

"Well, if you didn't realize from all the stupid-ass examples everyone just gave... Love seems like the shittiest bullshit ever, doesn't it?" We all turn our attention to Scott.

"No, no, that doesn't mean it's not real. Don't be like that because of what we're saying," Drew scolds him.

"Yeah, dude, what the fuck. It's not bullshit." Brandon ignores my question, again, and talks to Scott now.

"You're one to talk," Sam finally snaps and raises his voice at my boyfriend. *Shit, what else are we missing? What happened in New York?*

"Honestly, if you've never even said it, then don't even try to give him advice on it." I cross my arms in front of my chest, looking at Brandon.

"That's not what I meant, Olivia," Brandon argues in a slightly higher pitch.

"Oh? Or because you won't mean it, huh?" I'm not backing down until he explains.

"Hey, guys, just stop, please," Layla pleads in a shaky voice.

"Yeah, and what about you, who hasn't had a stable relationship and keeps coming back to her toxic ex?" Scott fires back at Layla. *Excuse you?*

"Scott." Sam gives him a warning look.

"What now, Sam? Do you want me to start with you because I think if we talk about love, you know more than anyone here, right?" He looks between Sam and me.

"For once, guys, stop with this lame-ass bullshit!" Scott storms out to the balcony. Sam gets up without saying another word, walking down the hallway and slamming the door to his room.

"I've had enough of this bullshit! How can you tell me this is nothing?! Scott's gone batshit, Sam looks miserable, and Layla's on her last straw. I am not leaving this apartment until you tell me what's going on!" Anger takes over logic as I yell at Brandon. I cannot take any more of this secrecy; it's too much.

"We're not doing this here." He grabs my hand, pulling me behind him and into his room. I sit on the edge of his bed as he shuts his door.

He stands in front of me, looking between the spot next to me and his desk chair. Deciding on the latter, he sits in silence. *Is he waiting for me to talk first or...*

"Well?"

"Look, it's stupid, okay? And I was going to tell you,

but then you had this whole party prepared and caught us by surprise. I was going to tell you tomorrow, I swear," he says all in one breath. I nod for him to continue, still waiting for an actual explanation from him.

"We went to Oscar's place a couple of times for these parties after recordings, meetings, or interviews. It's not that big of a deal."

"But if it wasn't a big deal, then why didn't you tell me? We talked almost every day, and there were plenty of times when you could've said something."

"I know, I know, baby, and I'm sorry." He leans over in the chair.

"Do you not trust me?"

"Of course I do—"

"Then what are you not telling me? Because a stupid party is just that; it doesn't mean anything. Why would everyone react that way about a party?"

He looks down, avoiding my gaze as I question him. Without looking up, he says, "Because these parties included groupies. And lots of alcohol."

"Oh," I breathe out.

"Hey, nothing happened, Ollie. I swear." He looks up and tries to reach for me, but I move away.

"Then why did you hide it from me?"

"I didn't—"

"Yes, Brandon, you did! You went out of your way to not tell me shit during your trip, even though you had endless chances to do so. And what about out there at your surprise party? Are you telling me that was your best way of trying to explain anything? You tried to shut everyone up!"

"Come on, that was in no way the time to have that conversation. We're all drunk and mad and tired of yelling at each other."

"Don't come to me with those lame-ass excuses." I stand up. "Yes, I admit it was not the best time to do it, but I was not the one to bring it up; the guys did. That just makes you seem even shadier for hiding it."

He stands up, too, towering over me. "It was a stupid party! And it's nothing. You're being ridiculous right now."

"So you're insulting me now? Nice move, Brandon." My breathing gets heavier, and my body feels like it's on fire.

"That's not—fuck." He brushes his hand through his hair, letting out a shaky breath. "You know that's not what I mean."

"No, I don't know what you mean. Like I didn't know what you meant with your answer to Layla's question."

"And, of course, you go there!" He laughs sarcastically.

"Well, you're the one warning me about *not loving me anytime soon.* How'd you think I would react?"

"You can't force feelings, Olivia. All I was trying to say is that the whole Anna thing damaged me, and it's not easy for me to say *I love you.* It doesn't mean I don't have feelings for you; I do. I just don't love you *yet.*" He turns to look at me.

"Hey, no, don't cry. Come here." He sits on his bed and pulls me with him. "I'm sorry, baby. I should've told you about the party sooner. And we should've had the love conversation at a better time."

He brushes my hair as I lay on his chest, soaking his shirt. "You're the best thing that's ever happened to me, Ollie. I don't want to ruin it by lying or rushing our feelings."

"It's okay, I understand." I sniff, calming down a little. "I don't want to lose you either."

"Hey, look at me." He tips my head up to face him. "You're not losing me; this can only make us stronger moving forward. I'm here, and I'll always be here."

He wipes the tears off my face and presses our foreheads together. He brushes his nose with mine, making me chuckle.

"I hate it when you do that." I laugh.

"No, you don't." He does it again.

"Stooop!" I try to get away by turning my head. He pushes me back, holding my face and tickling my nose with his.

"Never," he whispers. After a while, he passes from brushing our noses to leaving kisses all over my face, ending on my mouth. "I missed you," he mutters against my lips. "So much, baby."

He deepens the kiss, entangling one of his hands in my hair while the other trails down my sides, stopping at my hips. It may be the alcohol in our systems, but this kiss is heating up quicker than any other.

Our hands roam over each other's bodies, not wanting to be apart any longer. His hands slip under my shirt, caressing my stomach on his way to my chest, and my breathing quickens. I slip my hand under his shirt, scratching his back in an attempt to pull him closer.

"Can I take it off?" he whispers in my ear, his breath shaky and hot on my skin.

He continues down my neck, leaving a wet trail of kisses. I nod *yes*. He gets rid of our clothes and throws them on the floor. He pauses as he hovers over me, my chest heaving from my fast breathing.

"Have I told you that you're beautiful?" Again, I just nod.

He suddenly gets off the bed and walks toward his door, locking it. He comes back, sitting against his headboard and pulling me onto his lap. He kisses me like his life depended on it. Our bodies are so close together that you couldn't slip a paper between us. His hands travel down my body, landing on my hips to hold me even closer.

"If this is how every fight ends, then maybe I should make

you mad more often." He laughs against my neck as he shivers.

"Oh, baby, this is the alcohol talking. Next time"—I grab his face, making him look me in the eyes—"you won't be so lucky."

Chapter Fourteen

"Every morning like the last, a pair of brown eyes by my side."
~ My Confession, Alexandra Kessler.

OLIVIA – OCEAN CITY

THE SUN WAKES ME UP AS IT HITS MY FACE, and I look up from Brandon's chest, squinting. *We left the blinds open.*

I carefully get up to close them so the light doesn't wake him up. As I stand at the window, the unbelievable view of the marina stops me: how the sun reflects on the crystal water and the waves crash on the rocks, the calming sound of the ocean.

I turn around when I hear some shifting behind me, finding Brandon stretching as he wakes up.

"Why did you leave the bed, baby? Come back." He pats the spot next to him.

"Sorry, I didn't want to wake you," I say, leaning on the wall.

His eyes trail me up and down, a small smile forming on his lips. "What?" I look down at myself.

"Nothing, just that my dress shirt looks much better on you than on me." He crosses his arms behind his head.

"Really?" I say in a low voice.

"Of course, you should keep it."

I take a deep breath, savoring this moment of Brandon looking at me as if I am his world. *And he's mine too.*

"Have I told you that you're beautiful?" he mutters against my hair as I lay on top of him, his arms around me.

"Every day." I smile and look at him. "I'll make coffee."

"Okay." He presses a kiss on my forehead. I get halfway through the room when his voice pulls me back. "Aren't you wearing some shorts or something? You do know that other people live here, right? And that they're men."

Fuck, I forgot about them. I nod, throw on my shorts from last night, and walk out. Luckily, no one else is awake, or at least not in the kitchen.

I take the mugs from the cupboard and turn on the coffee maker. I left my phone, so now I have to wait in silence, all alone with my thoughts. That's a dangerous game to play. Especially when I still have so many unanswered questions of last night.

Why would Sam go off like that? What happened between him and Brandon on the trip? And why was Layla trying so hard to veer the conversation away?

"*Buenos días.* Can you make me one too?" Maia's groggy morning voice startles me.

"Shit, warn me first, won't you?" I turn around and take in her appearance: oversized shirt, socks, and messy hair. "Want to tell me what happened first? I know you like big shirts, but I know for a fact you do not own that one."

"I did say good morning first," her lips twitch as she tried not to smirk. "And nothing happened, so shut up. I didn't have anything to sleep in, so Scott gave me a shirt. But what happened with you and Brandon? From the looks of it, you definitely made up." She nods to the shirt. *So she's really not going to tell me, huh?*

"We went into his room, and yeah, we kept fighting, but talked it through. There's still some shit I know he's hiding from me, and my drunk self couldn't remember what to ask either. I ended up crying, and he comforted me."

"And nothing else happened..." She asks sarcastically, clear evidence that she's now awake.

"Well, we kissed and made up," I whisper, and she raises an eyebrow. "And other things." My cheeks must be tomato-red.

"Ooh," she says in a gossipy tone. "You little hoe."

"Oh, stop it." I slap her arm, laughing at the stupid comment. "We didn't, you know..."

"Yeah, but you're still a hoe." She shrugs.

Before I even get to answer, the machine dings.

"Coffee's ready." Maia gives me her classic, smug smile.

"Here, baby." I wake him up again, setting his mug on the bedside table.

He mumbles something incoherent as he sits up, probably a *thank you*. I walk around to the other side, sitting next to him with my legs on top of his.

He hums in approval as he sips his coffee. "You always make it how I like it. You should sleep here every day."

"That's just your excuse to get me in bed with you." I nudge his arm and smile.

"Is that a crime? Wanting to spend time with my girlfriend?"

"Why are you always this cheesy?" I rest my head on his shoulder, smiling.

"Only for you." He places his head on top of mine.

And we stay like that, entangled with one another as we finish our coffees in silence, enjoying each other's company.

"I'm sorry, Ollie."

"About what?" I ask, taken by surprise.

"Last night, the way I reacted wasn't the best. I hurt you, and I promise it won't happen again." He grabs my hand and kisses it.

"It's okay. We were all drunk, and I didn't control my

emotions either." I play with his fingers. "But can I ask you something else?"

"Go for it."

"What happened with Sam? Why was he being so rude and standoffish?"

He takes his time to answer, as if he didn't expect the question. The silence becomes deafening as I wait for him to say anything. The sounds of the waves and the birds outside the window are now annoying.

"He was being defensive of you back in New York because I never told you about the parties. And I reacted negatively when they were telling me how I was in love with you. And, you know, saying it's something I struggle with, so I felt pressured by them and exploded on Sam."

"But why would he get so defensive about me? It makes no sense to me."

"Because you're good friends. You went to school together. He knows you and some of the shit you've been through. He doesn't want to see you get hurt, so he reacted how he thought best." He sighs in defeat. "Or maybe he has some sort of territorial position over you because of it." His grip on my hand tightens.

"No...no, I don't think so."

But something still feels off; something doesn't add up. *Why would Scott stare him down like that? And why would he look between us so much?*

"I mean, he's been acting very weird lately. But that might be something with his parents, his job, or even with an ex. I don't know. Should I talk to him?" I release a breath.

"Give him time, babe. Whatever it is, it's been very stressful for him. And it's all very recent." He rubs my arm. "He'll talk to you when he feels ready."

"Fine," I groan, throwing my head back. "I'll wait, or whatever."

"Or whatever." He copies my tone.

"Are you mocking me?" I face him.

"So what if I am?" He puts his empty mug on the table, and I do the same.

"Then you'll regret it!"

"Then you'll regret it!" he mocks me again.

"That's it." I jump on him and begin my assault.

His loud laugh echoes throughout the room, maybe even the house. I tickle his sides, his stomach, his neck, all over. His hands come to my waist, and I prepare myself for him to flip us. But much to my surprise, he tickles me instead. We laugh and try to catch our breath.

"Okay, okay, I surrender." I hold my hands up, but he continues.

"No, I'll stop when I want to." He flips us, so now I'm trapped underneath him. "And I don't want to."

He takes both of my hands in one of his, holding them captive above my head. And with his free one, he continues his assault, making me laugh as never before. He also spreads kisses all over my face and neck, tickling me with his breath as he laughs too.

I gasp as his kiss on my neck is no longer a peck, and he stops tickling. His hand lies on my stomach, spreading apart as it slides up toward my chest. He continues his way up, tipping my chin up with his nose.

"You look so beautiful right now, with that wild look in your eyes, your flushed cheeks. I can't believe you're mine." He says before he kisses me.

It's fire and passion, burning with desire. He holds me there while we move as if I'll leave when he lets me go. He releases my hands, placing his on my hips to pull me closer. I clasp mine behind his head, entangling them in his hair. This seems to encourage him further, and he releases a soft moan.

Sure of where this is going, I start unbuttoning his shirt that I'm wearing. But his hands stop me after releasing the first button, and I give him a questioning look. *Maybe I was wrong.*

"No, leave it on. I like it when you wear my clothes." He moves to my ear. "Want to find out what it does to me?"

And with that, my self-control goes out the window.

*"I've never been afraid of losing someone as much as
I'm of losing you." ~ Mirror, Alexandra Kessler.*

OLIVIA – OCEAN CITY

PULLING ONE OF BRANDON'S SHIRTS OVER MY HEAD,
I walk to the kitchen and see Maia standing still, staring at nothing.

"Umm, good morning." No response. "Maia... hello? *Buenos días.*" I wave in her face. *What's going on with her?*

"Huh?" She comes back to reality. "Oh, sorry, good morning. There's coffee on the stove."

"Aww, thanks." I hug her but feel her drift off again. "Are you okay?" I ask while filling up our mugs.

"Yeah, yeah, I'm fine. Just tired," she dismisses me while grabbing hers.

Why won't she tell me what's wrong? Is it because the band is coming back today from another week in New York, and all we did was work? Well, all she did...

"So, what are today's plans?" Ella startles us as she walks into the kitchen. *What the heck? She never wakes up this early.*

"The world must be ending today," Maia mumbles and blinks a couple of times.

"Are you okay?" I touch her forehead to check if she has a fever, and she pushes my hand away.

"Can I not want one productive day?" she says defensively as Maia and I give her the same look: head to the side and squinting our eyes.

"Bitch, it's Saturday. You never do anything on Saturdays," I scoff while eyeing her up and down.

"Okay, okay, fine. I fell asleep earlier than usual because I was tired from doing my stupid homework."

"See, that makes more sense," Maia says.

"Ha-ha." Ella rolls her eyes. "So...the plan?"

"Well, if you need to know. We could do brunch, have some more coffee, maybe do a little shopping. And..."

I look at both of them, biting my lip and doing a drum roll on the counter for dramatic effect. "I made an appointment to get our tattoos!"

"*Siiii*," Ella screams. "Well, what are we still doing here? Let's go now!"

"Yeah, sure, let's leave in our pajamas: T-shirts and underwear." I gesture over us with my hands.

"Right, let's get ready, and *then* we'll go."

"What are you getting?" Ella asks as we flip through the book of pre-made designs.

"I don't know. I have a couple of ideas saved on my phone; not sure which one to get today." Maia nervously looks through the pictures.

I skip many pages, not interested in the big and showy ones or the wild animals. *No. No. Too many colors. Wait.* I stop flipping as my eyes land on the cutest colittle heart.

"We should get matching ones." I lift my head and look at them. "What do you think of this one?" I show them the page, pointing to the drawing.

"It's perfect!" Ella gasps and claps.

"Yes! And you know where we should get it?" Maia smiles like the Cheshire Cat. "On our fingers," we say at the same time.

"That's a great choice, ladies." Our tattoo artist, Camila, comes up to us from behind the counter. "Who's first?" She looks between the three of us.

"Me. It's going to hurt anyway, right?" Ella raises a hand as she volunteers.

Maia and I move to the couches in the waiting area as Camila takes her to the back. Silence takes over us as we sit down. It's like we don't know how to talk to each other since that morning last week at the guys' place.

"Are we not—" "So, listen—" We start talking at the same time, and she nods to let me know I can go first.

"I know something's going on. You don't have to tell me if you don't want to, but I'm here if, or whenever, you want to talk."

We sit in silence again, but this time it's not uncomfortable. It's not deafening, and I can feel her taking in my words. Maybe all she needs is for me to let her know I'm here.

"It's nothing, Ollie," she breaks the silence with a sigh.

Before I can say anything else, Ella comes back with Camila, showing us her finger. *That was quick...I guess it really was that small.*

"Guys, look! Isn't it pretty?" Her skin turned pink from the needle, but the bright red heart inked on her finger stands out more.

"I love it! Red suits you. Can I go next?"

Camila nods. "Perfect! Maia, you can come with us too, and I'll do yours right after."

She looks at me and then back at her. "Sure, let's do it."

"See you back here. It's going to hurt like hell!" Ella screams back as we walk through the curtains and into the back rooms.

I sit on the leather chair with my hand on the armrest as she disinfects my finger. What I love most about this place is how clean they are. Camila takes everything directly from the box: brand-new instruments and ink.

She takes the little piece of paper with the drawing, the same size as Ella's, and places it on the side of my index finger. "Is this good?"

"Yes, perfect! Can you do mine in black?" I smile as I see it. She nods and starts preparing the ink on her little side table.

"Ready?" I nod, waiting for the needle, and then…it feels like a million bees are pricking my finger. *Jesus, wait for me!*

"You know, it won't disappear if you stop staring at it," Ella whispers to me, though she's also doing the same thing.

"I know, I know. But they're just so cute!" I sigh in satisfaction and happiness. "I love that we finally did this."

We open our cameras. "Come on, let's take some pictures."

A whole thirty-minute photoshoot later, we arrive at the boys' apartment. Brandon and I barely spoke this week with them in the recording studio every day and us doing more photoshoots for the online store.

We ring the doorbell, and a couple of seconds later, Noah opens the door. "Hey, girls, what's up? We didn't know you were coming over!"

Ella looks at her phone, appearing confused. "Oh! Sorry baby, I thought I hit send…surprise!"

Her boyfriend playfully rolls his eyes, already used to her forgetfulness. "It's okay. Come on in." He takes a step back to let us through.

I spot Brandon at the kitchen counter, his back to us as he

sits on the stool. As I walk closer, I can see his earphones, which is why he didn't notice us coming in.

"Guess who?" I whisper in his ear after taking them off, startling him.

Whatever he's drinking spills all over the table. I hope it's just water. And I know I'm supposed to feel guilty, but this is too funny; I can't stop laughing.

"Shit! What the—" He turns around and stops himself when he sees me. "Oh, of course, it's you!" I'm bent over the stool, still laughing at him.

"Come on, baby, it's not that funny." He tries to stay mad, but I can hear him stifle his laughter. I look up and find him staring, a glimmer in his eyes. "I missed you."

This makes me stop laughing. And now I stand there with a smile on my lips, looking back at my beautiful man.

"I missed you too." I stand between his legs as he turns around to reach for me. "How was your week? Did you finish recording the album?"

"Almost there. We're still working on the first half of. We want to make sure that whatever we do is perfect before moving on with the second part."

"Well, it's still progress, right?" I give him a peck on the lips. "And I'm sure that everything will come out as amazing as you are baby."

He gives me a comforting smile before holding my face and pulling me in for a kiss. A lovely and tender kiss that makes my whole world stop.

"Can you guys *be* any cornier?" Maia groans as she watches us from the couch in the living room.

Now that I take a closer look around, I notice that neither Scott nor Sam are here. Maia gets what I'm doing as we make eye contact, and she shrugs in response.

I turn to Brandon again. "Where are the others?"

"In their rooms, I guess." He shrugs too. "They're tired from the trip." Right, they drove back early today.

"Aww, you guys worried about me?" *Speaking of one of the devils…*Scott walks into the kitchen. "Being a star is exhausting, you know? I need my beauty sleep." *I think we're getting used to his dramatics by now.*

"Then you should go back, don't think you slept enough." Maia gives him a smug look. But something else flashes in her eyes for a split second before going back to the smugness. *Huh, what's that aout?*

"Well, we drove for five hours. What's your excuse?" Scott fights back, but I notice him holding back a smile.

"I guess seeing you has that effect on me…" She leans back on the couch. *What is going on?*

"Hey, guys, what's up?" Sam comes in, saving these two from killing each other.

He looks at me for a brief second and nods, then moves to the living room. Brandon pulls me closer to him, hugging me from behind and kissing my cheek.

"Well, we have a surprise for you all," I announce with a smile since no one is speaking.

"What did you do?" Scott asks slowly.

"Well…" Maia, Ella, and I look at each other. Then we put our fingers up, and the room gets quiet. We look at each other, seemingly confused by the silence. *Well, this is not going like we thought it would.*

"Umm, what the fuck?" Noah says a little too loud. We turn to him, an excited look on his face. "When did you get these? They look amazing, I love them!"

Damn, for a second there, I thought he was mad.

"Really?" Ella turns to him, sounding like a kid. "Today. We just came here from the parlor. That's why our fingers are still red."

"You got a heart?" Scott scoffs as he crosses his arms. "I'm surprised Maia inked something so cheesy. I pictured something different on you. Well, at least it's in blue."

"And what would you suggest I get? Since you think about me getting tattoos so often, you must have some ideas." She smirks at him and raises her eyebrows.

"What—no, don't flatter yourself. You're not on my mind that often," Scott argues back, but widens his eyes. "Or ever."

"Whatever you say, big boy." Maia smiles proudly.

Seriously, what in the world is going on here?

"I think what Scott's trying to say is that they look very nice, and it's cool that you got them together," Sam intervenes, per usual, and smiles at all of us.

"Sure, let's go with that." Scott rolls his eyes.

As they continue their conversation in the living room and I tune them out, I realize Brandon's been quiet.

"Baby." I turn to face him. "What do you think? Do you like it?" I put my finger up.

He takes a moment to answer. "It's nice. And it's black; it fits you," he says with the driest tone I've ever heard from him.

"That's all?"

"What else did you want me to say?" He frowns at me.

"I don't know. That you liked it and it's pretty. Or that it looks cute on me. I don't know, you tell me." I raise my voice a little, catching the group's attention.

"Ollie, I said it's nice. I don't know what else to tell you," he says in a bitter tone while appearing calm.

"Yeah, but that's *all* you said." I try not to roll my eyes.

"Fine, I don't like tattoos. Is that what you wanted to hear? I don't like them, so all I can get myself to say is *fine*. Sorry if that offends you," he practically barks at me, throwing his hands up.

"What?" I say.

Sam quietly walks past us into the kitchen, grabs a couple of six-packs, and sets them down on the living room table. *Well, someone had to pull out the alcohol.*

"Yeah, Brandon despises tattoos. He doesn't have a single one and always gives me shit for mine," Scott answers and grabs a beer from Sam.

"Oh, why didn't you tell me that?" I look back at Brandon.

"We hadn't talked about it, and you never asked."

"How was I supposed to know I needed to ask?" I scoff a laugh, feeling everyone's tension from behind me.

"We've never talked about tattoos!" He releases an exasperated breath, leaning back.

"You do know this is not my first tattoo, right?"

"Wh—what? Since when?" He blinks a few times.

"Yes, I have a poppy flower behind my ear. It's been there since before we met."

"Can I see?" He pushes my hair back to see my inked skin. He traces the flower with his index finger, covering my body with goosebumps. "How have I never seen this?"

"You never asked," I repeat his words back to him. "And I guess I haven't worn ponytails around you." *Is it just me, or have we been fighting a lot recently? It's happening like every time we see each other now.*

He lets go of my hair, and now we're facing each other again. I stare into his eyes, many emotions dancing around in them. *But what is he thinking?*

"When did you get it?" he whispers, holding my hand.

"About a year ago or so."

"Why? What does it mean?"

"It's about my dad. Ever since my mom was pregnant with

me, he's sung me a song by Juan Luis Guerra called 'Amapola.' It means poppies in Spanish."

"Oh," he breathes out. His expression changes in a matter of seconds. "Is he–?"

"Oh, no. No, no, he's fine. This is just something meaningful between us, and I decided to tattoo it. But I should call him...we haven't talked in a while."

He stays quiet now. *Maybe too quiet and for a little too long.* My mind starts going a mile a minute, getting anxious from not knowing what he's thinking. *Does he like it, or does he not? Is he disappointed? What is it?!*

"Listen, I don't like tattoos, just like I don't do drugs. I believe each body is a temple, and you should love it as it is. But it's your decision, and I can't do anything about it," he explains in a calm tone.

I open my mouth to reply, but he continues.

"It's pretty, though. I like it on you." He moves closer to my ear. "A little sexy too. I could kiss it all day," he whispers, sending chills down to my toes.

"Brandon, there are other people here," I whisper back.

"I don't care." He kisses my cheek.

"You're lucky you're his girlfriend. I wish that all I needed to do was kiss him to get out of his speeches," Scott complains. "Now, can you stop it with the corniness? It's starting to get annoying and cheesy."

"Starting to?" Maia mumbles under her breath.

"Ha-ha, very funny." I stick my tongue out at them.

"One last, quick question. Did none of you think that getting matching tattoos was a bad idea?" Brandon asks as we sit on the couch.

"Oh no, we all did. We just decided to do it anyway," Maia answers with a shrug. Ella and I nod along, agreeing with her.

"That might be the dumbest thing I've ever heard." Scott releases a dry laugh.

"Don't worry, I've said much worse." Maia taps his knees.

"That's what I'm worried about, darling," he says with a slightly flirty tone.

"Aww, so nice of you to worry about me. My therapist warned me about people like you," she retorts.

Is no one else seeing what I'm seeing? These two are one step away from kissing, and we're all just quietly standing by?

"You see a therapist, huh? Didn't know you had problems." Scott props his elbows up on his knees.

"And they all come from nightmares about you." She copies his pose.

"Now you're flattering me. I didn't know you dreamed about me." He leans back on the chair, legs spread, and chugs his beer straight from the can.

"There has to be something wrong with you." Maia opens her bottle, shaking her head.

"Many things; I'm afraid you'll have to be a little more specific..." He takes the shades hanging on his shirt and puts them on.

"Well, first, you're wearing sunglasses indoors. That seems wrong to me."

Scott leans forward, staring Maia down. He's about to say something that I assume will be offensive, but Brandon stops them from going at it.

"How about a game of poker, huh? And let's spice it up a bit, make it drunk poker."

I raise my hand, asking for a turn to talk. Brandon rolls his eyes as he does when I do this and nods. "What makes it drunk, how does that work?"

"Right, the rules. First: anytime someone folds or loses

a hand, you drink. And to make it extra spicy, each card has a rule. If it's an ace of spades, everyone takes a drink. With a deuce—a pair of twos—the winner makes someone else drink." Brandon uses the cards as clear examples.

"If it's a split pot, all players involved must finish whatever's in their cups. Winning with a bluff or a high card, everyone takes a sip except for the winner. If it's a queen, girls drink, and if it's a king, boys drink. When a player goes all in, we all drink. And the last rule, if you win with pocket aces, everyone finishes their drink."

Brandon looks around the room as he's done explaining, and we all stare back. "Everyone got it?"

"Yeah, sure, what could go wrong with a little game of drunk poker?" I smile as I grab my cards to see what I have. *Easy, peasy, right?*

"Who said playing this game was a good idea?" Sam complains, staring at the broken wine bottle, liquid, and glass all over the floor.

"This guy"—hiccup—"over here"—hiccup. "Remind me not to"—hiccup—"trust him"—hiccup—"again." *Shit, I'm on my hiccup-drunk stage. How much have I had to drink?*

"Well…" he trails off. "No more alcohol for you, babe." He takes the glass from my hand.

"Oh, come on, it's not my fault we ran out of beer"—hiccup—"It was those stupid rules, and we *had* to spring for the wine"—hiccup—"So, technically, it's on you for getting me drunk and breaking the bottle." I give him my best persuasive smile, trying to stop my hiccups.

"Fine, I'll take the drunk part, but I was not the one who

tipped the wine over." He boops my forehead.

I lose my balance, enough to fall back onto the couch. "Okay...okay...sorry for being messy too," I drawl, my tongue twisting with each word.

"My clumsy girl." He pulls me up to him, puts an arm around me, and kisses me on the head. "Tripping over everything since the day we met."

I cuddle against him, looking into his eyes. "Give me some credit. I've been clumsy all my life." I can hear Maia and Ella in the background making fake gagging noises.

"I don't doubt that." He laughs against my hair. "I'm glad you're here; it was a sweet surprise after a very stressful week."

"Really?" I say in a low voice.

"Really," he whispers back.

"You promise?"

He grabs my face, tilting my head back and looking into my eyes. "I promise."

"Aren't you scared to make promises?" I whisper.

"No. As I've told you before, I'm not afraid. You already got me hooked." Before I can answer, he pulls me in, taking my lips in his.

In this moment, I realize this man right here makes me feel like the luckiest woman alive. And there's nothing else I need but him, right this moment.

Chapter Fifteen

"We had it all, but for you, I wasn't enough."
~ Sad Love Song, Alexandra Kessler.

OLIVIA – OCEAN CITY

THE MICROWAVE BEEPS, letting me know the popcorn's ready. I pour it into our movie theater-type bowl, set it on the table, and throw myself on the couch. I look out the balcony's doors as the sun sets on the horizon, rays reflecting through the window.

Instead of bringing me peace as it usually does, it gets me thinking about how painfully slow this day has been. Scratch that, this whole week was draining. And for no reason. I have a great job—which I do not even consider a job—a perfect support group, and a boyfriend.

Yes, we may not see each other as often due to the band recording in New York. And he did stay this past week, even though they leave again tomorrow.

Speaking of Brandon...how is he not here yet? Did he forget about our date night? Was he scared off by the fact that we have my apartment all to ourselves?

I jump off the couch as my loud doorbell rings in the kitchen. I walk across the wooden floor as I cross my living room to open the door.

"Hey, babe," Brandon says as he gives me a peck.

"Hi." I kiss him back. "What's that?" I ask while looking down at his hands.

"Ah, this? Well, it wouldn't be a proper date without the

finest wine and meal for my lady," he replies in a fake accent.

"Wine and pizza?" I mock his tone.

"The best of the best." He kisses my cheek and walks past me as I invite him in.

We set everything up next to the popcorn and sit back on the couch.

"Which movie?" I ask him.

"Should we clock in how long it takes you to choose?" He pretends to be serious, and I push his arm playfully. "We can even try and break a new world record!"

"Brandon, stop!" I laugh, pushing his arm again. "Come on, help me out here."

"Okay, okay," he surrenders. "I don't know. Let's pick something at random."

"Fine, give me a second." I pull out my phone and search for a movie generator.

"*A Beautiful Mind*..." he reads out loud. "Nice pick; I've been wanting to see that one."

I get up from the couch to put on the movie and turn the lights off. I sit back down, and we get started on the food and drinks as the opening credits roll through.

Half an hour goes by, and I can still feel the pressure from earlier, the same thought running around in my head. Adding to that tension is the massive elephant in the room.

Something is wrong between us. Neither of us wants to acknowledge it, and avoiding every situation for fear of confrontation only leads to more pain. I value our relationship too much not to speak up.

"Hey, baby?" I speak up. He doesn't reply right away, so I nudge his arm.

"Huh? What's wrong? Don't you like the movie?" He looks at me, a concerned look in his eyes. *What if this is really nothing and I'm just being stupid?*

"It's nothing, never mind." I kiss him and turn my attention back to the movie.

After it ends, the feeling is still there. I couldn't even tell you what it was about; that's how distracting these thoughts are.

I tap my fingers on my leg as I grow anxious. Only seconds have passed since the credits rolled in, but this silence is killing me. *How can he sit there and not notice this tension?*

That's it, I can't take it anymore. "So, listen," I start.

"Yeah?" He looks at me as he grabs my hand.

"What happened to you that day when we showed everyone the tattoos?"

He throws his head back as he breathes out and groans. "Here we go again!"

Every time he reacts this way, he makes me feel like I'm an annoying little girl.

"No, come on. I'm serious."

"What's more to know? I told you this already. I don't like them. That's it," he responds in an exasperated tone.

"You say this to me, but Scott has them all over his body, and you don't say shit to him." I try not to snap at him.

"That's different. He's my friend, not my girlfriend. And I gave up on giving him shit," he says like it's the obvious answer.

"What the hell, Brandon?" I let out a frustrated groan. "But you still ride a bike, don't you?"

"And since when do you use stereotypes to back up your arguments? What happened to you?"

I slide away from him on the couch. "To me? Are you kidding? Brandon, one of the things that made me fall in love with you was how much attention you paid to me. How much you seemed to care. And now you're telling me you never realized I have a fucking tattoo behind my ear?"

"I don't know what kind of perfect human being you expected me to be, Olivia. I can just not notice something that small; it's not that big of a deal."

"Fine, then, but you still complimented me on it. And now you're the total opposite." He stays silent. "Which one is it, huh? I would love to know where all this bullshit is coming from."

"Well, from you making it a big deal. Can't you drop it?" He slaps his hands on his legs.

"No, I will not. I won't do that anymore. I feel a strain in our relationship, and I've seen it for a while now. And, unlike you, I care enough to confront it." I take in a shaky breath.

"And it's been like that ever since the *not saying I love you* shit…" I mumble.

"God, Olivia, what? What strain? We talked about this last week. I thought we were fine." He presses his head into his hands.

"Damn it, Brandon, are you even listening to me?"

"What more do you want?!" He raises his voice, making me move away.

"I want you to be the same guy I fell in love with, the one who paid attention to me. Because lately, I've felt like I'm only your little fling. Always around, loving you, but who you never get too close to."

"That's not true," he says while pointing at me.

"Then why are you making such a conflict out of nothing?"

"I do that? Huh, I sound like a terrible person." He looks offended, his eyes piercing through me.

"Brandon—"

"No, no, Ollie, you're right. I am. But what I don't get is if I'm so terrible, why are you still here?"

"Wow, you're playing the victim card now?"

"No, I'm being honest. And that's what you wanted, right?"

He puts his hands in his pockets and gets up, acting as if nothing he's saying insults me.

I nod as I breathe in and think about my next words before I say them. "Maybe it's better if you leave."

"Of course you want me to go! Because you always need to have the last word, don't you?" He gets up from the couch and storms out of my apartment, slamming the door behind him.

The echo dissipates, leaving me alone in my living room. Me, the deafening silence, and its emptiness. Empty as I could ever be. Why is this even happening? What have I ever done wrong to deserve this? Just as I meet a guy who finally treats me right, who cares enough, and who my friends like.

Why is it that the only guy I love can't open up and have a serious conversation about something that means something to me? Is it me? All I want is to get to know him as profoundly as he knows me. *This is so stupid; this fight is stupid.*

"¿Qué estoy haciendo (what am I doing)?" I say out loud. I need to go, go to him, tell him I'm sorry and that I love him.

"And I know some first loves only last for a while."
~ Sad Love Song, Alexandra Kessler.

BRANDON – OCEAN CITY

I CAN'T BELIEVE THE BULLSHIT SHE JUST PULLED. Telling me that I don't care about her anymore, that she's only a fling. And what's wrong with not liking tattoos? Is that just a stupid excuse to resent me?

I slam the door to her building, the noise echoing through the empty street along with my feet hitting the pavement. *Maybe I should've taken my bike.* Whatever, I need a walk to cool down before going back home and having the guys bombard me with annoying questions. And I don't need any more bullshit tonight.

This is stupid, a ridiculous fight over nothing. So what if I didn't notice her tattoo? It's behind her fucking ear; only a pervert or a stalker would see it.

I'm now walking with bated breath, my thoughts agitating me. *Where even am I?* I don't even notice all the left and right turns, letting my feet guide me. I must be nowhere near our apartment by now.

My legs stop me dead in the tracks as I near a bush by the sidewalk.

"If I had a flower for every time I thought of you since that kiss, I would be as full as that bush!" I come up from behind Ollie as she's standing in front of it, smelling the flowers. Plucking one, I brush her hair back and completely startle her.

"Aye, warn a girl before scaring the crap out of her!" She

swats my arm away and then looks at my hand.

"But I will have the flower because it's very beautiful." She gives me a sheepish look as I place it on her ear.

"Not more than you." I snake my arm around her waist, turning her around and pulling her in.

"Is that the best you have?"

"I'm just starting." I lean down.

"What if I stop you?" she whispers, dropping her gaze to my lips, then back to my eyes.

"Trust me, you could never stop them from coming." And my lips are on hers. Ollie's soft lips move against mine, burning with that same fire from the party. Not even caring that we're on the street, I deepen the kiss.

And it's at this moment that I realize I can't control myself with her. Whenever Ollie is around, my body takes over, dictating my moves as if it knows what I want or need before I do. Maybe it's different with her; perhaps she won't hurt me but instead will teach me how to love.

Ollie...this is where I showed her how much I like her, how much I care. And now I've left her all alone. I pick a flower and breathe in its scent.

How could I have been so stupid? So naive to think that I don't love her...and say that to her face. *Idiot. Brandon, you're an idiot.* Even my body knew this before me, mere days after that first kiss.

I need to go back; I need to tell her. Dropping the flower, I turn around and start jogging toward her apartment. *Take the flower, you moron.* Right, yes, a romantic gesture! That could give me points. I go back to the bush to take another one and then run to her place.

She's going to love this, and she's going to love me. *Does she love me?* No, don't think like that! All that matters is that I love her. *Ollie, my Ollie, I love her.*

I burst through the door, running to the elevator and pressing the button incessantly. It finally dings. I'm moving so fast, as if she won't be there if I go any slower. *But what if she's not? What if I lost her because I was stubborn? Because I couldn't stay and talk it through?*

And why is this elevator so slow?! I look down at the buttons and notice that none of them are glowing. *Dumb, so dumb.* Seconds after I press the one to her floor, it starts to go.

Come on, come on, come on. Move faster, will you? My fingers start to get fidgety, playing with the flower in my hand. I don't even wait for the door to open entirely before I get out on her floor. I reach her door in seconds, raising my hand to knock but it creaks open without effort.

Shit, shit, shit, did someone break in? Fuck, Ollie...not again. "Olivia! Please tell me you're okay, please."

I walk in, looking around every corner of the apartment. Finding everything intact and in the same place as before, I take out my phone to call her. After two rings, she picks up, sounding out of breath.

"Brandon?"

"Ollie, baby, thank God. Where are you? Why was your apartment door open?"

"Shit," she breathes out. "I must've forgotten to close it after running out."

Running out? What? "Why? Where are you?"

"I'm by the flowers..." she says barely above a whisper, sighing. *If I couldn't love her more.*

"I was just there." I let out a breathy laugh, shaking my head. "But I came back for you. I need to tell you something, Ollie. Something important."

"Me too! I'll come to you; wait for me there," she says, and

I can hear her smile in her voice.

"No, no! I'll come to you!"

I don't even wait for her answer before taking off, closing her door first. High on energy, I run down the stairs. My legs ache, but I don't care so long as they take me back to her.

I push the building's door open, hitting the ground and running back toward the flowers. With each step I take, a drop of water hits my skin. I look up; the sky is no longer starry but full of dark clouds and rain starting its descent.

"Brandon!" Ollie's voice reaches me in an echo. I stare forward, seeing her power walk toward me, her clothes and skin as wet as mine.

"Baby, I'm so sorry. I don't know what I was thinking; it was so stupid," I breathe out as soon as she's within earshot.

"I'm sorry too. I don't care about a fucking tattoo; I care about you," she cries out, carefully stepping closer. "Please, let's not fight like that again."

"Never, never again, so stupid!" I yell as the rain starts pouring harder.

"What?" I barely hear her yell.

I walk even closer to her, our shoes now touching. "I'm sorry. Can you forgive me, baby?" I lift my hand, brushing the rain droplets off her cheeks.

"Can you forgive me?" she whispers, her breath trembling like she's crying.

I nod, cradling her face in my hands, and lean down to whisper, "I love you."

She sucks in a sharp breath, her hands covering mine. She parts her lips, and I see her bite down, making me want to do the same.

I close the remaining gap between us, leaning down just in time to swallow the *"te amo"* that pours out of her lips.

"My fingers your piano, my curves your guitar. My eyes the conductors of your symphonic orchestra." ~ Symphonic Orchestra, Alexandra Kessler.

OLIVIA – OCEAN CITY

THIS KISS IS RAW AND FULL OF NEED; it's desire meeting with want, all the emotions in one. Each of our kisses is magical, but this one's special, intimate. I don't know if it's the closeness or because we've confessed our love to one another under the rain. But nothing can beat this perfect moment.

He turns his head to the side to deepen the kiss. The intensity of the moment increases, making our breathing heavy and fast. He then pulls me closer, the water cold on our skin. A gust of wind blows around us, making me shiver and pull him closer for warmth.

"Are you cold? Maybe we should get you warm back in the apartment," Brandon jokes against my lips as he notices my reaction. His gaze drops for a second before going back to my eyes.

"Only if you join me."

He doesn't answer. Instead, he takes my hand and we take off under the rain, all the way to my apartment building. But he doesn't wait until we're inside. Once in the elevator, he presses the button to my floor and quickly pushes me into the back wall. He wastes not one second more, pulling my face to his.

If the last kiss was magical, then this one's astronomical. The heat of our bodies mixed with the water—the roughness of our clothes against our hands. Water droplets hit the floor as we move against one another, our bodies dancing in sync. A raspy moan leaves his mouth as I pull his bottom lip.

"You're going to be the death of me," he whispers against the skin below my ear. My breath catches in my throat as he plants a kiss right there, and a tingle runs down my spine.

"Ollie." He places his hand on the side of my neck, thumb under my chin. Staring deep into my eyes, he whispers in a raspy voice, "I want all of you. Every inch of you." He plants a kiss on my lips. "And it doesn't matter when or where; I will wait until my last breath just to have a taste of what it is to have you. All of you."

This is the moment where nothing else makes sense except the two of us. He looks at me as if I'm his world, his everything. Love, lust, desire, tenderness, and care; all these emotions swim around in his eyes.

And no other answer fits what I feel but this one: "You already have me."
There's something mystical about this moment, where everything is moving so fast but so slow at the same time. Brandon holds my body close to his while pushing me tightly and carefully against my bedroom door. He intertwines our hands above my head, joining our lips together in a tender kiss.

Our tongues dance together, a feverish feeling erupting from both of us. *Te amo,* he whispers against my lips, and I breathlessly whisper it back.

"Ollie." He sings my name as if it were a song, pulling me close and lifting me in his arms.

I wrap my legs around his waist, our slightly wet skin feeling hot against the other's as we get rid of our clothes.

"Brandon." I match his soft and breathy tone. Never has his name felt so beautiful as it leaves my lips.

He breaks our rhythm, pulling back from me and looking so intensely into my eyes that I might burn. He looks at me like I'm everything he needs, and I can't break away from his stare as he walks us to the bed.

Every day feels like spring, summer, fall, and winter; every season blends into one endless emotion. It may not make sense to everyone else, but it does to us. We're a perfect symphony: the velvety sound of a violin, the roughness of the drums, the darkness of the cello.

I fall on my back with Brandon above me, *just like I love*. He'll never let himself admit this, but he likes it when he's in control—when I give him the space and power to make me feel beautiful while we become one. Everything else disappears, leaving us alone in our bubble as we kiss and hold each other tight. Our bodies are intertwined, and our minds, hearts, and souls are one. In this moment, nothing else matters. All that matters is us.

Here, under my lamp's lights, my body and my heart light on fire. He straddles me as I look up, both of us in love, and I've never felt so alive. He leaves a lingering kiss on my lips, pinning my hands on either side of my head. Things start heating up as we kiss hungrily, rushed and messy but always in sync.

He moans my name, his voice low and his lips against mine. He trails wet kisses down my neck, on my chest, and my stomach, pulling my underwear. Never breaking eye contact, he makes me tremble—under his spell and willing to wait because every second of this is remarkable.

He trails back up, ending on my lips, and takes my hands from where he left them to entangle them in his hair. I chuckle as it elicits a moan from him. He doesn't meet my eyes straight away; his gaze fixates on the spot where our bodies touch. When he looks at me again, his eyes are now a very dark brown, so dark they might as well be black.

I crash his hips with mine as I wrap my legs around his waist after ridding him of his underwear. The atmosphere changes as we become intimately intertwined. Pulling each other as close as possible, I wrap my hand in his hair as he peppers my neck with innocent kisses. They slowly turn hot, leaving me panting under him. I whine as he detaches himself from me, reaching for his wallet on my nightstand.

He prepares himself and then turns to me. "Are you sure?"

Smiling as he cradles the side of my face and his thumb caresses my cheek, I nod. "As sure as I'll ever be."

He returns the smile before kissing me like the world was ending and we only have this moment.

"I love you, Ollie," he whispers against my mouth as he slowly enters me. "*Te amo*," he mumbles against my neck.

I whisper it back to him as we shut our eyes, panting and cursing as we rock our hips together. His tug on my skin gets rougher, leaving a mark; his way of saying *you're mine, and I love you*. I claw at his back, my way of marking him and saying it back.

Ollie, he whispers my name again and again as we move together, his forehead pressed against mine. A round of curses leaves his lips, getting lost in mine as he kisses me again.

A "*te amo*" escapes my mouth, eliciting a breathy groan from him.

"Say it again," he moans, letting go of my lips and holding my face. A devilish smile forms on my lips as I whisper it back.

Our breathing gets heavier as we move faster, climbing our highs together without losing synchronicity. Our vocabulary is reduced to our names and endless moans against each other's necks until we're over the edge. We press our foreheads, a breathless, panting, and sweaty mess.

∞

I lay on top of him while wearing one of his dress shirts,
with him brushing my hair with his hands and me drawing
circles on his chest with mine.

"You know what I want to do?" I tilt my head to look at
him.

"What?" He swipes some loose strands off my face.

"Surfing," I say without missing a beat.

"You, Olivia, want to surf again?" He smiles as he gives me
a skeptical look.

"Yes, me! Don't you remember how great I was the first
time?"

"The only time," he says with a laugh, the vibrations
running through me. "And I remember you falling on your face a
lot."

"Oh, whatever; I still want to go," I mumble, looking down.

He places his finger under my chin, tilting my face toward
him. "How about this Sunday? I can tell Sam to set it up just like
last time."

"Sounds like a plan." I give him a smug smile as if saying, *I
always get my way*.

"Just promise me you'll try not to fall on your face again."

"Sure, as long as you do the same." I hold up my pinky.
"Promise?"

"Promise." He laces his finger with mine, and we kiss them
to seal it.

I go back to laying my head on his chest, and he goes back
to brushing my hair. I slowly drift to sleep as he sings so low
that I can't hear the words, except when he mumbles my name:
Ollie...

Chapter Sixteen

"All I am is music. The one you are meant to love."
~ Symphonic Orchestra, Alexandra Kessler.

OLIVIA – OCEAN CITY

HAVE I TOLD YOU HOW HAPPY YOU MAKE ME?"

I stand on my tiptoes and clasp my hands behind Brandon's neck.

"No, but I'm sure it's not as much as you make me." He pulls me closer, kissing my forehead.

"Ugh, get a room, you two," Maia says breathlessly next to us, her recently re-dyed hair blowing back with the wind. "Or help out by carrying some bags to the car?"

"Oh, I wish I could, but I don't want to." I shrug with a smug smile on my face.

She pushes one of the bags into my arms. "Stop quoting *Friends* and put the bag in the trunk!"

I roll my eyes but help anyway. "Come on, there's a beach we need to get to." I urge Brandon to do the same.

"Do I have to? They're almost done packing up the car anyway!" he complains in a whiny voice.

"Yes, you do," Scott answers before I can. "Now move it, lover boy."

It doesn't matter how often I come to the beach; it will always be my happy place. The sound of the waves crashing as it roars. The taste and smell of the ocean's saltiness, as fresh as a cool summer's day. The roughness of the sand on my bare feet reminds me of how beautiful it is to be alive and to be able to experience this.

Brandon's arms hug my waist, joining in on my moment. We're breathing in the ocean-scented air and holding each other close as we gaze into the horizon. I smile, laying my head on his chest, feeling happy and complete.

"You know what I'm thinking?" he whispers.

"No, what?"

"How I could get used to this. Just you and me, being free together and loving each other." He plants a kiss on my shoulder. "There's no other place I'd rather be."

I turn around, hanging from his neck. "Me neither." Tickling his nose with mine, I go in for a kiss. "*Te amo.*"

"*Te amo más.*" He cradles the back of my head, deepening the kiss.

"Impossible, I love *you* more."

"Fine, fine, I give up," he surrenders, holding up his hands. "I guess I can accept that. It's not the end of the world."

"I know, and I'm always right. Face it, honey. You don't get to win anymore." I shrug, a smirk on my face.

"Hmm, I don't know about that. There's still something you can't win." Brandon leans down, aiming for my lips.

"What's that?" I close my eyes, waiting for the kiss.

But in a split second, I stop feeling him against my skin, and it's replaced with a gust of wind. I open my eyes and notice him running halfway down the beach.

"Not fair. You didn't give me a warning start!" I chase after him, leaving my clothes at our group's spot.

"Hey, careful!" Maia screams out as I kick sand all over them.

"Sorry," I yell back.

The salty, crystal-clear ocean water splashes on me as I run in and jump on Brandon's back. He playfully tries to shake me off, creating more splashes. I hide my face on the back of his neck, failing to keep the salty water out of my eyes.

"Fine, you win, okay? I give up; put me down."

"Oh, you do?" I can sense the mischievous smile forming on his lips. "What if I don't want to put you down now?" He holds onto my legs.

"And what if *I* want you to?"

"Okay." He lets go of me, and I immediately fall into the water, letting out a squeal.

I quickly cover my mouth and nose. Swimming to the surface, a loud gasp leaves my mouth as I take a breath of air, wiping my face and brushing my hair back.

"How was the water?" Brandon's arms engulf my waist as he pulls me closer, a faint smile on his lips.

"Very refreshing, a much-needed restart."

"No, no, you don't have to thank me." He bows his head.

I splash his face. "I was not."

"But you should." He splashes me back. "How else would you have learned to care for yourself if I hadn't thrown you in?"

A loud and shrill whistle cuts off the conversation. We turn to find Sam waving at us, surfboards and suits lined up by his feet on the shore.

"Let's go." He rubs my arms and pecks my lips.

By the time we reach the group, everyone's already zipped into their wetsuits and waiting for us. We decide to stay out in the sun for a while as Sam gives everyone a quick review lesson before they start.

"To start with the most important reminder, please don't forget to place the strap tight onto your dominant leg. The water is a little choppy today, so it's best to stay strapped in case of an emergency. Don't forget to breathe steadily and concentrate on your balance while popping up."

He claps his hands together. "Let's go in!"

I lie on Brandon's chest, and he brushes the hair off my back and starts drawing shapes with his fingers. The gesture makes me smile; I love when he does that.

"I know we came to surf, but right now, I just want to lay here with you."

He leaves a kiss on my forehead. "Me too. I could stay here forever. Just you and me."

"I wouldn't mind living on the beach. The happiest place on this earth."

He lifts my face, a baffled look on his. "Isn't that Disney?"

"Not to me, no. My happy place is the beach." I release a breath. "Where every single detail is painted to perfection. Where nothing can go wrong, happy places can't get ruined."

"What?" I ask as Brandon stares at me, a glimmer in his eyes and a calming smile.

"You're adorable."

"Stop." I playfully push his face away.

He evades my hands and holds my chin, "I love you, Ollie. And I especially love the little things that make you who you are. Don't ever doubt it." He leans in and kisses me.

No matter how many times we kiss or how much time goes by, he always erupts endless emotions through every inch of me. And everything freezes around us, leaving us in a world of our own creation.

"Can we come here every day?" I mumble against his lips.

He nods. "Whenever you want, baby, just say the word."

"Come on. We did come here to surf, so let's go surf." I leave one last kiss on his lips before standing up.

A few minutes and some zipping-ups later, we're running into the water, boards in hands. We follow Sam's instructions from the last time we came surfing: lying flat on the boards and paddling out to sea. But we keep bobbing up and down, way more than usual. Sam was right; the water was choppy. The salty water harshly splashing my face is more proof of this.

We try to catch up with the group, which has the advantage of an early running start. But the waves are so rough that everyone keeps falling over, and only Sam rides them perfectly for obvious reasons.

I fix my gaze on the clearing, finding a fascinating interaction: Maia and Scott splashing and pushing each other. But this is not like their typical interaction; no, this one seems playful and borderline cute.

"Hey," I call to Brandon as he paddles by me. "Do you know anything about that?" I nod to the pair.

He follows my gaze, furrowing his eyebrows and vaguely shaking his head. "No, not at all. And it's not like Scott would've told me anything about it; he always avoids talking about those things."

He turns back to me. "Don't you girls tell each other everything? Shouldn't you know if something's happening?"

I shrug. "I don't know anymore. But I'm pretty sure she tried to tell me something that morning after the welcome-back party. Maybe she needs her time and space to figure it out."

He holds my hand, caressing the back of it. "I'm sure she'll come to you when she feels ready. But, meanwhile"—he plants a kiss—"can we go back to surfing? I haven't seen you fall on your face yet."

"Oh, but I won't." I retrieve my hand. "Don't you know I'm a pro now?"

"Are you, now? Let's make a deal then." Brandon shows off his award-winning smile. "The first one to ride out five waves without falling over wins."

Hmm, this sounds like a trick. "Wins what?"

He waggles his eyebrows. "That's a surprise."

I pretend to think about it, knowing that I'll be the clear winner. Having made a decision, I extend my hand to shake it. "Deal. Let's go!"

We spend hours going back and forth between riding out to the shore and falling after ten seconds. The score? We're currently four to three, me being ahead.

"Yes, yes, I'm doing it!" I scream as I pop up on the board, riding out the wave like a pro.

A few seconds later, a splash of water hits my face, distracting me and making me lose my balance. Right before going under, I hear Brandon laughing as he rushes by me. *That fucker did that on purpose.* When I come up for air, he's in front of me.

"I hate you." I squint at him.

"No, you don't." He goes in for a kiss, but I turn my head, his lips landing on my cheek instead.

"No kisses for you, cheater."

He pecks my forehead before paddling away and mumbles in a childish voice, "Petty, petty, petty." I jump back on my board, paddling as fast as possible to reach the clearing. I cannot—will not—let Brandon win. *It's a matter of pride now.*

This time, as we wait for another wave, I take my time to reflect on Sam's lesson from last time: closing my eyes, breathing in and out, and moving my feet. I connect to the board and the water, preparing myself for the incoming perfect wave that will help me win.

A soft wind blows around me, and I know this is it. *This is my winning wave.* I open my eyes, looking back to the sea and sucking in a breath. The tide is getting closer and growing by the second. But it doesn't matter, I got this.

I give Brandon one last look before paddling out, winking at him in an attempt to distract him. And before he can react, I'm already moving, closing my eyes and feeling the water.

Everything flows like it is in slow motion. I look back at the water, nodding as the wave gets closer, *ready*. I push myself up, lifting my body in a swift, clean movement.

I hop on, coming face to face with Ella, and there is a look of surprise on both of our faces as we each stay balanced. We hit a small but bumpy wave, stumble a bit, and reach over to each other out of instinct. To my surprise, we don't fall, riding out to the shore.

"Oh, my God, we're doing it! Ella, I'm doing it!" I scream, excited as we almost reach the end—the wind blowing in our faces, salt in our hair, and water on our skin.

"¡Sí, vamos!" Ella yells out as we hold our hands.

Our boards stop as the wave dies near the sand—a sense of excitement, realization, and relief overwhelms me. Hopping off the board, I jump on Ella for a koala-bear hug.

"Can you believe it? Oh, my God, did you see what we just did? I never reached the shore before. This is so exciting!" My voice reaches an octave I never thought possible.

"I know, right?! Who would've thought I'd like surfing, barring all the fish, of course!" Ella matches my energy level.

"Where's Brandon? Did he see it?" I ask while I'm still hanging from Ella's neck.

"I—I'm not sure. Wasn't he behind you?"

And in the blink of an eye, the atmosphere changes from pure bliss to an air of uncertainty. The sky's no longer a beautiful baby blue but a pale and gloomy gray. The air's no longer fresh but stale and hard to breathe.

Something's wrong. Something feels off. Where's Brandon?

"Sway to this sad song that was made just for you."
~ Symphonic Orchestra, Alexandra Kessler.

OLIVIA – OCEAN CITY

ARE YOU SURE YOU HAVEN'T?" My chest compresses, and it's getting hard to breathe as I ask Ella again.

"Dude, *no*, I swear I haven't. He was right behind you, and then he wasn't." She hastily looks around the beach. "What if he's swimming or just left the water?"

I start spinning around, scanning over every region my eyes can reach. For some reason, I can't seem to move, like I'm stuck in place. The world fades out as I keep spinning, brushing my hands through my hair, and feeling like I'm losing my mind.

My lungs start burning as I scream Brandon's name over and over again. I don't even notice I'm moving until the water reaches my chin, and the girls pull me back.

A group of lifeguards rush by us along with Sam, and they search underwater; the high tide makes it even harder to look. A glimmer hits my eyes from my peripheral view. I turn my head to the source, finding a lonesome board floating around, and a sense of hope fills my heart.

"Sam, Sam, over here!" I scream out while I run after it. But I don't get very far as he stops and pulls me into an embrace—comforting and protecting me.

"It's okay, Olli. Let the medics do their job. He'll be fine."

As soon as the words leave his mouth, paramedics rush in while the lifeguards pull Brandon's limp body out of the water.

Dios mío, Brandon. My body acts on its own as it carries me over the sand, following the medics to the ambulance.

"Is he okay? Is he breathing? Please be okay, Brandon!" I don't process the words leaving my mouth. All I can think about is whether my boyfriend's alive.

"All we can say is that we'll do our best. And once we reach the hospital, we'll have more information about his state. Are you family?" one of the medics asks me as they roll him into the ambulance.

"Girlfriend. His family's not here."

"Then you can provide the nurses with his information and contact his nearest family member. You can ride in the back with him."

As soon as I sit down, I grab Brandon's hand—crying and praying. I don't even notice when we start moving. I just know that we are, and it feels like it's taking forever, and there's nothing else I can do but beg with silent prayers.

Please, God, don't take him yet. He still has so much to do. His whole life's still ahead of him. Please, please, don't leave me, Brandon. I just got you, and I'm not ready to let you go. Please.

A pang of hope hits my chest as his hand twitches in mine. I lift my head to look at him, watching him open his eyes and look around in confusion. I immediately try to stop him from taking the breathing mask off.

"Don't, there's something I need to say," he whispers in a hoarse voice.

"Brandon, no, you need it to breathe, save it for when you wake up again."

"Ollie." He squeezes my hand, a sad look on his face. "If I don't make it—"

"Stop it, don't say that." My voice trembles.

"If I don't make it," he continues, "don't forget I love you."

I shake my head, denying what he's saying.

"Promise me, Ollie," he begs, but I look away, lips quivering. "Promise me, please!"

"I promise," I give in, not knowing if this might or might not be his last breath. "I love you too," I whisper before kissing him, closing my eyes as he drifts back into unconsciousness. *I just hope that you heard that.*

I go back to my prayers and grasp his ice-cold hand, begging and begging for someone to save his life. The ambulance stops, indicating that we're at the hospital. Everything that comes next happens in the blink of an eye: doors opening, doctors running out, yelling medical terms that I can't even comprehend. But I refuse to leave his side, holding Brandon's hand for as long as possible—unwilling to let him go.

We reach a wide double door with a sign over the top that reads *Operating Rooms*. It doesn't take a rocket scientist to know that this is where I stay. The nurses' voices sound muffled as they explain what I already know.

I lean down, pressing a salty kiss on his forehead and whispering *"te amo"* with the hope that this is not goodbye. My body stills, and the world around me fades as they wheel him away. His hand slowly slips from mine, leaving behind a shadow of warmth and, with it, a never-ending numbness.

"And all they say is I should let go. But how do you let go of the one you love?" ~ Sad Love Song, Alexandra Kessler.

MAIA – OCEAN CITY

"HEY, WAIT. WHERE ARE YOU TAKING HIM?" I grasp the ambulance's back door as the paramedics are about to close it.

"Atlantic General Hospital in Berlin. It's a little far, but his injuries require a more specialized hospital. You should leave now if you want to arrive when we do."

"Thank you." I nod before turning around toward the group.

"What did they say?" Scott asks without missing a beat as soon as I reach them.

"Atlantic General, so let's pack everything as fast as possible. We'll have to take the highway."

"But did they say anything about his condition?" His voice breaks a little on the last syllable.

"I didn't ask. There's not much they could've said since we're not family. All I know is we have to leave now."

Within ten minutes, we are all packed into Sam's Jeep and hitting the asphalt. Sheer silence fills the air as we drive from the boardwalk and head to the bridge.

But who even wants to talk in a moment like this? Our friend just had an accident, and no one knows what to say. Our best friend, Ollie's boyfriend, is fighting for his life.

Fuck, Ollie. What could be going through her head? I've

never seen her so devastated, so broken.

What if… No, *no pienses así (don't think like that). Brandon will be okay; todo va a estar bien (everything will be fine).*

"Sam?" Ella's trembling voice echoes in the silence of the car. "Do you think Brandon will be okay?"

Sam looks back through the rearview mirror. "It's most likely a concussion. This kind of accident happens very often with surfing, more than you can imagine. I know a lot of guys that go through the same thing, and they're fine."

Ella nods, going back to Noah's comforting hug, a numb look on his face.

Scott sits next to him in the passenger seat. I can see from behind Sam that he's putting on his best poker face. *I guess he takes after his brother.*

His legs give him away, bouncing up and down incessantly. We're all worried and on edge, but there's nothing we can do but drive and wait in silence. No words could drown this awful feeling in our chests.

"I'm calling Ollie. I'm sure they've arrived by now." I dial her number, connect the phone to the car, and put it on speaker.

"Maia, hey, where are you guys?" Ollie's voice sounds raspy.

"We're crossing the bridge now, but what about you? Are you at the hospital yet?" Sam replies in one breath.

"Yes, we got here a few minutes ago, and they took Brandon right away—"

"Any updates? Is he okay?" Sam cuts her off.

She releases a shaky breath before continuing. "He's okay, guys. One of the doctors came out and talked to me right before you called. They think it's a concussion and that there's nothing to worry about; we can all relax now." Her voice comes out strained.

Silence fills the car; we can hear the wheels rolling on the pavement. A slight sense of relief surrounds us. *But why can't I shake this bad feeling that she's not telling us the whole truth?*

"See, guys? I told you it was just a concussion." Sam lets out a sigh, his shoulders visibly relaxing.

"Are they sure it's nothing more serious, Ollie?" I ask in a cautious voice, trying to hide my frown.

"Yes, I talked to the doctor. I'm sure if it were more than that, they would've told me; I would know. So, he's fine, okay? He's fine." Her voice breaks slightly at the end of the sentence, and we can hear a light sniff.

I take in a deep breath before speaking again. "Okay, we're about twenty minutes away. Try to stay calm, maybe drink some water, and avoid coffee. Please call us if you need anything at all."

"Okay, see you guys in a bit. But don't worry, okay? He's fine. I'm fine."

Ollie's heavy words echo in the car even after she ends the call; rounds of sighs and *phews* leave everyone's mouths.

Everyone relaxes while I'm still staring at her phone, pursing my lips and frowning. I lift my head and catch Sam staring at me through the rearview mirror. He opens his mouth, but before he can say anything, the sound of Scott cursing and yelling draws our attention his way. He presses down on the brakes as we reach a long line of cars with no end in sight and even more piling behind us.

"No, no, no, no. Fuck, this cannot be happening," Scott groans, leaning on the dashboard.

Dozens of horns resonate on the highway. Apparently, everyone has somewhere to be. Imagine if someone else is rushing for the same reason as us. Shit.

Sam honks as he spots a police officer a car ahead, calling

her over.

"Excuse me, officer, is something going on?"

"There's a pretty bad accident about five miles ahead. You better get comfortable; we estimate it not to clear out for another thirty minutes or more."

Sam nods at the officer, trying to keep his composure in front of the law. But all we want to do is scream or punch something to release the frustration.

"What if this lasts for hours instead?" Noah mumbles under his breath.

"No, do not say that." Scott turns around. "And Brandon will be fine. He'll be wide awake when we get there, waiting for us to hug him."

It's okay, respira. Brandon is fine. Just breathe.

∞

OLIVIA – OCEAN CITY

*P*LEASE, GOD, I CAN'T LOSE HIM. *I love him; I can't live without him. I'm not strong enough to live in a world that doesn't have him in it.*

I pray over and over in my head, hunched over the bathroom sink after ending the call. It's only been ten minutes since I talked to the doctors, and I already can't breathe—it's like the walls are closing in on me, and I can't escape them.

I pace back and forth, repeating the same prayer in an endless cycle. I sit on the floor, curling into a ball and dry cry—*breathing in, breathing out.* Nothing calms me down. Praying, splashing water on my face, pressing my nails into my palm, walking; it's all useless. Nothing short of knowing that he's awake will slow my racing heart and control my trembling hands.

I get up from the floor, dusting off my pants and splashing my face with water again. I give myself one last look in the mirror, fixing my hair and smiling before walking out. *There's no need to cry; the doctor said Brandon will be okay. He's fine.*

I take in short breaths and let out shaky puffs while counting to ten. By the time I reach seven, I'm growing anxious again. *Maybe I need some water.*

My feet start moving on their own in what I hope is the direction of a coffee machine. It's not long until I find one, and I immediately lift my hand to reach into my purse to get the money. I realize all I have with me is my phone; I fucking left my things at the beach.

Great, fucking great. A throbbing, pumping feeling settles on my forehead, making me dizzy. I slip onto the floor, resting my head on my knees as a way to numb the pain.

The sound of feet shuffling and rushing around me doesn't help, but I can't get myself to move. I should get off the floor, but it's as if I'm stuck. My body starts shaking again as desperation and exhaustion overwhelm my emotions.

Why can't the doctors come out already and tell me I can see Brandon? I can't take all the waiting anymore. I need some air, or maybe some water.

My legs shake as I push myself up, but I still manage to work. I end up outside, leaning against the wall beside the emergency doors. Following Maia's advice, I try to stay calm and steady myself.

My puffs of air are still coming out shaky, but my heartbeat starts to slow down. I close my eyes, allowing the memory of our promise in the ambulance to replay and flood my mind.

"If I don't make it, don't forget I love you."

"Promise me, Ollie. Promise me!"
"I love you."

Tears silently spill and stream down my face, and my shoulders shake, but no sound comes out. *I love you too, Brandon. Please don't leave me.* My whole body's trembling now, and I can't take it anymore; it hurts too much.

Standing hurts, breathing hurts, sitting hurts. And yet, the only position that comforts me is curling into a ball—a sobbing mess on the floor.

Okay, calma, Ollie. He's fine; the doctor said he was fine. Trust the doctors; he's fine…

MAIA – OCEAN CITY

ALMOST THIRTY MINUTES HAVE GONE BY, and we're not halfway through the drive.

Noah groans against the window. "Why isn't this fucking moving? We would be at the hospital already if it weren't for this damn traffic."

"No one else loves this either, Noah, and your annoying nagging isn't helping. So, shut up! And it's not like you're the one laying on a hospital bed, are you?" Scott yells.

"Stop the fighting, please. It won't make us go any faster," Sam says as he looks back. "There's not much need to hurry now, anyway. We heard Ollie; the doctors said Brandon is doing okay. We can trust her, right, Maia?"

I breathe in, closing my eyes and resting my head on the window. "Umm, well, sometimes Ollie—"

"There's a fucking open spot right there, and no one is

moving," Noah cuts me off.

"Would you shut the fuck up already?" Scott tries to lunge at him, but the seat belt stops him.

"Everybody calm their asses down!" Sam yells out. *Has he ever raised his voice at anyone before this?*

Next to me, I see Ella reaching out to Noah to calm him down. I ignore them all, zoning out as I stare at my hands. *Why can't I shake the tightness in my stomach?*

"Our bad, Maia. What were you saying?" Sam's voice pulls me back.

"Right, sorry, guys. It's nothing. If Ollie said she talked to the doctors, trust her. I just think that she might be painting a prettier picture than what is reality. That's all."

"Fuck." We all startle as Scott yells out and punches the dashboard before him. "Sorry," he mutters. "I just can't take this anymore, not knowing exactly how he's doing."

"It's okay." Sam pats his shoulder. "Let's just trust Ollie."

Sam glances back at me again, but I'm still feeling out of it. Glancing back at him, I nod to the road. "It's moving."

He doesn't think twice before stepping on the gas, merging into the left lane, and driving toward the nearest exit.

"Maia, call Ollie again. Let her know what happened and that we're almost there. She's probably feeling very lonely and anxious right now."

"On it."

The call rings and rings and rings, sending me to voicemail. I hang up and try again, getting the same result.

"Maia, what happened with Ollie? I don't think I heard you talk," Sam asks, and I realize we're now parked at the hospital.

I turn the phone to face them, showing them my call log with eight unanswered calls.

"She probably fell asleep." Ella shrugs as her leg bounces

nervously. "It's been a long day; she must be tired."

"Yeah," I say under my breath. "We're already here, anyway, might as well look for her."

We all agree, grabbing whatever's essential and getting out of the car to search for her. And we better find her fast; we need some answers.

∞

OLIVIA – OCEAN CITY

*O*LLIE."

"*Ollie, despierta (wake up).*"

"*Are you okay?*"

"*Olivia!*"

I hastily open my eyes in panic as I'm shaken awake, my breathing erratic again. I rub the tiredness out of my eyes, finding myself surrounded by my friends.

"Hey, you made it," I say in a groggy voice.

"There was an accident on the highway; it cost us almost an hour. But why are you sleeping outside? Did something happen?" Sam helps me up while looking very concerned.

"No, don't worry about it. I'm just very exhausted and drained. I came out for some air but ended up falling asleep. *Estoy bien.*"

We walk through the emergency doors, find empty seats in the waiting room, and settle in. After a couple of minutes of silence, Maia speaks up.

"Olivia."

"Yes?" I snap out of it, not even realizing I was zoning out. *Wait, did she call me Olivia?* No nickname, no tenderness;

nothing but concern in her strong voice.

"What exactly are we waiting for?"

"What do you mean?" I now notice that everyone has their eyes on me.

She sighs. "If Brandon has a concussion, and you've been here for an hour, shouldn't he be in a room? Or at least in the ICU, somewhere we could see him?"

I hear what she's saying, but the words start getting lost, mixing and becoming distorted—the hospital sounds, the sirens outside, and stretchers bursting through the doors. And in a blink of an eye, everything is frantic as doctors and nurses rush out to help.

Noah covers Ella's eyes as we notice the mangled and bloody bodies. "Wait, what's happening?" she yells, trying to pry his hands away.

"What's going on?" Scott asks a nurse.

"Car crash, excuse me," she answers before pushing past.

I can feel Sam fidgeting beside me. I turn my head to look at him, but he's lost in something else.

"Family of Brandon Collins," a deep voice resonates amid the chaos. We all turn toward its source: a tall and mature-looking doctor coming through the ER doors.

"Is it just me, or does he look like he realizes he chose the wrong career?" Scott mutters next to us, and Sam shushes him. *Not the time to make jokes, asshole.*

All I can feel right now is my heart beating a mile a minute, about to burst and stick in my throat as we run to him.

"You're Brandon Collins' friends?"

"Yes, doctor," Scott answers. "Family."

He takes a deep breath, and I hold mine. A warmth starts spreading through my hands as someone grabs them. I look down at them, noticing Maia has one and Sam the other. I silently thank them.

"From what we gather, it's presumed that Mister Collins hit his head with the surfboard from an abrupt wave. This accident affected his brain, a result of blunt force head trauma. I'm saddened to say that this caused some internal bleeding that we couldn't control. The blood pooled over the brain's surface, causing fatal, widespread effects."

We all jolt as a loud, crashing sound breaks the silence. We turn around to find Scott knocking over the trash cans.

"What are you trying to say?" he asks the doctor in an agitated tone.

"Yes, could you please be more specific?" Sam asks, standing beside me with a bone-crushing hold on my hand.

The doctor nods with a sad smile, causing my heart to drop. "We're very sorry. We did everything we could, but there was too much trauma. Mister Collins passed away from complications regarding his head trauma. We're so sorry for your loss."

My knees are weak and trembling, but Maia and Sam hold me up. "No, no, no. That can't be true," I say in between breaths. "No, this is not right. They told me he was fine, that it was just a mild concussion. He's fine, doctor. He's fine. You must have the wrong patient."

He looks confused. *But...he's wrong. I talked to them, and they said Brandon was fine.*

"I am sorry, miss, but we have not spoken to anyone else about Brandon Collins' condition."

"No! No, what are you talking about? He was fine," I yell, trying to free myself from their hold.

"Ollie," Maia says in a calm tone, her voice breaking too.

I block out all sounds as everything crumbles around me. My head spins, and my ears ring. I feel like everything's moving, and I can't control it. *No, no, no. This can't be happening.* I fall, not able to handle the crushing pain anymore, my knees crashing to the floor.

I'm paralyzed; I can't breathe; I can't see. Tears rush freely down my face. *No, this is not real. He can't be dead; he can't.* My chest starts hurting as it compresses, making it hard to take a breath.

"He can't be dead," I sob into Maia's chest, crumpling on the floor. "This isn't real."

"I know, Ollie, I know. I'm sorry," she says softly, holding back a sob. "*Lo siento tanto.*"

But nothing can numb this endless pain that's throbbing in my chest, in my soul. The world fades around me, leaving me to my sorrow as I weep. *He can't be gone, my Brandon, my love.*

"Why, God, why?!"

I hear the words I'm thinking, but they don't come from me. We see Scott trashing everything he can while Sam tries to stop him, both soaking in tears. Ella and Noah are curled up like Maia and me.

Ella catches my eyes, and I cry even harder. The sobs wrack my body, making me shake and break all at once. There's nothing else left of me, left of my heart, only pain, sorrow, an empty soul, and endless tears.

I can't believe—I refuse to believe—that he's dead. That Brandon's gone, and I'm all alone.

And I promise I won't forget our promise because I will always love you too. Except now, you can't love me the way I do you.

Chapter Seventeen

"There's nothing else left of my heart. You took every single piece of it." ~ Sad Love Song, Alexandra Kessler.

OLIVIA – OCEAN CITY

*I*T'S BEEN A WEEK. One week since he left us. I haven't said his name, not even in my thoughts; it would hurt too much. I even ask the rest of the group to refrain from saying it.

The funeral is today back in Salisbury, his hometown. I'll be meeting his family and more of his friends. But how will I face them after I couldn't save him? Maybe I could've warned him about the incoming wave if I had paid attention. He could've protected himself and untied the board from his ankle. And how will I face my friends after lying about talking to the doctors? But I could've sworn I did. It seemed so real in my head.

Too many *what-ifs* have flooded my head this past week. That's one of the reasons I haven't left my room or even opened the curtains and why it's so weird to see myself dressed in black, staring at the mirror from the comfort of my bed.

We're supposed to leave in the next few minutes, but I can't move, like I'm stuck in place again, just like back at the hospital. *Am I stuck, or is it an excuse not to go? I don't think I'll be able to handle it.*

I press my hands onto the bed, trying to lift myself and stand. *No, no puedo (I can't).* I fall back down. Why can't I do this on my own? Even changing into my black dress required help from Ella and Maia. I can't do this.

I drift back into reality when someone knocks on my door.

"Ollie, can I come in?" Sam calls.

"Yeah." My voice comes out barely above a whisper.

"Hey, sweetie, how are you holding up?" He comes in, kneeling in front of me. He's wearing a black suit, and his hair is combed back.

I slightly shake my head. "I don't know." My voice breaks.

"Hey, hey, it's okay." He sits beside me, pulling me into a hug and shushing me. "It's okay, Ollie. You'll be okay; the pain won't last forever."

"Then why does it feel like it will?"

"Because you love him, and love doesn't go away. I'm sure that you'll love him for however long you live. Which is how I know the pain won't stay because love will make it easier."

I wipe away the tears that silently stream down my face.

Sam kisses the top of my head. "Ollie, we need to go now," he whispers.

I nod, sniffling. "I'm ready." I don't even recognize my voice.

He holds my arms, helps me off the bed, and lets me go once I'm up. But I pull him back. "Please, stay with me."

"Anything you need." He holds my hands in his.

We walk out to the living room, where everyone's waiting for me. And now I feel awful, knowing they were here while I took my precious time.

"Sorry for taking so long." I look down at my feet.

"No, honey, it's okay. We weren't waiting for too long, anyway," Layla says in her sweetest voice, very different from her usually shrill tone.

"Come on, let's get going then." I nod to the door.

Minutes later, we're in Sam's car, buckling in for the hour-long ride. Sam's driving, and Scott sits in the passenger seat. Maia, Ella, Noah, and I take the middle while Drew and Layla sit in the extra row way back.

"Everyone settled in?" Sam asks, looking in the rearview mirror, and everyone answers *yes*. "Okay, let's go."

∞

"Ollie, hey." I slowly open my eyes as someone shakes me, my vision blurry. "We're here, sweetie."

I rub my eyes in an attempt to see clearer. *When did I fall asleep? How long was the ride?*

"Come on." Maia helps me get out.

I step outside, close the car door, and link arms with Maia. Everyone walks in silence, with the boys going in before us since they know the family. *I had never even met his family before today. What will they think of me now?*

We walk into the cemetery, and it's not at all what I expected. Although I didn't know what to expect anyway, most cemeteries I've been to are identical. But not this one. Parsons Cemetery is beautiful: vast open spaces, well-maintained green grass, big blooming trees, and flowers on every lot. Other families are also here, visiting their departed and paying their respects to loved ones.

Never, not even in my worst nightmare, did I imagine I'd be here today, saying goodbye to him. This is not how I wanted to meet his family, his best friend, or visit his childhood home. This is not how anything was supposed to go.

We silently follow the guys until we reach some chairs set up in front of a burial lot with a big, framed picture of him. It's a collage celebrating his beautiful life from when he was a baby, his childhood, high school and college, and even some recent ones. The guys must have sent those last photos over.

The chairs are mostly empty so far. People, whom I assume are family members, spread around talking, crying, or comforting each other. We slip into the third row, leaving the first two for the immediate family.

But with the first rows empty, I have a direct line of view to his picture. And it takes every ounce of my being not to burst into tears. I can't seem to turn away, to stop staring at his beautiful smile. It breaks my heart that this is how I see his life, his old self, his baby pictures. I glance away as tears threaten to spill over my eyes and stare at the freshly cut grass instead.

"Aunt Kathy, Uncle Robert, hi!" I hear Sam's solemn voice from next to me. "I am so, so sorry for your loss. We cannot begin to imagine what you must be going through."

"Oh, my dear boy. Always so sweet, Sam. Thank you for the kind words. But he was your friend too, or more like a brother. You boys have a right to be hurting just the same." I see them hugging from my peripheral view. *They must be his parents.*

"Thank you for coming. We're sure that your being here would've made Brandon very happy," a deep, manly voice says as he pats Scott on the back. He mumbles a *thank you* and sniffles, not raising his head to acknowledge them.

I shut my eyes, holding in tears as I hear his name.

"Layla, Drew, it warms my heart to see you again. You were always so good to my boy!" Mrs. Collins walks to the other side of the row to hug them tightly while Mr. Collins talks to Scott, Sam, and Noah.

How can they sound so calm? How are their voices not breaking after saying his name and seeing his portrait?

"No, Kathleen, he was good to us," Layla mumbles.

"He was the best there ever was, Auntie. There will never be anyone like him." Drew sniffles next to them.

I signal Maia and Ella to stand with me as I sense Mrs. Collins' silent gaze. Something tells me it's our turn next, even though we don't know each other yet.

"You must be Olivia." Her soothing voice reminds me of him. "Brandon told me so much about you. I'm so sorry that these are the circumstances we're meeting under."

I take a look at her: long, wavy, dark-brown hair with the roots showing, wrinkles around her eyes, and lines on her forehead. Her skin is slightly tanned, *just like his*. She seems to be around her late fifties, but her frame says otherwise.

I clear my throat, standing in front of her. "Yes, yes, I am. And you must be Mrs. Collins."

"Oh, no, please, call me Kathleen. Brandon would've wanted you to."

I immediately look down, sucking in a breath at the sound of his name.

"Oh, honey, I'm sorry. Did I say something wrong?" She steps closer, rubbing my arms in a loving-mother manner.

"No, no, it's okay. I"—I release a breath—"haven't heard or said his name since he—"

"It's alright, sweetie. We understand." Her hands slip into mine, holding them carefully. "I heard you were the one who found him and rode with him to the hospital. That must've been very hard and scary for you."

I just nod, and my lip quivers, unable to form any words, or my tears will burst.

"We needed to let you know how thankful we are for that. You are a courageous woman for going through that pain all by yourself. I can see why my son loved you so dearly." Her voice strains at the end, and I can't take it anymore.

I let the tears out and, with that, what little composure I had left. "Thank you, Kathleen. Will you excuse me?"

I know it's rude, but I don't wait for an answer before turning around and rushing to the nearest tree.

"And you must be her wonderful sister and best friend..."

I'm about to sit on the grass when I realize I have no coat to place on the ground. *Fuck, I'll stain my dress.*

"May I?" An unfamiliar, deep voice comes from behind me.

I look up at him. Dark skin, short curly hair, and almost as tall as Scott. He must be a friend of Brandon's from high school. He stares at me as if he expects some sort of answer.

Right, he asked me a question. I look at his hand and notice a blazer in his left hand; he signals to the ground with the right.

"Oh, no, it's okay. I wouldn't want to ruin your jacket. It looks brand new."

"It's not a problem." He sets it on the grass. I take a second to think about it but cave in and sit on it.

"Thank you," I whisper in a shaky voice while sniffling.

"Are you okay?"

"What?"

"Umm, you're—" He waves his hand in a circular motion around his face.

I touch my cheeks; *shit.* I wipe away the tears. *Great, and now this stranger has seen me cry.*

"Well, you know how it goes at funerals. There's always someone who can't handle the pain."

He sits on the grass next to me, "I'm pretty sure that's part of the full package, you know?"

I let out a small, breathy laugh. *So stupid.*

"I'm Jordan, by the way." He stretches his hand out toward me, and I shake it. *Why does that name sound familiar?*

"Olivia."

"I know." He lets go of my hand. "You were all he talked about on our calls or when we texted. He wouldn't stop."

He talked about me... My lips quiver again.

"Did you know he was planning a trip to visit me? I know it was a surprise, but, you know, he wanted you to meet me."

Oh, Jordan! "You're his childhood friend who moved away to Texas."

"Ahh, so he told you about me. I feel special now." He lays back against the tree.

"Yeah, he did." I force myself to smile a little. "He also told me the story about how you two met and the friendship bracelet you made."

"Did he also tell you how we kept falling over the railing? We never learned to do that trick; maybe we weren't meant to be skateboarders."

I let out a genuine laugh as I picture a young Brandon learning to skateboard but failing every time.

"Is that why he became a musician instead? The railing crushed his dreams of skating?"

His face turns a little more serious now. "Did he not tell you that story?"

"What do you mean?"

He scoots closer to me and lets out a sigh.

"That same day at the park, after we gave up and after scraping our knees, we walked home. We passed a small group of people jamming out with their guitars and some bongos on our way home. He was so immersed in the whole thing as if his body called out to the music and begged him to play."

"And that's when he knew..." *How did I not know this?*

"It was written in the stars." He smiles, clearly reminiscing. "You want to know the best part? That wasn't even the fastest way home. We took that path because we felt like it."

Music, indeed, was his destiny. We were all there to witness and help fulfill it.

"And why did you leave for Texas?" I change the subject; it's getting too deep to bear.

"I got into varsity football during high school. And during

one of our games, a recruiter was there. He offered me to play there for my senior year with the chance to continue in college."

"Oh, wow. That's amazing, congratulations! Five years too late, but still, it was a great opportunity. I wouldn't have passed it by either." I give him a tight smile.

"I almost didn't take it, though." He lets out a breathy laugh. "Brandon pushed me to do it. Something about it being my future and taking opportunities before they vanish."

And there he goes again, saying his name. I look away this time, not wanting him to see the tears pooling in my eyes.

"Shit, I'm sorry. I didn't mean to say it." The words rush out of Jordan's mouth.

"Don't worry about it." I wipe my eyes. "It looks like the service is about to start; we should take our seats."

I stand up, brush off any dirt from my dress, and hand Jordan his jacket. "Thank you again."

"My pleasure." He smiles as he takes it back and shakes off the grass. "And thank *you* for the chat. I guess we both needed something today."

We walk back just in time for the sermon by the officiant, the same generic bullshit they all say. *Thank you for being here; we have gathered today to remember his life; each of us feels the loss deeply. Give the family a shoulder to cry on; your presence is worth more than words.*

"And now, a few words from the family as we say our goodbyes to Mr. Brandon Collins."

Goodbye…I could never say goodbye to you. I just hope we meet again in another life.

We step out of the car in front of the Collins' home, a cozy two-story house with cream-colored walls and a brick-red roof.

A vast yard surrounds it, leaving it in the middle of a green paradise with one big tree behind it. The fading green of the leaves indicates that summer's ending. It seems fitting for the tragic occasion.

Maia and Ella support me as we walk up the small steps onto the deck around the first floor. Cream, white, and brown patio furniture decorates the space. Once inside the house, the same color palette fills the living and dining rooms with suede couches, the dining table set, and some touches of glass elements resting on different cabinets and accent tables.

Lots of food lines the table and the kitchen counters, as if they're expecting to feed either a very hungry or large crowd. *Or both.* We stand in front of the fireplace as the house fills with everyone who attended the funeral and others who couldn't.

"Who are all these people?" I whisper to myself.

"Cousins, uncles, aunts. Friends from high school and college," Sam hears me and whispers back.

"Did you know all of them?"

"Not the ones from high school. We know some of his family and some friends from college. But Scott knows more of them since they majored together."

How did I never meet anyone in his life besides the band? Was he embarrassed by me? Did he not want me to be in other parts of his life? But how come Jordan and his mom knew about me, but I didn't know more about them?

"Right," I barely whisper as I try to stay calm after the intrusive thoughts.

"May we have your attention, please?" A deep male voice echoes through the house. The Collins family stands in the middle of the living room.

"Thank you." Kathleen smiles and nods politely. "And

thank you, everyone, for being here today. We wouldn't have been able to do this if it weren't for you. I'm sure that my beautiful Brandon, wherever he is, would be thrilled to see everyone gathered here."

Can people just please stop saying his name? Does it not kill them inside every time they do?

"We know it's hard, saying goodbye to someone we love. And we will miss him more than we thought possible—the twinkle in his eyes when he plays, his handsome smile, and his beautiful voice. We'll miss everything about him. And we're sure we would have been proud of all of his success if he hadn't been taken far too soon."

Maia pulls me into a side hug as tears pour out of my eyes. I look to my right, noticing that the guys couldn't fight their tears either—even Scott, who hasn't allowed himself to feel anything until now, based on what Maia said earlier.

"All we ask is that you remember him for all the good things that he was. When you think of him, think of the thousand times he made you laugh or smile. Keep inside the memory of his beautiful soul."

I try, believe me, I try. But all I see and feel is his cold hand slipping from mine.

"We love you, Brandon, more than anything in the world. But it's time to let you go. May you rest in peace, our beautiful boy."

No, no puedo. I'm not ready; I can't let him go yet.

As the speech ends, I slip away from the crowd searching for a bathroom. I spot one by the front door, but someone's inside. *This might be inappropriate, but hopefully, they understand.* I take the stairs to the second floor and take my best guess.

I try the one on the right, and it opens. *Not the bathroom…*

The room is spacious, with a full-size bed in the middle and bookshelves on each side. In contrast with the rest of the house, everything is a shade of gray or black with touches of brown: the carpeted floor, the bedding, and the desk.

Once I spot the desk, I can no longer pretend this wasn't his room. Picture frames of his childhood, concerts, and college days, even some from the collage, line the table and shelves.

No, no, no. I can't be here. The back of my legs crash against the bed frame, and I lose my balance, falling on my back. I close my eyes as his scent hits me; *I'd recognize it anywhere.* He must have been here recently, maybe after one of the trips to New York.

I crawl onto the bed, clutching one of his pillows. *He's gone, really gone. My love is gone from this world and with it all that he could offer it: his talent, light, and music. Why, just why?*

"Ollie?" someone whispers, but I cannot figure out who it is from how loud I'm sobbing. "Oh, come here."

They join me on the bed, holding me in their arms, pillow and all. "It's okay, sweetie, it's okay. Let it out, let it all out." He rubs my back.

"He's gone, Sam. Brandon's gone." The mention of his name makes me cry even harder.

"I know. I'll miss him too." His voice cracks. "But I'm here, Ollie. I'll always be here."

And here I lie, sobbing while clutching a pillow in the love of my life's bed—so lonely and heartbroken, and yet, not alone. Sam keeps rubbing my back as I cry, but it's not enough; *it will never be enough.*

I feel myself drift to sleep as I'm hugged and soothed in the comfort of someone who cares about me... *But not the one I love.*

"How is it that when I'm in need of space, I'm the one full of remorse?" ~ Alone, Alexandra Kessler.

OLIVIA – OCEAN CITY

I'VE LOST TRACK OF THE DAYS OR WEEKS since the funeral. I don't even know what time of day it is unless Maia or Ella brings me food—letting me know if it's morning, midday, or night. All I know now is this room.

Eat, sleep, cry, take a bath, repeat: this is what I've become. I don't even know what's happening at work, and I don't care. *Nothing else matters ever since he left—since he died.*

I still can't say his name either. The last time I did was at his funeral. That was the day I locked myself in my room, which I haven't left in Lord knows how long. My bed and his hoodies are the only things that give me comfort. The feeling of the material against my skin reminds me of him.

I miss him so much. I miss how he held me and kissed me when he said "te amo."

My skin itches, my heart aches, my head hurts—my whole body burns with never-ending pain. It feels like the world has crumbled around me, yet it continues with a sense of normalcy; just not for me. It laughs at me while I drown in misery and self-pity, its mockery echoing over and over in my nightmares.

Why do they even exist? Why should we be tortured and hunted by our bad memories? Our worst fears, repressed thoughts, lousy karma—however you call it—it's paralyzing and destroys us from the inside out. But I welcome it, becoming accustomed to the pain it brings: a comfort zone, if you will.

"Ollie, can we come in?" Maia and Ella knock on my door, but I don't answer. *They're going to come in anyway.*

The door squeaks as they open it, a tray in their hands. "We brought you lunch. It's your favorite, Bolognese pasta."

It's midday, then. But I wouldn't know; my curtains have been closed for as long as I can recall.

"You can leave it on my desk, thanks," I mumble.

"Okay."

Their feet shuffle as they move to follow my instructions and leave my room. They close the door behind them, but the lock doesn't click, leaving a tiny space between it and the hinges. Meaning I can hear them whisper and mumble behind it.

"How long do you think she'll be like this?" Ella sighs and I picture her fidgeting with the ends of her hair.

"I don't know, man, but it's been three months. I don't think that letting her mourn on her own will work anymore."

What do you mean it's been that long? It feels as if the funeral wasn't more than two weeks ago.

"But what can we do? I hate seeing her like this. It's like she's lost her will to live." Ella cries, and Maia silences her.

"Maybe we should get her to see a therapist or a specialist," she says with a sigh, and I can picture her biting her nails. "She might also need it. I just got a call from the authorities; they can't find Connor after her assault. He hasn't been seen since that night."

Fuck, this man is getting on my last nerves. He better have left the continent and changed his identity.

And I don't need a therapist to tell me how I feel or how I should mourn. I don't need help.

"How? She won't agree, and you know it," Ella whisper-yells.

You know that's right. No one knows me as well as my sister.

The house becomes silent; I assume Maia's thinking of an answer that could convince me. The silence continues for an eternity, so I give up on waiting and stand up to get my food.

It does look and smell very appetizing. I grab the fork and spoon and start spinning the pasta. *Damn, this is good.* I sigh while savoring the richness of the sauce and the meat.

"Should we call our moms and ask them to take her to Miami? A change of scenery might do her some good, where their memories don't surround her."

The sound of the fork dropping on my plate echoes through the room. I finish chewing and immediately yell in a firm voice, "No!" *Where did that energy even come from? Maybe I'm not so hopeless after all.*

"Ollie, sweetie, it's for your own good. We love you and care about you. All we want is for you to know that about yourself and help you move on." They come into the room.

"And so do our parents," Ella says softly.

"I know you do, but I don't care. I don't need anyone's help or pity, so save it."

"*Pero (but)*—"

"*Por favor*, just let me be and let me eat in peace. You *do* want me to eat, right?" I raise my voice a little and sigh.

They don't say anything else. But their eyes speak louder than any word they can utter: they express pity, worry, doubt, annoyance. And I don't want any of it, not from them, my parents, a specialist, or God.

Sorry, Lord, I know you do what you think is best for us, but you took him. Was there a reason for it? I'll never know.

I finish the rest of my food in silence and place the tray outside my door. Instead of going back to my disarrayed bed, I take out some fresh clothes from my dresser and decide to take a bath.

I turn on the faucet and prepare the tub for a bubble bath in an attempt to relax. *It won't happen, but I should try.*

∞

As I leave the bathroom, they knock on my bedroom door again. *What the hell do they want now?*

"Hey, Ollie? Sam called; they're starting to clean up his room and send them to Mrs. Collins. He was wondering if you wanted to go and take a look at it first. It could be a good thing." Maia's voice echoes from outside the door.

I freeze in the middle of my room, wrapped in only my towel. *I haven't been in his room in…I can't remember how long. How will I even go in? How can I face it—face everything?*

She knocks again. "Are you okay? At least let us know if you heard me."

"I heard you," I mumble. "Can I think about it?"

"Of course. We'll be in the living room if you need anything."

Sitting on my bed, still in a towel, my head spins with doubt, memories, dread, and deafening voices begging me to stay. But on the other hand, what if this is what he would've wanted me to do? What if going through his room will also help me ease the pain?

Okay, I can do this. I have to do this—for him.

Five minutes later, I come out in joggers, sneakers, a loose T-shirt, and a high ponytail. I take my phone and put it in my bag, ready to fill it with items to remember him by. With a hand on the doorknob, I take deep breaths: inhaling and exhaling. *Come on, open it; you can do this.*

I slowly open my door, packing in all the courage I can muster, and step out. They haven't noticed me yet. How could they? I'm a shadow of who I once was; a weak, limp, and skinny body. *Not even I would recognize myself.*

"I'm ready," I whisper as I reach them on the couches.

We walk to their apartment instead of driving since it's close by. As we approach the building, I can't help but feel anxious. My heart beats faster, I breathe erratically, my hands sweat, and my legs tremble uncontrollably. *No puedo. I can't do this; I can't go in—I don't want to.*

"It's okay, take your time," Maia whispers beside me.

"Yes, we're here for you." Ella rubs my back as we stand at the building's door. "Whatever you need."

"It's okay. I have to do this at some point, right?" I take a shaky breath as I push the door open and head to the elevator with the girls behind me.

That's it: breathe in, breathe out. You can do this; stay strong, power through.

And without me realizing we're here, Maia's knocking on their door. A door I've grown used to, a door that holds so many memories behind it, memories I'm not sure I'll be able to face today. *Dios, give me the strength to do this.*

"Hey." The door bursts open to reveal Sam standing on the other side. "I wasn't sure if you would come, but we're glad you did it."

I barely give him a polite smile as a reply before he lets us in. The apartment looks the same since I was here last; untouched, not a thing out of place. It's like nothing has changed, but nothing is the same either. *I wonder how his room is now, if it's as if he never left at all—only one way to find out.*

"We thought you could go in first," Scott mumbles.

I look over at him, and he's unrecognizable: bags under his

                                          Book of You & I

eyes, disheveled hair, baggy clothes, pale skin. *Maybe we died with Brandon too.*

"Thank you." I give them a genuine and sympathetic smile, a sad understanding between us. *It feels like I'm dying too, but they were his best friends. And yet, here they are, helping me...*

I take my time reaching his door, holding on to the handle for longer than should be allowed. Sam walks over to me, placing his hand on top of mine.

"Healing takes time, Ollie, and it takes a lot of small steps. And it might feel impossible right now, devastating even. But the first step always looks tougher than it is. The important thing is that you're already trying, which is a huge step. We're here for you regardless of what you decide."

I don't know if it's because they came from Sam, but those are the words I needed to hear. They give me the courage I've been missing to face my fears, the pain, and the sorrow. I push through the voices in my head and open the door to his room.

His room is no different from the one in his childhood home. The only difference is that this one is not tidy. It has scattered papers, books, clothes, instruments, and a skateboard. It's as if he left in a rush with the intent of cleaning up later but never got to it. I close the door, standing in place while my eyes gloss over the mess.

I find an empty spot on the bed and take a seat. I don't know what I'm supposed to do, think, or even say, but this seems like my best option. What I don't like is the silence—it engulfs me and leaves space for dark thoughts to flood my mind. These past months were full of silence, but at least I was safe, hiding in my room.

Here in his room, it makes my chest heavy with pain. This room is full of memories of us, and yet, I can hear them, but they are just out of reach. His morning voice as we wake up, him singing me his new songs, or playing music we like. *But if I touch something, will I feel it? Will I hear the memory?*

I spot a brown leather jacket lying next to me on the bed. *Why does it seem so familiar?* Picking it up, I clutch it to my chest, his scent overpowering my senses:

"Do you trust me?" He grabs my hands and looks me deep in the eyes as I stand in front of his bike.

"I do." What I don't trust is the bike.

He puts a helmet on my head and kisses my lips. "Then hop on, baby!"

Baby, baby, baby. He called me his baby.

Hearing him calling me a pet name calms my nerves about riding a motorcycle, and I carefully hop on behind him. A warm feeling erupts and spreads through my body as I hug him tightly. Is the warmth coming from him or his leather jacket?

My body trembles as he turns the ignition and the bike revs. Why did I agree to this?

"I won't go too fast, okay?" he shouts over the motor.

"You promise?"

"Yes, Ollie, I promise!" He gives me the sweetest smile through the round rearview mirror. That damn smile and his promises.

I hug it tighter as I remember our first date, the first of many nights where it was just the two of us. Tears stream down my cheeks and spill on the jacket, and I don't even bother wiping them away. I'm sure many more will come; maybe it's better to let them flow.

I loved that date, how he made me feel that night, and why I fell in love with him. Just because he took me to my favorite place, and I never even talked to him about that, brings me to tears. It was the first time I'd ever felt seen, really seen, and all that mattered was my happiness. And I will never get that feeling back now.

Turning the jacket around, I put it on, letting it engulf my petite figure. I start sobbing again, feeling warm and like he's embracing me in his arms. This is the closest I'll ever feel to him, but nothing can bring him back or make it feel real. And I have to get used to that reality.

I get up from his bed, tears staining my face, and with his jacket on, like armor. *Where should I even start?* I look around, searching for something, but I don't know what. *What am I waiting for, some sort of sign?* And as if answering my question, my gaze lands on his dresser.

I start with the top right drawer, surprised by what I see. It's full of my things—emergency underwear, pajamas, basic shirts, and pants. I didn't even know he did this, was this supposed to be a surprise? *Well, I don't need to leave any of it here anymore, do I?* I take it all out and place it inside my bag.

Moving on, I open the top left drawer. I guess this is—was— the one for his personal belongings. I see papers, writing utensils, guitar picks, and some pictures. *Wait, those are Polaroids of us. When did he even take these?*

I grab one that I *do* remember: one night when we couldn't sleep, he picked up his guitar and started singing. I wanted to remember it forever, so he took out my camera and snapped one of us being goofy. He had his shirt off, but I made him promise to keep this one private, an intimate moment between us. *So many fucking promises.*

Putting it away in my bag, I look through the drawer. Something inside this called out to me, waiting to be found, so I have to keep going until I see it. Minutes go by, and nothing stands out. It would help if I knew what I'm supposed to find.

I groan out of frustration and start closing the drawer. In the corner of my eye, I notice something I swear wasn't there before. It's a piece of paper, but not like the others: it's another color and texture—a music sheet. With my hands now shaking, I take it out, unfold it, and read the title: *Ollie's Song.*

No, I must be reading this wrong. The tears must be making my vision blurry. Or worse, it's a figment of my imagination. It's just—there's no way he wrote me a song.

Is it even finished? And why didn't he show me earlier? So many unanswered questions float in my brain and make me dizzy.

Verse I:
The stage is not the same if you're not in there
Just like my life that turns to gray

Pre-chorus:
Frozen in time like a picture of us
Unlike the clouds that pass by,
My feelings always stay in line
And there is no one I can rely on
You change my life from gray to color
There's no one else I could fall for

Chorus:
Because there's no me without you
No melody that could be in tune
If I'm not with you, saturated, black, or white

Kiss my lips, say that you're mine
Let me keep you by my side
Make forever last a while
Make forever last a while, starting now

Verse II:
Just like the sunsets,
You paint my world around
We're a song, I hope it lasts

Pre-chorus:
Frozen in time like the story of us
Unlike the stars up in the sky,
I'm right here right by your side
And there is no one I can rely on
You change my life from gray to color
Ollie, you're the one I die for

Chorus:
Because there's no me without you
No melody that could be in tune
If I'm not with you, saturated, black, or white

Kiss my lips, say that you're mine
Let me keep you by my side
Make forever last a while
Make forever last a while, starting now

Bridge/Outro:
I promise, if you promise, not to let go
I promise, if you promise, to love till we're old
I promise, if you promise, not to let go
I promise, if you promise, for forever

And as I read over part of the lyrics, another memory floods my mind.

"Promise?"

"Promise." He laces his pinky finger with mine, and we kiss them to seal the promise.

I go back to laying my head on his chest, and he goes back to brushing my hair. I slowly drift to sleep as he sings something that I can barely make out:

Frozen in time, like the story of us,
Unlike the stars up in the sky,
I'm right here, right by your side,
And there is no one I can rely on,

*You change my life from gray to color,
Ollie, the one I die for.*

"Ollie, the one I die for." "Ollie." "Die for." The last verse echoes in my mind, like the memory of his hand slipping from mine in the hospital. A *song*, he wrote a song declaring his love for me and everything he couldn't voice before. *"The one I die for,"* but did he know he was going to? *Of course, he didn't.*

I can't, I can't handle this. I knew I shouldn't have come. I try to move, but I'm stuck on the floor, a shaking and sobbing mess. The music sheet drops from my hands, droplets of my tears staining it. I wrap the jacket tighter around me, trying to feel the comfort of his warmth as I bawl my eyes out.

I don't care if anyone hears me shrieking; I can't hold the pain in any longer. My chest heaves, my body shakes, and my breaths come out short as I struggle to suck in the air. *Why can't this stop? Why does it hurt this much?*

"Hey, hey, it's okay." Maia's soothing voice reaches me as she nears me, and I let her hug me.

As she embraces me, I can hear multiple people shuffling around the room. Meaning that everyone is witnessing my breakdown. I cry harder at that thought, that I'm now embarrassing myself in front of our friends.

"I can't, Maia, I can't. It's too much; this pain is too much. Make it stop, please." The words barely leave my mouth since I can hardly breathe.

"Whatever you need," she whispers as she cradles me.

"What's that?" Ella asks in a whisper, and something tells me she's pointing to the music sheet.

Scott kneels before me and looks into my eyes as if asking for permission. After giving him a nod, he picks it up and sits across from me on the floor.

He closes his eyes and sighs, a single, silent tear slipping from his eye. "Sam, this is the song." His voice comes out rough.

Sam comes closer, reads over the lyrics, and sighs, letting his head hang. "We have to tell her. It's what he would've wanted. No, it *is* what he wanted."

I wipe my tears as my curiosity spikes. "Tell me what?"

They exchange a glance and then look back at me. Scott starts explaining. "I wish it weren't me telling you this. He was writing this song as a surprise for you, where he'd tell you everything he felt. But now…" His voice breaks at the end.

I don't realize I'm sobbing again until I feel Ella on my other side, hugging and comforting me. She and Maia are crying too, but silently.

"I'm sorry, Ollie. We didn't know the song would be in his dresser, or I would've come in with you. We're sorry that you found out this way," Sam apologizes in a soothing tone.

I shake my head. "It's okay. There's nothing to feel sorry for. I would've found it eventually. It was meant to be this way."

"He finished it," Scott mumbles, an incredulous look on his face. "That's what he wanted to show us during rehearsal, the one we were supposed to have after the beach day. But—we—it didn't—"

"I know, we know. And all that's left is the music now," Sam sighs, placing a hand on Scott's shoulder.

"Can you do that?" I wipe away my tears, looking at Scott. "For him, if not for me."

He places his hand on my knee. "Of course. I'll ask Drew and Layla for help."

I thank him, holding his hand as a way to comfort each other. *I lost a boyfriend, but he lost a brother, his best friend. I don't even want to imagine myself in his position.*

"Do you think you'll have it ready for next week?" Sam asks.

"Yeah, I think so. But I'll have to start today," Scott answers.

"Wh–what's next week?" I interrupt, not knowing what the heck is going on.

"You don't know?" Scott asks, glancing at Ella and Maia.

"No, it's been tough for her. We thought it was best to tell her the same day," Maia answers, ignoring my questioning looks.

"What day? Can someone please tell me what you're talking about? Sam?" I turn to him, a guilty look on his face.

"I thought you knew, Ollie. But I'm still so sorry that I didn't talk to you about this sooner," he rambles. The look I give him tells him that he should get to the point. He takes a deep breath. "It's Brandon's birthday next week, and I'm guessing that you forgot. Or maybe you just lost track of the days, it's okay."

What? Is it his birthday? But we're not in September yet, or are we…? I check the date on my phone and it reads September 21. Sam's right, they all are. How did I lose track of this many months?

"But why does the song have to be ready by then? I don't get it," I ask, still dizzy from everything that's happened in the last ten minutes.

"Umm, we're doing a concert that day. It's a tribute to Brandon." Scott wipes his face as he explains.

A tribute to Brandon… How I wish there was no reason for one. "Oh." My voice breaks again. "Well, that's a wonderful thing you're doing. And you should sing it." I sit up in front of him. "Thank you, Scott."

He looks at me, both of us drenched in tears, and nods. "Anything for my brother."

I reach over and hug him. At first, he doesn't move, maybe shocked by the fact that this is the first time we've hugged. Or at least in this way, in grief. Seconds later, he embraces me back. We pull away after a while, and I sit back next to the girls.

"Is there anything I can do?" I ask the guys.

"Just be there. That's what he would've wanted." Sam gives me a sad smile, and I nod. "And what can we do now? Do you need more time in the room?"

I shake my head. "No, I don't want to be alone anymore. If today taught me anything, it's that even though I needed some time alone, grief shouldn't be this lonely. Not when we have each other to help everyone through it."

We all smile at each other, and I realize that we *are* some sort of family. A family that was pulling away and breaking apart, and I just wasn't noticing. But now I will, and I'll do my best to keep us together.

Chapter Eighteen

"Silently sobbing, wishing things could go a different way.
But I'll wake up with the house a mess and coldness in my bed."
~ Drown, Alexandra Kessler.

OLIVIA – OCEAN CITY

RIGHT THIS WAY." We follow a staff member to a secluded table on the far right of the club and next to the stage. As we sit down, he removes a reserved plaque.

"Thank you," we all say to them.

"Are you sure you'll be okay here?" Maia asks me for the umpteenth time. "I'll be right here. You can just holler, and I'll stay with you. I could ask someone else to take the pictures; it's just backstage stuff for now."

"Hey, no, I'll be fine. I am fine. And I'm not alone, remember?" I signal over to Ella, Noah, and Sam, who are sitting next to me.

"Yes, right. Just let me know, okay? Anything." She hugs me from above, being careful with the cameras, and leaves to do our job. *I should be helping her.*

I take my time to look around the room as Noah and Ella talk. We're the only ones inside besides the club's staff and the band. There's nothing much else to add; the club is the same as all the other times we've been here. The slight differences are the signs and banners announcing the tribute concert.

Brandon's tribute, with the song he wrote for me. Which he will never get to sing...and that thought breaks my heart.

"Ollie, are you okay?" Sam's voice pulls me back from

getting lost in my thoughts.

I've been doing that a lot lately—drifting into my mind with no real end in sight. It's hard trying to move on while still having all these feelings and unfinished business.

Ella and Maia even convinced me to try a therapy session during the week. But all I could do was stay silent as the therapist wrote down her notes and gave me space and time to open up. Maybe for our second session, I'll tell her something...if I ever go back.

"So far, so good. Don't worry about me." I look back at him, finding nothing but worry and care in his eyes. *Maybe I shouldn't have been so cold to him.* "Really, I'm fine."

"Look, we all know why we're here. But if for some reason you feel like you can't handle it, just say the word and we'll leave."

"Oh, Sam, no. I can't make you do that, especially not for me. He's your best friend." His face falls, and I realize what I said. "Was," I whisper.

"It's okay, it happens to the best of us." He tries to laugh, but it comes out dry and ragged. "And besides, even if this is what he would've wanted, he would've understood if you needed to leave."

"I'm not. I need to be here tonight." I place my hand on top of his.

He smiles back, a sad smile, but a smile nonetheless. We stay like this for some time, with Ella and Noah talking in the background, a soundcheck going on, and us waiting. It's as if he understands what I need, and maybe he needs too—silence, comfort, support.

We look at the stage as one of the staff members announces that the concert will start in thirty minutes. And with that, it's no longer quiet inside as the doors open to the public.

Ella looks back at me as I scoff, "What?"

Instead of answering, I nod toward some girls in the front. They wear T-shirts that read: *RIP. We will miss you. Your music will never die. We love you, Brandon.*

"Did you expect anything less? They all have fans, and they, too, have their right to mourn." She tries to speak calmly.

I know, I know; she seems to understand what I think as I roll my eyes.

"Would you like anything to drink? Compliments for the band and their companions," a waiter interrupts my thoughts.

"A Coke for me and a Shirley Temple for my lady," Noah orders for them. *Adorable, ugh.*

"And for the other couple?"

Sam starts talking, and I cut him off. "We're not a couple. And a strawberry margarita for me, thank you."

I ignore the hurt look on his face and the cold stare from Ella as I play with a napkin on the table.

"A Coke will be fine, thank you, Cameron." Sam places his order and turns back around in his seat.

Sensing his short-lived gaze, I continue to avoid it, and the mood at the table changes. But I guess it's on me for being so rude. It's not their fault I'm annoyed at these so-called *groupies* that came in. *And it's not their fault either.*

"I'm sorry, that was uncalled for," I apologize without looking at him.

"It's okay, don't worry about it," Sam says.

And we're back to the silence as no one seems to know what to say. I stare into the crowd as more people pile onto the dance floor and other tables.

"Here are your drinks." The waiter comes back and places our orders in front of us. "Enjoy."

"Cheers!" My attention comes back to the group as everyone grabs their drinks and waits for me.

I grab my glass and lift it. "Cheers." We clink the glasses and sip on our drinks.

"Ladies and gentlemen, the show will begin in ten minutes."

"Which song do you think they'll start with today?" Ella asks Noah excitedly.

"Either 'Twisted,' 'Fallen Obsession, or 'Elixir;' they always open with one of those. They're the most popular," I answer before he can and without looking at anyone.

I'm staring at the stage, drink in hand, as I recall all the times we've seen them play. *Always one of those, without fail.*

"No shit, really? I love those songs! How do you know that?" one of the annoying *groupies* asks from behind the velvet rope separating us from the floor.

I turn to them, a stone-cold look in my eyes as I answer. "It comes with the territory of working with the band and dating one of the members."

They squeal with excitement as if they were meeting the band itself. "OMG, you work with Reputation? Wait, who are you dating?! Can we gues?"

I breathe in shakily as I mentally prepare myself to say his name out loud, already expecting their pity. "I was. Brandon."

And just as I predicted, pity floods their eyes as they mutter, "*We're sorry for your loss,*" and return to their spot.

"I don't need your sorry's," I mutter against my glass as I take a couple of gulps. *This will bite me in the ass tomorrow.*

"It's not their fault; they didn't know. You weren't very public about it either." Ella says, defending the groupies.

"It's fine," I mumble as I finish my drink.

The lights dim as another voice announces, "Two minutes for Reputation on the stage."

I turn around and lock eyes with the waiter. "Another one, please," I mouth to him. It's not long until the empty glass disappears, and he replaces it with a newly-made margarita. If I'm going to make it through the night, I'll need my liquid courage for this.

"Guys, it's two drinks. I'm fine." I roll my eyes as I catch Sam eyeing Ella and nodding to me. "Besides, we already had dinner. There's nothing to worry about."

"Here's a refill for the rest of the guests." The waiter comes back to replace the other's orders.

"Thank you," they say together.

As he retreats, the rest of the club's lights turn off and the stage's colorful ones turn on, and the show begins. A round of clapping and the sound of cheers and excitement echo in the club as the band enters the stage. My chest constricts as I notice them leaving the space where Brandon always stood. Tears threaten to spill, but I blink them back and take another sip of my drink.

"Hello, guys, thank you all for being here today on this special day," Scott's voice resonates from the speakers. "As you might already know, or for those who don't, we lost a band member three months ago. But, more than that, he was our friend—our brother. And something more to someone else." He glances at me, and I return the smile, his usual glimmer missing.

"Brandon, wherever you are, I know you're watching over us right now, and I hope you know how much we love you. And there will always be a space where you used to be. This is for you. Happy birthday."

I look over to his place, a light-blue spotlight illuminating it. Someone who I assume is the new guitar player stands there next to it. *I didn't know they hired a new guy...I guess I did miss a lot.*

They start playing and singing, and they begin with "Fallen Obsession." It seems fitting as it's one of their first songs and one that *he* wrote.

As they enter the chorus, the new guy sings some harmonies and does the guitar riffs. He's good, but it's not the same. *It'll never be the same.*

I lock eyes with Drew as he carries the rhythm, and he seems to understand what I'm feeling. His eyes give him away: a little sadness with a touch of understanding. *Yeah, but he's not our Brandon,* is what I think he communicates through his look.

The crowd cheers, going wild as the song ends, and the band blends into the next one: "Twisted."

I drift into my thoughts again as they play their favorite songs, all of them fading into one in my head. I've also lost count of how many refills the waiter brings me. *Four, maybe five in total; it's okay.*

"Hey," Sam calls as another song ends. "Here." He hands me a glass of Coke.

I'm not that drunk; what does he mean? I take a deep breath; *calma, he's just looking out for you.*

"Thank you." I accept and drink it, the refreshing taste already sobering me up. *I guess I did need it.*

I look back to the stage and notice that Scott's missing, but the rest keep playing. *What's going on?*

"Ollie." His deep voice startles me as he whispers next to me. "Shit, sorry, I didn't mean to scare you."

"It's okay." I work on steadying my erratic breathing. "What's going on?"

"Can you come with me?" His face turns serious as he looks at me. "It's important."

I nod, drinking the rest of my Coke and leaving the glass on the table. Following Scott, he takes me backstage through a small door in the far back. Stopping right by the stage's stairs, he bends down and picks up a brown box, more like a small treasure chest.

"We found this under his bed after you left last week. It has your name written on top, but we didn't even dare to open it. I don't know what it's for or if he even meant to give it to you. But

I think that you should have it."

I take it in my hands and trace my name, which looks like he engraved it with his keys. Opening it, I let out a gasp. It's full of mementos of us: more Polaroids, movie stubs, tickets to the amusement park, and letters.

He kept this? My vision gets blurry as I recall the memories attached to each item inside. *I cannot believe he kept this.*

"We prepared something too." He stretches his hand to me as he climbs the stairs.

"I—I don't know." I shake my head as anxiety starts creeping.

"It's okay, and you don't have to talk or anything. You'll just sit there." He nods over to the chair placed on his spot.

Breathe in, breathe out. Slowly nodding, I take his hands, and he leads me to the front of the stage. I close my eyes and wipe away the remaining tears on my face as the soft spotlight hits me. *It's okay; estás bien. We don't know what it is yet, but we're okay.*

"Hello again, everyone. Before we go into intermission, we've prepared a surprise for a very special someone. Our dear Brandon meant a lot to our friend Olivia. Their connection and love for each other was bigger than any of us. And tonight, this song is about that: a celebration of his love. This one's called 'Ollie's Song'."

My hand grips the box tighter into my chest as they start the song, my breathing getting erratic again. Closing my eyes and tilting my head down, I listen to the beautiful lyrics he wrote for me, for us.

> *The stage is not the same if you're not in there,*
> *Just like my life that turns to gray.*

My mind drifts back to the times I watched him play. When he seemed to smile bigger and enjoy it more every time he looked at me. When he sang in my ear as we lay in bed, on the couch, or in the park. Scott's raspy voice harmonizes with Layla's soothing one as they sing the chorus.

Because there's no me without you,
No melody that could be in tune, if I'm not with you,
Saturated, black, or white,

Kiss my lips, say that you're mine,
Let me keep you by my side,
Make forever last a while,
Make forever last a while, starting now.

I look up and notice a reel playing in front of me on a screen with pictures and videos of us. I look at the guys and see them playing behind us too. *When and how did they get all this? And who made the video?* I turn back around and spot Maia in the crowd, taking pictures. And I see it in her eyes— she did this. *For me, for him, for us.*

Tears start to spill, and I don't even attempt to stop them. *I have to let them flow if I want to heal, to feel something again.* This is us; it's our memories and our little moments. Snippets of who we were together and who we could've become in the future. *But this is not how I wanted to see this, my feelings and our story put on display this way.*

Of course, I hope that we didn't have to end this way—so tragically. But at least I got to experience what it was to love him and have him love me. *And I promise, Brandon, I won't forget you. I won't forget our story, the book that you and I were meant to write.*

Suddenly, they stop singing, but the music continues, leaving me confused. It feels like I've stopped breathing as another voice starts singing. It sounds like it's coming from the video and not the stage, it's from a studio recording. *Brandon...my Brandon is singing. He's singing my song to me.*

> *I promise, if you promise, not to let go,*
> *I promise, if you promise, to love 'till we're old,*
> *I promise, if you promise, not to let go,*
> *I promise, if you promise, for forever.*

I feel a hand on my back, comforting me as I let the sobs out, crying so hard it hurts. My heart, chest, head, and soul; everything hurts as I cry and forget how to breathe. I cover my face with the inside of my elbows, screaming into them. I can't take it anymore, can't take the pain and the reality underneath their well wishes.

His voice, it is Brandon's voice. A voice I didn't think I would hear again, talking or singing to me. His songs are still out there, but it's not the same.

As the song ends, everyone's cheering and clapping. Others are also crying. Except I have three people comforting me on stage. *I can't be here; I need to get out—I need to be anywhere but here.* I take advantage of the lights dimming and run backstage, taking the box with me.

"Wait," I hear Scott calling out and following behind me. "What's wrong? Didn't you like it?"

I stop, my hand on the door, and turn around to face him. "Why did you do that?"

"Do what?" He looks confused, his voice unusually soft.

"That. Put me on stage and put my feelings on display. That was private; those pictures and videos you used were only meant for us. That was our relationship, Scott. It wasn't yours to show."

"But I thought—"

"Well, you thought wrong." I stare at him, tears running down my face, my heart pounding.

He looks hurt and defeated. "It's a tribute, Ollie. To who he was and who he was with you. He wrote your song for a reason, and we tried our best to do him justice. What's so wrong about doing that?"

I stay quiet, not having anything else to say. *But I can't be here. I've had enough, and I need to go; run.* Shaking my head, I barely whisper, "I can't."

Pushing open the backstage door, I cross the dance floor, not caring if I'm pushing and bumping into people. I reach our table and grab my things without any explanation to anyone. *I don't owe it to them, anyway.*

"Wait," someone calls out to me, but I'm too far gone to turn back and find out who it was.

I'm out of the club in a matter of seconds, running without thinking of where to go. *As long as I'm far from the show and the constricting feeling it brings, I'm good.* So, I run and run, letting the wind blow my hair back and wipe my tears away.

My lungs burn, my legs hurt, and my vision blurs, but I can't stop. Not until I reach my destination, wherever it is, wherever my feet are taking me. Suddenly, the smell of saltwater hits me, and I realize where I am. Slowing down, I reach the sand, the crunching sound echoing in the air.

No, no, no, I don't want to be here—too many painful and bitter memories. I need to run again and find another place.

I turn around to leave and bump into someone. Lifting my head, I lock eyes with a sweaty and panting Sam. *Damn it, why did he follow me? I need to be alone.*

"Ollie, what's wrong? Why did you run?"

I shake my head, letting it hang as I catch my breath. "I

couldn't be there anymore. It was too much to handle: the box, the song, the video, hearing him sing it. I–I can't."

"Hey." He reaches for my face, lifting it and looking deep into my eyes. "It's okay not to be okay; we each have our own mourning process. But you could've told me you wanted to leave, and I would've taken you home."

I suck in my bottom lip, trying to stop more tears from flowing out. "I just felt like I needed to leave, to run. My feet took control, and I let them lead the way. But I can't be here either; it holds too many memories." And as if it's a sign, my breathing starts to get out of control again.

He looks behind me and seems to realize where we are, where my subconscious took me. It's our spot on the beach, the place we've been to countless times, where we surfed, *the place that took his life.*

"I think I know a place you'd like." He nods for me to follow, and I take off my shoes, letting him lead.

We walk for about five minutes and reach a part of the beach where no one goes anymore. I don't even remember being here ever before. All I know is it has an old lifeguard house that my friends and I always thought was creepy, we were always too cowardly to even be close to it.

Wait, that's where we're going? Oh, heck no! I stop, paralyzed and staring, feeling panicked.

"What?" he asks as he notices me stopping and looks between me and the lifeguard house. "Ollie, come on, don't you trust me? It's not haunted; it never was." He offers me his hand.

I eye him suspiciously but eventually take it. *I do trust him.* He pulls me behind him, walking toward the creepy-looking structure. *I cannot believe I'm doing this.*

As we walk in—Sam first, of course—I gape at what I see. It's not what I expected. It's not like I would've seen spiderwebs, missing floorboards, or something from a horror movie. But this isn't it either: the walls are painted white, and the borders on the small windows are red. He installed a lightbulb and electric ports, where he connected a speaker. Gray blankets and cushions line the floor. *What is it with these guys and the color gray?*

"Told you it's not haunted," he whispers. "Do you like it?"

"Sam, I—this is beautiful. How? What?"

"I've been coming here for as long as I can remember. At first, it was empty, just a lifeguard house that they stopped using. So, over the years, I took over and made it better. It's where I come to escape."

"Escape what?" I turn around and suck in a small breath at how close he is. *He needs to stop doing that.*

"Life, reality, anxiety, *feelings*."

As he whispers the last part, something flashes in his eyes. It's swift and fleeting, and I can't describe what it is.

"Here." He grabs my hand again, pulling me to the floor.

I follow his lead, landing on a very comfortable and fluffy blanket. *This is what I needed*. We sit in silence, enjoying the sound of the waves crashing on the shore. It used to be calming for me, my happy place, my comfort. But now, all it does is remind me of what I lost—what we lost.

"Is it okay if you put on some music? It's just that, umm, the waves—"

"Of course." His hand slips from mine as he stands up, setting up the speaker and putting on some calming music.

He sits back down in front of me. I can feel his gaze but don't return it, hiding more tears that slip out by looking away.

"Do you want to talk about it?" he asks in a soft voice, and I nod. "Okay, take your time."

Taking a couple of deep breaths, I start. "Everything reminds me of him here. The beach, the boardwalk, the flowers, the coffee place. It's as if we went everywhere in this city and left nothing untouched.

"Don't you sometimes get that feeling of running away, leaving everything behind? A burst of energy and desire to change, to start over somewhere new?" I release a shaky breath, body shaking.

He shakes his head, and I continue. "Well, that's all I've felt since he died. I've always wanted to travel, but this place would always be my home to come back to. And now...I don't know anymore.

"Is it wrong to want to leave everything and everyone behind? I just can't do this anymore."

"Oh, Ollie." He scoots over next to me, pulling me into his embrace as I sob. "There's nothing wrong with wishing for change. No, it won't be easy, but it doesn't mean it's wrong. And we will always be here for you; you're not abandoning anyone."

I keep sobbing as he comforts me, rubbing my arms and back. *This is what I needed to hear.* He doesn't stop me. Instead, he cuddles me while I let it out: the pain of leaving the memory of Brandon, abandoning my sisters and my home. After lying on the floor with Sam hugging me while I cry and listening to music, I calm down.

"Damn it, I must look like a complete mess. Getting all blotchy and red while bawling my eyes out in your arms," I mumble against them. "Shit, did I ruin your comfort place?" I lift my head to look at him as the thought pops into my head.

He lets out a breathy laugh, his minty-fresh breath fanning my face. He lifts his hands to my face, brushing some wet strands from my cheeks and forehead. The feeling of his touch sends shivers down my arms.

"You didn't ruin everything." He smiles and looks at me like Brandon used to do when we met. He caresses my cheeks again, wiping my tears away. "And you do not look like any kind of mess. You could never, not to me, Ollie."

My chest rises and falls rapidly. I don't know if it's the look of sheer adoration on his face or the way he caresses my face, but it's making me nervous. His hand doesn't leave my cheek, and I start to lean into it, liking how it feels. I close my eyes, enjoying the quiet moment and what erupts in me.

When I open them again, his eyes are closed, and we're closer to each other, our noses almost touching. *What are you doing? He's not Brandon; this is Sam. He's your friend; he's always been your friend. Get out, run!* My thoughts scream at me, loud and shrill screams that I can't seem to shut up.

He opens his own eyes again, staring right into mine. And his breathing is just like mine: heavy and all over the place. His gaze drops to my lips for a second and goes right back to my eyes.

Get out, get out, get out! These damn thoughts, I just need to shut them up, but how? Sam seems to read my mind as he moves closer. *Wait, what is he doing?* He leans in and pulls me with him as he does. Our lips touch, and with that, the voices in my head are no longer screaming at me.

Okay, you kissed, we can stop now. I ignore the thought, tilting my head as I keep kissing him. I know this is wrong, that what we're doing is wrong, that we shouldn't do this. But it feels right; his lips feel right against mine. We should stop, we shouldn't go on, but I don't want it to stop. And he doesn't seem to want to either, as he pulls me closer by the waist.

The kiss gets heated as we press tighter against each other, and he lays me down on the blankets. And I don't stop him, enjoying the feeling of his body on mine. His lips move to my neck. I sigh as he kisses me right on the spot below my ear. He stays there, giving it more attention.

"Sam," I groan. *We shouldn't be here.*

"Hmm," he sighs, his breath on my neck making me tremble.

This is wrong. Leave. Fuck, just shut up! How can I shut you up?

He suddenly stops and stares into my eyes. My breath catches in my throat as I look back at his: they're dark and full of desire, lust, love—all for me.

"Are you sure?" he asks me, holding my face.

No, stop this! Instead of answering, I pull him back down, crashing my lips into his. *Maybe, just maybe, giving in to the desire will shut up the voices in my head.*

"Making me believe that we're more than what it is. A desire, a crave, a cry of love from an unlovable girl." ~ Stage 2: Him - Not Again, Alexandra Kessler.

SAM – OCEAN CITY

*I*S THIS REAL? AM I DREAMING? Someone, please pinch me; I need to know if this is happening.

No, scratch that. If I'm sleeping, then I don't want to wake up. And if this is a dream, it's the most beautiful one I've ever had: Ollie's here, in my arms, how?

No, I know how, and it was the most unbelievable night. I mean, how or why is she here with me?

I don't want to move or leave because she's still sleeping peacefully and beautifully in my arms. How can someone be so beautiful while they sleep? And how can someone's skin be so smooth and soft? I just hope I don't disturb her and wake her.

Oh, last night… It took everything within me to take it slow, to not rush her out of excitement and ruin the moment. But how could I not feel like that? With her skin pressed against mine, my name slipping from her mouth, and the sweet sounds she made. All I could think about was keeping her here with me for as long as possible. And how I could never get enough of her lips on mine. *Damn, those lips; I could love them forever.*

Fuck, love? Did I just say love? Of course, I did because I love her. But she doesn't love me back; she still loves Brandon. *Shit, Brandon. How could we do this to him…on his birthday?*

As if fate is playing some twisted game with us, she stirs next to me and sighs. *Here we go…*

"Ugh, my head," she groans, placing a hand on her forehead with her eyes still closed. "Water, I need some water."

She starts rubbing the sleep from her eyes and slowly opens them. As she looks around, confusion is written on her expression. *Does she not remember last night?* My heart drops at the thought.

"What–where?" She looks around and sits up on her elbows. Her eyes land on mine, eyebrows furrowed. "Sam, what—" As the realization hits her, her eyes open wide. "Oh, umm," she stutters.

Fuck, I knew this was too good to be true.

She looks down at herself, finding only a blanket over her and her clothes in a pile on the floor. Letting out a gasp, she drops to her back again and covers her face. "Shit," she mutters.

I stay silent, letting her process what went down, *how I went down…no, focus!* Neither of us moves or talks, too scared of what this means and what will happen next. I take the first step toward the awkward conversation, moving to put on my underwear and hand her hers.

"Thank you," she says in a shy voice. Before changing, she looks at me for a second, asking me to turn around.

Not that I didn't enjoy what I saw. But I do what she asks, respecting her wishes for a bit of privacy. *What I would do to wake up next to her every day…and, yet, she's not mine; never was., maybe never will be.*

"I can get you some water if you want," I mumble, treading carefully around her.

"Please," she whispers while avoiding my eyes.

I put on the rest of my clothes from last night and walk down to one of the carts on the boardwalk. After getting a bottle, I go back to the lifeguard house. When I close the door behind me, I find Ollie already changed.

"Here." I hand her the water and her phone.

She nods instead of answering and takes them from my hand but doesn't look at me once. Chugging the water, she sits back down on the blankets. Her silence is killing me; I need to know what she's thinking and feeling.

"Ollie," I whisper, but she doesn't look up. "Can you please look at me?"

She shakes her head, hugging herself. I think she's about to cry. I sit in front of her and place my hands on her knees to comfort her.

"Talk to me. What's wrong?"

"Last night," she barely whispers. "This, us. That's what's wrong, we shouldn't have done that.."

Ouch. But I don't think it's wrong; it doesn't feel like it.

"Please look at me, Ollie," I whisper again, and she raises her head, her eyes teary. "Do you really feel like that?"

She takes her time to answer; I can see the wheels turning in her head. When she opens her mouth, my heart breaks into a million pieces. "Yes. That's how I feel."

"It doesn't mean it was wrong, that we're wrong."

"Yes, it was—is."

"Ollie." I lift my hand, reaching for her face, but she moves away from me.

"It was his birthday, Sam." Her voice trembles. "It was his birthday, and I ran away. The band prepared something special, something to honor him with, and what did I do? I ran off to sleep with his best friend."

My face drops. *Sleep with his best friend...that's all it was.* But she's right; that part was wrong. It was his birthday, and we disrespected and dishonored that—him.

"You're right. We shouldn't have done that to Brandon's memory. I'm sorry."

"Please, don't say his name. At least not while we're in here," she begs with a sad look.

I nod and go back to being silent, not knowing what else to say now.

"I should go," she whispers but still doesn't make an effort to move. "I shouldn't be here, Sam."

"I can't say the same." I try to read her face, but she turns away, hiding herself.

"I'm sorry," she mumbles as she stands up and quickly grabs her things. She stops at the door, a hand on the knob, and looks back at me. "Goodbye, Sam."

A single tear rolls down her cheek, and she wipes it away, then leaves. And I let her go, wiping the tears off my own face. *I'm sorry, Brandon, I'm so sorry.*

OLIVIA – OCEAN CITY

HY DID I DO THAT AND ALLOWED MYSELF TO STAY?
It was Brandon's birthday, his fucking birthday, and I slept with his best friend.

Poor Sam, I know it meant something to him. But it didn't mean the same to me…he's not Brandon. *He was good—it was great—but it's not him.*

I need to get home. *No, not home. It's not my home anymore; I have to leave for somewhere far away. I need a change, and I need it now!*

I reach the building and run up the stairs. I don't want to wait for the elevator today. Opening the door, I run straight to my room in an attempt.

"Did you think that was going to work?" Maia's stern voice stops me right at my door. "Living room."

Shit, so close. "Yeah?"

"¿Dónde estabas? (Where were you?)" she asks, her arms crossed in front of her chest.

"*La playa.* I needed an escape from last night. It was too much, too soon."

"And we get that, but all night? You never disappear for that long," Ella comments now, squinting at me. "Why are you lying to us?"

"I was with someone." I look down, ashamed of my confession—of what I did last night.

Ella's eyes open wide. "Don't tell me it was—"

I nod. "Sam."

"Fuck," they mutter as they sink into the couch.

"I know," I whisper.

"But how, why?"

"He followed me when I ran, and I ended up at the beach, on *the spot*. He recognized it too and took me somewhere else, some sort of comfort place for him. The old lifeguard house at the far end of the beach." My hands begin to shake.

"I was venting to him about everything I couldn't say to the therapist, and he just listened. I ended up crying, he comforted me, and one thing led to another..." I suck in my bottom lip to stop myself from crying, *again.*

I don't even look at them, not wanting to know what they think of me now.

"We get it," Maia says, and I lift my head. "Yeah, it was his birthday tribute, and that was wrong. I won't sit here and tell you it doesn't matter; it does. And it matters because you still love him; you don't love Sam."

"But *he* loves *you*, Ollie," Ella says in a soft voice. "And that was probably the best thing in the world for him. Tell me you at least talked about it."

When I look down again, ashamed, they gasp and groan. "Are you serious? So, you just ran away?!"

I nod, pressing my head into my hands.

"You have to talk to him. You'll break his heart, Olivia," Maia scolds me, standing before me now.

"I think I already did," I mumble against my hands and look up at them. "I treated him like shit when I woke up. Fuck, the look on his face when I told him how wrong everything felt. How will I be able to look at him when I stomped on his heart?"

"Just tell him the truth and be as nice as you can. He'll understand." Maia smiles sadly, rubbing my shoulders.

I shake my head. "No, and I can't, he won't. And I won't stay here very long, anyway."

They exchange glances, not knowing what I'm about to share. "There's something I have to tell you."

∞

"Are you sure you have everything? Anything you forgot?"

"Girls, you helped me pack. We've checked and double-checked; I'm fine. I have everything I need, and then some," I groan as they ask me for the hundredth time.

"*Lo sé, lo sé*, we're just making sure." Maia turns around from the backseat to hug me. "It's just, you know, we've never been apart for this long before."

"I know, it's hard for me to." I sigh, pushing back the tears as I hug my best friend. "But I have to do this, now or never."

"Hey, wait for me." Ella unbuckles her seatbelt and joins in on the hug. "Gosh, I can't believe my sister is going to Europe without me."

Maia and I laugh as we wipe away the tears. "It's not like I'm leaving forever, and I'll be just a call away."

Ella steps back from the hug, teary-eyed, and looks at me. "Bitch, I know you. You'll fall in love with one of the cities and decide to stay. I bet you'll meet someone and fall in love, that you'll be *living the dream*."

I roll my eyes at my dramatic sister and pull away from Maia, trying to replace my sad look.

"Damn it, sorry. Too soon?" she mutters, closing her eyes.

I shake my head. "No, no, it's fine. I'll be fine. But I don't want to meet anyone, not so soon and not after everything."

"Have you returned any of Sam's calls or texts? It's been days," Maia asks.

"No, I still can't face him. And I can't just tell him I'm leaving the country. No, the continent. He'll think it's his fault."

"I mean…" Maia mumbles.

"No, it wasn't. That night just made me realize what I needed: to leave. I've spent my whole life saying how much I wanted to travel but never actually did it. But it's time. If I don't do it now, I never will."

We stay quiet as I take in what this means and what I'm saying. *I'm leaving. Not only what's been my home but the people who mean the most to me.*

"Have you talked to Mom yet?" Ella asks as she looks back at me.

I smile and nod. "Yeah, I called her last night. And then I called Dad."

"Oh, no," Ella laughs. "What did he say?"

"He was supportive and proud that I decided to do it. Something about growth and learning to be alone."

"I bet he did," Ella laughs, but I can sense it's fake.

We go back to the silence, just enjoying each other's

company. An alert on my phone lets me know I should get moving.

"I have to go now, or else I won't make my flight to Spain." *Sunny Barcelona, as he once told me when we first met—my first stop on a long trip.*

We look at each other and melt into another hug, crying in one another's arms. I bask in this feeling of love and endless support. The feeling of knowing that no matter where we are, the others will always be there. No matter what.

"Well, this is it," I sigh as we separate. I get out of the car and take my bags from the trunk.

"Don't forget to keep us updated with everything: when you're at the gate, when you board, when you land, and when you get to the hotel. Everything!" Ella says with a shaky voice as I lean on the window.

"Yes, *moms*." I pretend to be annoyed. "Of course I will!"

I turn my head to the airport doors and remember something else. "Can you do me some huge favors?"

"Sure, what?"

"Tell Scott and the band that I'm sorry. What they did for Brandon was beautiful, and I did appreciate it. I didn't mean to ruin it like that."

"They'll understand." Maia smiles and nods from the driver's seat. "And what's the other one?"

"Keep an eye on Sam, will you? I messed up, really messed up with him. And if he comes looking for me, tell him I'll call him when I'm ready."

They nod, and I look at the time again. Shit. I really have to go now.

"I love you, girls. Thank you, for everything." I smile, trying not to cry again.

"We love you too." They smile back, blowing me kisses as

I walk away. I keep this in my memory, giving them one last look: a bittersweet moment where it's just us three, like always. Except, now, it'll be different. This moment, me leaving, will be one for the books, marking it as the catalyst for our futures.

But this is not the end of our story, our book. No, this one is never-ending; it'll last a lifetime. And yet, it's the end of something, *of someone*. Because this is when I move on, and where we cease to exist—*ending the book of you and I.*

Epilogue

"I promise, if you promise, not to let go. I promise, if you promise, to love 'till we're old." ~ Ollie, Alexandra Kessler.

OLIVIA – MILAN, NINE YEARS LATER

*T*ESORO, I'M HOME! *DOVE SEI (WHERE ARE YOU)?"* Lorenzo's voice echoes through the house after he shuts the front door.

"In soffitta," I call out from the attic as I stand on a chair, trying to reach a box from the top shelf.

Footsteps run up the stairs, and after a couple of seconds, a pair of hands helps me out. "Here, let me." He pulls the box out and sets it on the floor.

"Always the gentleman. *Grazie, tesoro.*" I kiss his lips and wrap my hands around his neck as he carries me off the chair.

I do a once-over of my husband, still not believing how handsome he is. His dirty blond hair, heartwarming smile, piercing blue eyes, and tall, muscular figure—*perfect*. But that's nothing compared to his kind heart, ambition, talent, and protectiveness over us. *How did I ever get so lucky?*

"Sempre, amore mio." He returns the kiss as my feet touch the ground. "And I was the lucky one," he whispers.

I have no idea how he always manages to do that. But I'm not complaining. It was hard for me to admit at first, but Ella was right. It did take me some time—years—but it happened: I found love. Or, better said, it found me—*he found me.*

"Ti amo, sole mio," he whispers against my lips, melting me into his arms.

I shake my head. "I love you more."

It wasn't simple, and it definitely wasn't love at first sight, *or even at second sight*. But it happened. I found myself, found him, and found love. We even made something out of it… And as if the universe could read my thoughts, she calls out to us.

"*E io (and me)?*" Mia's sweet and soft voice reaches us, calling our attention.

We part from each other and kneel in front of our beautiful four-year-old daughter, the light in our lives.

"*Certamente, ti amiamo, tantissimo (of course, we love you so much)!*" We pull her into our lap, hugging her tightly.

"How can we not love the most beautiful girl in the whole wide world?"

"*Mie belle ragazze (my beautiful girls).*" He plants kisses all over our faces.

She giggles into our chests as her father's beard tickles her face, and it's the sweetest sound I've ever heard.

"*Papà, no,* it tickles!" As the words leave her mouth, he starts tickling her for real. I join in on the fun, wanting to hear her laugh forever.

This, right here, is happiness. This life, this love, was worth everything I've gone through. And if I had to do it all over again, just to get a glimpse of it, I'd do it in a heartbeat.

As she wiggles around, trying to escape our attack, so do her adorable pigtails. And that's another thing I love about her, how she's the perfect mix of the two of us. My dark brown hair and green eyes, her father's expressions and skin color, but she has a smile of her own—the best in the world.

"Okay, okay, *andiamo.* We have some work to do in this attic. The decorations won't find themselves." *Nothing like a garden picnic on a fresh summer day in Milan.*

I stop tickling her, and she stands up, walking back to where she was before, still giggling. We get up from the floor too, going to the box he helped me pull down. Opening it, I start searching for what I need.

"*Che stai cercando (what are you looking for)?* And what's in the box?" he asks as he helps me.

"A dress," I sigh, moving things around. "It's olive green and wraps around the front. I thought I could use it for your family's picnic this Sunday. And it's full of clothes my sisters sent a long time ago."

"This one?" He pulls something out, and I peek at it.

"Yes, that's it!" I take it and stand on my toes to kiss him. "Thank you, thank you, thank you."

"Always, my love." He makes his thick accent sound more Italian, and I smile. He does this on purpose, knowing how much I love it.

"*Mamma,* who is this? That is not *papà.*" Mia's voice pulls us apart, our attention now on her.

When I turn around, the sight of something I haven't seen in nine years makes me suck in a breath. My eyes get glossy, my hands tremble, my heart beats faster, and a fond smile forms on my face.

It's the chest, Brandon's chest, the one Scott gave me that night—the night that changed everything. But how? How is this still here? I don't remember keeping it after all the moving and traveling around.

Sitting next to her, I notice what she's holding up. It's Polaroids of us: on the beach, on top of the Jeep, the one when he played his guitar.

"*Mamma, chi è il ragazzo (who's the boy)?*"

Coming back to reality, I kiss the top of her head. "*Vieni qui, ti racconto una storia (come here, I'll tell you a story).*"

"Let's call it… *book of you and I.*" Before starting, I look back at my husband, searching for any resistance.

"*Va tutto bene, tesoro.*" He smiles at us.

"This is also the story of how life led us to each other. It's perfectly fine that you tell her why I met you, my love." He winks at me, and I shake my head at his silliness, knowing how much I genuinely enjoy it.

"But if that's not *papà*, how did you find him?" Mia's confused voice makes us chuckle.

He sits next to us, taking our hands into his. "That, *amore mio*, is a story for another time."

Acknowledgements

To my mom, for her endless support, advice, guidance,
and her understanding;

To my dad, for his mentorship and for being my
sounding board to bounce off ideas;

To my sister and best friend, for their inspiration
and motivation;

To my partner, for the encouragement to publish
my words, for his undying support, and for his love;

To all my author and book besties for always being there;

To my colleagues and friends for cheering me on;

To my editor, for your advice and patience, for the courage to
make changes, and for believing in my story;

To Alexandra Kessler, for the honor of using your lyrics
and for writing "Ollie's Song."

To my readers, I wouldn't be here without you!!